Already Taken

CAROLINE
GRACE-CASSIDY

POOLBEG

Published 2015
by Poolbeg Press Ltd.
123 Grange Hill, Baldoyle,
Dublin 13, Ireland
Email: poolbeg@poolbeg.com

A catalogue record for this book is available from the British Library.

ISBN 978178199-931-8

Printed and bound by CPI Group (UK) Ltd, Croydon, CR0 4YY

www.poolbeg.com

About the Author

Caroline Grace-Cassidy is the author of four novels: *When Love Takes Over*, *The Other Side of Wonderful*, *I Always Knew* and this new work, *Already Taken*.

She is a Creative Director of Smart Blondes Productions and a regular panellist for *Midday* on TV3.

Caroline lives in Knocklyon in Dublin, with her husband Kevin and daughters Grace and Maggie.

Also by Caroline Grace-Cassidy

I Always Knew
When Love Takes Over
The Other Side of Wonderful

Published by Poolbeg

Acknowledgements

For my beloved best pal and hubby Kevin and my two unique, amazing, wonderful, beautiful daughters, Grace and Maggie.

The rest of the fam'bly: Robbie Box, Noeleen Grace, Samantha Grace-Doyle and Keith Grace. Mia, Zoe, Cillian, Olivia, Conor.

Thanks to the Smart Blondes: Sarah Flood, Sorcha Furlong and Elaine Hearty. This is a business, girls ;)

All the brilliant TV3 *Midday* ladies I have the banter with and the boss woman Elaine Crowley!

Contrary to popular belief wine is not my only friend! To all my fabulous pals: Lisa Carey, Ciara O'Connor, Maia Dunphy, Susan Loughnane, Louise Murphy, Leontia Ferguson, Tara Durkin, Gail Brady, Amy Joyce Hastings, Marina Rafter, Nicola Pawley, Ciara Geraghty, Steve Gunn, Kieran O'Reilly, Graham Cantwell, Paul Buckland, Claire Guest, Maeve Callan, Neil & Jenny Bedford, Caroline Cassidy, Ali Canavan, Fiona Looney, Barbara Scully, Tara Flynn and thanks to all at Park Pictures, Kevin, Emmet, Paul, Erik & John.

To my 'Secret Authors Club' – you all know who you are and thanks so much for all the support.

Big thanks to Tara, Amy & Honour.

Thank you to Paula Campbell for giving my stories a shelf to wave from and to Gaye Shortland for all her hard work on this, and all my novels.

To Margaret Kilroy, my Ringsend Rose.

My biggest thanks are to all of you who buy and read my books. THANK YOU! You can contact anytime me via Facebook AuthorCarolineGrace-Cassidy, Twitter @CGraceCassidy or my website www.carolinegracecassidy.com

All my love,

Caroline xxx

In loving memory of Sarah Knott
"*You have three choices in life:
Give up, Give in or Give it all you've got.*"

Chapter One

KATE WALSH
Ringsend, Dublin 4
April 2015

"Howrya, I'm Kate," I practise into my freestanding full-length mirror in the bedroom, smiling brightly. 'Shine bright like a diamond.'

"How's it goin' – my name's Kate." Soft tone.

"Nice to meet you. Kate Walsh." Strong tone. I extend my hand to my reflection, a strong, rigid movement. Very businesslike. Taker of no shit.

I am practising for my new job. It is an unusual job, yes, I will freely admit that. It isn't innovative in its creation, it has been done before, but I've never known anyone with the job so it is new to me. I feel like I created my own version of it. I feel like the man Zuckerberg and his book of random faces. I don't really have a proper name or registered title for this job of mine. I am inventing my own rules and regulations. I am creating my own world. A much-needed change.

"Sorry, that is not in my job description." I affirm my rules into the mirror seriously. Lips pursed together. Bit too Khloe Kardashian so I part them slightly. I want

1

serious businesswoman. I channel my inner Melanie Griffith in *Working Girl*.

"I think you may need to read the small print again, sir?" Much more Mel-like.

Just in case any of my clients get the wrong idea which, I am pretty convinced, will happen sometime. It is sort of a risky job, yes, agreed. It is probably kind of stupid in a lot of ways to offer myself as an escort. An escort to events. But, I am simply providing the service of accompanying people to events who need my support. Simply put, I am a paid-for companion. I have changed my life to this independent freelance job because I was sick of being me. So sick to tears of it all that anything was worth risking to get that sense of actually feeling alive again. I was sick to death of the crappy deck of cards life had dealt me, bored of being in shit form, mainly because of my shit job.

I'm not one to moan – I know it doesn't sound like it right now but I rarely do. I live on my own so there's no one there to listen to me really. Here is the thing though: I am a completely contented and committed loner which I am surprisingly proud to admit. I do love life, don't get me wrong. It's just that I like my own company a lot more than other people's most of the time. Life hasn't exactly shown me many warm hugs and compassion so sometimes, I will admit, it would be nice if I felt life loved me back even just a smidgen.

I became so fed up last month I was close to the running-away-and-joining-the-circus state of mind. I didn't expect to go straight to the trapeze – I'd sweep up the elephants' shit for a few years but slowly I would make my way to the Big Top. I could clearly see the faces of the punters below me, mouths agape at my fearlessness and raw talent. Standing ovations as I glided through the air to be caught on the other side by a Jamie Dornan lookalike in dark tights.

"I need you, Kate," my Dornan lookalike would whisper with his hot breath into my ear as he held me tight, high above the normal world. Suspended in love.

Anyway, I did something about it. I did something about my shit life and lack of warm hugs. I made a new plan. I was more than ready for a bit of life's widely reported adventures. I was truly bored with the banality of my daily existence. I was at a stage where I had to push for more.

"I am simply an escort to events. A companion. I am no prostitute!" Firm, in control, tell them out straight. No crossed wires here. Set the ground rules down immediately. Cop yerself on, pal. Bag full of illegally purchased Pepper Spray.

"I do not have any type of sexual encounters with my clients, sir!" I put my shoulders back, my head held high, and the mirror tells me I look pretty good.

I could no longer face getting up every morning and feeling like gluten-laden brown bread. (You know the type – sure you do. That type of very serious-looking, darkly coloured brown bread that only whole-foods shops sell. People who buy it always look healthier than you. It weighs your bag down. A big brick of brown bread. It isn't too hard to picture the transition of the bread from mouth to toilet bowl.) I was completely bored of still having to penny-pinch after such a long-drawn-out week's work. Bored out of my unfulfilled mind, bored of knowing where almost every solitary penny I earned was going. A rainy day would be very, very wet for me. The type of rain people say soaks you to the bone.

I had never known quite what I wanted to do for a living, granted, but I had always known just what I didn't want to do, which was working in the dead office I had been inhabiting for the last twenty-four months. I always, without sounding like some kind of do-gooder, wanted to work at a job that made some sort of a difference to people. Something worthwhile. Just something that meant something, however big or small. I suppose I presumed, after all I had gone through growing up, that something better had to be out there for me but, like so many of us, I thought it would just land in my lap. I thought I bloody deserved it. Fate. That magical four-letter word. A word that when whispered made it hard not to believe in it. Top teeth hitting bottom lip and tongue clipping the roof of the mouth. If it was for me it wouldn't go past me, right? I so wanted to believe that. I didn't think I had the power to make the changes until I flicked on an episode of *Oprah* one lazy Sunday afternoon. Sprawled across my sofa eating chocolate spread on a thick cut of toast as my ears pricked up. It was a simple thing she said – I wasn't even looking at her – I was concentrating on licking my fingers carefully – but she said: "*No one is going to make things happen for you. Only you have the power to do that for yourself.*" It just resonated. I'm not getting all *The Secret* on you now. It's just that in the end that's what happened. (I haven't read *The Secret* but it does keep my couch level because one of the mini-wheels fell off and the book sits in its place, so technically it is keeping me upright. It was a birthday present from my younger sister Ciara – she loves it. I am polite and love her enough to

4

listen to her constant glowing reviews of it but I make no comment when she informs me of the true-life success stories of the asking-the-universe theory. She needs to believe it. God knows Ciara needs to believe in something.)

"It was a pleasure doing business with you." I practise my professional voice as I move away from the mirror.

I turn back and smile at my reflection.

"It's been an absolute pleasure to do business with you." I try out my posh accent now but sound slightly Liz Hurleyish.

I flop out across my freshly made bed. I'm a devil for new bedding. Ciara would go so far as to tell you I'm addicted. Bit dramatic, I'd say. I rub my palms over the softness of the duvet cover. This one is all white with a red satin trim on the edges and across the middle. The pillowcases match. Is there anything in the world as relaxing as snuggling down onto new fresh sheets? I think straighter. I sleep better. You know, when I told you I carefully account for every penny, well, I have a small confession to make: every week I put a two-euro coin into my old plastic brown-boot moneybox to go towards new bedding. I inhale the fresh scents now before I rummage in my cardigan pocket and take out my iPhone. I click on the little white envelope secured in the middle of its blue box to open up my emails and see if I have any new jobs in. I turn around on the bed and put my legs up against the wall.

I am at work now, you see. I am four weeks into my independent life as my own boss. I never give out my phone number or home address obviously, so all my work is through carefully placed advertising with my email address (eventcompanion@gmail.com) as point of contact. Obviously I need to be careful about who I do business with but so far so good. I have my business cards and flyers printed – '*Event Companion Available*' – and I put them up myself in places I consider safe and where I feel my product might be seen and needed. I have flyered the Ringsend area in particular, the local college evening classes, stuck business cards up in the local shops in Sandymount and the St. Andrews Resource Centre. I'm not throwing them around town in derelict phone boxes or anything. I'm pretty clued in like that. Street smart.

I scan the black lettering on my email account. A few bits there to go through. I am building an empire one shy email at a time. The shyer the email the smaller the font size I have noticed. The cowering font size. I understand inwardness and insecurity. You see, everything in my life to date has pretty much been total shite. But I've always known, no matter what other crap I've had going on, the one thing I didn't want to do was to be stuffed into the rat-race suitcase, the zips pulled together, and then fitted with one of those tiny useless gold suitcase locks.

Shit happens. I have the T-shirt. I had no choice over the years but to take a series of shit jobs, the brown one being the last in a long line. As soon as I could fly the broken nest I went out to work to earn money to support myself. That was exactly how I had felt before I created my new job. An irrelevant part of the rat race. My alarm sickened my ears at seven a.m. every morning. I smacked it a box then trudged (some ladies might say 'padded' but I never pad ever, unless it's my time of the month and then I just am padded) to the loo, showered, put on my brown skirt, brown shirt, brown tights, brown shoes and yellow tie. I ate a bowl of Crunchy Nut 'Corn*fakes*'. I could never afford the luxury of the original brand of anything. I washed my bowl and spoon and left them to drip-dry on my bare sink surface. I got my keys and I got my bag and I got my exact change in bus fare from the circular glass key-holder on the hall table and I got myself out the door and I got myself to the overly crowed bus stop. I tried to shove my way on the bus. Sometimes I was successful, other times I used incredibly bad language when I was not successful. The rage I got from packed-bus syndrome was high emotion. I could have walked into town to the brown job in twenty minutes but I just didn't want to walk. I wanted to read on the bus. Walking gave me time to think. I only allowed myself to think when I wanted to think. I didn't like being forced into it due to the woeful service Dublin Bus provided. Whenever I got on the bus I then got off at the end of Suffolk Street and I went up the somewhat shaky, battered wooden staircase to the small square office that I worked in. Photocopiers Services. Yes. It did exactly what it said on the tin, or on the small chrome plaque on the navy door. We serviced photocopiers. We sold photocopiers. I sat in between Shannon and Linda under the small window with the peeling off-white paint and constant pigeon pooh.

Shannon was the most boring girl I had ever met in my entire life. She quite literally had nothing to say. She wore her long thin black hair down around her face and applied bright neon-pink lipstick throughout the day, never managing to miss her very crooked two front teeth. Shannon also ate bags of Bombay Mix from nine to five all day long. *Crunch. Crunch. Crunch.* She didn't sell the photocopiers – she did the very small accounts and fucked

7

Mr Brophy the owner every Friday night after their book-club cover-up. They were both in their forties. They were both unusual people. They were both people I really did not want to surround myself with.

Linda was okay actually – it's just I had no interest in seeing people I had to see every day again at night or on my weekends. She did try in fairness to get me out for a piss-up but I always declined. Linda was from Tipperary, an only child, and she supported her mother who was caught for pension fraud and had her pension revoked. Linda was small and wore bright electric-blue-framed glasses with tiny plaits in her hair. She sold a fair amount of photocopiers; she did better with the country people than I did. Honestly, in Tipp she had sold photocopiers to farmers and old age pensioners – she sold to people who simply had no use for them just because she told the story of her poor, pensionless, swollen-ankled mother.

Anyway, to say I can't look at the colour brown any more is an understatement – but back to my new job. Although my brain was in overdrive to think of a way out of the Brown Job, this job had kinda fallen into my lap by accident.

This girl Marina Rafter from my dance class in Townsend Street was chasing some girl in her job.

"Ya wouldn't do me a massive favour, would ya, Kate?" she asked.

"If I can, Marina," I said as I dragged a towel across my sweaty forehead. "What is it you want?"

"Just sit with me in a bar and laugh a lot. I want it to look like we're a couple. I want you to look like you're having fun with me. That's all I need you to do."

So a week later we were sitting in the beer garden of

O'Donoghue's on Baggot Street on a busy Thursday evening and I was there to make this girl, Sorcha, jealous. Well, I say 'jealous' – Marina preferred 'interested'. Marina bought me two pints of Coors Light in return. I'm by no means a big drinker but she insisted on me drinking a second.

I couldn't believe it but it worked.

"Hey, Sorcha, what are you doing here?" Marina had feigned great surprise as she took my hands across the table and rubbed her thumbs across my fingers. A subtle inner-actor she was not.

"It's my local, Maro," tall Sorcha told her as she sparked up a Marlboro Light. The cigarette hung from the corner of her mouth for a few seconds before she removed her matches from her pocket. She cupped her hands and flicked the match, with her hands shielding it from any wind. She dragged hard.

Sorcha was a very lesbian-looking girl. Hear me out for a second here. She wore tartan jeans ripped at the knees with high oxblood Doc Marten boots and a black-and-red lumberjack shirt with a very large Gay Pride rainbow pin on the left collar and a Marriage Equality badge on her right collar. Sorcha had a piercing in her nose, in her chin, in her eyebrows (I'm guessing the tongue and down below but I cannot confirm that) and she had blonde peroxide short hair, shaved at one side but with a sweeping fringe that covered one eye. In her back pocket a neckerchief in paisley poked out.

"God, so it is . . . where is my head at, at all, at all?" Marina pulled my hands so far across the table I nearly lost my balance on the high stool. "We've just been in a bubble these last two weeks, haven't we . . . Samantha?" She smiled at me.

"Yes. Totes . . . totes bubble of love," I offered and they looked at each other strangely. I'd said the wrong thing obviously. Too girly maybe? They weren't girly lesbians, Marina and Sorcha.

Sorcha offered Marina a drag off her cigarette by reaching across me to insert the white stick into Marina's mouth. Marina sucked on it like it was Sorcha's lips.

"We should hook up later if you're still around." Sorcha had cut me out of her frame. Her director's cut of this moment in time did not have me in the scene. I was on the cutting-room floor.

"Deffo," Marina gave back and blew her smoke out, I have to hand it to her, very seductively.

"Laters." Sorcha crushed the fag under her heavy Docs and strode away.

So there and then I had the thought about charging people money to do this sort of stuff. They are back together now the last four weeks. However, Sorcha still thinks I'm jealous every time I cross her and the worst part is, she comes to the dance studio now. She stays at the back of every dance class to keep an eye on me and make sure I don't try and steal her bird back. Marina has begged me to keep it up so I do. I feel like I'm charging their chemistry a bit. There's nothing like knowing someone has a huge crush on your partner to keep you on your toes.

So the idea for this job just sort of snowballed from there. Marina's sister Noeleen was my next job. Marina, in confidence, had told her sister what I'd done for her with Sorcha, and Noeleen told her she could use my services if I was willing. Marina asked me and I agreed to let her pass on my details to her sister. Noeleen wanted me

10

to go with her to a work pitch she had to attend. She was pitching her kitchen interior-design plan to a building firm for a new renovation on a huge house in Blackrock. She needed it to look like she had an assistant working with her in her company '*Combined*'. I played the part of her PA. I went all out in power suit and glasses she loaned me. It made her look more professional at her pitch and she got the gig. After that, Noeleen's friend Emmet needed a female to go with him to an art exhibition at the Hyde Gallery. He was mad about the girl who collaborated with the artist and was too shy and unsure of his place in the art world to go alone. I looked up some details about D Fitzpatrick, the artist, and briefed Emmet. I briefed him really well. He ended up taking her to Chapter One for dinner a week later.

I made a few more possible girlfriends jealous and then it really took off. That's when I got my flyers and business cards made up, with my tagline of, '*Event Companion Available*'. I started getting lots of emails asking me to help out on a whole range of situations. All very innocent stuff, just like the sitting-in-a-beer-garden with Marina – emails from guys asking me to come along to a certain nightclub and ask them to dance in front of the one they really wanted. It was just all a bit of craic in the beginning and I was making a bit of extra money to save towards some Debenhams bedding. I would tell Ciara about it just to keep her amused when she was feeling really sick, just to make her laugh. It was Ciara who suggested I shouldn't be mad and that I should go for it full time. A new and unique business venture. She knew how miserable I was.

"It would get you away from Brown City," Ciara told me as she lay, white, pale and cold under her huge duvets.

11

"I never thought of that," I said as I took her hands in mine and blew my hot breath on them as a mammy would do with a small child. Long, lean fingers. I took each of her fingers and massaged them slowly.

"But if they expect you to sit in beer gardens or nightclubs they need to pay you a lot more than what you're charging. A twenty euro here and a fifty euro there isn't enough. Set a standard price. This is a service they can't go elsewhere for so they have to pay for it. That's the brilliance of the job. You can't be out-priced. It's not like they're plying you with booze because you're not really a drinker. Two or three is still your limit, am I right?"

Her voice was dragged out and I realised she needed to sleep so I popped her hands back under the heat of the covers.

And so I decided to charge top rate for my event-companion services.

My first proper well-paid job was Aidan Guiney. I had left flyers in the hospital canteen at St James's and he got in touch. A thirty-something. Actually, as it turned out, Ciara knew him from the hospital. He was in research, in a lab all day, and in fact looked like he had never seen the sun in his entire life. I met him in Bewley's Grafton Street one Friday evening after the Brown Job to discuss. He was sitting upstairs by the window over a fry-up and a pot of tea. He was a nice guy – a bit shy and shaky but decent enough. We talked it all out – what he wanted from me. I had to 'bump' into him at the top of Grafton Street and make out like I was a disgruntled ex-girlfriend. I had to tell him that I wanted him back. That I had never stopped loving him. His dilemma was this. Sue, his girlfriend of a month, was proposing they should 'take a break'. He, however, was madly in love with her.

"I just thought if maybe we bumped into you by chance and it was obvious that you were an ex-girlfriend but that you really wanted me back, it might make her think I was worthy boyfriend material." He swallowed hard as he pierced the egg yolk with his fork and the orange oozed over his button mushrooms.

He wore thick dark-framed glasses and was very thin for a fry-eater, very softly spoken and balding rapidly for one so young. It was the fact he was in denial about his balding that caught my attention. He had about four strands of wispy hair covering the baldness at the front, and like every man before him who has tried to cover the obvious, it looked pathetic.

"Can I make a suggestion, Aidan?" I removed the white ceramic teapot from between us and laid my cards on the table. "I will be happy to pose as your tortured, love-struck ex-girlfriend but I think you need a bit of a makeover." I chose my words as carefully as I could. I didn't want to hurt his feelings but I did need to help him.

"A makeover?" Some egg had dribbled and hardened slightly on the warmth of his chin.

"Aidan, why do you like this girl?" I passed him a purple napkin and pointed to my own chin.

He grabbed it and wiped the offending egg-stain clean away.

"Sue is the best thing that has ever happened to me. I haven't really ever had a girlfriend – I have always been too caught up in my studies – but we met in the hospital canteen – she works behind the counter there. I'd spilled my milk all over my tray, onto my Shepherd's Pie, and she came to my aid. She handed me out a tea towel and gave me a fresh portion. So we got to talking and then began to meet in the evenings. She is sweet and we get on so well, but I know she's losing interest in me and is starting to just see me as a friend. I really want to make this work. I know I'm not the strong doctor-type she thought she might meet in there but I am kind and I will treat her like a princess." He skilfully speared four mushrooms with his fork and ate them.

"You can't make someone love you, Aidan," I said gently.

He chewed with his mouth closed and then swallowed. "But you see, Kate, I think she is falling in love with me but I think she never thought she would. I know she is probably getting some slagging about me too – I hear the chefs ripping it up for her every time I come to the counter. They call out 'Sue, quick, here's Wally' or stuff like 'Sweet sweet Waldo's hungry'. I know it's all aimed at me. Lately she's been blushing and I've become more and more clumsy, so that's when she suggested we take a break." He opened two tiny gold-wrapped pats of butter, peeling the sides away carefully. Then he scraped both pieces of foil clean and covered his toast in creamy butter. "But, okay, a makeover, I get that – tell me more." He chewed and stirred his tea.

There was a unique quality in how confident he was around food. In control. If only I could channel this into his everyday life.

He crunched another bite.

"Okay," I said. "So let's start with the hair. It has to go – all off – it's going and it's never coming back."

He nodded in agreement and chewed some more.

"Next the glasses, and I love glasses, but maybe we can, if you have the money, fashion them up a bit, ya know? Take a look at some Red or Dead or Ted Baker frames. You have a quirky lab job – you can carry them off."

He was trying to open one of those tiny jam pots now. The strain showed in the veins on his neck as he struggled with it.

"Why do they make these so damn hard to open?"

It popped just as I was about to open it for him and I was relieved.

"Go on, I'm listening, and I've loads of money, loads of it. I just never know what to spend it on," he told me.

"Okay, finish up and let's go. We have a few hours of late-night shopping to do and a date with the Grafton Barbers." I put my phone in my bag and pushed back my chair.

He licked his fingers and thought about finishing the jam on the remaining piece of toast but my eyes told him it was time to press on.

I took him first down Grafton Street to River Island. I dressed him in tight (not drainpipe but fitted) black trousers and a tight fitted light-blue V-neck jumper. He wasn't convinced as we both looked at him in the mirror but I assured him it was the right look. (I had actually seen it on the mannequin in the window – I was no personal stylist.) Then I sent him off to Specsavers followed by the Grafton Barbers – I had to get to dance class. We were to meet at the newsagent's on the top of Grafton Street in the morning at precisely eleven fifteen.

I actually almost fluffed the job up. I honestly didn't recognise him. I stood outside our destination and watched with interest this tall, slim, trendy hipster-type guy, with a closely shaved head and slate-grey designer glasses come towards me, his arm loosely slung over the shoulders of a very small mousy-haired girl.

Then I jumped. It was Aidan.

"Aidan?" I stepped in front of them. "Aidan? Hi . . . I can't understand, Aidan . . . why do you never call me back? I know you say it's over but I just wanted one more chance. I'm so sorry, Aidan. I can change, I love you so much. You were the greatest thing that ever happened to me." I turned to Sue, whose mouth was literally catching flies.

Yeah, a fly flew in and she started to cough hysterically.

"I'll get some water!" Aidan ran into the shop.

"Sorry, I swallowed a fly," she gasped, pulling herself together. "Ugh, don't you just hate that? What if it's flying around in my belly right now?"

"It's not – it's well dead, believe me."

Aidan, her knight in shining armour, galloped up and handed her an open bottle of water. Thank God he had no trouble twisting the cap off.

"Drink it all!" He pushed the bottle up to her face. "If by any chance he's still alive flying about your stomach we'll drown him."

A match made in heaven.

"So how do you two know each other?" she said when she had drunk the water and caught her breath. "I feel like I should leave you to it."

"No," Aidan said. "It's over between Kate and me – it has been over for a long time. You are a great girl, Kate, and I loved how we – how we dated so well together – but – but I have moved away – on, I mean . . ." His performance was less than convincing.

"You look so well . . . what we had, Aidan, it was incredible." I let my lip quiver a little.

"I know . . . that it was . . . passionate, wasn't it? All fireworks and cream crackers . . . but sometimes that's not what is right . . . I have found someone who I am with now. Her." He pointed out the bleedin' obvious and tapped Sue on the head.

"Listen, I'll be in Top Shop, okay, Aidan? Follow me in." She turned and looked up into my eyes. "Kate, is it?"

I nodded, suitably upset.

"I'm sorry you are heartbroken, I really am, but Aidan and I are going out together now. I really like Aidan – he's taken, sorry." She clutched her brown leather bag tightly to her chest and headed off. Good for her.

"She really likes me," Aiden said too loudly and I shushed him.

"She will look back – pretend we are still discussing our relationship!" I hissed at him.

Aidan started wagging his finger at me and saying "*Rhubarb, rhubarb, rhubarb, red leather, yellow leather, red leather, yellow leather*" over and over again and I hung my head. Through gritted teeth he then said, "Yes, she is looking back. Mission still not completed, I repeat mission still not completed." We stood for a few more minutes until he said, still through gritted teeth, "She's gone into Top Shop. Thanks, Kate, thank you so much – I can't thank you enough –"

"You can speak normally now, Aidan," I told him fondly.

"Oh . . . right . . . sorry." He let out a breath. "Oh, your money, Kate."

I almost told him to put his wallet away but I couldn't

– this was my new job now. I needed to make a living if I was to quit the Brown Job. I ushered him around the back of the shop so we couldn't be seen and he handed me a wad of cash. Hundreds.

I flicked through the notes. "Where are you going with all this? I told you eighty-five euro!"

He walked away as he said, "Take it, you earned every penny. I'll keep Ciara updated with how things are going, okay?" And he strutted away towards Top Shop, a new man.

And you know what? I felt I did deserve it.

Three hundred euro he gave me. I counted it all out when I got home. I only came out with three hundred and nine euro after tax in the Brown Job. This job had taken me about three hours in total.

The second big job I did after Aidan I charged even more: one hundred and fifty euro. I was also propositioned.

Dan Gunn had been handed my business card from a friend who had picked it up in a local Yoga studio. Dan wanted to take me to his brother's wedding. Grand, I thought. It was only by the airport and it included a free meal and some free champagne. Bonus. Keeping my costs down all the time, I borrowed a dress from one of the girls in my dance class. She left it for me at the dance studio. The agreement, aside from the fee, was that he would collect me in a taxi the morning of the wedding and pay for my taxi home.

Dan was wheelchair-bound and the nicest fella you could ever meet. He had been a perfect gentleman throughout the day but, at the end of the night, when he'd had a few too many, he asked if he could also pay me for sex.

"I'm sorry – that's not in my job description," I told him, my mirror-acting paying off beautifully. Fail to prepare, prepare to fail.

"Sorry," he bowed his head, "I have no idea why I asked you that. You must think I'm a right prick." He was mortified.

"No – no, not really, Dan. It's a very unusual service I provide and I have no problem telling you it doesn't go anywhere near you and me having sex. I think you're a really attractive bloke but this is the nature of my business. I don't offer sexual favours."

Dan paid me my one hundred and fifty euro and asked me to push him back to the table. To be honest I didn't feel uncomfortable – I was glad he had brought the sex question up. I was prepared and felt in control of myself and my business. I'd handled it really well. I'd been expecting the question. Sex wasn't a huge thing to me – it just was what it was. But this was my business and I'd never had enough interest or, if I'm honest, pleasure from sex to even think about doing it. Oh I had rumbled around the sheets quite a few times thank you very much but I rarely, if ever, thought about sex. Before I left, Dan asked me to another wedding in a few months and I promised him I would go along with him again.

The last email I got from him made me laugh. He apologised profusely again but he'd become more adventurous and he wanted me to say I had changed jobs from the last time and I was now modelling for Assets. Now, bless Dan, but I'm no model. I'm not exactly model-thin – I was once, but it never bothers me in the slightest that I am not now. I associate thinning with ill health, hunger, dissatisfaction and unhappiness. I am a happy size fourteen, which I consider by the way to be a normal size. Ciara tells me that a ten is a normal size. Ciara is probably a size six now. Maybe even a four if such a size exists. My stomach is pudgy, I will admit that. It rolls, just slightly, over my waistband and therefore I don't wear tight tops so I don't subject others to it. It is most likely due to the amount of Chinese takeaway food I eat. I'm not a big drinker. I enjoy a few drinks socially but I never really drink at home or alone. I have a rule: no drink during the week until Friday. Anyway, I'm quite happy with the way I look. My hair is a very light brown and wavy to my shoulders. No problem to maintain; I rarely straighten it. I have a pretty enough face and I am always complimented on my full lips – torturous innuendo of insults as a teenager but now all worthwhile. If I was to tell you who I have been compared to, you might take it as gospel but, believe me, it's not. I have a very, very faint look of Kate Winslet when she is at her 'normal' size, a size fourteen. I wear comfortable clothes that suit my shape. I usually just wear jeans and white vest tops with loose cardigans over them. I love coloured cardigans. Someday I want a red cashmere cardigan. There was one in Avoca opposite where I used to sell the photocopiers – I used to go in on my lunch break and just stroke it. Like a child in a petting zoo.

Did I mention yet I also have a very strong Dublin accent? A *hard* accent, I'm told, as though it's not a good thing. I happen to like my accent. I am who I am. Ciara practises her vowels. She sounds like Eliza Doolittle up in her bedroom drawling on about 'The Rain in Spain'. She sounds ridiculous. You might say 'That's not fair – isn't she trying to better herself?' Right, but why? Her accent is perfect. How is she bettering herself by her sounds leaving her mouth differently? She's still saying the exact same things. I love Imelda May – I keep leaving articles on her lying around for Ciara to read. She doesn't have to better herself. She is the best by being herself. I have been told on occasions at various interviews that my accent is difficult to understand. It really isn't. Ciara wants to have a more cosmopolitan accent, she tells me.

When I was eventually able to move out, I didn't stray too far from the small terraced houses where I grew up. I just popped over the bridge to the fancy new apartments there. A six-minute walk but worlds apart. I love Ringsend. It is part of me, but, as I said, I'm a bit of a loner and you can't be a loner in Ringsend. Everyone knows you. Everyone knows your ma and your da, yer granny and yer granddad, yer first-second-third-fourth cousins once removed, what brought you into the chemist yesterday – and they all stop and talk. They like to natter. I could have got a flat in the block directly opposite our house, when Mrs Heaney in No 142A died, but I didn't want it. I wanted to live around the area yet still be a stranger in Ringsend. The new apartments were perfect. The blow-ins, as they were referred to locally, all lived there. The day I moved in I cried. I cried a lot. Bucket loads. I couldn't believe I had it. It was mine. It didn't smell of his shit.

I have one other thing about me I should probably tell you now. I kind of see flashbacks. A lot. It's become quite normal to me now – I no longer worry I'm losing my mind. In fact, I find it quite peaceful, but it might seem slightly strange to you. Whenever something dramatic happens to me, good or bad, I tend to see an image in my head of Jennifer Beals in the movie *Flashdance*. Not all the time but quite a lot of the time. If it's bad I see the image of her falling down at the dance audition in her black leotard and black leg-warmers, her curly black hair framing her beautiful tanned face. If it's good I see her moving across the dance floor like a goddess and pointing those dancing fingers at the judges, her feet kicking out in time to the music. I don't think it's weird; it's just me. You see, I love dance. I love it like Oprah loves books. Like Bono loves sunglasses. It happened to me completely out of the blue the first time I saw *Flashdance* in the Metropole cinema on D'Olier Street when I was fifteen years old and feeling completely hopeless. As I sat in the dark, alone and frightened, it blew me away. It took me out of my world into somewhere so free and magical. If you're not familiar with the film, it's based on the real-life story of construction worker/welder turned dancer Maureen Marder. It's about a girl with no family connections, a Pittsburgh girl with two jobs, one as a welder and one as an exotic dancer. She has a dream to get into a certain prestigious ballet school. Now don't get me wrong, I don't want to be a professional dancer, God forbid, and I'm not that delusional! I just want to dance. For me. For no-one else. My guilty pleasure. I never want to dance in front of other people. I dance a lot now. I still can't believe I'm doing it when I do it. It's private. I never really tell anyone about it apart from Ciara. It's mine. Personal. Precious.

I didn't take the plunge into dance after Ma left – I had too much responsibility minding Ciara and him to do anything else. I was a wife and mother in a young girl's head. But, years after, when I was a full-grown woman, I took myself into an internet cafe and googled Dublin dance classes. There were a lot. Then I googled: '**What type of dancing is the dancing in** *Flashdance*?' My answer appeared in various forms and I read them all slowly on the screen: '**Flash dancing began in the 1920's and 30's as a combination of dancing and acrobatics . . . tap dancing . . . modern dance . . . a combination of movements . . . free-style dancing . . .**' and so on.

I loved that it was a bit of a mix-and-match. It wasn't classical in its origins. It had evolved. Just like me.

I picked up a pink flyer in Lily Bon Bon's café one Saturday morning. I was sitting in the window seat with a pot of tea and a pancake with chocolate sauce. I was watching the world go by. I turned my attention to this couple at the bus stop. They were besotted with one another. They couldn't stand near enough to one another, they couldn't stop smiling, and they reeked of happiness. I hated them. I tore my eyes away and dipped some pancake into the sauce as I tried to focus on the flyer under my plate. I pulled it out and read it. It was advertising a small dance school, above Macken's, a bar in Townsend Street, that offered classes in modern dance, hip hop, tap and ballet. The image on the flyer, completely illegal, I imagine, was of the poster of Jennifer Beals in *Flashdance*: the iconic image of the water scene, where she is on a chair, her body arched, drenched in water. I reacted to it immediately. I wanted to go. So I made myself go along that very Saturday evening.

I walked into town slowly but determined to go inside and take a look.

The dance studio was run by a very flamboyant redheaded gay man called Phillip Stark. Phillip was extraordinary and I fell in love with him from the word go. He exposed me to a kind of personality I had never encountered before. He exposed me to what I had been missing. I just felt I had met my match. He was what I was always looking for in a friend. This was quite unlike me. I never usually trusted people until I got to know them really, really, really well. Like me, he wasn't from the type of background that saw him having a career in dance. He was originally from Salford, in a rougher part of Manchester in the UK, and was bullied for his sexuality most of his life, even ending up in hospital once when they cut his Lycra silver short-shorts off him with a Stanley knife in the Salford precinct and managed to give him a six-inch cut up his leg to his groin in the process, resulting in him losing one of his balls. (I suppose when I tell that story I should say testes?) He will show you the scar if you ever meet him. Readily. He is always draped head to toe in Pineapple Dance Studio clothes. Yellow mainly. He loves teaching and he's brilliant at it. Never, ever, ever does Phillip lose his patience teaching a step or a movement. Never does he give you the impression you simply aren't good enough or you just can't do it. He is encouraging and accepting and fabulous. Phillip knows what dance can give you. I go to his place on a Friday night most weeks, sometimes after a class or sometimes, if I'm not at a class, I'll just call into him. We open a few bottles of wine and watch 1980's movies, like *The Breakfast Club* and *Pretty in Pink*. His favourite is *Ferris Beuller's Day Off*; he has a mad crush on Matthew Broderick and on Sarah Jessica Parker.

That first evening I crept into the back of the studio (it is a function room with a wooden floor but Phillip insists we call it the studio), my face burning red. I was mortified. I saw a few people warming up and I went to run for the door. What was I doing here? I couldn't dance! I was such a freak! As I put my hand on the dark, tarnished, once-gold doorknob, I felt a hand on my shoulder.

"Hey, chuck, why don't you just sit this one out and watch?" He gave me a huge smile.

I shook my head. "Ah no . . . thanks. I think it's a waste of time, I . . . I have . . . I have never danced," I stuttered. Jesus, but my face was red – it was burning off me.

"Oh, you have, chuck." He raised his hand very slowly and isolated his index finger from the rest of his fingers. Then he brought it to the front of his head and tapped it ever so lightly about twenty times before simply saying, "In here."

I sat. My life changed.

Chapter Two

So I had a job where I ended up in Deansgrange Cemetery yesterday. Work had been flooding in but this was the first job I'd had since I quit the Brown Job a month ago that didn't sit with me very well.

I was a mourner. I had been asked by Jimmy in the Pork Shop in Ringsend (it sold every type of meat under the sun but it was known locally as the Pork Shop) to come along to his Auntie Dolly's funeral as a mourner. He had heard about what I did from Ciara over the phone. (I'd have to start giving her a cut of my wages soon.) He let Ciara ring in orders and then he'd fly down on his push-bike to the house and deliver the meat. I had just popped into the Pork Shop for some white pudding. I was a big fan of white pudding. I loved white pudding on toast, spread with Heinz tomato ketchup. Delish! I'd never cooked it when I was living at home because I'd associate the smell with *him* and I didn't want to ruin white pudding for myself. (It's not exactly PC to say you like white pudding, is it really? It's up there with tripe. I don't like black pudding on account of it apparently being pig's blood. I don't know what white pudding is made of but don't tell me if you do know. I have managed to avoid knowing for this long.) There were few things I could eat now. I could no longer look at boiled meats. He loves boiled meats – like corned beef, ham, bacon ribs, and pig's feet. Bits of it would stick to the side of the sink where the water couldn't wash it down. Hardened puke.

We would sit at the table every Sunday, as was his wish, at three o'clock, him in the kitchen serving the dinner Ciara and I had prepared. Usually corned beef, boiled potatoes and cabbage. Sometimes turnip. Sometimes cauliflower.

He would put on his best face.

"Here we go, isn't this nice?" He'd sit heavily.

Me da. The state of him. The smell of stale cigarettes and booze stuffed up my young nostrils. No matter how much Impulse I sprayed on myself I could still always smell him.

"I always sit down with me family of a Sunday," he'd croak through his hangover.

Asshole. Pig. How he could even say the word *family* I could not understand. As delusional as a child putting a tooth under its pillow.

His yellow stained fingers shaking as he gripped his water glass. The liquid flowing from side to side.

"What time did ya fall in at?" I'd ask, stabbing at my cabbage with my fork. Light green on top of dark green. Pure Irish in its heritage and colour but I felt no love for it.

"Ahh, wasn't too late. Went forra bit of a stroll down be the docks b'fore I came home." He'd push the food around.

We always knew he was too hungover to eat it but he liked to pretend. Helped with his fear. He'd force some in near the end and it always came back up. Most fathers excused themselves from the Sunday dinner table to let the dog out, or to watch Manchester United. Ours excused himself to puke his guts up.

"Ya did in yer shite." I'd stuff the foul cabbage into my mouth. Chewing through the greenery.

"Ah, here, stop, will ya? Will you, Kate?" Ciara would implore.

Me and him would stare at each other. Our love for her burying our hatred for one another. And we did hate one another. That was a fact. I started hating him way before he started hating me though. I hated him way before Ma left and continued to hate him all the way to my current stage in life. Why? He is an alcoholic. Dad has a disease. Sure he has a disease, a disease he also infected me with. No, I'm not an alcoholic but alcohol has traumatised me. My memories. It has hurt me so badly. Robbed me of a youth.

Anyway, fuck him, I was telling you about the mourner's job. I told Jimmy I'd do it but that all he had to pay for was my taxi there and back. It didn't feel right to ask for a fee.

"Why exactly do you need my services?" I'd asked him as he sealed my white plastic bag of pudding with red tape and slid it across the glass counter top.

"Because I'd like a few people in the church for her – look good, ya know?" He wiped his bearded chin with the white sleeve of his not-so-clean coat. "She was always on her own, our Dolly. Never had anyone in her life – only child, never married, had never even been across Ringsend

28

Bridge, ya know, in eighty-five years. Born, raised and died here. Angela, the wife, would send across her dinner every day with one of the kids through the park to the cottages. One Sunday we were there and she was sitting in her usual spot in front of her open fire, hands black as soot. A woman of few words normally. Her face as crinkled as an old pound note and her hair down to her arse but always rolled up on top of her head in one of them bun things. All she'd ask for was a cigarette or two. She never wanted us to bring her a whole packet. Anyway, this Sunday she surprised us all.

'I'd like a ring,' she said in her very hushed voice. She whispered like.

'A what, pet?' Ang asked her, leaning in closer.

'A big fancy diamond ring,' says she.

It was all me and Mary could do not to break our hearts laughing, bless her!"

He wiped the counter top with a pink cloth. Big, sweeping motions taking in the whole counter top with one sweep.

"'Alright,' says we and we arranged to bring her into O'Connell Street to the Happy Ring House to have a look. Nothing mad, ya know, not the real thing. Though she had a few bob put away, did our Dolly. She is burying herself, so she is. Not costing us a penny. Never wanted to be a burden to anyone. Anyway, right, there we were the three of us at the No. 3 bus stop outside the library. We'd wrapped her up in an old grey shawl we found in her drawer. Shoes worn and brown. The bus pulled up. We eased her on, up the two steps and sat her down but when the bus pulled off she started freaking out, screaming her head off.

29

'Get me offa this thing!'

The bus was just coming up to Ringsend Bridge and I wanted her to make it over. Who'd have known her voice could reach that level?

'Hold on, Dolly, two more minutes!' I gripped her tiny wrinkly thick blue-veined hand. Veins like them big noodles ya get in that place Waggomammo, she had.

'No!' says she. 'Get me off now!'

We had to stop the bus . . . anyway, sorry, that's two euro eighty cents, please, Kate love – special price today just for you – when yer ready." He then nodded at my purse.

"Oh right, yeah." God, there must be a queue behind me for him to stop so abruptly. I'd been so immersed in Jimmy's tale I hadn't thought of that.

I turned. I caught my breath and coughed.

There stood a guy I had never seen before. One guy. That's considered a queue in the Pork Shop. Rule of thumb: someone behind you, you stop talking, pay and get out.

I couldn't take my eyes off the guy. Of slim build, yet he seemed to occupy the entire space of the small shop. Striking presence. A blow-in by the looks of him.

"Sorry," I managed, catching my breath eventually as I stuck my pudding under my arm and struggled with the change in my purse.

"Not a problem, please, do take your time. I'm in no rush."

Me and Jimmy both stopped now and I turned back to look at him again.

A blow-in. I was indeed correct. A definite blow-in with an accent Prince William might have. Or Hugh

30

Grant. A voice that could address a nation. There he was. A fish out of water. I paid Jimmy and took a longer look at Hugh Grant as I stepped out of the way to let Jimmy serve him. He was wearing a black tight-fitting round-neck jumper, jeans and black runners. Light-brown hair kinda like that Bradley Cooper actor guy. Thick and messy. Deep brown eyes. Deep dimple in his chin. He was holding a copy of the *Irish Times* and his brown leather wallet.

"May I?" he said, hesitating about stepping forward.

Jennifer Beals' dancing fingers engulfed my mind. *Flashdance* . . . 'What a Feeling' . . . Jennifer was bouncing along in front of the line of judges, on fire. Ah, not now, Jennifer! I shook my head.

"Yeah, yeah, ya may, work away there . . . see ya, Jimmy!" I moved back towards the open door onto the lane.

He moved to the counter.

"See ya, Kate! Enjoy yer puddin', pet!" Jimmy roared.

Cringe. Cringe. Cringe. Pudding is a private thing. It's not something you share with every Tom, Dick or Hugh Grant type. It is the type of food people judge you on. I once knew a girl years ago who had a guy break up with her over breakfast when she ate the pudding. It was apparently acceptable to have pudding on your plate, but never, ever to actually eat it, or so he'd told her. I know times have changed with the trendy pudding dishes now but back then it was food for thought. I still didn't feel my love of pudding was something I wanted to share with the world. Quinoa yeah, pudding no.

I walked home after that encounter, a little shocked and bemused at myself. I didn't suddenly fall for guys. I didn't get hit by Cupid's arrow. Oh I'd like to, don't get me wrong. I would love to want to have sex with someone. I just didn't. As I already told you, I have *had* sex obviously and even had sort-of-boyfriends that all lasted about two months or so. I've had sex with about six guys, and every time it has just been okay. I never felt that explosion of wonder that other women say they experience: the opening of a flower, the magnificent discovery of the G spot. I suppose, as Ciara tells me all the time, it's because I've never been in love. True love where the love and lust is all-encompassing. It just wasn't in me to fall in love. The boyfriends that did last a few months saw me becoming needy. I hated needy. I figure I just never wanted them not to want me so I'd cling on for all the wrong reasons. I'd had a belly full of not being wanted by both my parents. But I have never had that 'Oh, look at him! Drool! Swoon! To die for! OMG!' making-a-heart-shape-with-both-hands-and-instagramming-it emotion in me.

So what had happened in the Pork Shop just then, I questioned my still beating-at-a-fast-pace heart as I pounded the pavements home. That man had caused my dancing Jennifer to appear and he had kinda stopped me in my tracks. This was all a bit too swoony for my liking. The blow-in guy was attractive, yeah, but what had Jennifer joined in for? How could he have that effect on me when I'd only seen him for a few seconds? Put it this way: I actually felt like going back towards the Pork Shop to see if our paths crossed again. To get another look at him. Was it fate? Were we destined to cross? I was distracted thankfully as I said hello to Old Mr Dent outside the chemist's. He wanted to stop and chat, so I had to pull my phone out of my cardigan pocket and pretend it was ringing. He was stone deaf so he'd never know if it was ringing or not. That was the problem with Old Mr Dent: people stood on the street literally screaming into his face as he nodded and kept asking them questions. He couldn't hear a word of the answers but he let on he did. We all knew he couldn't hear a word but we all let on too. He wanted it that way. Probably sounds mean now that I pretended to be on the phone but it was half an hour once you stopped and I had to get home to get changed for the removal in an hour. I looked down at my pudding and for some reason suddenly the hunger had gone off me.

A removal and burial later, I'd done my job to the best of my ability and given Dolly a good send-off. With my bum numb on a hard wooden bench I had sung along to her favourite hymns, joining in in a loud voice wherever I could. I tried not to think about the occasion. Death. The readings. The life that was. What it was all about. Who knew?

I saw Old Mr Dent across the pews and shimmied my way across to him. I'd been feeling guilty about not stopping for him the day before. I smiled at him and sat in close beside him. I let his body tip off mine and I'm not sure why but I imagine he liked the human contact. He had no one. He hadn't had anyone since he was a young boy. Wasn't it a pity he and Dolly couldn't have shared their lives together? I wondered now if their paths had ever even crossed. "Brought himself up so he did," was the tale around Ringsend. His parents had both died within two weeks of each other when he was thirteen years old. His mother had been nursing his father who had passed away with tuberculosis and his mother took a massive heart attack a week later. Not much in the way of social services in those days. The corporation let him stay in the house and the boy Dent worked his fingers to the bone down on the docks morning noon and night to keep that roof over his head, turf on his fire and fresh fish in his belly.

I tipped him on the shoulder at Communion to alert him and walked up beside him. I didn't normally go to Mass and I wondered why I was going up to receive Communion now. It was a beautiful church and I felt peaceful in it.

When we laid her to rest and left Deansgrange, I shouted at Mr Dent for twenty minutes. He removed his tweed cap, twisting it between his old hands, and was delighted with the bit of company. Lips smacking, spittle flying. I felt better about myself. Doesn't cost much to be nice.

I hailed a taxi on the road and hopped into the overpowering heat in the backseat.

"Ringsend please – the new apartments before the bridge."

I sat back. Death was too hard for me to think about right now. It loomed too heavy over me. I needed to dance. I hadn't been to a class in a few days and I needed to release. I closed my eyes for the journey home, safe in the knowledge old Mr Dent would be enjoying a few 'wake-ing' pints of stout in The High Chaparral. The traffic was heavy down Beech Park Road and the driver swore under his breath. The heating was stifling. I wondered if Dolly was anywhere right now. Was she being reborn as a screaming new baby? Was she galloping through open fields as a horse? Was she looking down from a heaven in the skies or was she just simply gone? Gone. Forever. Jennifer Beals fails, falls flat on her face in the audition room, her perfectly shaped legs twisted underneath her. *Get up!* I urge her in my head. *You can do it. I'm rooting for you.* She remains on the ground, head bowed as the taxi driver swerves in and out of traffic and eventually drops me in a sweat at my apartment.

I paid him out of the fifty-euro note Jimmy had given me – always a bone of contention for taxi drivers. I was keeping busy but I couldn't really relax, I needed to get a few more jobs in. My funds were doing alright but it was the reassurance of more work coming in I needed – otherwise I'd be looking for a Blue Job. It would be great if I could do some kind of extra advertising. The carefully placed business cards and flyers were working really well, but I was thinking about taking out a Facebook or Twitter ad. Would I be mad? It was such a sensitive job it could be a dangerous thing to do. I could only work for people I trusted – so far it had all been locals. To open myself up to the big scary web would be a mistake – I knew that deep down. I needed to come up with a clever way to get more advertising for my services that completely ruled out any social media. A radio ad perhaps? Something like the dating websites had, serene but clear and to the point.

I jumped out of the taxi and strolled down towards my home. On the approach to my apartment block I avoided all the white lines. I was a bit OCD, I must admit. I touched wood a lot. I shook my own hand and spat discreetly when I saw a magpie. Don't ask me why. I counted up the numbers on the registration plates of cars. I tried to avoid anything adding up to thirteen all the time.

I had to brush my hair an even amount of times on each side. Weird shit like that.

I got to my apartment-block door entrance. I keyed in the code of the main door and stepped into the marble lobby. The smell was always so clean. Slightly industrial and more than likely way too many chemicals sprayed all around, but it appealed to me. Every time I stepped inside it was like a dream. I loved it so much. I checked my little letterbox. I still got a buzz from putting the teeny tiny key into the box and looking for my mail. It made me feel so independent. Just to be clear, I was only renting, I hadn't actually bought the apartment, but it didn't matter to me one bit. It felt like my home. It was my home. My landlord was a local lad from up in Sandymount who I sort of knew growing up. He lived in Dubai with a local Sandymount girl and they had five kids. He had told me that someday they would come back but not for quite a few years yet. They wouldn't be able to live there in any case when they returned as it was too small so I was perfectly confident they would buy a large four-bed detached on the Strand Road and leave me paying off their nest egg. I just had this feeling that me and my apartment could stay together forever if we wanted to.

A few flyers and a Vodafone bill.

"Black or white?" a voice asked me out of the blue.

I jumped and let out a little yelp.

"Oh, dreadfully sorry, I didn't mean to startle you." Hugh Grant. Standing there at a letterbox, a little key in his hand. In my building!

'Wha'?' I was about to ask but I stopped mid-thought when I got it. The pudding. I was as clever as his Royal Plumness, no doubt.

"White. Don't like black, do you?" I shut the small metal door with a bang and twisted the key as I pulled it out.

"Oh black, without a doubt, absolutely delicious." He smiled at me. "I recently tried Clonakilty black pudding with blue cheese and baby beetroot toasties. Have you tried that?"

"I haven't." I felt a bit dizzy – the heat in that taxi must have really taken it out of me.

I smiled back at him now because I didn't know what else to say. We stood smiling at each other, boxes now closed, letters in his hands, flyers and the bill in mine.

"Okay, see ya." I walked to the lift, my mourner's shoes squeaking on the posh parquet floor beneath me. I pressed the little orange button. I pressed it a few times. I looked at my reflection in the gold lift doors as I awaited its arrival. I could hear it whirring its way toward me and it couldn't come soon enough. The black suit I was wearing was old and looked misshapen and baggy in the reflection. It made me look way heavier than I actually was.

"It's such a tiny elevator this, isn't it?" he said, standing next to me now.

I could smell what I thought was chlorine.

"Yeah," I answered, looking down at my shoes.

"I'm Hugh by the way . . . Hugh Clover." He extended his hand.

I couldn't believe his name was actually Hugh.

"Kate." I shook his warm hand.

"I mean, it says a maximum of three persons. I would question that though and say two, wouldn't you?"

The accent was pretty sexy. I hated to admit such

fickleness in me that I could be won over by an accent.

"Yeah," I answered.

The doors opened. We both got in. The tiny space closed in on me. He was wearing a grey-and-red Adidas tracksuit and carrying a large navy gym bag.

"Level?" he asked me.

"Four, please."

He hit four with his thumb, holding it on the button for longer than he needed to. He must be on the fourth floor too, I thought.

"Have you just moved in?" I asked.

"Yes . . . well, just over a month ago. I haven't ventured out much," he said with a smile.

To be honest, I tried not to get to know anyone in the building. There was one girl who always tried to talk to me, some model. I was polite but distant with her. She was too tall and too thin and made me feel like someone had stood on me and squashed me.

We rose up in silence. I wasn't much of a conversationalist with people I didn't know. I was bad enough with people I did know.

My phone rang. Praise be. I rummaged in my suit jacket pocket and pulled it out. Ciara.

"Hi," I said, pulling my hair from my mouth.

She wanted to see me later that evening, she told me through cracked words. She had something she wanted to talk to me about. She sounded weak and the coverage in the lift was crap. I agreed I would try and stop by later and rang off as the doors opened.

"Goodbye now, Kate." He smiled at me again, remaining in the lift.

"Oh, are you not on this level?" I stepped out.

"No. My place is up on six." He shifted the gym bag higher up onto his shoulder.

The doors started to close but I put my hand in between them, waving it up and down as it re-opened.

"Why did you press four then?" I asked him.

"Because you said you were on four." He looked puzzled. "You are on this floor, are you not?"

"And wha'? Ya wanted to see where I lived?" I moved back now. I had no idea why I was saying this to this strange man. No idea whatsoever.

"Em . . . no, I just thought it mannerly to press the button for you. Isn't that how it's usually done? And now that you've got out, I'm going to continue up two levels to my own place. Doesn't that make sense to you?" He looked slightly amused at me now.

"That's just weird," I told him. Why was I still talking to him? What was I saying to him?

I had embarrassed him now and his skin flushed a little. I took my hand from the door.

"Oh right, sorry . . ." he said.

The door shut slowly and muffled the rest of what he said.

I entered my apartment. My sanctuary. I leant my back against the door. I threw my keys on the small glass hall table. What did I just say to him? What on earth was that all about? He let me out of the lift first, so what? Of course he did. We hadn't come to his floor yet. He must think I'm a total lunatic. What were the chances he lived in my building? Well, every chance, dopey, since he was shopping in the Pork Shop yesterday! Duh!

I shook my head clear of him and went to change my clothes. I pulled off the horrible old black suit but couldn't throw it away. I changed into my jeans, white T-shirt and a navy cardigan. I looked in the mirror in my bedroom. I looked a lot slimmer than when I was looking at myself in the reflection of the lift. I hung the suit back up anyway. I didn't know how soon I might need it again and this sent a shiver right down my spine. My entire body shook as I slid across the wardrobe doors.

I would have loved Ciara to move in here with me but she just wouldn't leave him. No matter how many times I asked and begged she just wasn't budging.

I came out into the bright living room. 'Sparse' was certainly a word you could have used to describe my place. I had a two-seater brown-leather couch in the main room, a plasma TV and a cream rug on the dark wooden floors. No curtains on the windows. Why would you? I could see it all up here.

I knew Ringsend like the back of my hand but this was a different Ringsend. A new Ringsend with new inhabitants. Gone were the dockers and fishermen and in were the IFSC workers and the staff of Google. People who could walk to their jobs now located here. In the library I taught myself more about my area. My history. My Ringsend, situated in Dublin, its geographical coordinates 53 degrees 20' 31" North, 6 degrees 13' 35" West. I'm fascinated by its history and the realism of its people. There is a no-bullshit law in Ringsend. A no-asshole policy.

From my fourth-floor windows I could see right into Ringsend Park, I could see as far as the Poolbeg Towers. The sea of blue. The seagulls soaring. The lights of Dublin illuminated my nights. I had my own personal light shows up here when darkness fell. Ringsend is so flat I could see for miles.

I headed into my small kitchenette. I was like one of the seven dwarfs: a small table for two, two small black IKEA seats. Mini-microwave. Mini-fridge freezer. I did everything small. I had two small cups, two small plates, two small bowls. Two knives, two forks and two spoons.

Tea seemed like an option so I filled the kettle and popped the button on. Not many people would really believe, or could really understand how I loved this silence, but I truly did. I made a green tea (look at me!) and decided to call it a night. I could do that. I could just switch it all off and sleep. I prayed in thanks that I could sleep anytime and anywhere, knowing that nothing's as awful as insomnia. Ciara suffered from it badly and it was beyond dreadful. I planned to call and see her the next day – I was too tired to go around there tonight. I stripped naked and crawled under the pristine covers and onto my soft cotton sheets. My legs spread the width of the bed and I buried my face into my goose-feather pillow. Before I turned off my bedside light I stared at the wall. I had a poster. Just one. *Flashdance*.

Chapter Three

The heat of my apartment calls me up from an unplanned nap on my couch and informs me summer has arrived alongside it. I tear my tongue from the roof of my mouth and shift my dead-weight body parts. The late afternoon sun streams colourfully into my living area and it's such a beautiful light. Yellowing and peachy. I watch it dance for a while as my limbs come back to life. Fresh. Soon Ringsend will be full of those bright nights ahead. I love the long evenings. I wriggle my fingers to rid them of the pins and needles as I reach for my iPhone and click to refresh the email account. A few beep-beeps sing out. Wonderful. A new job has come in. It has to be acknowledged, however small my advertising campaign is, it is working. I'm getting work. I need to order new flyers and business cards as I'm almost all out. I'd like to make them even better, make them stand out more. I'm proud of my self-employed state. The more I work the more work I seem to get. It is incredible the amount of service I am providing to people who just need a body beside them. An ally. I cast my eye over the mail as I stretch and yawn loudly.

***

Hi there, Event Companion,

My cousin has passed me on your email details and filled me in on what it is you do. He saw one of your flyers in the IFI cafe in Temple Bar. I think you might be the very person I am looking for. Here is my dilemma: my fiancée left me last year after having an affair. They now both live together in his house and I can't sell the house I am in that we built together as the market value is still so low. My best mate Seán is getting married on Friday 21st April in the Central Hotel in town and my ex-fiancée is going to attend as she is still very good mates with his missus-to-be. I don't want to go but I have to because he has always been a great friend. But I need a date. I couldn't face them on my own – she is bringing him with her, they have told me. I would like to employ you to escort me to the wedding (it's all in the hotel, no separate church). I will need you to stay until after the meal when I too am leaving. My cousin suggested we can bluff that you are a doctor and on call? That way we can leave whenever we want with a perfect excuse. Let me know your price and if you are available, will you?

Cheers,

Mark McMahon

***

Hi Mark,

Thanks for getting in touch. I'm really sorry to hear what has happened to you. That's really shit but then again life just is really shit sometimes. Yeah, that's all fine with me. I will put it in the diary if you are okay with my fee. For a wedding, including clothes etc, I charge two hundred and fifty euro. If you are okay with that, will you collect me or do you want to meet me there?

Your Event Companion

* * *

Hi Event Companion,

Thanks a million – that's perfect – two hundred and fifty is fine – and cash okay, I presume? I will pick you up at twelve if that's okay? Just email me back your address, yeah?

Mark

* * *

I unfold myself from the couch and rummage for my diary in my bag on the floor. I write in the details carefully. Then I email him back with my name and address and tell him cash works for me! Pulling my hair up into a messy bun I head into the bedroom. Slipping into my change of clothes, jeans with a grey sweatshirt, I slide my feet into my flat grey pumps. I pop my phone into my back pocket and head into the kitchen. Opening the fridge, I rummage for my last bit of cheese. I find it at the very back. I peel my small piece of red cheddar with my potato peeler. Growing up, the potato-peeler in our house always double-jobbed. That booking with Mark is next Saturday so I'll need a new dress for it, I think. I want to look the part for Mark. He sounds sweet. What a terrible thing to happen – to be engaged to someone and have them cheat on you like that! Just have the balls to tell the person it's not working and leave them upset, yes, but with their dignity for God's sake. Love really is a fool's game sometimes.

I'm not exactly getting rich from my new job, yet, but I'm ticking over and that is just fine with me. What is rich anyway? Healthy organs? And in fairness two hundred and fifty euros for a day's work, free food and a drink or two isn't too shabby, now is it? Just the cost of the bloody dress is a problem. If only I had girly mates I could borrow off. I can't ask that girl, Sarah McDowell, in my dance class for another loan of her dress – she was the one who gave me her dress for Dan Gunn's wedding but last week she emigrated to Dubai. Maybe Phillip might know someone who would lend me a pretty frock?

My phone beeps again. I pull it from my back pocket. It is Ciara, demanding my presence tonight. I am being summoned to meet with her this evening in the house. In fairness I do pretty much see her every day – this week has just been a bit mad so I didn't see her yesterday. Ciara has no dresses. Ciara hasn't had the need to wear a pretty dress anywhere in a very long time. I always have to go over there to see her nowadays; she simply isn't up to coming over to me any more.

I turn on my gas hob. *Click. Click. Click.* The blue flames flicker on and it hisses loudly at me. Digging my index finger into my tub of coconut oil I put a good lump of it into the pan. It slides around, the hard mass becoming a liquid in nanoseconds. I chop up my pudding and put on six good-sized pieces. I cut two thick slices from a Vienna Roll, hoping I'll be able to stuff them into my toaster – I always wish someone would invent a toaster for thicker slices of bread. I flick on the radio. It's a really old silver standing machine I've had for years. I had saved up to buy it in Dixons when it first opened on Henry Street. I had then, and still do to this very moment, adore it. I flick the dial a few times. I miss Gerry Ryan still. No one does morning radio like Gerry Ryan did. No one had that ease with listeners that Gerry Ryan had. Although, like most of the nation, I never actually met him but I still missed him for a long time after he left us. I settle on some easy listening with Andrea Hayes on Sunshine radio and music fills my space as I flip my pudding and hum along.

The doorbell rings and I freeze. No one rings my bell. Like no one. Ever. My bell has honestly never belled out in the two years I have lived here. My pudding sizzles. I stand still and poke it with a black burnt spatula. It rings again. Shrill through my ears. Who the hell is it? No one could get in the door downstairs without the code so it wasn't Jehovah's Witnesses. I turn off the blue flames and push my pan to the side. I walk to the door.

"Yes, hello, who is it?" I call through the door.

I close one eye and look through the peephole. I see a person. These peepholes are bloody useless.

"Couldn't fry up my black for me, could you? I've no cooking oil left!" comes back to me, heavily accented.

I know immediately who it is and I yank open the door.

Hugh Grant. Pork Shop pudding in the red-taped white bag in his hand.

"How d'ja know what number I lived in?" I hold onto the frame of the door.

"Pardon?"

I can't take my eyes off the dimple in the middle of his chin.

"How – did – you – know – what – number – I – lived – in?" I repeat more slowly.

"Simple . . . I used my nose."

He grins at me and I feel all woozy and a little giddy. What is going on with me? I must be starving. I ate very little yesterday or today. I have an overwhelming sense of déjà vu but I don't believe in déjà vu. I don't know why. Well, I do. I'd googled it before – when in doubt, google it out. It's the phenomenon of having a strong sensation that an event or experience has been experienced in the past. Probably not the case, the experts believed.

"I'm sorry – I can't – I'm in a real hurry." I want to say yeah, sure, of course come in, sit down, take your hoody off, put your feet up, watch the telly, make yourself at home – but I don't. I am way too shy.

"Of course you are, how silly of me, apologies – I'm sure you have plans – I'm so sorry – well then . . ." He tosses the pudding in the bag from one hand to the other. The plastic bag rustles. The relief of its noise filling the dead air is overwhelming. I can't speak.

His presence is again looming and I realise with a jolt it's all a bit thrilling that he has come looking for me.

"I'll just . . . well, perhaps I'll just go to Lily Bon Bon's for a fry-up." He backs away from my door.

"It's a nice fry they do . . . they give you loads of . . . beans." What the fuck am I saying?

"That's true . . . they do. I have eaten in there quite a bit . . . sausages are good too." He has stopped now, pudding tucked under his arm.

"Yes, indeed, very nice sausages." I'm starting to burn up.

"Well, goodbye then. Have a good evening." He turns and walks towards the lift.

"Okay." I shut the door quickly.

Appetite gone.

I walk slowly to the window and stand tight against the stark white wall. I usually only touch the walls when I have washed my hands thoroughly, I love them so much. The cleanliness of them. Perfection. Unspoiled.

I wait. First I see him and then my eye is drawn to his long narrow black shadow that follows him. He has put on a leather jacket, brown, old-looking, and he has a baseball cap on now. The cap looks like the nose of a Concorde in his long shadow. His body is tall and wiry. I have some sort of unhealthy, weird interest in him and this bothers me. Why? I haven't fancied anyone in so long. How can I fancy someone I don't even know? Surely that is weak and stupid and I am a brighter woman than that? Whenever I see myself with a man it is always because we have a meeting of the minds.

I need to dance. I need to get to a class.

I watch him press the lights at the pedestrian crossing; he stands still even though no cars are coming and he could have just jogged on across. Still he stands there waiting. Waiting. The Green Man flashes and he crosses and disappears into Lily Bon Bon's café.

I slowly move away and into the kitchen. Chucking the pudding into the bin, I scrub the pan. Jennifer appears as I use my Brillo pad with force. *Flashdance* . . . 'What a Feeling'. This is completely ridiculous.

Chapter Four

HUGH CLOVER

Dear Mr & Mrs Collins,

I have no words to express my deepest regret and sympathy. I have gone over and over the events of July 11th in my head, played it out every night, and I can only put my mistake down to a serious lack of sleep. I had worked 48 hours straight. But that's no excuse to offer for what you are now going through. I can only tell you . . .

Hugh Clover pauses before throwing his ballpoint pen on the table and pushing back his chair in Lily Bon Bon's. The squeak from the rubber bottoms on the chequered linoleum floor is enough to make the elderly gentleman eating his small fry look up and grimace. Hugh holds up his hand in apology and goes up to the counter.

"May I have another black coffee, please?" he asks.

"Have a seat, I'll drop it down ta ya, love," the waitress replies with a smile.

Black coffee. Maybe that was it? Maybe he just hadn't drunk enough black coffee.

He returns to his table and sits again. The mainly un-eaten fry sits in front of him as he gazes out the window. His head aches now and he rubs his temples.

"Have ya a headache, love?" the waitress asks as she places the black coffee in front of him.

"A bit . . . yeah." He was still getting used to the people of this area. It had dumbfounded him in the first week how they all interacted with one other on a very personal level. A customer with a headache in a London caff would never be noticed.

"Ya hardly touched yer fry either! D'ya want two Solpadeine?"

"No, thank you, I'll be fine."

She moves away to serve another customer.

He crumples the letter up, tight into a tiny ball in the palm of his hand. He squeezes it so tight it hurts. What is this? The one-hundredth letter written, never finished and never sent? He drops his head into his hands. It is all completely irrational, he knows that. He needs therapy; he needs a lot of stuff. What he is doing is beyond sick – God, he knows all that, but he simply can't stop himself.

He watches the steam rise from the coffee cup and inhales the familiar smell. He needs to find a way to stop what he is doing. It is becoming out of control.

Chapter Five

KATE WALSH

"Darling!"

Air-kissing. Always lots of air-kissing. Air-kissing suits me. I'm not one for people's wet lips on my face. Tactile is not my middle name. I think it's most inappropriate when strangers kiss each other. Ciara does it all the time.

"You will not believe who came into the studio last night? Well, that girl I met you with that time we went to *Rock of Ages*, at the Bord Gáis Energy Theatre, the one from the Brown Job, you know the one I mean, the one with a criminal for a mother, the one with the tiny plaits in her hair? Linda, is it?"

Phillip is walking away from me now. I always think he expends too much effort on his walk – all those jerky hand, hip, bottom, leg and neck movements.

"Breathe, Phillip, you really need to take a breath," I say as I follow him, dropping my dance kit onto the floor.

We go into his office which is in fact just the space behind the old empty bar with a flap for letting servers in and out. He perches on a high stool and begins to tap on his MacBook which he has placed on the counter. He peers at it with his eyeliner-tattooed eyes over un-needed, prescription-free glasses with their John-Lennon-type frames. He is wearing a bright green tight Pineapple T-shirt, long black shorts with green trim and pumps on his feet. Sockless. I have never seen Phillip wearing socks. Even during that really bad snow of 2011 he refused to be socked. "To be socked is to be mocked," is all he would say. Today he sports a bush-load of red stubble to match his hair.

I pull out a high stool and sit beside him.

"Yeah, Linda. What did she want?" I ask.

"To dance, darling, what else?" He tip-taps on his keys. "I put her off – as much as I need the money from her I knew you wouldn't be comfortable with her here. The Brown Job is so behind you we don't need any reminders of it, do we?"

Tippy tap tippy tap. All seemingly very urgent tapping, peering over his glasses until he gives in and takes them off altogether.

"So, let's concentrate, we need to get this fundraiser idea off the ground, Kate. I'm now three months behind on the rent here and that red-rimmed arsehole of an owner Donal wants me out. He can't see what I'm creating up here. He says he can use it to store kegs. Kegs! Stinking barrels! In my dance studio!" He pants before continuing. "He said these words to me on the phone earlier: *'Just pay me what you owe me or I'll get the RA onto ya, ya mad queen!'*"

He jumps down from his stool now. He loves a bit of drama all the same, although I know even this is too close to Shakespearian tragedy, even for him.

"The RA! A mad queen? *Moi?*" He sucks in way too much air through his nose until it is pinched and red. Exhaling a draught, he says: "He basically said he's going to have me shot, Kate. I told you that *Love Hate* was a deadly dangerous programme." Sharp intake of breath again. "Come . . ." He curls his index finger at me over and over.

I follow.

We leave the office and walk out onto the wooden floor.

Phillip has had bars attached all around the sides and has erected a full mirror wall. He has spent a lot of money on this place. Phillip worked for years as a travel agent in Manchester. He made pretty good money. He came here for a dance competition in 2009 and returned the year after to set up this dance studio. He still does some work for the travel agency in Manchester online, although he won't admit that. It does, in all fairness to him, look like a proper dance studio. What am I saying? It *is* a proper dance studio. Our dance studio. I am more than proud to be a part of it.

He stands in the middle of the floor, doing a ballet plié. This was how he thought, how he came up with his ideas, we were informed – they came easier to him while he was in dance positions.

"See, Kate, we need to bring people here, to see what it is we do. I need to raise six grand – six thousand euro – to get a proper lease off this homophobic tit-bag Donal Dick-face – Donal Dipstick – downstairs. I imagine secretly Donal Dungpile wants me. This pub has been here for forty years, it's a listed building, and it is, simply put, never going to close down or be sold, so if I could give Greedy Guts a lump sum and get him to sign a lease for the next ten years we'd be sorted. I'd be legal. Just think of what we could create here if we knew we had it for the long term? We could build a proper dance company." He stops now and begins to raise his leg. He is extremely flexible for someone who is actually a slight bit overweight for a dancer. He holds his left leg up high in the air with his right hand. Straight as a ruler.

"I dunno 'bout that, Phillip – why don't we just look for some other premises that we can lease? Maybe an old dance studio already fitted?" I go to get my dance kit.

"Never! This is our place – it's where we first met, Kate, it's special. I don't belong anywhere else. I belong, we belong, here. Dancing on Townsend Street. Its location actually means something to me. Its history, its bravery, its resilience, all inspire me."

I am pulling off my jeans and slipping into my pink Aertex top, pink leggings and dance shoes. It's the only time I would wear pink leggings obviously. I never mind undressing in front of Phillip. I begin my own warm-up. I slowly rotate my neck from side to side. Looking from one corner of the room to the other. Shoulder rotations now. Up and down. Arms swinging from side to side. Loosely without tension.

The door opens and Maura walks in. I say walks but she kind of hovers. I love Maura. She was once a ballet dancer and then a teacher and she is very ladylike and very quietly spoken. Maura spends a lot of time in the studio. We are like her little family.

"Lunch today, dears, if you're both free and lounging around until then?" she says.

We both nod. We regularly eat early lunch together after class.

Now, if I'm perfectly honest with you, Maura is, or

should I say was, the type of woman I considered to be an 'intellectual' and totally out of my league. She lives alone too but every day her day is pretty damn lovely. She is happy like me to live alone. She has a Shih Tzu called Chang that she adores. She rises at seven every morning, makes a green tea and lets Chang out into the back garden. Then she dresses in her leotard, tight black leggings, black pumps and sprawling woollen shawls and walks Chang to the local organic supermarket beside her in Dalkey and buys two fresh free-range eggs and some Irish smoked salmon. She crosses the road and buys the *Irish Times*, making pleasantries with people as she passes. She returns home, makes her scrambled eggs and salmon and more green tea and reads her paper in her conservatory until ten o'clock. Then she gets ready for her dance class. When she arrives at class she always puts down her bag and makes plans for lunch. At lunch a green tea is always taken and then back to the studio where she lies down and sometime dozes but mainly watches the dancers for an hour while she digests her food and then she dances and by God can she dance! She is seventy-three years old with the body of a fifteen-year-old *Teen Vogue* cover girl. Flexible and lean and full of hard muscle. She's told us she was once a well-known ballerina – that was how she had made her living for years – but she never elaborates. There is no doubt she was once an incredible dancer but I will admit Phillip and I googled her and could never find anything on her. She chooses to tell us no more about her youth or in fact much about what had happened in her life up to the time we met her. Maura is a private person and I felt bad about googling her so we agreed never to do it again.

After class Maura returns home to her routine. She takes Chang for his regular walk. They walk up through Dalkey Village, past Finnegan's pub and on up to the sea front where they stroll the beach for an hour or so. Maura likes to chat with the other dog owners she has become friendly with. She collects seaweed whenever she can. On the way home she does her light shopping for her dinner, usually a piece of fresh fish or breads and cheese and some Parma ham. After dinner she lets Chang out the back for a while and prepares for bed. I love this bit. She's told it so often I can say it word for word with her now when new dancers join the studio or join in on our lunches: "Bedtime preparation is vitally important. One must take it very seriously. One must change one's sheets and pillowcases every night. I do try to always air them on the outside washing line, weather permitting. So once I have changed my bed, I turn down the cover and pop a hot-water bottle in. I leave a pint of water by my bed with lots of sliced lemon. I close my curtains and turn on my bedside lamp. A high-wattage bulb is frightfully important. Then I retreat to my bathroom to begin work. I lie in a lukewarm bath, no bubbles or any of that toxic stuff, but I do wash with some bicarbonate of soda and wash my hair with tea-tree green shampoo. I emerge and rub some olive oil over my skin then slip on my pure silk nightwear. I dry my hair, let Chang back in and then it's straight into bed. Then I read. I read and I escape into a world I have never known, can never know, and situations I'd dearly love to still be in but with my age I can't. Harry Potter and Jason Bourne live in my head. I must rest the body as much as possible, but not my mind. I never rest my mind."

I think she's fucking deadly.

I continue to do some stretching and then I do some squats before I start to dance. I pull legwarmers up over my pumps and begin. It is a class and it is, I am delighted to see, quite full – about twelve people in the studio, some beginners, some ex-professionals. You see, Phillip's classes are a bit different to other classes. He teaches movements and you can copy him or you can just dance your own dance. There are no rules. It's a free class. Phillip has put on music and it is mellow and easy. I concentrate on Phillip at first and let my limbs follow through with fluid movements as he is doing at the top of the room: the much-laughed-at swaying of a tree in a warm spring breeze and then all the way to the violent shaking of a tree in a December storm. Phillip is now being battered by a storm. His body rocks and shakes fiercely. My mind clears instantaneously.

Jake beside me, the plumber from Cabra, uses the class to make shapes that are both ridiculous yet heartfelt. He is releasing. Jake jumps in the air and then he rolls on the floor. It is his dance. Maura uses the bar, as graceful as a white swan on an early Sunday morning, gliding down the canals. We roll and stomp and glide and jump. I dance. Phillip and Maura never look at me, everyone is lost in their own dance moves, doing their own thing.

I move in front of the mirror. Slow fluid movements. If you had no idea about dance you'd think I dance terribly, just moving my arms in weird directions and rolling my neck and my head. I am doing modern dance. A free-expression style of dancing that developed in the early 20th century as a reaction to Classical Ballet, Maura had explained to me. Follow-through actions. Every movement was followed through. It compels me to watch me in the mirror. I look like a dancer in a dance studio and that never ceases to amaze me. I take long slow deep breaths and forget about everything as I let the music move my body. I can do certain 'proper dances' that Phillip has taught me. I can do the tango and the foxtrot and the cha-cha. I can do a lot of 'proper dances'. I focus on my shapes.

"Drop at the waist more!" Phillip approaches me now. He holds my hip bones and twists my torso around. "Trust your mind, Kate, trust where it's taking your body." He flutters away.

I don't dance all the time. I dance whenever I want to. Because I can and that is the most freeing thing for me. Sometimes I come here twice a week, sometimes I don't come for weeks on end. All depending on how stressed I am. My mind tells me when I want to dance. A few thoughts come into my head now and they are most unwelcome. Him. The blow-in. Hugh. Hugh Clover but now he would always be Hugh Grant to me. It was as though we knew each other or something. I couldn't put my finger on it but all I knew was I would be lingering in the foyer now whenever I could and that was just daft. I spin myself around the floor, tying to remove his image from my mind. What was it about him? Good-looking sure, but it was more than that. I fancied him. I suppose I had to admit that now. After three meetings I very seriously fancied the arse off him.

As we wipe down after class Phillip approaches me.

"I've had an idea, chuck – you know what we could do in here – what we could all do together to raise the money we need? Well, we were just talking there, me and Maura

. . . we could hire a bigger venue and put on a show, *Swan Lake* perhaps – end of June?" His eyes are all excited.

"I don't dance in front of people, Phillip, you know that!" *Flashdance* Jennifer falling over on those perfect knees at the audition. Her record skipping as the needle painfully scratches the vinyl. Her black legwarmers fill my mind. I pull my hair up into a bobbin on top of my head and wipe my neck. Unfortunately I have to walk home from here as the lack of showers means a bus journey is out of the question – and it is spitting rain now despite the day's sun-filled promise.

"No, I know, I know, I know, I know, I know. I know. Maura and I and some of the others could dance and you could be the producer? Maura has loads of contacts in all the ballet schools she taught in and she says she could get some of them to come and dance. I thought we could use those and put a show on around them with our gang?" His eyes are wide and pleading. The tattooed eyeliner done in his teens fading now. So cheaply done it's fading more from his right eye than the left, making it look even stranger, as though he has one eye bigger than the other.

"I don't think enough people would come, Phillip," I tell him. "We wouldn't make anywhere near the target. That's a lot of bums on seats – to raise six thousand euros!"

His hand flies up and covers his face. "Stop with the negative vibes already! We can at least try? We could book the theatre in Belvedere College – it's a local theatre, a five-hundred seater, and we could raise the six grand. I am not the Scarecrow, I do actually have a brain. I relate to Dorothy for a whole other variety of reasons too, you know. Sooooooo, all we need is to sell at least four hundred tickets at fifteen euros each and there's our target. Anything over and above is profit."

"I'm not being negative but like I said that's an awful lot of bums on seats, Phillip. Four hundred people! Are you listening to yourself?"

"Where is your sense of Carpe Diem? I'm finding this all a little too hilarballs coming from you, Little-Miss-I-invented-my-own-job! I can do anything if I put my mind to it. You must believe. But if you don't, then, as my Cher would say, '*I don't need you any more, I don't need you any more!*'" He makes a fist with his left hand, raises it to the centre of his forehead and closes his eyes.

"Stop, Phillip, stop being so melodramatic!"

He jumps in the air then and flitters his feet as gracefully as any prima ballerina.

"Who wouldn't want to pay to see me at work?" He is only half joking.

"But what kind of a show? You need to put on something substantial to use a big theatre and get people out for a night. Have you thought that through? How would you advertise it? Where is your budget for that going to come from? Insurance?"

"Negative, negative!" Phillip chants.

"It's a huge ask to get four hundred people out of a night, that's all I'm saying. Our dancers here are not those types of dancers, as far as I am aware. The one-time professionals dance purely for themselves now – they have no interest in performing in public ever again." I tell him this because I don't want him to be disappointed and get his hopes dashed by this ginormous idea.

"Well, isn't it about time they did then? They are all still marvellous dancers! Perhaps this is all happening for a reason. The God of Dance wants us all to re-shine." He stares up at the ceiling, clasps his palms together in prayer under his chin and closes his eyes.

"There is a whole lot involved in putting on something like this." I sigh as I realise there is little point in trying to talk Phillip out of this. I muse as I watch him 'pray'. "The only thing that might work is if we ask our ex-pros to help us out, maybe pay other professional dancers, and use our amateur dancers as background."

"What do you mean 'pay other professional dancers', Kate? We *are* all dancers! I hate the word 'professionals'! Dancers are dancers." He flicks his hair with his hand. Nothing moves.

"Can you dance *Swan Lake*, Phillip?" I am stern with him now.

"No, but I have choreographed it in Manchester twice, dear."

Touché, he thinks.

"Not the same," I say.

"What do you mean?"

"Who did you work with on it?" I try to make this as clear as I can for him. Break it down.

"The local dance schools," he tells me.

"So would you say it was an amateur production of *Swan Lake*?"

"Yes."

"Did people pay to see it as an amateur production?" I hope I am taking him on this journey of realisation with me. We need to make it crystal clear it is an amateur production. That way we'd have small expectations from our audience who'd be just buying tickets to support the cause. I'd be happy to be involved in that.

"They did, actually. We sold out the Scouts' Den two nights in a row!" He throws his hands out wide in his defence.

"Right, well, that's a positive, but we need a target audience like the Scouts' Den had. So who came? Who paid for tickets?"

"Every parent of the students, every cousin, brother, sister, friend." He counts on his fingers and runs out even though it was only a five-finger count.

"Well, there you go: that's all we can do here. We advertise the show as an amateur production of *Swan Lake*. There is less expectation that way. First we must get some of our ex-pros to sign up and see if we can get even one professional who we can pay if necessary. Then we use the ballet schools Maura suggested, dance college students, our amateur people and any other dance studios that might like to get involved. Just like with the Scouts' Den, here's the trump card: all the dancers involved must each sell a certain number of tickets, that's the deal. We need them to dance for free and we sell it to them that the pay-off is they get to dance *Swan Lake* in a huge theatre in front of their family and friends whilst saving the dance studio above Macken's!"

The penny drops but he will never admit this was my idea.

"Exactly – that is just what I was trying to say. So let's set up a meeting for next week . . . after the next Beginners' Hip Hop Thursday evening, in the Beggars Bush?" He bats his eyelashes at me. "I think this *Swan Lake* idea of mine might just work."

"Grand, okay," I say.

"I am a genius," he self-professes.

"You are. One other thing though, Phillip: you don't

dance in it, you choreograph it – you have done it before and you are a brilliant choreographer."

"As you wish." He bows before me.

This is a little family to me now. I owe it to them to turn up and help plan this fundraiser. I will try to be positive that we will manage to raise the money to keep our dance studio.

"I think I'm going to eat now. I know it's still early but I'm suddenly starving," I say as Maura approaches.

"That's fine with me," Maura replies and throws her dance bag across her shoulder.

We wait for Phillip to talk with the remaining, straggling dancers. There is usually a small bit of flirting involved with the ones who wait behind. When he is done, the three of us head downstairs where we always go. Macken's Pub. We dance up above and eat down below.

The pub has a patriotic history dating back to 1916 when Michael Collins apparently hid out in the basement for seventy-two hours. It was your typical old-fashioned pub – bit of an overpowering smell of bleach, wooden floors, high stools with carpet-covering and high tables with a row of booths at the back where once they thought it might take off as a bigger eatery. Dozens of faded pictures of Michael Collins in cheap thin gold frames grace the walls. His name is mentioned in high glory in here as it should be. Occasionally a tourist bus will stop by. Basically the pub just has a load of aul' lads up at the bar supping Guinness with 'the ginger ladies' (i.e. whiskeys) sitting patiently nearby awaiting their turn to be necked. The lads let the cold air in as they stand at the doorways puffing fags. The odd few office workers who want to get away from the Starbucks crowd to have a gossip about Pamela in Accounts and her new boobs come in too.

We slip into a booth now and the smell of the newly opened carvery fills my nostrils. But I usually just go for the excellent toasted cheese-and-ham tomato sambos Tom makes.

Maura always has the same thing. "Two slices of brown bread, some beetroot, and a green tea, please, Tom," she politely requests.

Tom the chef had to buy green tea in just for Maura and she keeps count in her teeny tiny diary and warns him when they are down to the last seven teabags.

I watch Phillip as he jumps up. Gliding his brown tray down the line, he poses at the carvery.

"Five minutes, Phillip! It's not twelve yet!" Tom roars at him from behind the carvery as he removes tin foil from silver trays and steam gushes up.

"That's fine, Tom. I am aware of the rules of the carvery. I am just eager to be top of the queue, that is all. I don't want any pushing and shoving when the clock strikes twelve." Phillip then turns around and gives a double take as though he is confused as to why there is no one else in the pub queuing for food, only him.

I laugh. Tom throws him a filthy look. I continue to observe him as Maura pulls out her miniscule notebook to mark off yet another green tea bag. Phillip rises up onto his tippy toes and back down as he waits. He couldn't care less what anyone thinks of him and it is inspiring to me. So inspiring.

"Two slices of the roast beef, trim the fat, no gravy, Tom," his voice booms then. "Some mash, no roasties, some carrots, no peas. And can I have just a handful of skinny chips on the side purrrrlese and *merci beaucoup*!"

Tom grunts at him. Tom and his scowl. Tom would never get a job in Happy Chef because Tom isn't and never will be a happy chef at all, at all.

Maura and I order from Áine, the waitress, and we chat about my *Swan Lake* idea for the fundraiser. She says she will get her thinking cap on and is happy to let us use her contacts.

Soon we are all eating in a comfortable silence. I can't eat with many people. I find it uncomfortable. I always feel I'm chewing too loudly. That's why I sort of admired Aidan Guiney: he ate that fry in front of me with gusto. Apart from being with Phillip, Maura and Ciara, I really preferred to eat alone.

When we have finished, Maura says, "Just musing there, dears, and although I do love the *Swan Lake* fundraising idea, you really do need a proper hold on a premises, Phillip. That Donal man is quite the ignoramus. I could help you put a deposit on another studio, you know, I'd be happy to . . . I have some money . . ."

Phillip clatters his fork down on the table. "Not in a million years am I taking a penny of your pension, Maura, noway-dot-com-forward-slash-over-my-dead-rock-hard-abs-body. I said to Kate only earlier that this place is perfect for us; we just need to raise enough to secure a proper lease. Don't tell me we can't raise six poxy grand between us? Sorry, Maura." Phillip placed his hands over Maura's – she absolutely detests swearing. I sometimes wonder what my da would make of Maura.

"I'll start to jot a few ideas down for the meeting next Thursday," I say. "Oh and Phillip, would you know anyone who could lend me a fancy frock for a wedding on

Saturday? I borrowed off Sarah McDowell last time and she's gone to Dubai now." I wipe my mouth with my purple paper napkin and place it across my empty tomato-juiced plate. Delicious sambo as always.

"Oh fabaroodoo! Another wedding gig, tell me all?" Phillip leans in on his elbows, chewing his beef quickly but with his mouth shut tight.

"This guy's girlfriend . . . no, actually, sorry, she was his fiancée, had an affair and then dumped him and moved in with her new boyfriend. They had only built a house together and all. Anyway, they're all going to be at the same wedding – it's his best friend's. I'd like to look nice for him."

"Slag!" Phillip spat. "Oh! So sorry, Maura!" He slaps his wrist hard.

"It's understandable, dear, under the circumstances," she tells him.

But I shut my eyes tight. "Phillip!" I despise that word. I had heard my dad hurl it at my mother and bowl her over too many times. *Strike! Emily is down!*

"I could have some suitable garments, dear," Maura surprisingly pipes up. "I mean, they are hanging there donkey's years but some are very beautifully made."

"Thanks but I'd never squeeze myself into your dainty clothes, Maura," I say with a laugh. "Okay, I have to go, emails to answer this afternoon, apartment to clean, family commitments and all that jazz." I pull on my cardigan and throw my €5.50 down for my sambo and water.

"Goodbye, Kate, dear," Maura says.

"See you for our Friday night, chuck, yeah?" Phillip rises to his feet as I nod.

I air-kiss him and take my leave.

Chapter Six

"I'm here, Ciara!" I call up the stairs as I slam the front door of my da's home behind me. My old home. Ciara's home but I always call it his. The loose glass rattles in the wooden doorframe. It is freezing in here. He never allowed us to turn on the heating as kids, and over the years we just didn't put it on because we knew it was another bill he would ignore.

I stand in the hall and wait for her to come out of her bedroom. It's the only place she can stay warm. I hear the door open and the old floorboards' familiar creak as she comes down. She is looking deathly pale and swamped in huge old woollen cardigans with black leggings and oversize Homer Simpson slippers on her feet. Everything dwarfs her.

"Jesus, you look like . . . like shit," I tell her.

"Cheers! I'm grand, stop fretting, just a bit off me – off *my* game today," she corrects her inner Eliza.

We head into the tidy old-fashioned 1970's Deco kitchen. Yellow presses, yellow-and-brown lino on the floor and yellow and brown sunflowers print on the torn, faded wallpaper. Ciara has bought a new oilcloth for the kitchen table, I notice, a deep red pattern with small black birds soaring high. It seems so out of place amongst the retro mellow-yellow.

"Where is he then?" I enquire as I remove two mugs from the rusted stainless-steel draining board, turn them the right way round and give the kettle a good shake. Satisfied with the weight of water, I replace it and click it on.

"He's in Dirty Nelly's with Luke Griffin," she manages.

"You want me to take you to outpatients?" I ask her now. Her colour is really that bad.

"No, I'm goin' – I am *going* on Friday. I'm just going to go back to bed today. I got the new Marian Keyes book from the library, ordered it weeks ago, so I'm looking forward to that." She runs her cupped fists over her tired dark circled eyes.

She sits now. Slowly, as an older lady might sit after receiving the worst of news.

"Where were you last night? I asked you to come over."

She puts a coaster in front of each of us as I sit opposite her. They are green with a pattern of tiny high rise buildings printed in gold. So familiar they look strange to me now.

"Weirdest thing ever . . . wait till you hear this." I am about to tell her all about Hugh Grant as we wait for the kettle to boil but she doesn't give me a chance.

"I have news on Mam." Her voice is slow now. Her words carefully considered. Deliberate.

Silence fills the small space as the kettle screeches to boiling point. It's one of those kettles that doesn't turn off itself. Steam rises around us. I catch my breath.

"Huh?" I get up and click the kettle off. I leave the tea unmade as I pull out one of the old wooden chairs at the table beside her, reposition the worn-out, stuffing-deprived cushion and sit beside my darling sister.

"Auntie Brenda wrote to us – look here." She pulls a crisp white page from her cream bobbled cardigan pocket. If she had read it a lot it didn't show. It was in pristine condition. Folded over, twice

"Mam is in Connemara – that's in Galway, Kate," she continues in this put-on low voice.

"Connafuckingmara?" I spit at her.

"No, just plain Connemara." Her self-taught voice lessons are really paying off. She is clipped. *Con. Eh. Mar. A.*

"So what, Ciara?" I stand up now and turn to the sink. I fish two cheap tea bags from the cream ceramic tea jar (is there anything worse than cheap tea bags?) and I fling them into the mugs. They land slowly and delicately. I pour the water in and watch them darken and then swim to the top. I push them around with the teaspoon, stirring them in the hot water, turning it darker and darker with every turn.

"So what? Are you serious, Kate? So what? Our mother is back in contact with us after twenty-eight years and all you say is 'so what'? Our mother is back. She wants to see us." She struggles to her feet. "Fuck, you are so bitter it's not true. I should be bitter! *I'm the one who should be bitter!*" She is screaming at me now. "You have it all, Kate! You just fucked off outta here and left me to take care of Da an' I'm fuckin' sick, I am really fuckin' sick and you couldn't give a fuck!"

White foamy spittle gathers at the corners of her small rosebud mouth. Ciara almost never uses bad language.

"You are so selfish, Kate!" She grips her forehead with her splayed fingers as though her head is about to burst open.

I know she will calm as quickly as she exploded – she always does. So I say nothing more and I wait. I turn back to my tea-making duties. I always knew we'd find her one day because I knew Brenda knew where she was. I also knew she wasn't evil. Oh, of course I'd go with Ciara to find our beloved absent mammy, of course I would. After all, we'd been actively looking for her for the best part of the last five years, to help us, since Ciara was diagnosed, after a bone-marrow biopsy, with aplastic anaemia. She was gradually becoming sicker and sicker and we were told she would need a bone-marrow transplant to save her life. This cruel disease, in which the bone marrow and the blood cells that reside there are damaged, was slowly killing my sister.

We had sat opposite the consultant, Doctor Doyle, in St James's hospital and fearfully asked all the questions, Ciara and me.

"It's a bit extreme – a bone-marrow transplant." I was horrified.

"This is the only potential cure," he told us out straight. "A stem-cell transplant, commonly called a bone-marrow transplant, will replace Ciara's failing bone-marrow cells with new ones from her matching donor. These multipotent stem cells in the bone marrow will reconstitute all her three blood-cell lines, giving her a new immune system, red blood cells and platelets."

"So can I donate my bone marrow?" I asked him without a second thought.

"Yes, siblings usually have the best chance of being a complete match. A successful bone-marrow transplant requires the donation of human leukocyte antigens, or as we say HLA, near-perfect-matched bone marrow. Family members are our best bet."

"What are the risks to her?" I had asked.

Graft failure was the first, he told us. The fear was that if graft-versus-host disease set in, this would be a real setback. This was where the immune cells in the transplanted bone marrow recognised the recipient's body as foreign and attacked it.

We had moved fast and both me and the da had all the HLA-typing required tests done. We were both matched donors for bone marrow and Ciara and me were ecstatic. I couldn't believe Da was considered healthy enough but he was. He'd donated first, believe it or not, but four weeks later she got an infection and his donation was unsuccessful. Ciara spent three weeks in intensive care. Then I donated and the same infection set in after twenty-eight days, my donation also proving unsuccessful. Again we were back in intensive care. We were back to square one. The Irish Unrelated Bone Marrow Registry hadn't found a suitable match, yet. While we waited Ciara had regular blood transfusions and a heap of medication. Surely Mommy Dearest would be our saviour?

I squeeze the bags against the ceramic of the cups and let the hot spoon burn my fingers. It feels good. I turn to the fridge, remove the milk jug and put it on the table. I carry both mugs and a spoon to the table.

"Calmed diddly-doodly-down yet? At least that outburst put a bit a colour in your cheeks. Sorry – I shouldn't have said 'So what?'. Of course it's a big deal – because hopefully she'll be a match for you. So of course I'm going to go see her with ya – what d'you think I am?" I blow and sip the hot tea and it tastes of nothing.

I hate the words 'bone' and 'marrow'. The bone. The marrow. The fact my sister will surely die if she can't get a bone-marrow transplant to take. Even though my donation didn't take for Ciara I remain on the donation register. Maybe I'll be a match for someone else someday.

I let my mind go there. To the two nights I spent in James's Hospital. It was hard. I had more obligatory tests, chest X-ray, ECG, urine analysis and more blood tests, and it all still looked good. When I was admitted into hospital for the operation Ciara never left my side; she slept on the hospital floor both nights on a blow-up bed, even though she had her own hospital bed down the hall. I had the operation under general aesthetic so felt nothing during the donation. Lying on my front, the two needles were inserted into my pelvis to extract the bone marrow. A doctor inserted one syringe, a nurse the other. I woke up with two simple sticking plasters over the mark where the needles went in. Slightly pathetic-looking. The next few days I did feel some pain in that area and general tiredness but was so anxious about Ciara being prepped I never gave it a second thought. Ciara was taken straight into hospital as I left to have her immune system wiped out in preparation for my donation. A donation which only lasts for 72 hours outside the body so it was time-critical.

We knew all the risks from before. While the transplantation is a lifesaving therapy not all recipients survive. Sometimes a patient's body cannot withstand the procedure for a variety of those reasons Doctor Doye had told us about on our very first visit. Ciara, like the trooper she is, came through after my donation. So nothing hurt as much as when, twenty-eight days later, she suffered another major setback. She was rushed into hospital with a serious infection. Despite the fact we did everything by the book, the transplant was unsuccessful. I was so careful of her. I showered her meticulously the first few weeks she was home, she painstakingly cleaned her gums and teeth, avoided all fruit and vegetables. Still, it was not to be. Ciara's operations had both gone really well in theatre so Doctor Doyle, who performed the procedure, was very upset but positive we go again.

Doctor Doyle was emotionally attached to Ciara's case now, I knew that. He had taken her out for dinner last year when she had recovered after my donation failed. He wanted to see her again but she wouldn't. I know it wasn't because she didn't like him but because she didn't think it fair on him. Ciara was just like that – she was always thinking of others – she rarely thought about herself. I could really do with taking a leaf or a tree or the entire forest out of her book.

"Kate? Are you listening to me? She was our mother for a long time, Kate. She loved us. I want to see her again, anyway, not just because . . ." Ciara trails off, stirring her tea some more before banging the spoon off the side of the mug and placing it down on the table.

"She left us," I say.

"Move on, Kate," she tells me.

"With an alcoholic father and no money." I continue to stab the words into her.

73

"Move on, Kate," she repeats and lifts her mug between her hands.

"No, why should I? What kind of a person does that, let alone a mother?" I pick up her spoon and stir my tea hard. I whisk my tea basically. I am stirring for no reason except that the continual stirring is giving us something to focus on.

"You can't stand to be with him either so what's the difference? You left me here with him too." She puts her mug down.

"Take that back!" I bang the spoon on the table and send droplets of tea spinning through the fraught air.

"No." She folds her arms.

"Take that back right now, Ciara Walsh!" I am livid.

"No! It's true." She sits back into the wooden seat.

"How many times have I asked you to move in with me? How many times have I begged you to leave him and come live with me?" I shake my finger at her.

"But you know I can't," she says.

"No, that's not true. I know you can!"

"No . . . no, Kate . . . I can't leave him here alone . . . he would burn the house down." Her accent is sounding more like her own now.

"Let him!" I spit.

"He's my father!" she spits back.

"He's a prick."

"To you maybe."

"What does that mean?" I am incredulous.

"He's . . . nice to me," she says, a bit quieter.

"He's nice to you. Am I actually hearing this shite? Are you fucking serious right now? He is nice to you?"

"He just is." She swallows hard, making a gulpy noise

as she does it, and picks up her mug again.

We both look into our mugs, now studying our tea intently.

"Was he nice to you when we had to take our duvets down to the car and sleep on the road most nights because we were so afraid of him and his drunken rages?" My voice is more controlled now.

She has no answer.

"When, Ciara?" I lower the tone of my voice. "When is he nice to you?"

"When he's sober." She looks into the distance, not blinking.

"When he's sober, yeah, and how many hours a day is that?" I reach for her cold hands.

"We have breakfast together. He is lost, Kate. He hates who he is . . ." She shrugs my hands away.

"Well, that makes two of us," I say as I move my hands back to pick up my mug of tea.

"He has a disease, Kate, the same as I have this disease."

Ciara has been trying to preach this line to me for years, I know that.

"Oh, come on!" I smash the mug down on the table now. I am not buying this. "Get the feck out of it, Ciara, please! Daytime TV is wrecking your head. How can you compare alcoholism to aplastic anaemia!" I am incredulous. Too much Dr Phil. Talk-show overload.

"Honestly, Kate, when he's sober, for that while in the morning, we talk about all sorts – mainly about his mistakes and his illness. Just last week he said, for the first time ever, that he'd really like to stop drinking." She is animated now.

"Well, I'd really like to ride the fucking Grand National winner but that's not gonna happen anytime soon, now is it?" I wipe the spilled tea with the palm of my hand, clearing the drops off the high-soaring birds. I wipe my wet palms on my jeans.

Ciara gets up slowly and moves to the sink. She throws her tea down the plughole. I can't help but be shocked by her skinny bony frame. I'd do anything for her, of course I would.

She rinses her mug over and over.

"Here, showiz the letter, will ya?" I say eventually.

She turns off the tap and puts the mug upside down on the draining board, then wipes her hands dry with the tea towel. She hands the letter to me.

51 Devonshire Road
Bispham,
Blackpool,
Lancs
UK
Tel: 00445694372933
14th April 2014

Dear Kate & Ciara,
You mother, Emily, has asked that I write to you to let you know she is living in Ireland, in Oughterard in Connemara, Co. Galway. Should you wish to contact her at any time, please just let me know. I have all the details.
Auntie Brenda

I read it just the once. I refold it neatly along its grooves and return it to Ciara. She puts it back in her bobbled cardigan pocket. My sister is now a whiter shade of pale. She leans up against the sink.

"I mean, how completely bizarre that she gets her sister to write the letter? Can she not hold a pen? So now we have to get useless, nosy, English-accented-even-though-she-only-moved-there-at-thirty-three, bitch-face Brenda involved to get to Mommy Dearest. All seems very Jane Austen, doesn't it? 'Madam has returned. Stop. She requests her daughters visit. Stop. Come by carriage this very evening. Stop.'" I'm tired now. I've had enough of this. I want to go and stalk Hugh Clover. "You need to get to bed, Ciara."

The door rattles and rattles again with the noise of someone struggling to put a key in. I freeze.

"Why is he home at tea time?" I stare at the clock on the yellow kitchen wall, the straight line of the black hands confirming the time of six o'clock.

"He makes himself leave the pub at ten to six every night now, Kate. That's what I've been trying to tell you when I said he'd really like to change his ways. I've wanted to tell you this for ages – that he comes home early, but you just won't listen when I try to talk about him. He gets home, in time for the first bell of the Angelus, every night." She gets up and goes to the door.

I lean back in my chair and peep into the hall. I watch her slowly open the door for him. He stands swaying from foot to foot and nodding stupidly.

"Is de key . . . is de key, love . . . me key . . ." he slurs at her.

Ciara pulls the key from the door and he leans on her. He leans on her. I actually can't swallow and for a moment I panic. I'm choking but then I manage to swallow. Slowly, slowly, they walk into the kitchen. I stare at the pathetic image. Her sick bony frame holding up this piss-head.

"Kate, could your pour a glass of water while I get him up the stairs? In his plastic beaker, please – it's on the draining board."

He squints behind his broken glasses. Black gaffer tape holding them together. I stare at his clothes. Old. Ancient. His grey slacks, the thread so cheap and nasty. They are so short they reveal his off-white socks and his dirty scuffed black shoes. His green anorak hangs off his skinny frame. What's left of the limp greasy grey hair covers one eye. A face so worn by alcohol, it's the face of any alcoholic you have ever seen. Individuality lost a long time ago.

He turns and slurs at me. "Izha ya, Katie? Katie Walsh . . . izha? Ahhhh, howya, chicken?"

"Oh spare me!" I stand up.

"Whatza say, love – say 'gain ta me?" He holds his hand behind his deaf left ear as I push past his greasy body. I leave the kitchen and the hallway and slam the front door behind me.

The glass rattles so hard I am expecting it to fall out. It will one day. It will shatter everywhere.

Chapter Seven

I can feel the rage building up inside me. *Flashdance* Jennifer is on her knees, her head bowed down and her fighting spirit broken. Curled up in an embarrassed ball. *Get up!* I urge her. *Get up, Jennifer! You know you can do better than this.*

So I know I need the walk. Walking and dancing. They both eliminate my baggage if you will. I shake Jennifer out of my mind and take myself down the long street of Stella Gardens, up the steps and along the river and down towards Bath Avenue. I see the crowd on the way to the dogs at Lansdowne. I pound the pavements, my temper still at high levels. That man. That *thing*. That excuse for a human being. The traffic is heavy and people are pissed off. I like this. I want to whole world to be angry right now. Why won't Ciara get out of that house? I know I'm going to have to move back in soon because he can't look after her. None of us know what way it's going to go with Ciara. This maddens me even more. I worked so hard to get away. This is killing me. I walk faster, the wind cutting my face and it is cold now against my skin. I like this too. The stinging of my skin. My nose runs and I don't even bother to wipe it. I walk up Shelbourne Road and keep walking until I finally find myself outside Beggars Bush. I'm out of breath now, my eyes watering and nose still running. I need a strong black coffee. I pull a tissue from my pocket and wipe my eyes and then blow my nose. I push the doors open and the bar is quiet. It smells how I expect it to smell. Pubby.

It's warm inside and I see him immediately sitting at a low brown oak table reading the *Irish Times*. Hugh Clover. I cannot believe this. My heart goes a little flippy. A half-pint glass of Guinness rests dangerously close to the edge of the table. He is engrossed in reading. I don't know how anyone reads the *Irish Times* – it's not that I'm incapable of understanding the articles in it, I am a clever girl – but it's just so big it wrecks my head. It's too messy.

I order a black coffee and I'm aware he looks up, hearing my voice in the otherwise quiet bar. I stare straight ahead.

"Milk and sugar?" the bar girl asks.

"Just milk, please." I run my hand across the smooth gold-chrome bar top and continue to stare straight ahead. Rows and rows of shiny bottles of alcohol. So innocent, almost alluring, until you ingest the bastards.

"That is two euro and ninety cents, please, when you're ready." She smiles at me.

Clear braces but I notice them.

I hand her three one-euro coins and I pick up my coffee. The white cup rattles slightly on the small white saucer and the sugars tumble from the side. I said no sugar.

He's on it like a boy on a flash of white knicker. He smells of shower gel.

"I got it." He's on his knees collecting the sugar sachets, then standing up he takes the cup from me. He stuffs the sugars in tight under the cup.

"Will you join me?" He points to his messy *Irish Times* table.

"Sure, okay, if you like," I manage and I realise I really do want to sit and talk to him. This is so unlike me and I wonder if it's not just because Ciara told me she actually likes Da. Maybe I need to vent? To a stranger. Maybe. But no, I know I fancy him.

We sit and he tidies the paper up a bit to make room for me.

"Nice bar this . . ."

He trails off as I viciously shake my sugar sachets and dump them in. I don't take sugar. I didn't ask for sugar. What am I doing? I lift the cup and blow at it, pretending to Hugh Grant it's too hot.

"Our paths seem to be crossing a lot . . . lucky me," he says with a wink.

He smiles. I stare back at him, expressionless, and he swiftly moves on.

"Did you read that story about the undercover cop who was shot by a gangland member in Naas last night?" He rummages through the pages now to find it for me, messing the paper up all over again.

"I don't read or watch bad news, Hugh," I tell him and it feels sexy to say his name. Hugh. I like the way it rolls off my tongue. Hugh. *Do you, Hugh, take . . .*

"Why not, Kate?" he asks me and I focus again after my crazy last thought.

81

I absolutely adore the way my name rolls off his tongue.

"Because I simply choose not to. My right, eh? There's enough bad shit in my life without me taking on other people's bad shit. Selfish, maybe?" I recover well and watch him closely. In fact I stare at him. He's so very good-looking. Features all the right shape and size. Body in proportion. Dark stubble building around his face. Shadowy. Those deep-set brown eyes study me back. A strong nose. Prominent is the word. I wonder if he's thinking the complete opposite about me. I tug at my cardigan and drag it down further over my roundy belly.

"No, no, it's not selfish – it's a good idea," he manages. He joins his fingers together and cracks his knuckles.

"*Urgh!*" I say and fling my hands over my ears. Da always did it. I fucking hate the noise.

"Sorry! Sorry! Awful habit . . . It won't happen again." He goes a bit red and I feel bad.

"It's grand . . . it's just . . . ahh . . . my da does it. I hate it . . . because I . . . well . . . I hate him." What on God's Green Earth am I doing? Why am I telling him this? What is going on with me? I lift the cup again by the tiny handle and it's awkward. My finger doesn't fit. My hand shakes so I put the cup down again.

"I see. That's terrible, Kate, I can't imagine . . . but . . ." He licks his lips and goes on, "Well, I'm lucky . . . my father and I, we're pretty close. He's a doctor too and I think very highly of him . . . I'm not sure . . ."

"You're a doctor?" I bet he's a head doctor, knowing my luck.

"Surgeon . . . was . . . was a surgeon. Not now. I don't practise medicine any more."

I need to move on from my Da Blurt-out.

"So, you said that you are here just over a month – but where are you from originally, Hugh?" I lift the coffee cup in my whole hand and I no longer shake.

He seems to relax a bit too. "Well, okay . . . you want my story? Here we go . . . Yeah, I arrived here in March . . . um . . . I am originally from sunny Blackpool, born there thirty-six long years ago. My folks born there, their folks before them too. A fantastic town to grow up in thirty years ago but a bit of a shell of a place now. It was once very magical."

He lifts his glass and shakes it gently. He's no stranger to a glass or two of Guinness, I can tell. But not its best friend either – I can tell that too immediately.

"I suppose I had an idyllic childhood," he continues, obviously in the mood to talk about himself. "One older brother. We were adored, loved, pampered, our house was full of laughter, Christmases were wonderful experiences, holidays in the sun, allowed our first glass of wine with Sunday dinner at fourteen – the excitement – unusual Sunday dinner in ours – my parents were vegans so –" He stops mid-sentence and looks at me. "Sorry, I'm making a huge mess of this. Why am I talking about my wonderful family and childhood after what you just told me? I know you asked but still, well, I should be asking you about you. Why do you hate your dad so much?" His dark eyes lock into mine.

"Alcoholic." I don't blink.

He nods very slowly.

"Abusive?" he asks very quietly after a few seconds pass us by.

"I would say yes, abusive. No, he didn't batter us, beat

us up, but I was always afraid that he would. It was always a very real looming threat." I can look him in the eye with great ease. This very rarely happens with me and a stranger.

The door opens and two young girls enter. Dressed in skinny jeans, Ugg boots and black puffer jackets. Hair swinging in high dark ponytails. College-studenty types. They walk past and don't even notice us. I'm used to not being noticed but I doubt Hugh is. He sits upright and stares at them as they pass. His stare lingers on them for a second too long than I am comfortable with so I break it.

"You alright there? Want a pair of binoculars?" I am jealous and sarcastic and he swings back to face me.

"Oh no – God, no – I'm not looking at them like that – they're kids – they just remind me of someone, that's all." He is edgy now and I have managed to embarrass him yet again.

"So why don't you practise any more?" I quickly try to move on and get the conversation back to him.

"I'm not able for the business, I guess." He still seems uneasy and looks away, then he turns back to my gaze and gives me a sad, very forced grin.

I finish my coffee and don't ask him any more. He finishes his glass and doesn't ask me any more. I start to feel a bit self-conscious.

"I better go, Hugh, thanks for the chat." I push the small stool back and zip up my high-necked woollen cardigan.

"Yeah, me too." He gathers up his paper. "Are you walking back to Ringsend or driving?" He shoves it all under his arm.

The mess of it. I'd love to tidy it up. Smooth out each page and put them all back in the correct order.

"Walking. I don't drive." I move away.

"Me too – I mean, I'm walking too. Can we walk together?"

He picks up my coffee cup and his empty glass and takes them back up to the bar. The waitress is all smiley at him and he thanks her and hands her a tip.

I am at the door.

"So may I walk with you?" he asks again.

I say yes and we do. In silence.

Chapter Eight

"So heresdedeal."

Ciara is looking upbeat. A bit happier. Her dark hair is scooped up into a high ponytail. Some foundation on and mascara has been applied to her apple-green eyes – the creamy foundation brings out her sharp bone structure. Ciara is stunning but so thin it's hard to find her beauty right now. She looks in need. Desperate. All of which she is. She is wearing a long red gypsy skirt from Zara children's department and a black polo neck, on her feet red flats. Her nails are beautifully kept and polished as always. Today's colour is blue. The type of blue that looks like a Canary Island sky. A no-worries kind of blue. The type of blue us Irish just want to escape to.

"So – here – is – the – deal." She repeats very slowly, vowel-conscious, and blows air out long and fast through a tiny hole in her mouth. She pours us each a glass of 7UP. "If we get the train to Galway we can get the bus to Connemara from there. The travel time from Galway is about fifty minutes to Oughterard. I called Auntie Brenda, ya know? We had a good chat. She really isn't a bad person, Kate. She didn't want to go into too much detail – she said she'd let her sister do that. I have the address from Brenda. It's a small cottage by all accounts – Ivy Cottage – so she gave me the number of a B&B in the town. If we leave late Friday evening, I can go to the clinic first thing and get my blood transfusion and weekend meds."

I sit at the kitchen table and take the chilled 7UP from her. "I have a job. A wedding on the Saturday," I tell her as I sip the bubbles, making my nose itch.

"Well, you'll have to cancel, won't ya – won't you!" She puts her 7UP on the table on a high-rise-building coaster.

"I can't," I say.

"Oh, seriously, Kate Walsh, you'd try the patience of Mother Teresa. Okay. So it's Sunday then – we leave for Oughterard on Sunday morning."

She jerks her head upwards and, before I know what's going on, the stairs are creaking.

I can't move. I stare at her and she avoids eye contact. The steps get louder and louder until the handle on the kitchen door is pushed down very slowly and it walks in.

It speaks. "Katie, howrya, love? Cuppa tea, Ciara, if there's one goin', pet."

My da. My father. Maker of misery. But, hey, Ciara gets on with him. Ciara likes him. He is by all accounts nice to my sister. Could it all just be me? Am I the one responsible? Was it all in my head? I bark out a laugh.

"I believe I owe ya an apology about the state I fell home in the other night," he says, looking down at the floor, "and I –"

87

I cut him off with a long-drawn-out "*Noooooooooooooooo* – sure yer grand so ya are!"

I confuse him with my sarcasm but then he looks up and continues. "I hear yer ma's back." He coughs hard into his cupped hand. His skin is as grey as an Irish winter sky, his eyes so yellow it's like someone has been drip-feeding orange cordial into a large pint of water.

"Dad was home at six o'clock last night!" Ciara jumps in.

"Good lad, Dad. Good lad yerself!" I begin a very slow clap. Each slap of my hands echoes around the silent kitchen. The noise is horrible even to my ears and so I stop.

He gives me a weak smile and the kettle roars at us. Ciara unplugs it and fills the pot. He always insists on a pot for himself. I watch the stream rise and cause condensation on the window. I sip my drink. I have an urge to write my name with my finger on the window like I used to do.

He pulls out a chair at the table and his knees crack loudly as he sits down. I try not to look at him so I glance around the walls. My eyes land on the framed photo hanging slightly lopsided on the wall. Our token family photo. I stare harder at it, and from the corner of my eye I see him as he hands his mug to Ciara as is his habit and then accepts the tea. I am surprised he can hold the mug so steady. She cuts a large slice of bread off the turnover on the table. He reaches for the butter. He is hungry? Miracle of miracles. I look back to the family portrait on the wall. The four of us. The Walshes. He'd been drunk in the picture, I remember now. We were to be in the photographer's studio in Ranelagh at ten in the morning.

Mam had won it at some raffle in Quinnsworth, the old supermarket. She had bought a frame and entered a competition to win a professional family portrait. There had been some hassle on the day as the photographer tried to charge Da for extra prints or something like that. I can't recall the exact problem but across our family framed portrait is clearly marked *Sample Only*.

I remember it all now like I haven't done in years.

"Everyone has to wear white tops. Come on, Eoin, please, we need you to get changed," Ma had told him as she dragged him from the couch in the front room. He was a drunken mess.

"I'm not goin' to some poxy photograph place, Emily . . . piss off . . . I'm tired . . . I need me kip," he had slurred back at her as he grabbed for the banisters, missed them and fell in a heap at the end of the stairs. He missed hitting his head, by an inch, off the side of my steel roller skates which were lying there.

My young self had stood at the top of the stairs and looked at him for a long time. Ma just stood over him but Ciara tried to pull him up.

"Please, Da, please get up! Please? We want to go to the photo place!"

He had done it for Ciara.

My memory whirrs back and I recall the night before that now.

We'd all been to bed early – well, the three of us had. He'd been propping up the bar somewhere, putting the world to rights.

I even remember what we'd had for tea. A ham salad. Mam did such tasty ham salads. Old school. Baked ham and that old-fashioned lettuce with sweet baby tomatoes and beetroot and crusty bread. Salad cream lashed on top of the lettuce to mask it. Sometimes she bought a jar of pickles for herself and I would laugh hysterically at the contorted faces she would pull when she ate the bitter food. I crinkle a smile now in the moment in the memory.

"*The A-Team* is over, Ma!" I had called up the stairs to her that night as she was drying Ciara's hair. Murdock was so funny! I fancied Face but I never let on to Ciara that I did. I was too cool for Face.

The noise of the dryer ceased.

"What did you say, love?" Ma called down the stairs, leaning over the banisters.

"I said *The A-Team* is over – will I come up now and get washed?"

"Oh yeah so, love, come up and hop in while the water's still warm! Don't touch your dad's shirt hanging in the bathroom. I'm just steaming it – there are still some creases in it. And will you put those skates away in your room? Someone's going to break their neck on them." She'd pointed to my skates on the hall floor. Pity her premonition hadn't come true.

I couldn't have been more than seven. I remember the gentle way she pulled my rough school jumper up over my head. She pulled my arms out of the sleeves first, then pulled the jumper up and over, and kissed my nose. She was pretty, was Emily. My mam. Before. Before all the hassle.

So there was a 'before', I realise now. I hadn't thought of the 'before' in an absolute age. I had completely blocked out the 'before'. I had demonised her as I saw fit.

He speaks and removes me from my Johnson & Johnson powder-smelling, isolated memory.

"Yer gonna go see her and see if she can help our Ciara then, Katie, right?" he asks me. His dark facial shadow is grey and dirty-looking.

"My name is Kate." I do not make eye contact with him.

"Kate," he says slowly in his heavy Dublin drawl.

"*Whaaaaaaah?*" I drag the word out, as boring as I can make it sound, mimicking his accent.

"Are ya bringin' Ciara to see Emily, else I'll have ta?" he repeats slowly.

I laugh one of those guttural sarcastic noises people who can't stand another person's last comment make.

"Oh Daddy, you do enough . . . please, think of yourself for a change . . . you put your feet up and –" I don't get to finish.

"Go fuck yerself, Katie! Yer a pain in the fuckin' hole, so ya are! I dunno how Ciara puts up with ya – she's a saint!" He pushes the chair back – it screeches on the tiles and falls over onto the floor with a clatter.

"Lads, please," Ciara implores, her face reddening.

I know this is uncomfortable for her but I can't help myself.

"Going to the pub, Papa?" I say the words *pub* and *papa* in a clipped British accent and I hold a fake Joker-type smile.

"I'd go anywhere to get away from you!" he throws back at me and heads out of the kitchen.

"Toodle pips! Have a nice day in the office now, you hear?" I shout after him as he climbs the stairs.

"Nice one, Kate! Come on, he was only trying to be nice." My sister shakes her head slowly but I can see her chin is quivering. She is biting her tongue and fighting to hold back the tears as she begins to clear off the breakfast table she has laid. She grabs my unfinished 7UP and throws it down the sink plughole. The noise of the gushing taps washing it down drowns out her heavy breathing.

I suddenly realise this was all planned as I smell the cooking for the first time. The fizzy, newly opened 7UP. A daddy-daughter breakfast. She moves to the cooker and turns the black knob to off. She pulls out the tray with half-cooked rashers sizzling on tin foil and stands her foot heavily on the pedal of the bin. I watch in silence as the greasy rashers slide in. So long, piggy.

Ciara opens the back door and stands in the open space, looking out to nowhere.

"Ciara, I can't stand him, I can't bear him, I get hives when he's near me . . . don't . . . please . . . I love you so much, you know that I do . . . please don't expend any energy trying to get us to patch things up. It will never happen. Ever." I sigh deeply.

Then I stand up. I'm cold.

"Will you close that door?" I ask her as I go to her.

"I want to feel alive." She looks at me through her sad green eyes. The tight black polo neck reveals just how thin she is.

I have to be there for her. I have to do what she wants. I will try to try harder.

"I'll meet you at Heuston Station Sunday morning – just text me the time, okay?" I gently move her back in, close the back door and turn the key.

I pull my arms into my cardigan and swing the long strap of my bag over my shoulder. I settle the strap in between my boobs.

"Will I stick on a few more rashers for you before I

go?" I ask her as she sits at the table. I want her to eat.

"Thanks, sis." She gives me a watery smile.

"For what?"

"For coming with me."

"Of course I'll go with you." I put my hand on her shoulder. "Now, will I stick you on a few rashers?"

"I used them all," she smiles up at me.

"A boiled egg?" I offer.

"No, thank you, I don't really have an appetite today so I think I'll just go up and rest. You go."

She rises and we walk out of the kitchen and stand in the hallway together. He's moving around upstairs. Getting ready for his day on a bar stool. We kiss and I leave. I rattle the glass behind me.

I'm not sure what I want out of life, I realise, as I walk again. Pavement-pounding. I'm not sure what I am achieving by hating him so much. But I know I can't help it. When I see him I am flooded with anger. I can't let it go. He was such a terrible da. Such a terrible husband. He is still a state. I try not to think about him. It's my life now. I am in charge of it. What am I expecting for my future? I wish I could put it into words but I can't. Do I want a husband? I certainly don't think I do. Do I want children? I honestly don't know. Could I cope with kids? I don't know that either. Do I want to be alone forever? I don't think so. No. I pause at the lights as the red man stares me down, daring me to move. I punch his button rapidly. No. I can answer that one. No, I don't. I don't want to be alone forever. A lump rises in my throat and I am appalled. How pathetic. Then I remember it's Friday. I can go to Phillip's tonight and watch DVDs and laugh and not be one bit lonely. I turn on my heel and head to happiness.

Chapter Nine

I put my finger on the bell on the side of the small basement-apartment door on South Circular Road. The hall door is painted a gorgeous luminous yellow and the bell sings out 'Mustang Sally'.

He opens the door wide into the hallway.

"Darling, you look enterable, perfect, come in, come in, come in, I have some miserable movies for us to watch, I have a really saucy lasagne in the oven and a warm Olaf-type heart."

We air-kiss and I go in. I take off my coat and hang it on the coat-stand from Liberties in London in the hallway. Phillip dances up the narrow hall. He's wearing an orange track suit with cream pumps on his feet.

"What's up?" He leads me into the small living area. Candles burn brightly.

"Oh, ya know, the usual shite – wow, that smells incredible, Phillip." I flop onto his low-slung sofa and kick off my runners. I curl my odd-stockinged feet under me. One is black with little white stars and the other is navy with two thick black stripes at the top.

"Doesn't it – it's Jamie Oliver's recipe – I realise the only reason I cook Jamie is so I can prop up one of his books and look at him whilst licking the end of a spatula with my tongue guilt-free."

He lights a zillion more candles as he talks and I watch him. He has one of those oversized matchboxes with the huge matches. I always find them slightly comical, I don't know why. When the room is shining as brightly as a Christmas cathedral he collapses into an oversized multicoloured beanbag beside me.

"You know, I think I'm ready to fall in love again, chuck." He props himself up, hands me a huge thick Waterford Crystal glass from the table and pours me an obscene amount of wine.

"Wow, steady – that's too much!" I panic.

"Jesus wept, girl! It's a glass of wine on a Friday night – lighten your load. I want to talk about falling in love again – drink with me to that!"

He always scoffs at my ritual of panicking over wine in his house on a Friday night. It's just he fills the glasses up too much. I'd really prefer a glass of apple juice tonight but I'd take my life in my hands if I said that. Wine o'clock is his very best time of the day. His sunrise and sunset.

"Oh, what do you want to fall in love for again, Phillip?" I sigh heavily at this unwelcome news. "Aren't you happy enough already? You'll only get hurt again. What's the point?" I am incredulous he wants to go down this road again.

"So you aren't my Fairy Godmother then? I shall return the pumpkin, the six white mice, the brown rat in his cage and the six green lizards promptly!" he says sarcastically and doffs an imaginary cap at me.

"Now come on . . . that's not fair . . . you know how much I support you and want you to find your prince, I just hate seeing you get so hurt, that's all."

"Love is supposed to hurt, Kate," he whispers dramatically. "Barry Manilow, the greatest love lyricist of all time, told us so. Take Mandy, for instance. Love is simply supposed to be painful."

"Is it though, really?"

"Of course! Just look at all the poets, the writers of the greatest love poems of all time– they were all hurt in love at some stage, right – to write like that? Take 'I Tried So Hard' by Whitney Barton or 'To a Young Girl' by WB Yeats. To feel, to really feel that all-encompassing hurt you have to have experienced and felt the all-encompassing love first and truly there is nothing in the world that feels as good as being in love, no matter what my sweet Kate Moss says." He lies back on the beanbag and stares up at the ceiling.

"What did Kate Moss say about love?" I ask him.

"Nothing tastes as good as being skinny feels," he replies instantly in a version of Kate's accent.

"So nothing to do with love then?" I point out.

"No, but I sometimes get confused between love and food, that's all!" he says with a laugh.

"I'm serious, though – you are happy at the moment, aren't you? Bobby destroyed you." I lean over and look at him.

"He did but that's what I am trying to tell you, Kate – he also made me feel alive in a way I just don't right now. And it's not the sex. I can have sex anytime I like. But being in love sets off the most miraculous endorphins." He places his hand across his heart before getting up off the uncomfortable beanbag and joining me like a grown man should on the couch.

I raise my eyebrows at him as he pulls his tiny T-shirt down over his exposed belly.

"I just worry about you, that's all." And then I get it. "Is there someone already?"

He shakes his head and I look at him through narrowed suspicious eyes.

"What?" He pushes his glasses up his nose and smiles at me. "Okay . . . I'll have you know I did meet someone and we had sex only last night and it may, just may, be the next train to Love Town!" His pink tongue points at me accusingly.

"With who? And it isn't!" I take a drink and it's warm and comforting.

"I so totally did, girl, and it totally could be!" He clicks his fingers and stands up again.

I hold onto my glass which almost spills as he gets up.

"Oh, will you just relax, Phillip!" I say, exasperated.

"I bet Jules doesn't talk to Jamie like that? My gooey grub awaits my attention – I must attend – my love life will wait, but wait only for pasta . . ." He glides into the kitchen.

I don't want Phillip to have a new boyfriend. Simple as that. No one gets him like I do. I wish they did but they just don't. After a few weeks he falls really hard and ultimately starts to get on their nerves. A casual thing becomes all-consuming for him. He can't help himself. He sends ridiculously extravagant gifts to workplaces and offers romantic gestures that are far too sweeping and

OTT. There is absolutely no talking to him when he is in the throes of his love affair. He literally becomes obsessed. He starts to annoy his love objects and then they become really mean to him to get rid of him and I hate it. I absolutely hate it.

My phone beeps with a new email. I open it. A new job. I'll look at it later.

I stand and make my way into his kitchen, swirling my wine. "So who is this lucky man then?"

"Well, you know the guy who does my hair in town?" Phillip is lathering butter on bread. There is a huge plate on a silver tray with diced carrots and hummus.

"Yeah, him?" I lean against the fridge and sip. The kitchen is so warm and welcoming on this night. I feel the tension ebb away. The soundtrack to *Chicago* plays low on the stereo in the background.

"God, no! Is you mental! Well, is you?" Phillip puts on his best Ali G impression. He does a lot of Ali G impressions. Another thing I have seen irritate previous boyfriends.

"I don't think you can say 'mental' any more, Phillip – it's not PC." I dip a carrot into the hummus now and crunch noisily.

"Hands off. These are for our supper." He waves the butter knife up and down at me. "Well, anyway, he has a friend who does home extensions –"

"So it was the extensions guy?" I butt in.

"Is you drunk? Like is you total pissed up or wha'? Gavin the extension guy? Really? You think I'd touch him with a barge pole? Seriously, Kate?" He picks up the silver tray with the carrot and hummus and moves it to the kitchen table. "Let me concentrate on my cooking, please."

I am lost now. There is no point to the conversation and the start would have nothing to do with the end. So I leave it. Knowing full well he will pick it up later.

He dons two massive oven gloves and, bending from his knees, removes the bubbling lasagne from the oven and sits it on the side counter. Then he takes out two massive baked potatoes. He kicks the oven door closed.

"Here, split them and throw a bit of butter and cheese in them, will you?" He nods to the butter and block of cheese on the counter and hands me the butter knife. I run it under the hot tap.

"I don't got no cooties, ya know, ma'am."

The accent sounds Texan but I have no idea who he is taking off.

He dishes and I pop the potatoes on the side of our plates overloaded with melting butter and cheese. We take our food back into the living room. We always eat on the couch off our knees.

"So go on, what ails you, Kate Walsh?" He mimicks a Dublin accent now and blows on his hot spoonful as he finally settles down for the night.

"Ahh, everything, nothing, just life, ya know?" I blow now too.

"*Hmmmm?*" he pushes me.

"*Hmmmmmm,*" I say back and chew. "My God, this is too nice!" I pant short breaths on my forkful as it's still so hot.

"God bless Jamie and all who sail in him!" He opens out his overloaded potato with the knife and adds some of his mince in there. "So go on – I can't start the film until you tell me what has happened to you. My love life can wait. You are quite right – I shouldn't jinx this by overthinking it. I slept with a guy. End of. I've picked a goody for tonight by the way. It's Tom Brady – he appears shirtless at seventeen minutes and one second in according to Rotten Tomatoes movie fan site, and I will pause for no one."

"Okay, well, my ma is back on the scene – her sister wrote us a letter – she's in Galway and by all accounts via a crispy An Post letter wants to see us," I tell him.

He doesn't really react to this big news. He knows my life story inside and out so I'm a bit surprised.

"*Hmmmm,*" he repeats but asks me nothing.

So I continue. "Well, I mean I have to go see her because as you know she is probably Ciara's last hope. But I think I might want to punch her in the face."

"*Hmmmm,*" is all he gives me back and he chews slowly.

I lean forward and put my plate on the glass table.

"Phillip, why do you keep making that *Hmmmmmmmm* noise?" I take a long drink from my glass and hold it in my mouth for a moment.

"Isn't this the best thing that could happen?" he says. "I can't figure out why it's getting you down rather than up?"

I swallow. "She left us. Do I really need to go over it all again?" I feel my temper rising at him.

"But she is back and she wants to see you again and you have to see her for Ciara's sake," he says softly.

"I am still so angry, Phillip." I feel the tears suddenly exploding down my face like a dam bursting.

For such a drama queen he is marvellous in a crisis.

"Of course you are still angry, chuck. Your mother abandoned you when you were eight years old. She also left a sick five-year-old. Worse than that, she left you both in the care of your alcoholic father. You have every right in the world to be pissed! Mightily pissed! Brenda refused for years to tell you where she was, despite Ciara's condition. I know I keep saying it and you brush me off every time but therapy would be the makings of you. I'm no therapist, I can't give you professional answers about your feelings, but what I can tell you is that you are my dearest friend and you have every right to feel this hard done by." He takes my hand and squeezes it.

"I don't believe in therapy, you know that." I sniff and blow my nose in a sheet of the themed kitchen roll on the table. Winnie the Pooh.

"You will one day." He tears off an extra sheet, folds it neatly down the middle and hands me that too.

"I have to go see her on Sunday. I will be face to face with her again." I'm telling myself this more than him. I'm going to see her again. A flock of birds crash in my stomach and I can't eat another bite.

"Let's just watch the movie," he says gently, knowing that is exactly what I want him to say.

"Okay." I nod slowly. Exhausted.

"Oh, by the way, I got you a fabulouso frock for your work wedding." He can't help himself, he finds it impossible to stop talking. He holds the remote control up high, finger paused above the play button.

"Well, thank you, that's so nice. From who?"

"You know Rita who's in my recycling art club?"

"Well, thank her from me, won't you? I'll be sure to dry-clean."

"Is you mental? Well, is you? You honestly think Rita is a frock-wearing person? Rita who hasn't not worn a

101

man's suit with a black tie and runners every single day since she was nine years old?"

I hold my hand up. "Whoever it is, thank her. Now please let's just snuggle up and watch the movie." I rest my head on his safe warm shoulder.

Chapter Ten

HUGH CLOVER

Hugh Clover sits in the corner of the Beggars Bush bar, holding his *Irish Times* up to hide his face. He occasionally sips on a half-empty glass of Guinness. His eyes repeatedly dart to the door and back down to the swimming black-and-white small print. They are late today. He knows they take extra classes in the college on a Saturday. Their routine has been the same for the last three weeks. He scans the front page now – another murder – my lord, but Dublin is a dangerous city in 2015. Gangland killings every other day, innocent bystanders and passersby being gunned down in broad daylight on open streets. Drugs, guns, no value on human life. It sickens him to the pit of his stomach. He picks up his Guinness and swirls the glass slowly. Where are they?

He glances at his watch just as the door opens and they walk in. Dressed again in their V-neck jumpers, skinny jeans, Ugg boots and their two high ponytails bouncing happily. Victoria and Alison. Two beautiful girls. Just as she had been. Everything to live for. They sway through the bar and sit in the opposite corner. Huge gently pulls his iPhone from his back pocket and hides it behind his paper. His heart begins to race. They are chatting easily. One – he thinks that one is Victoria – pulls her ponytail loose and gathers her hair up in a bun on top of her head. He swallows bile.

That's how her hair had been. He remembers because he had jokingly asked her about surgically removing the pineapple on her head. She had roared laughing. The most infectious of laughs.

"It's greasy, that's why," she had told him, patting it down.

The waitress hands the girls a menu each and they look for a moment, not letting her take her leave. They don't need to look. They have ordered the same thing every lunchtime, every day he has been watching them. Two pint glasses of water with ice and lemon and the soup of the day. They never eat the brown bread but they do put it in their bags and break it up for the birds on their way back to college. He subtly moves his phone up to his face as though he is studying a text message or an important email. The camera is a bit far out for close focus so he drags them closer in to him on the screen.

Click. He takes their picture.

Chapter Eleven

KATE WALSH

I stand in front of the mirror at 11.55 a.m. and it doesn't often happen to me but I think I look really pretty. Phillip has done really well. It's a vibrant red silk dress. It is a halter-neck and billowy, doesn't cling anywhere. I put my feet together and study the strappy black sandals I bought yesterday in Next. Not too high – 'kitten heel' I think the sales girl called them. This morning I popped into Maeve Callan's in No. 54 Stella Gardens – she does blow-drys in her house for a tenner. She did a lovely job, sleek and shiny. My make-up is my own and is minimal but I hear lads prefer minimal make-up anyway and today I am working for Mark McMahon. He is my boss. I wonder how his ex-fiancée is feeling, getting ready to go, knowing he is going to be there today? My buzzer. Two people wanting me now in a short space of time. I pick up the phone and speak into the receiver.

"Hiya, Mark," I say cheerfully, "I'm on my way down."

"Cool," his short to the point reply.

One last check in the looking glass. I'm pretty sure he

will be happy with me. I stuff my purse and keys into the ridiculously tiny red bag which Phillip also managed to blag for me and I'm off to work.

Mark is sitting in the passenger seat of a taxi. We make eye contact as soon as I open the back door. We smile at each other.

"The Central Hotel now, please," Mark tugs at his seat belt and it keeps getting jammed with the force. Poor love is probably up to high doh. I need to do my job here.

"Mark, wanna stop at Beggars Bush for a quick pint before we get to the hotel? The civil Mass isn't till half past twelve, right? We'd easily make it."

He puts his arm around the back of the seat, holds onto the silver pole on the head-rest and turns to face me.

"That'd be deadly Kate, thanks – I'd mill a pint." He swings back around to face the driver. "Could you wait for us – we'll only be ten minutes or so?"

The driver nods. He pulls up after a few minutes, punches his hazards and tells us to mind the road getting out.

We jog to the doors of the pub in our wedding finery.

"Thanks for this. Will I pay you now or later? I'm a fuckin' nervous wreck . . . I can't believe I have to look at them together." He pulls at his bow tie as though it's choking the life out of him.

We stand at the bar.

"No, pay me later, get yourself a pint . . . it will be fine . . . they probably feel as nervous as you do. Maybe it's just something you need to get over and done with." I put the miniscule bag on the bar top.

"Pint of Heineken and – sorry, what do you want, Kate?" He pulls his wallet out.

"Just a sparkling water is fine for me, thanks, with fresh lime," I say and turn to lean back against the bar.

And that's when I see him. Again. Hugh Grant. I lose a beat of my heart and a breath swallows the one before. I shake my head firmly to cop myself on. He is doing the exact same thing, sitting there reading his *Irish Times* and sipping his glass of Guinness. He doesn't see me. Probably not the time to go over and say hello to him even if I had the nerve. I am Mark's date.

The drinks are put up on the bar in front of us and Mark takes three massive gulps.

"That's better already – you are a genius, thanks," he says.

"All part of my job description." I toast him with my water and bobbing segment of lime.

"How do you get over losing someone you love so much, Kate? I adored her. I worked my arse off to get her the lovely home she wanted, the home we built. I gave her everything. I can't believe I lost her, I really can't. We were made for each other, everyone told us that. I dream about her every single night – almost a year now and I still dream about her every night! Am I going nuts, I wonder?" He gulps more of the pint now, leaving its contents below the halfway line. On the verge of tears.

"Hey, there!"

We both turn.

Hugh Grant. Hugh Clover. Kate Clover. Oh for God sake, stop, I say in my head.

"Oh hi, Hugh," I say. "Sorry, it's not a good time for me to chat . . . I'm working . . . em . . . this is in fact work . . . em . . . drop in to me tonight, yeah . . . after nine? That okay with you, Mark? We'll be done by then, right?" I am trying hard not to blush and I fiddle with my earring.

"God, yeah," he says. "I'll be long gone out of there by then. I'm planning to go just as soon as we can leg it." He finishes the pint.

"Okay, well, that's . . . okay," I say.

Hugh Grant is just standing there staring at me and I feel he is staring at me because he thinks I am attractive. The blush escapes and I feel a hot rush run from my neck up to my face.

"Super," is all he says and turns and retreats to his paper and Guinness.

"Mate?" Mark asks and squashes up his face.

"No – well, yeah, he's a neighbour really." I wish I didn't embarrass so easily.

"Bit odd, is he?" he asks.

"Dunno, don't think so. I don't know him that well."

"He looks a bit dodgy to me." He looks after Hugh. "Will we go and get this crap over with so?" He rubs his hands together.

I was wrong: the traffic is really heavy and we are late. We have no choice but to walk in during the ceremony which is in the Davenport Room of the hotel and everyone turns to look at us. Scarlet.

"Big smiles!" I whisper into his ear and we both grin like we'd just been riding in the jacks.

We slip into two spare seats in the middle of the room. Mark immediately nudges me, hard in the ribs, and nods to the top of the room. It doesn't take more than a quick glance around for me to spot her near the top. The ex-fiancée. No question it has to be her because she is staring hard right back at me. She has a contorted look on her face, a mixture of shock and awe. I really must look alright. I put my head on Mark's shoulder. I leave it there for a few moments before I sit up straight and tall. Good posture. She is staring straight ahead now. Pretty alright: that chic elfin look that not every woman can pull off. The look Phillip is convinced most heterosexual men are physically attracted to. A tweed cape covers her dress so I can't see that. She turns around now and we stare into each other's faces. I really dislike her yet I have never met her and this is unfair. I don't usually judge. She looks away first.

I take Mark's hand now and his palms are sweating.

"Ya have to do all this?" he whispers in my ear.

"This is my job, Mark," I whisper back into his ear, smelling his strong aftershave.

"If you're sure, then great, I can show her I have moved on." He looks so forlorn.

When the ceremony is finished we all clap as the beautiful bride and the dashing groom kiss. Mark high-fives the groom a little awkwardly – they nearly miss hands on their way past – and we are escorted out to the dining area by ushers. Lots of people come over to Mark and he introduces me to them all as his new girlfriend. We hold hands.

It appears Mark is a very popular guy amongst these people here today. The general chat is built up of:

"We never see you any more, Mark!"

"Where are you hiding?"

"Thought you'd immigrated with the rest of them, man."

He's holding it together pretty well despite his very sweaty palm and the more I look at him the more handsome he is. Poor Mark, what a dreadful thing to happen to him!

"Are you hungry, Kate?" He smiles at me.

"Starving," I tell him and I am.

I see her approach from the corner of my eye and I know before I do it that this is totally not in my job description: I take my two hands and hold Mark's face in between them. I smile at him and I time it to perfection so that as she walks by I am kissing him on the mouth very slowly and very seductively.

"Mark?" she still says as she stops just past us and her shaven-headed companion keeps walking.

Cheek of her.

He pulls away too fast at the recognition of her voice.

"Oh! Wendy . . . what . . . what's the craic?" His face now goes a little red but not too bad.

I take his hand and squeeze it tight. She has removed the tweed cape thing and is in an incredibly stunning black skintight sleeveless dress and she has arms like Michelle Obama. She has the body of a swimwear model.

"You look . . . great," she tells him.

She smiles then and looks to me for an introduction, I know, so I save him because in that moment I am quite sure he has forgotten my name.

"Hi, Wendy, I'm Kate. I've heard a lot about you." I extend my hand and we shake.

She, like me, possesses a good firm handshake.

"Well, it's so lovely to meet you, Kate. Do try call me back sometime, Mark, won't you? It would be really nice to talk to you." And she leaves us.

He is breathless so I march him down the stairs of the Central Hotel and we cross over the road and sit on the window ledge of Dunnes Stores while he composes himself in the fresh air.

"So she's trying to get a friendship going with you, is she?" I ask him.

"Dunno. I guess so. I never answer her calls or listen to her messages. I can't." He skids his foot over a plastic crisp bag on the ground. Tayto. "She's a total ride, isn't she?"

"She is gorgeous, yes, but that's a look that has deceived you," I tell him.

"You think I was always out of my depth, Kate?"

"Not at all, Mark," I answer honestly.

"Thanks, I thought I'd won the Champions League getting her. I chased her for ages. I know – old ground. Okay, let's get this meal over and done with. Then I am out of here. I've done my bit. I showed up." He picks up the Tayto packet and puts it in the nearest bin as we cross back into the Central Hotel.

We find our names on the guest-list chart at the door and make our way to Table 16.

It's one of those weddings where everyone is beautiful and trendy and nice. The atmosphere is fun and light and the music is pop. It's arty.

"Which one is the boyfriend?" I have to ask even though I really shouldn't. I'm guessing it's the man who walked past when she stopped earlier. They are seated at the very top with us at the very bottom, praise be. I open my white linen napkin out over the dress. That is the worst part about borrowing – the panic all day. I really needed now to invest in a nice take-me-anywhere *gúna*.

"The one with the shaved head. He's a shrink – he was her shrink."

As the wedding reception and speeches get under way we both relax a bit more. The table is lots of fun, good people, and I take a glass of red wine and it unwinds me greatly. I love this job. I could be seated in the Brown Job now, staring out the bird-shit-stained window. There is no smell of Bombay Mix. I am suddenly filled with pride in myself. I know a lot of people wouldn't call what I'm doing a proper job but it is paying my bills and I am enjoying it. A win-win for me. I was thinking outside the box. I always wanted to be a 'thinkeroutsidetheboxer' type of person and now I am. Mark is knocking them back rather speedily, I notice, as he tries to pour another glass and a dribble of red trickles out from the empty bottle. His jacket is off now and he is okay. I'm betting he won't even leave now after the meal. Out comes our gorgeous tomato-and-basil soup which of course I immediately splash on the top half of the borrowed dress. I knew I would. It's just tucking napkins up there is so ridiculous-looking. I make my excuses to Mark who is starting into a new bottle and I run to the toilet to try to wash it out. The toilet is empty so I take off the dress and wash the stain out with soap and water. I have a nude-coloured strapless body on so I'm not too naked. I look on in delight as the tomato and basil takes its leave and I have it under the hand-dryer in seconds.

Then the door opens and Wendy saunters in. Coincidence, I immediately wonder?

"Oh now, what's happened here?" she asks me.

"The tomato-and-basil soup," I answer, slightly but not overly embarrassed for some strange reason. I am basically in my underwear and I am no swimwear model look-a-like. "I guess the dress was hungry too," I say. Why did I say that? Why did I just make that stupid comment?

"And such a beautiful dress," she says. "The colour is magnificent on you. Did you get the stain out?"

I take it away from under the dryer and we both study it. I was wrong. Dried, the stain is still very much there.

"Hang on a second," Wendy says and trots to the door.

I take it back to the sink and wet it again as she arrives back with a glass of white wine and a linen table napkin.

"Always works for me." She smiles at me before dipping the linen napkin into the wine and rubbing it gently across the soup stain. Slowly the stain begins to fade away.

I feel very awkward now. "God, thanks, that's brilliant. It's borrowed, you see."

"Done it a thousand times." She washes the napkin which has turned lightly red under the tap. "I am the world's messiest eater – if it can be spilt, you can be sure I will." She pulls at what bit of material she can grab from her skintight dress. "Black, it's all I can wear. I simply don't trust myself. I cannot even drink takeaway coffees in my car in the mornings any more either because every single time I dribble on myself."

We both laugh.

"I apologise for standing here in my undergarments," I say.

"Not at all . . . you remind me of Kate Winslet, if you don't mind me saying so," she says with a smile.

"Not at all," I repeat and we both laugh.

"So, I hear you're a doctor?" She leans her perfect torso against the sink now, her back to the mirror as I stare into it.

I pretend there's an eyelash or something gone into my eye. I remember this is what Mark told me he was telling everyone so that if he really needed to leave we could pretend I was on call.

"U – huh." My mouth is open wide.

"What type of medicine do you practise?" She turns now and looks at me looking at her in the mirror.

Fucking hell, I wasn't expecting this.

"Em . . . I work in St James's Hospital . . . in the blood-transfusion department . . . I specialise in aplastic anaemia," I bare-face lie.

"Oh. I've never heard of that condition. What is it?"

I close my eye and make it obvious I have now fixed the eyelash problem by blinking rapidly before stopping. All better.

"It's a deficiency of all types of blood cells caused by failure of bone-marrow development," I quote and then feel the need to carry on. "Basically the body's bone marrow doesn't make enough new blood cells – that is the bottom line. It's life-threatening."

She is buying it. "So do most of your patients die?" She is interested enough to move even closer to me.

I realise it's a question I don't want to answer. Ever. I can't. I freeze.

"I lost my sister last year, Kate," she whispers to me in the mirror. Why, I do not know.

"Oh God, I'm so sorry," this is too close for comfort and I am starting to sweat. *Flashdance* Jennifer falls at the beginning of her dance audition over and over again, the needle on the record skipping and scratching, agonisingly loud in my head.

"July 11th last year. She was in London for a summer, working with her friends. They worked in a telesales company. One Friday after work, they had just been paid and went out. They got really drunk and she . . . fell . . . anyway, sorry, but the reason I'm telling you this is I sort of lost my mind. I'm sure you think I'm the biggest bitch for doing what I did to Mark with Stephen, but he couldn't understand my pain. And Stephen could. She was just amazing, only twenty-three, second year in college, in UCD, studying music and literature. My parents couldn't get over it . . . they broke up . . . in fact, just today our family home sold."

Wendy doesn't show her emotion on her face, just in the tone of her voice. She licks her index finger and runs it under both her eyes now even though she isn't crying.

We just continue to look at each other in the mirror.

"Mark was the best thing that ever happened to me, Kate. We were so in love. I was totally besotted with him. Are you in love with him?" She audibly gulps.

"No," I answer. It's gone far enough.

"Oh." She twists her head from side to side.

"I can't really say any more, Wendy," I tell her as I move into a toilet and pull a sheet of toilet paper even though I have no need for it. I hate this job now. This isn't right.

"I still love him, so much . . . I made a dreadful mistake . . . an unforgiveable one apparently . . . I get that." Her voice rises here. "You see, I know Deirdre shouldn't have died – it's been proven and my anger at the negligence just ate me up. Mark couldn't understand it – he just kept telling me to let it go. I couldn't. I never loved Stephen, but he understood me – he never told me to let it go . . . let her go . . ."

She is angry now. I can see it in her.eyes.

"Does Mark know all this?" I ask her.

She eyes me suspiciously for the first time in this compelling bathroom-sink drama.

"He didn't tell you?" she queries.

"What?" I say.

"I shouldn't tell." She pushes in the soap dispenser and the pink liquid drips speedily onto her hand. She hits the tap with her elbow and washes her hands.

I watch her, saying nothing.

The hand-drier roars around us and when it stops she says, "He cheated on me first, Kate. Well, it was a kiss . . . he kissed someone in a sleazy nightclub and came home and he told me about it because he said he felt so guilty. It wasn't the kiss so much, it was what he said after that that really pushed me into Stephen's arms – he said she was happy, this girl he kissed – and that's what had attracted him to her – he told me that he missed being around happy people. I told him I'd never be happy again and I left. I went straight to Stephen's and cried on his shoulder. That was the night I started the affair with him." She examines her nails now. French polish.

The door opens and an older lady comes in.

"Hate chicken, why they do chicken on a wedding menu is beyond me. Beef or salmon, that's the rule, is it not?" She clip-clops on shoes that are far too high for her into the loo and slides the lock across the old wooden toilet door.

I have to get out of here.

"I'm really sorry, Wendy. I'm so sorry about your sister and about Mark. But maybe you should just be on your own for a while? I won't breathe a word of this conversation to Mark, okay . . . if you don't want me to." I move to the door.

"I kind of hope you do. It's totally up to you. So why are you with Mark if you don't love him?"

She puts her hand on the door so I can't open it.

"I really like him," I finally answer her honestly and she moves away to let me exit.

Back at the table, I sit back down and Mark looks a little drunk now.

"Where were you? I thought you had gone – your chicken's going to be freezing." He pokes his finger into it, ensuring I most definitely won't eat it now. He cuts his, adds potatoes and vegetables to his fork-load and stuffs it into his mouth.

I've no appetite any more anyway but I know I have to try to eat something. I pick up my glass of water and down it before picking at the food on my plate. I manage some potato.

"Look normal but I just had the longest chat with Wendy in the toilet," I whisper through gritted teeth, a smile plastered on my face as I watch her pass us and take her seat beside Stephen.

Mark's eyes cloud over – an Oscar-winning actor he will never make.

"What?" he spits.

"I don't think she loves Stephen as much as you think she does." My teeth are still clamped together.

"What – did she tell you something – what, Kate?" His eyes are blazing now with suspense.

"Firstly tell me what happened to her sister."

Mark sits back and throws his napkin from his lap onto his plate.

"Listen, it was horrific. Deirdre was in London for the summer – she got drunk and fell off a wall and broke her leg. No biggy. The girls were all a bit drunk but they rang an ambulance and went with her to the hospital. The doctor operated, put plates in, but forgot to prescribe antibiotics post-op and she contracted septicaemia and died. Horrific. Absolutely horrific, Kate. But, Wendy just couldn't let go of the doctor's negligence. She researched and googled and somehow got hold of his phone number and she hounded the poor guy, really hounded him. She became so bitter and twisted. It was me who suggested she go see someone. It was me who told her she needed to get on with her life . . . and this is how she repaid me! By fucking off with her shrink!"

Suddenly I understood Wendy better than I ever wanted to.

"As soon as you want to leave, Mark, just let me know but obviously I'm happy to stay for as long as you need me." I'm not. I really want to leave. I can't eat much more and it's cold now anyway.

"Thanks. What did she say about me though, Kate?" he implores.

"Nothing," I lie. "It was just something I picked up on. A vibe if you will."

"That she doesn't love Stephen?"

"Yeah, I really don't think that she does, that's all." I am quite strong in my delivery.

"Sorry, Kate. This all got a bit heavy . . . the speeches are starting after dessert and coffee and then you can slip away. I'll stay another hour or two, I think." He removes his wallet from his suit-jacket pocket.

"Not at the table Mark! Don't pay me at the table!" I whisper.

"Sorry! Don't know where my head is at. I'll walk out with you when you're leaving and pay you then."

"Grand. I'm glad you're staying for a while – your friends are really nice people." We both reach out and pick up our drinks. "Maybe go sit and chat to her for a bit after the speeches, yeah?" I lean across the table, take a bread roll, tear it in half and begin to eat it.

"Maybe." He picks up his wineglass and puts it to his mouth.

Chapter Twelve

I ring Ciara as soon as I get into the taxi. Kitten heels, me eye. Nothing kittenly about them. Killing me they are.

"Hi there," she says after two rings.

"How's it going? Are you all packed?" I check the stain on the dress. It's almost impossible to see where it once had been.

"Yeah!"

She sounds happy. Buzzy. I can hear it. Hopeful. I can feel it.

"Okay, well, I'm just leaving my wedding so I'm going to go home and pack when I get in and get an early night. How long do you think we'll stay down there?" I look out the window as South Great George's Street meets Dame Street.

"As long as it takes," she replies.

"So you're assuming Brenda told her about the worsening of your condition? She may not have, you know, Ciara. She may know nothing or not want to help in any way." People fall in front of the taxi on Dame Street as we turn into it, heading for the Quays. Town, even this early on a Saturday is never pretty in my eyes. I lock the door from my side.

"I don't care, Kate. I just want to see my mam."

We are both quiet and I bite my tongue.

"Okay, see you at the top of the escalator to Heuston in the morning." I ring off abruptly.

I have to pay the taxi with one of my fifties. He grumbles about me taking all his change.

I make my way into my apartment, close my door behind me and flop onto my couch. I kick off the kitten-heeled shoes and untie the back of the dress, relieved that there is no more sucking-in to be done. Suckfree. I can't really think about tomorrow. I stretch out on the couch and flick on the TV. I watch nothing in particular for a while before I get up and head to the bathroom to run a bath. I pour gallons of smelly coconut bubbles in, and when it's full I sink into the whiteness of them and soak for an age. I dunk my head, fingers pressed into my ears and listen to the sounds of the water. I stay in the bath until my fingertips crinkle before getting out and drying off. I slip into my Adidas red tracksuit and flip-flops. I am suddenly starving again and I go about making myself a toasted ham-and-cheese sandwich. There is one slightly hard-cornered slice of ham and a sliver of cheese. I really need to do a shop. I put the ingredients between two slices of batch bread and I drop the mayonnaise-soaked knife into the sink just as the door is knocked upon.

I am startled. Who is at my door? In my building? I reef my tracksuit sleeve up and there is the time. Nine bells. Nine o'clock. Fuck! Penny drops. *Clang!* Smashing of cymbals off both sides of my mutton head. Hugh

Grant. Was I out of my mind?

He knocks again.

"Hello?" I rest against the hardness of the door.

"Hi . . . um . . . Kate, it's me, Hugh . . . Hugh Clover." His voice is deep and muffled.

"Oh right, yeah, sorry." I open the door slowly. "Come in."

He has a carry-bag with two bottles of wine in one hand and a block of very white-looking cheese in the other.

"I come bearing gifts." He laughs as he holds them up.

We walk inside, side by side.

He turns in the small living area.

"My mother mailed these today," he tells me.

"You can post wine?"

"Well, it was part of a hamper," he explains. "It didn't travel in its bare bottle. I hoped you might have some crackers?"

I laugh. There was something so very adorable about him. Innocent. Sweet.

"I'm sure I have a packet of Jacobs' finest in there somewhere. I'll go get some glasses, shall I?" I say.

"If you would, thank you."

I rummage and find half a box of Carr's water crackers. I pull the top one out to see how soft they are. Not too bad. I throw away the top three and spread the rest on a plate. I grab the opener and the potato peeler and the glasses.

"Is it red or white?" I can't tell by the bottle – it's an odd colour.

"It's a rosé actually, a beautiful wine – she's sent it before. I can't afford these wines any more, I'm afraid. Thank you so much for the invite – I think this is my first outing at night since I've lived in Dublin."

"Really? And you're not stir crazy?" I hand him a glass and the opener.

"Um . . . a little, I suppose."

"Is it that you can't find work or you just don't know what you want to do now?"

He uncorks the wine with a pleasant pop.

I'm drinking too much lately, I tell myself.

We sit.

"Well . . . I'm on a bit of an unknown path really. . . I'm thinking of writing a novel perhaps." He sips.

"Cracker?" I offer.

He accepts. He removes the cheese from the packet and I offer him the potato peeler.

"What's this for?" He turns it upside down.

"For cutting the cheese." I thought he was supposed to be the cultured one.

"Oh, brilliant idea – a potato peeler that slices cheese, okay, thanks."

He cuts half a dozen or so slices and we eat.

He is in my apartment and it feels nice. I'm not uncomfortable.

"So how was work today then?" he says.

My mouth is full of cracker and cheese as he asks this, staring at me, and I swallow too fast and a bit of cracker goes down the wrong way. I start to cough. Mildly at first but then my eyes start to water. It's stuck and I can't catch my breath.

I have to stand. He doesn't move. I know I'm not choking for real but he doesn't. He looks like a rabbit in the headlights. The blood drains from his face. I point to my wineglass but still he doesn't move. I reach for it and down the wine, taking the obstruction with it.

123

"Jeez, thanks for nothing!" I splutter at him. "No wonder you don't practise medicine any more – you must have been a really shit doctor!" I gasp the words out.

He doesn't react for a few seconds but now he laughs. A huge laugh. Really contagious and I start to laugh with him. We roll around the place in stitches.

"I love your attitude – your straightness is so refreshing," he says after we wipe away our tears and he pours me another glass.

He pulls off his black round-neck jumper and sits now in just a tight white T-shirt and black jeans with black runners. Three white stripes down either side of them. He is simply gorgeous, I finally admit, and my heart sinks into the toes of my flip-flops. I fancy the absolute pants off him. Shit. I look to the floor. Just as well I had that wedding today – I'd made a half-decent attempt at painting my toes red last night.

"So what is it you do, Miss Smarty Pants?" He sits back into the couch and crosses his legs. The couch seems way too small for him.

"Well . . . I am currently self-employed . . . that is . . . I work for myself," I say with pride. No Brown Job to explain here.

"Yes . . . yes, thank you. I do know the definition of self-employed, Kate. So who was that chap with you today? Why were you all fancied up?" He is peeling more cheese now.

"That was Mark McMahon . . . Mark was . . ." I struggle to answer this one. "Well, I suppose you would say . . . I was his date. It was work."

He stops mid-peel and the half-cut piece of cheese falls on my spotless floor.

"Your date? You mean to say . . . you're a prostitute?" he asks, deadpan.

I don't know what is amusing me more – the fact that he thinks I am a hooker or the fact he doesn't seem remotely shocked or upset by this.

"Yeah . . . I'm a hooker, Hugh. High-class obviously." I remain deadpan too.

"Right . . . okay . . . I didn't know honestly . . . that's not why I'm here . . . I don't pay for sex, Kate . . . I don't want to have . . . I . . ." He moves to get up and grabs his dopey-looking jumper.

"Relax. I'm joking. I am not a hooker, Hugh, but I am deeply offended you thought I was."

"Lord, this really isn't going well, is it?" He throws his jumper to the end of the couch and drops his head into his hands. Speckles of fine dark hair cover the back of his hands. "I mean it wouldn't surprise me in the slightest if a frightfully annoying TV presenter jumped out from behind the sofa and shouted 'Caughtya!' Or some other dreadfully annoying slogan." He looks at me. He's cringing.

"Relax, it's fine. I do have an odd job. I escort people to events. No sex. No kissing, unless I want to kiss them. Just my company."

I sit beside him again now, our thighs slightly touching. Electricity shoots through me.

"Wow, super – now that's a way to make a living." He turns to look at me. "Will you escort me to dinner tomorrow night?"

"As an employee?" I ask.

"Oh. Well, no . . . as my . . . date? Or am I being exceptionally presumptuous? You are not spoken for, are you?" He looks shy now.

I am taken aback and I get a wave of that fuzzy feeling in my tummy.

"Yes . . . no . . . oh no, I can't," I stutter.

"Oh." He moves his thigh slightly away from mine.

"No! I can't tomorrow night – I'm going to Galway with my sister," I clarify as quickly as I can, words hurtling out of my mouth. "Next week maybe?"

"Great – okay – how about next Friday night? Say I pick you up at eight?"

"Are you leaving now?" I say.

"No, why?"

"Those are the kind of plans one makes when one is leaving, no?" I joke.

"Are they really?"

"Well, yeah," I say.

"So do we have a date?"

"Well, yeah," I say again.

"Do you want me to leave now?" His voice drops and suddenly, just like that, it is heavily tinged with lust.

It's too soon. Way too soon. So why does the next word I utter leave my big trap.

"No . . ." I breathe the word out slowly. I really should say, 'Yes, please, goodnight, see you next Friday'. But I don't.

He moves in closer, our thighs and knees squashed together now. I put my empty wineglass on the table. *Flashdance* Jennifer dances like she's never done before across that floor, her perfect non-cellulite bottom protruding in the tiny black leotard. He leans in. I lean in. His lips are inches away and I can smell his aftershave. Something not too sweet, manly. It's been so long. His lips touch mine and as our mouths open his tongue gently nips into my mouth and mine into his. It's warm. We lean back into the softness of my couch. He puts an arm tight around my neck. I put both of mine around his even tighter. The kiss is moist and sexual and it gets faster and faster and rougher and rougher. I stir down below. I pull away. My mouth is dry and I lick my lips for moisture. His brown eyes are heavy.

"Follow me." I curl my index finger at him.

We hit my bed like a ton of water. All over it. Falling from side to side. Waves of bodies crashing around. Top of the bed first then sliding down to the bottom. He unzips my track suit and feels my breast inside my T-shirt.

"It's been so long," he huffs at me now.

"Same here," I puff back.

I pull off his tight white T and fall into his manliness. He removes my T and kisses my boobs slowly, licking around the nipples until I can't take it any more and I grab his head and push my entire small breast into his mouth. He moans. I straddle him. We are kissing so hard my lips hurt. They sting. He removes my tracksuit bottoms and I am knickerless under them. He moves down and it's too much so I pull him up.

"I want you to make love to me," I tell him.

"I don't have a condom," he tells me.

"*Ffffuuucckkkk!*" I flop back. *Flashdance* Jennifer falls at her dance audition. The judges stare at her accusingly. Hateful judges. Spiteful faces. They say: 'You are not good enough – why are you here?'

"Next time," he promises me and teases me with his tongue and I float away to a place I haven't been in such a long time.

When he's done I ask him what he wants.

"No . . . nothing," he replies and holds me tight.

"But that's not fair," I tell him.

"Kate, this has been one of the nicest experiences I have had in so long. The slower the better for me. The first time I saw you in that butcher's shop that morning something triggered in me. I wanted to talk to you, I wanted to get to know you, I thought you were so gorgeous, so intriguing . . ."

He moans loudly now as I kiss him long and hard.

"I promise you I cannot wait for the next time," he says as I pull away and the words 'next time' dance around a maypole, waving glorious coloured flags high in the air in my head.

I rest in the crook of his arm and it feels so safe. His eyes are kind and I still can't quite figure out why I like him so much. I liked him the second I laid eyes on him, I admit to myself now. It's as though this was just how it was supposed to be. He seems a little lost like me, non-threatening, vulnerable maybe – that is it. Also I know he drinks glasses of Guinness and I think that can only be a good thing. Maybe, just maybe, this is meant to be.

Chapter Thirteen

"Shit! We must have fallen asleep!" I grab my alarm clock and try to focus on the numbers. That bloody rosé not so rosy now. The bright green light flashes 7:15 a.m. Balls! I have nothing packed yet even and I have to be at the station in forty-five minutes.

"Wake up, Hugh!" I shake him.

"What . . . oh . . . good morning . . . what time is it?" He's very groggy as he tries to lift his head.

"Sorry, I know it's a Sunday morning but I am going to Galway on the quarter to nine train. I'm so late Ciara will go through me for a shortcut."

"Oh no – can I do anything to help?" He rubs his tired eyes with his index fingers.

"Yeah, make me a cuppa tea and ring me a taxi. I need to pack. Milk no sugar. Cups and teabags in the press above the cooker and milk in a jug in the fridge."

"I thought you took sugar?"

"No," I say.

I hide my nakedness with my throw and escape to the

129

bathroom. I shower quickly and dress, then run around throwing bits into my big duffel bag.

Hugh, now fully dressed, hands me a mug of tea and a slice of toast.

"I'll get out of your hair," he says.

I lean up on my tippy-toes and kiss him on the mouth. It feels like a very natural thing to do.

"So I'll see you next Friday then for some dinner?" he says.

I nod happily and he leaves, closing the door very gently behind him.

The taxi hits every bloody red light and I am a sweaty mess by the time I arrive at Heuston Station to find my sister in a panic.

"You're late, Kate! Run! They're closing the platform in five minutes! Honestly, Kate!" she throws her hands up in the air in sheer frustration with me.

I don't blame her. I know she can't run so I have to run to the gate with both our bags and tell them to wait for her. She walks very slowly as fast as she can.

When we finally take our seats opposite each other, I put the bags up and I drop my head back on the headrest.

"Why were you late this morning of all mornings?" Ciara demands.

"I had a man in my bed, sister dear," I reply with a dodgy grin all over my face.

She literally spits her water out and the couple opposite look at us in contempt.

I laugh out loud.

"Really?" Her white pale face lights up with a flush of beautiful pink in interest.

"Yes, as a matter of fact this sister got it on last night." I am grinning so wildly it hurts my face.

"With the wedding guy?" she probes, twisting the cap carefully back onto her water bottle.

"No. With my English neighbour, the very posh, once-upon-a-time doctor, Hugh Clover!" I reveal my trump card.

"Go – a – way!" She flicks her hand at me, clearly enjoying the much-needed gossip.

It can't be much in the way of 'girly fun' having me as a sister, I acknowledge.

"I'm serious, Ciara . . . he's so lovely . . . I . . . I think I like him," I tell her, biting my bottom lip.

"I'm thrilled for you, but what does he do? This once-upon-a-time doctor of yours?" she asks.

"Nothing," I answer.

"Impressive," she nods.

"He's in between jobs, I guess. We didn't really get into the nook and cranny of why and what next . . . although he did say he was going to write a book." I reach over and take her bottle, twist the cap off and take a drink.

"Did he now?" She yawns widely.

"Yes, what's wrong with wanting to be a writer?"

"Absolutely nothing, unless you were once a doctor," she replies.

"Maybe he's going to write a book about being a doctor?"

"What, like *Doctor Doolittle*?" She bites her bottom lip now.

"Doctor Doolittle spoke to *animals*, Ciara," I say.

"Did he though? Really?" She raises her eyebrows.

"Yes, he did!" I raise my voice.

"Animals can't talk, Kate – you must know that?" She leans in closer to me across the small white plastic table.

"Yer annoying me now, Ciara – shut up!" I snap.

"AnnoyING," she says and repeats the word 'annoying' over and over, her mouth as wide as Julia Roberts at the opera in *Pretty Woman*. *La Traviata* if I'm not mistaken. "I admire the way you never drop your ING's, Kate," she says, grinning at me.

"Let's change the subject," I say. "I'm not looking forward to this. I really don't know what to say to her."

"Don't say anything you don't have to," she says. "Dad gave me a letter for her."

"I'd love to read that," I scoff.

"No. It's private. It took him hours last night," she says, with definite pride in her voice. She opens her mouth to say something else and then coughs – a fake forced cough, before she says quietly, "I just want to see her. Apart from the fact she could save my life I have never stopped thinking about her. I don't have as many memories as you – I was only five when she left – but what I do have are nice ones." She leans her head on the window.

I don't answer this. But I think about the night she bathed us before the photo shoot and the soft kisses she dropped on my little-girl nose.

County Dublin flashes by in all shades of green as I look out the window. Telephone poles and flocks of birds. Wires and wires. Blue skies. I remember how she tried to keep it all together. She did try to be a mother and father to us and she did try and protect us from his drunken rages and from slipping on his vomit in the bathroom of a school morning. But still she left us. Why didn't she just

132

take us with her? Ciara hadn't been fully diagnosed then but she was never well as a child. She left a sick five-year-old child and an eight-year-old in the care of a raging alcoholic. Who could do that? I'd called our Auntie Brenda over and over to see if she knew where our mammy was the first few weeks. "No, I haven't heard from her, Kate," was all she would say. I told Brenda about Da and all she said was for me to be patient and give my mam some space – she'd be back soon enough when she was well, when she was fitter. Brenda did send Social Services one day soon after but we lied, said Da was gone to the shop, and when they returned the next evening he was having his dinner. He told them he was okay. They never returned. I didn't want them to. As bad as it was, for some reason I didn't want to be separated from the family unit – not until I was much older.

I glance over at Ciara. Her eyes are shut. What a shite hand she has been dealt. Totally shite. If she ever gets better I am going to take her everywhere. We always talk about going to Ibiza, the two of us, and dancing the week away. Or winning the Lotto and going to LA, staying at the Chateau Marmont and visiting the homes of famous movie stars. That'd be the craic. Seeing how the other half live. Someday. Maybe.

I take out my iPhone and text Phillip. I still intend to help him as much as I can with this fundraiser idea. But I'm suspicious he's going to ask me to dance. That will never happen. Don't ever ask me to dance in public – so he better not.

"Maura had a bit of a turn in the studio," he texts back, **"but she is fine now. I am in her house in Dalkey staying overnight with her. I'm going to cook for her."**

I tap back, **"Oh no, poor Maura, give her my love. I'm on the train here. Get her some shopping in too maybe? The essentials: toilet roll, brown bread, beetroot and a box of green tea. I will go and see her as soon as I get back."** I press send.

I wonder now exactly why I'm so fascinated with Maura. I'm not normally the nosy type at all but I am deeply interested in where she came from because she doesn't ever say. I think I respect her lifestyle. She lives alone and is perfectly contented as far as I can see. I want to be like Maura when I'm Maura's age and younger.

I look at Ciara again, her head bobbing around now as sleep takes hold of her. I'm glad. The more she sleeps the better, we are always being told. I think of Wendy. How could you go back to normal when you lose a beloved like that?

I lean my head against the window and with an open mouth stare at my teeth – the reflection makes it seem like I have layers and layers of bottom teeth. I can't stop looking at it. I just hope and pray that this is all happening for a reason and Mommy Dearest is here to save us.

Chapter Fourteen

We disembark from the train at Galway and walk around onto on a sunny Eyre Square.

"Fancy a coffee?" I ask Ciara.

She looks really tired – huge black rings under her eyes now.

"Tell you what – I could do with a cold glass of vino?" She looks at her watch "Why don't we get ourselves to the bus station, get our tickets and then go for a drink?"

I take her case and she tries to protest but knows she can't carry it. We walk to the bus station with the sun at our backs. Galway smells of roses and mint chocolate-chip ice cream. The place is very busy. Throngs of people move through the square. We buy two tickets to Oughterard for the three o'clock bus and head back to sit outside a packed bar. Diddly-idle music rings out all around and, even though it's only early, pints are flying around on trays. We order and squeeze ourselves around a large barrel onto two high stools. It's a little heat trap and I hold my face up to the sun.

"I wonder what she looks like now? I wonder what she'll say?" Ciara says.

"She'll probably look the same, only either fatter or thinner with more lines on her face. She'll tell us the stories Brenda told us about how she had her reasons to do what she did. She'll tell us of the times when we were very young and she was almost always on her own as Da was in the pub until closing every night. She'll tell us how in the early years she would sit up all night worrying he had been in some type of accident when he never arrived home after work to his new wife and new baby." I want to go on but I stop because I don't want to wind Ciara up.

Our drinks arrive. The grungy-looking waitress, with dreadlocks and almost every orifice I can see pierced, gives us a great big smile and says in an Eastern European accent, "Who is for the wine?"

"Me, please," Ciara tells her and I immediately see the look of pity on the waitress's face as she puts the wine down. So does Ciara.

I hand her a two-euro tip and I continue.

"She will tell us how she had his dinner ready every night but he never came home to eat it, how he would then wake her all hours of the night demanding his dinner, telling her *'I'm entitled to me dinner '*–"

Ciara butts in. "God, I don't really remember anything, Kate. Did Ma make him his dinner in the middle of the night?" She swirls her wine, her nails painted black, as I nod.

"Well, she'd have to get up and reheat it. Oh, he was such a prick, Ciara, when he came in stocious – he really couldn't care less if he woke the entire house on a school night." I can see she doesn't want to hear it.

136

We drink. We sit in silence for a while, watching the happy tourists snapping pictures and drinking Guinness. I'd love a pair of sunglasses. Someone dressed as a leprechaun dances down the street holding a sign for a *Trace Your Family History Tree* shop.

"I remember the dread when it was coming up to St Patrick's Day. You don't. Every other kid in my class would be so excited about the parade, the green ribbons in their hair, the shamrock pinned on their new coats, the badges, and all we had was two full days of Da absolutely wrecking our lives through his drinking. That was the time of year she finally left. It was of a St Patrick's weekend. I know you can't remember."

Ciara slowly shakes her head at me.

"Mam had us ready for the parade. He'd been in the pub since straight after Mass and we were just getting our coats on when he fell through the door. We were going to walk in to O'Connell Street and Mam had made us sausage sandwiches and 7UP to take with us in her bag. He was so aggressive. He demanded to know where we thought we were all going? Then he demanded money off Ma, and when she told him she had none he picked me up high in the air by the collars of my new £2 Oxfam coat and said "Where'd this coat come from then, eh? Ya have that Children's Allowance, I know ya have – I want it!" He dropped me so hard I fell against the bottom stair and I really hurt my back. I cried out. I remember the exact words he snarled at me then, close to my face, the smell from his breath hideous. I could see the dried vomit on his shoes. 'Stop making this worse like always, ya fuckin' little drama queen!' His eyes told me how worthless I was to him. 'Leave her alone!' Ma shouted and then he saw her bag on the hall table. I always remember she had the small carpet-covered-looking suitcase by the door too. He didn't see that. He just grabbed her handbag, snapped back the gold clasp and pulled her wallet out. 'No!' she shouted at him. 'Give me that back! Ya bad devil, ya!' He stuffed it under his coat and staggered out, slamming the door so hard that the picture of The Sacred Heart fell off the hook in the hallway. No money. No parade. No Mam. She took off."

I close my eyes and still feel the pain of that afternoon.

"I don't remember any of that, Kate." Ciara swirls her wineglass.

"Should you be drinking wine?" I ask her.

"Are you serious? I should be taking bloody cocaine!" she says, laughing.

"Point taken." I lick the cold froth from the back of my coffee spoon.

"I'm sure she had a hell of a good reason to go, Kate – what do we really know?" Ciara says.

"Look, I know she had her reasons to leave, Ciara. I'm not saying she hadn't, but how could she have left us behind? I mean what kind of person, what kind of a mother would do that to her own two children?" It still freaked me out.

"But he wasn't violent, Kate – he was just a . . . a drunk"

I know she tried to choose these words carefully but they hit a nerve.

"Ciara, were to listening at all to what I just described? We were terrified of him! I know he didn't punch us in the face but he manhandled me lots of times and the fear of him snapping was nearly worse. The fear we would push him over the edge. I had to step into her shoes, left, not you. I had to learn how to be a mother. Get you up for school, make your lunch, cook your meals, do your washing, try and protect you from him. I know after she left he wasn't as bad as before, after Brenda got Social Services to come by – I know then the threatening behaviour stopped but he was still a horrible, drunken mess." I lift my face to the sun again and exhale heavily. I am fed up of these conversations with Ciara trying to defend him.

Ciara keeps looking at her watch now and I know she's incredibly anxious. She just wants to be sitting at the bus station reading a *VIP* magazine so we drink up and leave.

Once seated on the rickety old bus I am interrupted by the beep-beep of my text-message alert. Now I know most people will find this hard to believe but I mainly only ever get texts from Ciara and Phillip so now I assume without doubt that this is Phillip as Ciara is sitting opposite me. I pull it from my cardigan pocket and slide the arrow across. I was indeed correct.

"OK, I'm getting a bit worried about Maura, can you call me?"

I press call.

"Hi," he answers after the first ring. "I didn't know if you might be in your mother's by now?"

"No, just on the bus to Oughterard. What's wrong?"

"She's just so sleepy, Kate. I mean, I came in before class and made her breakfast and she was in bed – again at lunch I woke her and she sat up – but I've just let myself in again now and her lunch isn't touched and she's back asleep."

"Hmmm, I think you'd better call the doctor, Phillip."

"Who do I call?" His voice is rising.

"Calm down, it's fine, she more than likely has some virus. Maura's not getting any younger – she may need to slow down a bit. I would google Dalkey Doctors and see who does house calls, yeah?"

"Okay," he agrees.

"Keep me posted, won't you?"

He has already rung off. Googling Dalkey Doctors no doubt. Phillip never says goodbye at the end of a phone conversation. I close my eyes now as the bus bumps its way to a destination I am terrified of reaching.

We sit in the bedroom of the quaint Oughterard B&B with our coats on and say nothing.

"Well, this is it," Ciara says after a while.

"Not necessarily . . . we can still find an anonymous match . . . the doctors tell us that all the time. It happens – people donate all the time."

"I know they do and I know my chances too, Kate," She's very apprehensive.

I get up and she follows me across the room to the small wooden wardrobe. We unpack our clothes, both deep in thought.

We walk down the stairs. The friendly landlady has already told us where Ivy Cottage is – basically down the road – a five-minute walk. So we begin our walk.

It is still a warm afternoon; the birds screech above us and circle us wildly. It is slightly medieval. The ground is stony and hard and puffs of dust arise as we walk. Blackberries grow wild at every corner. The thing that strikes me most is the quietness of the town. The stillness. There is a convenience store called Mulvaney's and a couple of bars but it's so still. Trees hang above us, branches and leaves motionless.

Ciara is slightly ahead of me for a change. She looks really smart. She's in dark denim wide-fit jeans with a white man's shirt tucked in, and flip-flops. Dreadfully thin, yes, but alert. Oh so alert. She stops suddenly. I almost bang into the back of her.

We are standing in front of a small white picket fence and in sprawling red paint, handwritten on the gate, we see *Ivy Cottage*.

"Let the games begin," I mutter as I raise the white latch and push open the squeaky gate.

She must have been alerted by its noise as the front door opens before we ring the bell and there she stands. Older for sure. Same size, though, I gauge, and her hair, once chestnut-brown and bouncy, is now grey and short and flat. Her blue eyes still and wary. She wears a green dress with a blue apron on over it, thick tan tights and on her feet are white sandals. Those of the orthopaedic type, ones you might buy in a chemist shop. Not cheap but last a lifetime. Her face is make-up free and she looks like a photo-fit twenty-eight years on. Except it's not a photo-fit, it's really her. My mother. She pulls the apron off roughly now as though it wasn't part of her plan. She crumples it up and her fist grabs it tightly. She misses one of the ties and it hangs by her leg, swinging gently. We all focus on it. She catches it and adds it to the rest of the apron in her tight fist. We all stare at each other. No one moves. No one speaks. No one knows how to do either simple action.

Eventually Ciara breaks this. "Can we come in, Mam?" she says gently.

"Of course . . . Jesus . . . what am I like . . . of course.

Please, girls . . . come in, come in." She stands aside and we go in past her. I gather her scent in my nostrils as I pass. I had forgotten her smell. It gives me a great big lump in my throat. I swallow hard and take a deep breath in through my nose. We enter into a small living area and, despite the heat outdoors, she has a small fire lighting in the grate. Turf piled up in a tin box beside the fire. There is a wooden kitchen table and four chairs in the living area and a small TV on top of a glass cabinet and inside the cabinet the glass doors squeeze in many, many ornaments. The table is laid. The oilcloth looks brand new and a plate with a fruitcake on it lies in wait. Recently baked, I can smell.

"Tea?" she asks, rubbing her hands down the front of her dress.

"That would be lovely," Ciara answers and pulls out a seat.

I remain standing. It is so tense I feel a bit nauseous.

She makes herself busy in the tiny kitchen off the living area and Ciara and I talk to one another with our eyes. She looks okay, doesn't she? Yes. Nice place? Yes. Ciara's eyes jump out at me, asking if I am okay. I nod my head three times.

Emily returns with a blue-tea-cosy-clad teapot and puts it on a coaster in the middle of the table before returning and bringing in the cups, saucers and plates. The milk jug and sugar bowl are already out. Matching. White with three blue stripes.

She sits. I sit. She gets up again.

"Spoons," she tells us.

She returns and sits. Then she pushes the chair and gets up again.

"Knife . . . to cut the fruitcake," she explains and returns to the kitchen and comes back with a sharp red-handled knife and she sits again.

She pours and we all add the necessary amounts of milk and sugar and sip. It is like being at a job interview. A clock ticks so loudly on the mantelpiece that we all look at it. It ticks to the beat singing in my head, a sound-alike of 'Awk – Ward', 'Awk – Ward', 'Awk – Ward'.

"Fruitcake?" She offers some slices she has just cut and laid out on a white plate.

It is slightly crumbly, I notice, and splits when she tries to lift a slice.

"No, thank you," Ciara says.

I just shake my head. The fire spits.

"It looks great, though," Ciara adds. "Did you make it yourself?"

"Yes, I did . . . just this morning."

"It looks so nice. I would have a slice – it's just that I feel like I'm the same as every other woman out there if I don't . . . if I avoid sugar, if I calorie-count, if I deny myself, it makes me feel less of an outsider, you know?" Ciara doesn't seem sure herself of what she is saying.

Emily nods, unsure also. She then replaces the plate and clears some of the crumbs that have fallen with her fingers. She licks her index finger but the excess crumbs still stick to it. She flicks them towards the fire.

She lifts her cup. Still no one speaks.

"I am so sorry," she eventually blurts out and shakily puts her cup back down and repositions it on her saucer. Turning it around and around.

"I'm sick, Mam," Ciara says now, holding back tears, "really sick."

"I know . . ." She has to gather herself together. "Brenda told me. It's why I wanted you to come to me. She only told me very recently, mind you . . . I have mostly lived down here since I left you, when I have been out, but I had asked her not to tell you where I was . . ."

Ciara interrupts her. "Will you help me, please?" The words tumble from her mouth and she is begging.

I wasn't aware Ciara was this desperate. She hides it so well. Don't get me wrong – I'm not stupid – I know she's terrified out of her mind – but I thought that, more than anything, she just wanted to see our ma. I realise right now that it's what I wanted too. I shiver at the acceptance of my wanting. I look at my mother closely and I flashback all the good times. Jennifer Beals stands still in my mind. Frozen. She's not pointing those fingers nor is she on the ground. She's just still. She hardly ever had been still in my mind before. How do I feel, Jennifer? I need you to tell me.

"I will, of course I will, pet." She reaches across to put her hand on top of Ciara's but Ciara's hand has flown to her mouth so Ma's hand just lies in the middle of the table.

Do not ask me why but I place mine over it. Just like that, I think, I am forgiving her. It's the look in her eyes. Emily has the look of a broken woman, so shattered and so scared. I don't want her to be scared any more.

"Thank you!" Ciara jumps up, runs around the table and hugs her.

"I will do whatever you need me to do. I'm here for you both . . . I'm so, so sorry." Emily sobs and sobs now and I get up and go find some tissue in the kitchen and give it to her. She blows her nose noisily and wipes her eyes with her hands. She pushes herself up from the chair, goes over to the cabinet and slides across the small glass doors. She removes an old biscuit tin and then another. One is faded red with a picture of chocolate biscuits on the front but sellotaped around the tin in white paper is the name **KATIE**. The other, a blue tin, has a small boy eating a biscuit and around this one, sellotaped on the same white paper, is **CIARA**.

"Here ye go." She hands us a biscuit tin each.

I pull at the lid and it pops open. I look in. Letters. Loads and loads of letters. I look at her.

She says, "I know how much you must hate me, Katie. I couldn't blame you one bit, but I'm hoping what's in these will help you somewhat."

I pull a random letter from the middle and begin to read it.

"*When you were both very young I was always on my own as Eoin, your dad, went to the pub every night straight after work. I would sit and worry and wait for him to get home after I put you both to bed, usually after midnight. In the beginning he was full of excuses – Robert the foreman had to have a meeting with the lads after work about health and safety on the site or Robert has marriage problems or Robert had a funny turn on the job earlier, excuse after excuse. I'd heat his dinner up every night as he was always starving with the hunger. He'd be kinda sorry he hadn't seen ye all day or at night and he knew he'd be gone again before the pair of ye got up in the morning and soon he really never saw you girls at all. On a Saturday he'd have drunk so much, into the early hours from the Friday night, he'd be throwing up all day so I'd have to get you both out of the house. I didn't drive.*

He barely gave me any money. Sunday he was in the pub all day again. I remember sitting in the kitchen in the freezing cold because we had run out of oil and I had no money to order more. My hands would be so cold I had to keep boiling the kettle to warm them over the steam. That's why I put ye both to bed so early, because it was so cold."

I look up. Ciara's head is buried in a letter and Ma is sitting back, watching us read.

"It's all there in the letters – you'll get to read it all," she says then, "but, if I may say this much . . . I don't know if you remember but I had to get a part-time job when you were in school in the mornings, things got so bad. I cleaned houses in Dalkey. Rich people's houses, and I have to say they were all so lovely to me. One lady owner even became my friend. Some mornings I had to walk from Ringsend to Dalkey as I had no fare for the bus. The cleaning job was the only way we could survive because Eoin had stopped giving us any money at that stage. The bills were unpaid and the fridge empty. I never told him about the job for fear he'd take our money. He'd stopped talking to me altogether at this stage too. But the anger had set in on him. The jealousy. He'd accuse me of all sorts. He'd threaten me. I was terrified of him. He would tell me I was turning into my sister Brenda who he always called 'the ugly bitch'. There are hundreds of letters, girls, it will takes you months to read them all, but they kept me going. Read them in your own time . . . but if you will allow me one last chance to explain in my own words face to face?"

We both nod, our hearts breaking at what she has already told us.

I fold the pages and push them back into my box. My

precious box. I close the lid firmly and hold my box tight to my chest.

"I had a nervous breakdown that St Patrick's Day. A full-on breakdown. When he grabbed you, Kate, and threw you against the stairs, when he took all the money I had in my bag. One lady – the friend I cleaned for in Dalkey – I had confided in her and told her my situation and she gave me money, a lot of money in those days, to leave him. You see, that day I had all my cash, changed into fifties, in that wallet. I was going to get us train tickets to Galway, I had it all planned. Two years of saving and kind, wonderful Maura's money. I'd packed the small carpet-covered case for us. But he cleaned me out. He took it all. It wasn't a fortune by any means but it would have been enough to get us set up. Brenda was going to put us up in Galway – this was before she moved to Manchester. Ivy Cottage was, still is in fact, Brenda and David's. I still rent it from them. Anyway, I felt myself shatter. It was the strangest feeling and weirdest experience in the world. I wouldn't wish it on my greatest enemy. I could no longer cope. I stood in that hall but I felt like I was falling off the Empire State Building. It was the most debilitating dizziness. I simply can't describe it. I had nothing left."

She presses her hands together under her chin before she goes on. I get the deep feeling she hasn't spoken this much in a long time. It's literally wearing her out.

"I knew you weren't well, Ciara – you were never well as a baby – and I was so frightened for you. Eoin never shared the worry – I tried to tell him how concerned I was, but think deep down he couldn't cope with the fact you were getting so ill all the time. Anyway I somehow got the two of you in front of the television – that programme you loved was on, what do ya call it, *Grange Hill*? Funny how I always remember that. Anyway I managed to call Brenda and I told her of my situation. I told her my thoughts and my plan. She immediately told me to walk out, to go and wait in Ringsend Library and she would get someone to meet me there. She called a friend of hers who was up in Dublin on business and that evening her friend drove me to Galway – a saint that Gail O'Callaghan was, and still is. My head was still spinning when I got to Galway. Brenda took me to all the doctors in Galway city and in Oughterard, and two psychiatrists that week. No one helped me. I knew I was losing my mind if it wasn't already lost. I was prescribed medication for anxiety before eventually being admitted to St Kevin's hospital for mental illness where I remained for the next seven years. I tried to take my own life several times – every time I was released – so I always ended up back inside. I felt I was done. I was no use as a mother. I had technically failed at life." She tries to give us a weak smile.

As moved as I am, for some reason I still want to shout at her 'But how? How could you leave us with him?' But, looking at her now, I just can't. I suppose I've just realised after her speech just how she could. Ma was sick too.

"I decided to never go back to you when I finally got out, when I was finally deemed fit." Tears fall now, huge free-flowing sorrow-filled tears. Down her face onto her wrist where the skin is thin and white.

We sit very still and watch her cry. She sobs and sobs again. We aren't ones for emotional behaviour – it's unfortunate and cold but it is who we are. We've been robbed of a mother's love and it shows. I know if I offer affection I'll be mad with myself. I'm not cleansing this woman and in a way she owes us these tears. She eventually pulls the old tissue from up her dress sleeve and wipes her eyes before blowing her nose.

"So many tears, I have cried so many tears." She sniffs.

"You and me both," Ciara replies.

Emily sniffs repeatedly. Over and over as a child might do.

"How awful was it . . . your lives?" She breathes the words into the palm of her hand as though she might throw up.

"Awful," I answer straight away.

"Worse for Kate," Ciara answers honestly and I'm surprised at how moved I am by her support.

"I can't believe he's still alive." She says this with her eyes shut tight.

"I know," I say.

She shakes her head repeatedly. "I thought the drink would have killed him years ago. I'm so sorry . . ." She sits up straighter.

I feel it's a therapist's move. Accept what you have done, Emily. Apologise and move on, Emily. It happened. You can't pay for it for the rest of your life, Emily. Apologise and move on, Emily. Forgive yourself, Emily. You deserve a life too you know, Emily. The past is in the past, Emily. Sit up straight, Emily. Love yourself, Emily.

"Emily," I say although I don't mean to.

"Yes?" She looks me in the eye.

"It's okay," I say and I hear Ciara swallow – it's that hard a gulp.

"Wh-what?" Emily stutters.

"It's okay," I repeat, slower and in a softer tone. I feel

slightly like the late great Robin Williams as Seán in *Good Will Hunting*. It's not your fault. It's not your fault. It's not your fault.

"No . . . Katie . . . I know it's not okay . . . I know what I did . . . I've known what I did every single day . . . I abandoned my babies to an alcoholic brute . . ." She almost gags now on these words and coughs sharply.

"It's okay, I mean it . . . Mam." I take a deep breath and exhale slowly.

"I never stopped loving you both." She is engulfed in emotion again.

I feel for her now. I really do. I want to go over and hug her but I just can't.

"We need to get you up to Dublin to St James's Hospital as soon as possible, to Ciara's doctor," I hear myself say and I know it sounds so cutting and clinical but I don't mean it to be. It's just who I am. I don't know how to be any other way. She doesn't seem to notice.

"Yes, whenever, can you drive me?" She has a determined look about her now as she pushes the plate with the cake to the edge of the table. Clearing her way.

"We don't drive, either of us, but we can take you on the bus and then the train? We can get you a B&B beside the hospital. There'll be a lot to go through obviously."

"I have been reading up on it – I'm a walking encyclopaedia on aplastic anaemia, Gail says." She sniffs some more.

"That's great," I say. "Well, first you will be assessed to see if you are a HLA-matched donor? You know all that this entails though, right?"

She nods her head.

"So, after all that, if Doctor Doyle is happy with you

to go ahead, you'll have to stay in St James's hospital for two nights – one night before the procedure and one night after. I have done it and it's a simple enough procedure. I had very little pain after, was just tired for a few days, that's all. Then we or I, I should say, can bring you back down here on the train and the bus."

"Well, I'm sure Gail will drive up and collect me." She seems to be thinking aloud as she folds and refolds the soggy tissue. "So, yes, absolutely, when do we go?"

She seems so emotionally fragile that I wonder if she can even travel. She is only sixty-two but looks so much older. Her state of mind is concerning me.

"I think we need to ring Doctor Doyle this evening and see what he says," I say. "The most important thing we need to know is if you are on any medication?"

"Yes, I'm on antidepressants and occasionally Valium," she tells us matter-of-factly.

"Okay, well, I need a full list of your medical history," I say as I drag a pen and notebook from my bag.

"We can take a walk to Doctor Ashmore's down the town – he can provide you with all that information," she says. "But are ye hungry? I made a fresh coddle this morning – I can heat up a few bowls."

Ciara and I look at each other and nearly burst out laughing.

"We are literally allergic to coddle . . . eh . . . Mam . . ." I say. "It's all I could make after you left so we lived on it for months. It was kinda horrible – I was only eight after all!"

She looks afraid again.

Ciara helps her out. "Is there a pub or a café open nearby?"

"Yes, Yellow Posies will be open. Gail runs it – she does lovely homemade scones and soups." Her eyes seem to light up a little.

"Great!" Ciara says. "Let's do that and we can talk you through the procedure, from our personal experience anyway, and what will be expected of you. But are you really sure, Mam?"

"One hundred per cent!" She tugs at the collar on her dress.

"Thank you," Ciara replies simply.

"I've been praying like a mad thing that I am compatible – that I am a HLA-matched donor and we can get you better. I'll just get my hat and coat." She pushes back the chair and gets up.

"It's really warm outside." I tell her.

"I haven't been warm in years."

Chapter Fifteen

HUGH CLOVER

Hugh sits in his apartment in his bare feet. Last night was
the first night he had actually slept through the night in
the past year. He had found comfort and great peace in
being physical with Kate but mostly in the tender human
contact. He loves her honesty and her individuality. He
cannot wait to see her again. To smell her and touch her.
She is so easy to be around.

His nerves are up once more now though. He wishes
she hadn't gone to Galway – he misses her. He pushes
himself up with the palms of his hands and paces the
room. Round and round he goes. Like a fenced horse. The
rest of the day looms long ahead. Endless. He stops
circling and gazes out his long window. Looking out over
Ringsend it is all peaceful. A regular lazy Sunday
afternoon of people taking walks with children on
bicycles with cute safety helmets, and teenagers flirting
outside the taxi depot. He closes his eyes tightly and leans
his head against the cold glass. Then he lifts it slowly and
goes to the bookshelf. The nine months he had spent

curled up on his bed or couch in London after it plays in HD through his mind. He takes down the red photo album. He holds it in his hands for a few minutes and wills himself not to open it.

He crosses back to the couch and folds his legs under him. He rests the red album on his knees.

"Put it in the bin!" he cries into his open hands and runs them roughly down his face. "Stop being a crazy man!"

He stands bolt upright and goes towards the bin. Then he drops onto his knees on the cold wooden floor and opens the album up. He has to stop this. He opens the first page and the glossy photo stares back at him.

Alive. She is alive. There she is in Beggars Bush eating soup but leaving the brown bread, drinking the pint glass of tap water with ice and lemon with Victoria and Alison. All three of them together again. He turns the page. There she is now on the campus green with Victoria and Alison and a couple of lads only last week. There she is. Alive. She was in a picture taken just days ago, the far right-hand corner of the *Irish Times* dated in the picture proves that. He touches her face with the tips of his fingers. How happy he is that she is alive.

Chapter Sixteen

KATE WALSH

I have to admit it's the sweetest scone I have ever tasted.
Ciara has the leek and potato soup and Emily just has a
peppermint tea. Gail made a big fuss of Emily when we
came into Yellow Posies and Mam seems very fond of her.
I could tell immediately she knew exactly who we were
but Mam didn't introduce us. I was exceptionally glad of
this. I am settling on calling her 'Mam' now. Ma is the
past.

"Cute place," Ciara says as she blows the soup on her
spoon. It ripples.

"Yes, isn't it? This is where I write to you both every
day," she tells us.

"You don't write to us every single day?" I raise my
eyebrows.

"Oh, I do – there are boxes and boxes of letters,
biscuits tins and biscuit tins – that's only the beginning
I've given you, the first batch if you will." She dips her tea
bag up and down. An expert at it by the looks of her.
"There's even a biscuit tin for . . . for Eoin." She squeezes

the tea bag now and pops it on the side of her saucer. The smell of the peppermint is calming.

"You write to Da?" Ciara places her spoon in the bowl and I wish she'd place it beside her bowl like I showed her how.

Seriously, Ciara, where are your manners?

"All part of my therapy," Emily says.

Bingo! I shout in my mind. B.I.N.G.O.

"He'll be thrilled." Ciara smiles. "He wrote a letter for you too," she rummages in her bag. "Oh, it's back in your cottage in my make-up bag. I forgot to pop it back into my bag when I did my lippy."

I'm starting to get wound up. I can feel it. My mouth is going dry and my neck wants to move, my neck wants to warm up. My body needs to dance. I need to release inner tension.

"I'm just going to use the bathroom." I stand.

Emily points me the way. "Back of the café to the left – mind your head – the ceiling is very low. Gail really needs to stick up a sign about it. I keep telling her."

In the tiny toilet I splash freezing cold water on my face and pull my iPhone from my cardigan pocket. The place smells of too much lavender air-freshener. It catches in the back of my throat. No coverage. Shit. I want to see how Maura is. I think of Hugh. In a pathetic way, I know, he's calmed me down today. Without that intense intimacy last night I'd be feistier, angrier. I'm so ridiculous. I look at my reflection. I'm blushing. Am I falling in love? Hugh has been fantastic and I really like him. I really, really like him. I can tell he really, really likes me too. There are very few people in the world I am truly comfortable around, and I know this for a fact. If I am comfortable, like when I'm around people like Ciara and Phillip, I can look them in the eye all day and all night. With other people I can't even hold their gaze for ten seconds. I could look Hugh in the eye forever.

When I return to the table they are laughing. I sit and finish my sweet scone and we ask Gail for a pen and some paper. I write in my notebook, Ciara on the sheets of paper and we make a list of what is to be done as we talk Emily through all the medical procedures Ciara has been through. We tell her loads. We talk over each other, interrupting each other. We tell her our Leaving Cert results and she claps her hands and throws her head back, obviously over the moon, even though we'd both barely scraped a pass. She is proud of us. She orders pots and pots of hot strong tea for us and more scones. I drink cup after cup and eat another scone. We tell her all about our friends, various jobs, our Debs and basically all about our lives. Neither of us mentions a man of the boyfriend variety and I'm sure she feels that is her fault. Sworn off men for life. I'm keeping Hugh to myself. For now.

"Brenda wasn't sure – is he still drinking?" She dips her tea bag up and down in her fresh cup of peppermint tea as I spread more freshly whipped local cream thickly onto my fruit scone.

"Not anywhere near as bad," Ciara jumps in. "I still live with him."

Emily takes a very loud breath in through her nose.

"It's okay, Mam. I'm okay with Da. He doesn't stay in the pub after six o'clock any more – he comes home and has his dinner and goes to bed. He wants so badly to stop, I can't tell you . . . he's a broken soul." Ciara, who has also moved onto the scones after her soup, licks the cream

157

from the tips of her fingers.

"He's still a massive prick." I can't help myself. "I can't stand him, Mam." I feel better. I can't play this happy family routine much longer. Baby steps.

"Himself and Kate don't get on, that's for sure," Ciara tells her, "but as I said to Kate only recently he's okay with me. I think . . . I *know*, sorry . . . that Kate took the brunt of the really bad years and sheltered me from them as much as she could and then when I got really sick he stopped the anger and started to see his disease for what it is. He knows he's pathetic – he tells me often enough." She rests back into the chair.

Emily opens her mouth to say something, closes it then opens it again, now ready to speak. "You know, he took his first drink not long after you were born, Kate – did he ever tell you that? I knew he'd had a tough childhood and his father had a problem with the drink but both his parents had passed by the time I'd met him and he didn't really want to talk about it. He wanted so badly to be a great father and he had so . . . *we* had so many plans . . . and when we got the corporation house across from the flats we were thrilled. By then we had moved out of our one room on the top floor of the house in Townsend Street to the flats in Ringsend. Then over the next couple of years I lost both my parents and I became very upset and down and he couldn't really deal with me so he just never talked to me. Just like that. He literally went inside himself so much we basically stopped talking altogether. Then sometime after you were born he started to drink. He drank and drank and I cried and cried. He never stopped and it got worse and worse. It got so bad, that is why I just wished us all dead."

She stops suddenly as her last word hangs in the air, and a shocked expression comes over her face.

"Us all?" I'm on it so quick and me never having had a day's therapy in my life.

She knows she's caught.

"Yes," she says, lowering her voice.

"Huh?" Ciara is mopping the almost clean bowl of fresh cream with a thick broken piece of scone.

Emily and I stare each other in the eye.

"That Patrick's Day . . . when he took my money . . . I thought about it . . . I thought about killing you both . . . and then taking my own life." She pants the words in short breaths.

Bile rises in my throat. Fucking hell. I swallow it back.

"That is the truth. That's when I called Brenda, and she told me to get out, to get down to the Ringsend Library as fast as I could and not to go back near you. Brenda told me that I had no right to end the lives of my children." She is at whisper-level now.

The café is full and there is something comforting about the bustle of life and sweet smells around us when our own mother is telling us she thought about killing us.

"That's so fucked up, Mam," Ciara says. Her mouth hangs open, a flash of chewed scone still inside her mouth.

Emily nods slowly. "Very." She drops her head.

"How were you going to do it?" I ask.

"*Kate!*" Ciara shouts and all the people in the café look at us.

Gail studies our table before smiling at her customers and ringing up a bill at the till with a ding-a-ling-a-ling.

"I was going to strangle you in your beds with the belt from my good cream dress," Emily whispers across to us.

"Nice," I whisper back.

"*Kate! Stop, please!*" Ciara shouts again and again all the heads turn. She sticks her fingers into her ears now. She hums.

I fix the sachets upright in the sugar bowl. I line them up in the bowl. My OCD raging, all the sachets in a nice four by four by four formations. The brown sugars to the back, whites to the front. I have the urge to go around all the tables and line all the sugars up that way too.

"Will I get the bill?" Ciara asks as though the previous conversation had not just taken place.

"No – no, please, it's my treat," Emily says.

The word '*treat*' sounds almost comical coming from a mammy who almost strangled us both in our sleep.

She pulls her old-lady bag from the back of her chair and undoes the gold clasp. I stiffen as I recognise it. It's the same bag she had the day she walked out. My eyes focus in on that gold clasp before she removes a large brown leather purse and unzips it halfway across. She removes a twenty. She zips it back up, replaces it in the bag and clicks the clasp shut again. The familiarity of her closing that clasp sends shivers up my spine.

"Excuse me, please, girls." She goes up to the till.

"Well, this is lovely, isn't it?" I smile and make it a huge grin.

"I . . . I want to go home, Kate." Ciara is biting her bottom lip, turning it half-red half-white. It's a real pity because her lips supply the only real colour in her face.

I need to step in . . . again.

"Hey, listen, we're not going anywhere. We came here for a reason, remember, and that is the most important thing. She is the one who's going to make you better. I just know it. I think it's called Karma. Look, I know what she just said . . . it's pretty brutal but she was sick . . . you know, the way you are always banging on about Da having a disease? Telling me over and over that he can't help the way he is as he's sick? Well, she had a disease, still has in a lot of ways, I am sure. I imagine she was ill anyway before she met Da but I can as sure as hell tell you that our da pushed her right over the edge. She'd never have done anything to harm us – all she is trying to say to us is that the thought appeared, and when a thought like that appears you have to go. I think I finally understand her and Brenda too. I'm glad she went. I'm actually glad she left us, Ciara."

Ciara listens intently to me, her big sister, and 'mom of sorts' and she sits upright and stretches.

"Okay, but that seriously freaked me out. I need to take my meds and then to lie down." She stands.

"Okay," I say. "Let's go." I stand up too and push my chair in.

I check we haven't left anything under the table. Emily is talking to Gail in hushed tones and they are very close, I can tell. Gail is what I'd describe as 'homely'. A set hairstyle and still a good colour in her hair with just speckles of grey. She has a large bosom and is wearing a white coat with *Yellow Posies* embroidered across the left-hand side and oversized yellow buttons up the front. Her face is friendly and warm. I bet she is a great friend to Emily. We push open the door and wait for her outside in the sunshine. The smell of the café's cooking, cinnamon and vanilla, rises on the warm breeze.

I look around. It's a beautiful place. I'd love to bring Hugh here.

Emily comes out and we all walk slowly back to Ivy Cottage together, just commenting now and then on the scenery.

When we arrive back into the unlocked cottage Ciara gets her make-up bag. I couldn't imagine an unlocked door in Dublin any more.

"There's a double bed made up . . . if you . . ." Emily offers.

We both shake our heads.

I say, "The B&B is perfect. We'll come and see you tomorrow first thing with the arrangements and hopefully get on our way back up to Dublin late morning. I have pretty limited coverage in here so need to make my calls back in the B&B – the coverage is perfect there." I study the one bar on my phone.

"Yes, Gail always says that. I don't have a mobile phone so it doesn't bother me," Emily says.

"You should get a sure box, you know," Ciara says.

"A what box?" Emily looks confused.

"It's a box to make sure your house will have full signal . . . well, that's if you're planning on getting a phone . . . now that we . . ." Ciara trails off.

"Oh right. Of course, that's a – a given. I didn't think of that. Yes, girls, I really should do that." Emily removes the fireguard from the dying embers. She places the hat and coat over the fireguard now. I suddenly recall her always doing this with our coats when we were kids, to keep the coats warm for when we were going outdoors again.

Ciara has unzipped her overflowing make-up bag. She takes out a white envelope. "Here it is."

Reluctantly, it seems, Emily stretches out her hand and slowly takes a loose grip on the letter.

We leave without any sort of goodbyes.

Back in the B&B Ciara takes her meds and is straight on her phone to Da.

"Hi! It's me . . . She was great, Da . . . I mean, nervous but . . . huh? Yeah, well enough, I mean older obviously . . . her hair? It's short . . . yes, she did . . . and Da . . . shush, can I talk . . . she has boxes and boxes of letters for us and letters for you . . . I can't . . . oh, I'll bring yours back if she wants to give it to me . . . we are coming up tomorrow hopefully . . . no, we didn't book a hotel as she'll stay in a B&B, I imagine . . . Kate is calling Doctor Doyle now . . . she is . . . she did . . . she can't . . . she knows . . . I gave it to her . . . Okay, bye, Da." Ciara rings off.

"I don't want to know." I hold up my hand as I dial and perch my iPhone between ear and shoulder.

Philip answers.

"Hi, how is she?" I ask.

He tells me the doctor came and is slightly worried about her blood pressure so he's put her on medication and he will be back tonight. Maura keeps telling him not to fuss. I chat with him for a few minutes before he hangs up on me.

I am suddenly hit with exhaustion. I strip naked and climb into the spotlessly clean single bed and pull the crisp white sheet up over my face.

"Are you not getting into your pyjamas?" Ciara asks me.

"Nope," I answer her.

"Are you going to sleep already?" Ciara asks as she throws her head forward and scoops her hair up into a high ponytail.

"Yes, I want to – is that okay with you?" I really don't want to talk about what has just happened and what we have just heard. I know it's selfish but I'm so tired of the horrible past. I just want to wriggle my tired feet in this blissful bed and dream. Of Hugh. And sex.

"Sure. I just want to get lost in this book. My brain is fried."

I watch her as she changes and I try not to wince at how thin she is. She slips into her pink cotton pyjamas and slides herself between the sheets. My eyes are heavy as I see her open her massive Marian Keyes novel.

"Night, Ciara," I say, almost already asleep.

Chapter Seventeen

HUGH CLOVER

Hugh walks several paces behind Victoria and Alison and he's relieved it's sunny so he can wear his dark glasses. Not that they have any reason to recognise him, he hopes. But he's wearing the glasses just so he can hide his red eyes and his shame. He didn't sleep a wink last night. They're heading for the dance place in that old pub, Macken's, again. Every Monday morning after ten o'clock, for the last three weeks, they have gone there. They must have no classes until the late afternoon when they saunter back to the college. It's the class she had been telling him about. He remembers the conversation so clearly because she told him about the guy who ran the place. He was called Phillip and was a riot he was so brilliantly camp. He recalls how she kept him amused as he sat filling out her paperwork, with her description of Phillip's flamboyant clothes and tattooed eyeliner, and for some reason an image of this Phillip had stuck in his head. Most likely because that was the paper that he should have prescribed her antibiotics on.

He thinks again about Kate Walsh. He doesn't know how long she's going to be in Galway but he wishes desperately he'd thought of getting her mobile number before she left. He misses her. As crazy as that sounds, he does. He's glad he's being honest with her and is telling her that the moment he set eyes on her he felt this was something different. He hopes he has the confidence to tell her all the other truths in his life. But then she'd be gone too. In fact, he's surprised he has followed through and had the confidence to go up and speak to her in the bar when she was with another guy, and then even to call in to her flat. Where that had come from he doesn't know. Apart from the butcher in the butcher's, the bargirl in Beggars Bush and Lily in the café, he can't remember anyone else he's had an extended conversation with since he moved here.

They cross the road and he follows them. Into the old pub. They go straight upstairs. He sits downstairs with the local lads and orders a glass of Guinness. He finds a copy of the *Irish Times* on a table and opens it. He finds peace sitting here, knowing they are upstairs and if she were here that is where she would be too. Giggling, no doubt, at the flamboyant Mr Phillip. When they come down after class they'll have pints of tap water with ice and lemon before heading off to college. That's when he'll snap a picture. Maybe this will be the last picture?

Chapter Eighteen

KATE WALSH

The hospital appointment is full steam ahead. Everything is booked.

The trip back up to Dublin is long. Emily is as nervous as a newborn kitten. Not about the procedure – she seems very brave about that – but she seems nervous at the mention of Dublin. This woman who was reared in the heart of Dublin. A Ringsender through and through. The once tough-talking, job-doer, single parent of a woman is not the same person now, I know that. Old Emily is long gone.

We all travel in relatively good spirits, considering. I don't talk much on the journey, but they do. Instead I rest my head against the window and think about Hugh. I wonder where it will go? I wonder if I need to protect myself and I am reminded of Phillip's attitude to love. I think it's time I listened to advice, not a therapist's advice but that of someone who actually knows and loves me. I need to love and I need to feel love and if I get dreadfully hurt, well, at least I'll have loved and lost and we all know what they say about that.

"This will work, Ciara, I know it will. It's God's way of bringing us all back together. I'm a perfect HLA-matched donor!" Emily is thrilled as we settle her into her cosy B&B in Inchicore after the hospital and the routine tests. "That Doctor Doyle was delighted with me, wasn't he – did you see the smile on his face? He said I was very brave." She pulls up her sleeve now and shows us the small piece of white cotton with clear tape over her vein as though proving she really is telling the truth.

Both Da and I had been the recipient of Doctor Doyle's praises before. I choose not to remind her of this.

We all had a meeting with Professor Doyle (we just call him Doctor Doyle because he prefers that) at the hospital this evening. He is still an incredible help to us, and goes over and above for us all when he really has no need. But of course he has a special place in his heart for Ciara.

Mam has passed all the tests with flying colours – bloods, urine, X-ray – and she is due back in tomorrow morning to have her procedure done. This is it. Mam has to fast after ten o'clock so I am planning on asking her what she wants to do for dinner? I am literally itching to get back to my apartment to see if Hugh is home. This is the strangest thing, I know, but I decide not to let myself think too deeply about it because I know that after one more date I will feel we are kind of seeing each other – and I know nowadays that simply isn't the case. It is how I feel around him though, girlfriendly and almost, dare I say it, confident? I feel relaxed and the way he looks at me I feel that I am somehow a catch! I get that fuzzy feeling in the pit of my stomach again.

I pull the curtains for Emily.

"Gail will be collecting me after so I won't be around

too long. I need to get back home to rest and collect my disability allowance," she tells us.

"You won't be here for my operation then?" Ciara looks deflated as she sits on the edge of the bed.

"No, sweetheart, I won't. I'm not able. I need to be in my own home. I need to be there for my head – it's so, so difficult to explain to you, pet. You are sick and we can all see it – it's a sickness that is life-threatening in a very different way to mine . . . Oh Lord, I don't mean that to sound so selfish but I just need you to understand how ill I still am. I struggle daily. Mental-health sickness is never taken seriously enough as far as I am concerned. I have mental-health issues, I probably always had long, long before I ever met your father. I am managing it with limited meds, lifestyle choice, good food, routine and proper sleep in my own bed. Once all that is taken away from me I can get seriously ill."

"Cop out." I don't say it aggressively. I just say it because I am thinking it.

"It isn't actually, Kate." She seems a bit more defiant.

"It is a cop out. You're going to leave your youngest daughter before a life-threatening operation and go back to Galway to eat nice food in a calm relaxed environment?" Surely a week isn't too much to ask her for? Ciara needs her.

"It's not like that at all." She is still strong.

"It's okay – I understand," Ciara says.

"Well, I don't." I am truly puzzled by this. I expected her to be all over us, to tell us she'd be here for as long as we needed her. "I understand you're sick, of course I do, Mam, but you're saying you can't stay here for a week?"

"I don't expect you to understand, Katie – I barely

understand it myself – but if I could stay here and stay well I would. You have to believe me – I swear to God that's the truth."

I'm not angry at her, I realise. I'm just frustrated because we've only just got her back and now we're losing her again.

"I will be on the end of a phone morning, noon and night. Gail has already enquired about that box . . . the sure thing . . . and she's taking me shopping in Dublin before we head home to buy me one of those mobiles and a tablet. So I can talk to you face to face on the tablet." She seems proud of all this.

Ciara nods.

"Now, if you will excuse me," Emily goes on, "I'm having dinner with your dad at seven o'clock in Clery's in town. I have to fast after ten. I'm going to try to walk in and perhaps we can share a taxi home together." She settles her soft-bristled hairbrush and some sort of night face-cream on the dresser.

The fact that she so casually mentions the taxi home takes the explosion out of the sentence. Like it's not totally mental that they're going out to dinner together after twenty-eight years. Like it's a normal night out.

Ciara actually stops herself mid-sneeze to start clapping her hands like a six-year-old at her first ever pantomime. "Oh my God, that is absolutely fantastic!"

"Why?" is all I ask Emily.

"His letter." She smiles. "He's not a monster, girls. He was preconditioned too."

Uh oh. Therapy talk. I have zero interest in her therapy-bullshit talk any more. My anger rises again that she can go and meet Da but can't hang around for a week for Ciara. I've had enough of this. I just don't understand it all, I guess, but I can't shake the feeling that she is letting us down all over again.

I'm out of here. I grab my cardigan and my bag. I kiss Ciara on the head.

"I'll see you in the morning, Mam," I say and I leave the B&B.

I stomp the pavements all the way back to my apartment. How can some people be so selfish or am I wrong? Am I the selfish one who is misunderstanding her needs? Is she telling the truth? Is she really so sick that this is her only option – to abandon her youngest all over again at a time she needs her most? Maybe I need to ask an expert. A doctor perhaps. The walk will help clear my head, I know, so I pick up the pace.

When I get in the lift I press Number 6 immediately. I get out on the sixth floor. I have never even been up here before and I realise I have no idea what number he lives in. Then I see, almost like a *Charlie and the Chocolate Factory*, *Alice in Wonderland*, *Being John Malkovich* moment, there is only one door on the sixth floor. I spin around. One door on the entire floor. It's bizarre. I listen and I hear nothing but the sound of silence.

I knock three times. *Knock. Knock. Knock.* I look down at myself. Jeans, runners, a baggy sweatshirt and a grey cardigan. Not exactly Audrey Hepburn.

The door opens. Hugh stands there in his bare feet. Navy tracksuit bottoms and topless. Mother. Of. All. He is sweaty. Very sweaty and out of breath. I stir below.

"Kate!" He is more than surprised to see me at his door. He runs his hands through his damp hair. It is slicked back and shows his face even better. His strong

171

jawline and those deep brown eyes.

"Hi!" I smile brightly and then it rubs itself out slowly as realisation dawns. Oh no, he's riding someone in there. I panic.

"Ohh . . . listen . . . sorry . . . it's a bad time . . . sorry . . . I . . . I . . ."

Not so confident now, my girl Jennifer Beals is back and she is flat on the floor, the glaring judges at the forefront of my mind. Their eyes mocking me. You are worthless. What were you thinking? Why did you think for a second he would be interested in you? Who is he having sex with in there? I feel perspiration settle in on my top lip. I wonder is it that model girl who lives on my floor. The Pilates freak.

"No, no, not at all, please, do come in. I was just on the . . . on the . . . well, on my exercise bike. Not very macho, is it?" He laughs and stands back from the doorway.

Relief floods through my veins and I walk into his apartment, his penthouse apartment, and the views literally take my breath away. If I thought my little view showed me the sights I'd grown up with and loved from a height, this is something else. This view is extreme. I can literally see for miles. Dublin and the docklands sit out there to be stared at. The people of Dublin 4 are scurrying like little ants around the land. It is almost voyeuristic.

"The view up here!" I walk straight to the sliding door that opens onto a patio area. I pull it hard and it opens with a gush of noise. The warm breeze dries my sweaty lip in seconds. I remove my grey cardigan and tie it around my waist.

"It is a super spot all right." He is pulling on a

matching navy tracksuit top and zipping it up.

The words are out before I can check them. "How can you afford this?" I blurt. "I mean, it must cost you an arm and a leg?" I swing around to look at him.

"My folks pay for it for me . . . well . . . no, that is not altogether true . . . they feel they have to pay for it. You see, they simply don't know what else to do with me, Kate. I'm a bit of a nuisance to them at the mo . . . it's all a bit messy in my life . . ." He scratches his head and sits on the white leather couch.

The couch is one of those that you see in showrooms where you always hear yourself say: "Who would have a room big enough to fit that couch into?" Hugh Grant obviously. Or Mr & Mrs Grant Snr.

I come back in and slide the door closed behind me and immediately the noise of the city is shut out.

I sit on the other end of the couch, literally miles away from him. I want to be nearer. I want him to look at me with desire. I want to sit on his knee and have him cradle me in his arms. I want to touch his face, his stubble, feel the tautness of his arms. I want to get on top of this man and let him make love to me right here, right now. I most of all want to know why his life is messy.

Instead I say, because I'm really not sure what he is talking about, "Bit of a mummy's boy, are we?"

I laugh. He does not.

He shifts his position on the couch and says, "I'm surmising that a thirty-eight-year-old man is slightly too old to still be a mummy's boy, no?"

He looks so serious now and it occurs to me that he doesn't want me here. I am interrupting him. What am I doing here? Muppet!

I stand, untie my cardigan, shove my arms quickly through the sleeves and wrap it tightly around me.

"Listen, I'm sure you're up to your eyes – I'll head on," I say quickly.

"No! Please . . . Kate . . . I don't want you to go . . . really I don't. Can I make you a quick coffee? Tea? Which would you rather?" He leaps up from the leather couch. "Please stay . . . well, only if you can, I mean . . . if you have the time?"

I am suitably convinced that he wants me to stay.

"A coffee would be lovely so." I smile at him. "Just a drop of milk –"

"No sugar," we say together.

He heads off to the kitchen and I look around his place. It's bare like mine and I notice he doesn't even have a TV unless it's in his bedroom. God, I want to see his bedroom. His apartment smells just like him and it's very comforting. Almost like what you see is what you get. I stare out at the view.

When he returns with two white mugs in his hands, steam rising from them, he says, "Don't you think it makes us weird that it is five o'clock on a Monday afternoon and we aren't in a job? Don't you think we are a pair of misfits? Shouldn't we be part of the turning wheel of the economy? A pair of worker bees?"

He speaks now with a very serious look upon his handsome face. Of all the conversations we have had, both light and dark, he's always hard to read expression-wise. Not right now though. I know this look. The look of inner angst. I have seen it in the mirror many times. It's the look of inward unworthiness. Your face becomes a painting, perfectly still. Lips locked and turned slightly downwards, brows furrowed, eyes heavy, mouth dry.

"I thought you were going to write a book?" I say quietly.

He twists the handle of the mug towards me and offers it. I take it.

"Yeah," he scoffs, as he sits down with his coffee, both hands wrapped around the white ceramic.

I sip. It's piping hot so I blow easily before I realise he is waiting for me to say something, so I do. "I did the rat race, Hugh. I had a brown job, a brown life, a brown outlook on life and I chucked it all in. I have colour in my life now. I weighed up the life I was living. Nine to five every day, same alarm-bell sickening my ears, same bus stop, same cold breeze, same long bus delays, same crap heavy traffic, same smell of BO on the bus, same thing in the job, same buttons I pressed every day. Same lunch at my desk. Homemade ham sandwich and a cup of tea. No crisps or soups allowed because the boss hated the smell. Same journey home. Same, same, same, same, same all over again and again and again . . ."

He interrupts me now. "I hear you. Mine is a bit more complicated – not to belittle yours at all – it's just that I left quite a mess behind me . . . but I will write a book, Kate. It won't be a medical book. It will be a book about regret, a book about self-hatred, and a book about loss . . ." He is reddening in the face and his breath is heavy. "It will be a book about murder." He gulps as he swallows the last word.

I feel a shiver start its journey slowly at the base of my spine but then rocket up to the hairs on the back of my neck. I stare at him. He is looking down at his bare feet, bending over, holding his coffee in one hand now and his smallest toe in between his index finger and thumb with the other. Then he looks up and I see it. Terror. Fear. Absolute fear. He is wrapped in fear. And suddenly I am too. I have no idea what is going on here but my hands, wrapped around the warm mug, are suddenly stone cold.

"Wow . . . okay . . . what does all that mean, Hugh?" I set the coffee cup down on the dark wooden floor. Position myself bolt upright now, my hands pushed together at the palms and pointing in between my closed knees down to the floor.

"If I tell you . . . the first part anyway . . . you will hate me . . . and then you will be very afraid of me . . . because I feel both those things about myself." He too now places his coffee on the floor.

I know I probably should make a very fast excuse and get the hell out of here. But I don't, I can't, and I wonder now why I feel strongly for him? I barely know this man. Yes, we had been naked together but I'd done all that before and could never wait to bail my way out of the guy's apartment or dodgy house-share. I'd only met Hugh, what, four or five times, but the second we looked at each other in the Pork Shop that day, there had been a connection. Whatever he was about to say I needed to hear it. I was scared but composed.

"What? What are you telling me?" I say softly.

He pushes his top and bottom lip together as though trapping the words from escaping. The sun beats in through the massive glass windows and I have to squint to see him properly so I shift position to get it out of my eyes. The leather of the couch crunches a squeaky noise beneath me.

"What?" I repeat, even quieter this time. My heart is

racing and my mouth is now as dry as a sandpit.

"I killed someone." His chin with that adorable deep-set dimple starts to quiver.

I try to coax saliva into my mouth. "How?" I can barely hear my own words.

"In the hospital. I was negligent. I operated on a girl – she was an Irish girl actually, Kate, and I was so exhausted – I hadn't slept in forty-eight hours – I had covered a double shift. I left the hospital without prescribing her antibiotics . . . she got septicaemia and died . . . she was so young . . ." The chin continues to make jerking movements and his brown eyes seem lopsided, he's trying so hard to stop the dam bursting. If he was a wrestler he'd be lifting his world-record weight right now – that was the struggle of emotion on his face.

So it was an accident. I can't tell you the relief I feel ooze through my pores. I rub my sweaty palms on my jeans as discreetly as I can.

"You can't say you killed someone, Hugh. You didn't. And the way you said it made it sound like you murdered someone. It was an accident." My mouth is so dry I simply have to pick up the coffee mug and I hope he doesn't think I am trivialising his confession by my actions.

"But, you see, I was responsible. I always knew I should never have been a doctor – it was always too much for me – I'm not mentally or physically strong enough, it has been proven. My parents . . . pushed me so. They were both MDs, my folks. They always made it clear that they would be so, so disappointed if I didn't follow in their footsteps. Yes, I told you we had a great upbringing and we did – our home was so full of love and they gave us everything – but I always felt there was a price. Revise. Revise. Revise. Sport is not something the Clovers do. A career in medicine, that is us. And they would half joke with this but I knew deep, deep down they would be dreadfully let down if I didn't go to medical school. My teens were taken up with study; I was always the chap who was studying. I never went anywhere, Kate, I never did naughty things, got up to mischief. But for my *Horrid Henry* books, which I'm dreadfully ashamed to say I read into my teens, I'd have no idea of how misbehaving went . . ." He crunches up the skin on his face with his hands now and then throws his head back and says very loudly, "Oh, for God's sake, Hugh! Why am I telling you all this? I – I – I know I need to go home and restart my life but I just can't seem to pull myself together, Kate."

"G-go home?" I stutter. "Wwwhy?" I'm such a loser. Had I conjured up some visceral romance because we had spent the night together one time? Had I made this into something it was absolutely not? I almost whimpered there when he said he wanted to go back to London. I want him to stay here with me, forever, and I know how ridiculous I am being.

"I'm losing my mind here, Kate." He shifts again, unable to sit easy. "I'm really scared I'm losing my mind. I know this is going to sound insane but I'm constantly thinking about you and that has been helping me. I know we have only just met . . . what I'm trying to say, I suppose, is I'm exceptionally fond of you already, Kate. You are the person I always wanted to be with. Honest and real. Grounded. Why I'm telling you this now after what I have just told you I do not know. I'm sure you want to run a mile. See, I'm an absolute mess. Look, I'm not stupid – I know these things, negligent accidents if you will, have happened before and will happen again but it's what I'm doing here, in Dublin, that I'm most frightened about . . . it's how I'm coping with what I did that's really frightening to me. I can't tell you, so please don't ask me . . . not yet, not today . . . this much is enough." He tries desperately to hold back the tears again.

But I do need to know. It's just not in me not to ask now. I'm an all or nothing kinda Ringsender.

"Tell me. I want to know it all." I get up now and move over to him.

He stiffens and I slowly lower myself beside him. He likes me and I like him so I want to know it all.

"Did you hear what I said? I like you, Kate." He holds a strand of my loose hair.

"I did and I'm crazy about you, Hugh," I say and the relief of his words fills me up beautifully.

I can cope with whatever he has to throw at me because I'm so into him. I don't think he's weird for feeling as bad as he does about the girl. In fact, I think it's a pretty damn normal way to feel. And I have never had therapy as you know. I look at his stubble and his soft brown eyes under the floppy hair. I so want to taste his tongue.

"Tell me," I urge instead.

He gets up and goes across the room to a bookshelf where he stands on his tippy-toes and takes down a red old-fashioned photo album. Circa 1980's type. I haven't seen a photo album like it in donkey's years. It reminds me of one we had once – I have no idea where it went. He walks back, never taking his eyes off the album, and sits beside me.

He hands it to me.

"Open it," he says as I hold the cover, "but before you do, know this . . . after July 11th when it happened I took to my bed. I – I stayed there for weeks and stayed virtually locked up in my flat for almost nine months. I thought coming here would help me . . . but . . . well . . . see for yourself."

I feel the weight of the cover as I open it onto the first page. Two glossy pictures look back at me, so well kept, the plastic over the page without a single crease over it or air bubble under it. Both pictures are of three pretty young girls and they seem to be eating lunch. Soup.

The same in the next.

I don't ask him anything as I slowly flip the pages. This time a double spread and again my eyes do a rapid scan. They seem to be the same three girls, this time sitting on the grass. And again. And again. Much the same pictures of them eating lunch and sitting on the grass. I flip through.

"I don't understand, Hugh," I say as I look up at him.

"That's her. There with her friends." He leans over me now and points to the prettiest of the three girls.

She has her chin high in the air and is smiling widely, with a row of perfectly white brace-trained straight teeth. Dark brown hair with a heavy blunt fringe and charcoaled eyes. She is wearing a yellow sleeveless dress with a thick black silver-buckled belt and her tanned slim legs are crossed. On her feet are cute silver-studded ankle biker boots. I can't take my eyes off her.

"That's the girl I killed. The three of them were in London together. I came here to – to – to see what her life was like. I follow them, Kate. Her friends Victoria and

Alison. I have spent all my time in Dublin following them. I've spent three weeks stalking them." He gulps loudly as he swallows tears. "I'm a fucking psychopath!" The dam bursts now and he cries heavy, heavy, weighty, panting, choking tears. Frightening sounds fill the living area.

I don't know what to say because I have no idea what he is talking about. I thought something about the pictures wasn't right but my mind can't whirr into action. I'm just holding the album and watching this man. He cries and cries. I'm not the type who can cuddle and go hush, hush, there, there. So I just sit and look at the pictures until she goes in and out of focus. The sound is so horrible. This man's cry is so deep and earthy. So full of perpetuated sorrow.

Eventually he stops. He walks to the door at the end of the apartment and pushes it open. I see a tiled bathroom and hear him pulling at the roll of toilet paper. He blows his nose. Then he runs the tap and returns wiping his face with a small white facecloth.

He stands in front of me and looks down at me.

"Oh believe me, Kate, I know how crazy I am . . . but I can't seem to cope if I'm not keeping her alive . . ."

Album still open in my hands, I stand up and face him, still unsure of what he is trying to explain to me.

"So where did you get these pictures?" I ask, choosing my words carefully.

"I took them. On my iPhone."

"What? When?" I still can't grasp this.

He points to a photo. "This one I took the day you met me in Beggars Bush, when you dropped your sugar sachets and then we walked home together in wonderful comfortable, silence . . . when I went up to return the cup and glass and to tip the barmaid, remember?"

I nod. "But how is *she* in the picture, Hugh?" I'm completely and utterly lost.

"I Photoshop her into all of them."

I know he knows he's just confessed by the way he falls back onto the couch and his head leans back on the cushions, tilted up to the ceiling.

"Jesus Christ," is what I say and I sit then – not too close to him but not that far away either.

"Yeah, Jesus Christ is about right." He still has his eyes shut.

We just sit. That's it. I cop it suddenly – what I couldn't put my finger on. She's wearing that same yellow dress in every picture. It's the same picture of her in all the photos. She looks sort of familiar.

"I know you must want to leave, Kate, so please just go." He reaches out and takes the album from my hands. His are icy cold.

Then something hits me. It has been gnawing at the back of my mind. Oh my God, it couldn't be! Could the world be this small?

"Did her sister hound you after . . . the girl died . . . Deirdre?" I ask the question slowly, recalling my conversation in that bathroom with Wendy in vivid playback now. They look so alike, Deirdre and Wendy.

As I say her name he literally goes white. His eyes pop open and he jerks upright. The blood drains right out of his face like from a close-range bullet wound to the neck. He tries to catch his breath but he can't and he is hyperventilating slightly. I try to put my hand out to reach his knee but he jumps.

"How . . .?" He pulls back away from me.

"I honestly can't believe this – this is the weirdest thing ever – but Mark – you know, the guy I met you with in Beggars Bush last week, the time after the sugar sachets, after the silent walk home . . . well, his fiancée, his ex . . . Wendy . . . Deirdre was her sister. I never met her before but she, Wendy, told me this story last Saturday in the hotel bathroom at that wedding." I'm a little spinney now myself, my mind throwing details and facts out of the overly packed suitcase that is my brain. I think of Wendy and her anger and I feel somehow I am exactly where I am supposed to be. I'm not religious but I'm exceptionally spiritual (I know but that's who I am) and I think paths cross for a reason. How else can I explain a coincidence of this magnitude? Such extreme crossing of paths?

"Are you telling me the truth, Kate? This isn't some kind of trap Wendy has set for me?" He drops the album onto the floor and drags his hands through his hair – he leaves them there on top of his head, squeezing his brain hard. "How does she know I am here? In Dublin?" He rises fast and paces the room.

"I don't think she does, Hugh." I get up. I hold him by the shoulders. His body is shaking. I want to protect him so badly. This is not a bad man. I know a bad man. I speak softly. Motherly tones. "Listen, Hugh, she's angry with every right, but you didn't kill her sister – it was a mistake, a terrible mistake granted, but mistakes happen every day of our lives and there isn't one single thing you can do about it."

"She made my life hell for months after. She somehow got hold of my number through the hospital – no one will admit to giving it but someone did. She rang my flat all hours of the night every night, screaming 'murderer' at me

183

through my answering machine speaker as I lay huddled in my bed. Then she got my parents' number and rang their house all hours of the night. She . . . she had every right, I know. After a while I answered every call, every night, and I listened on the other end of that line to her screams of pain. I always asked her, when she ran out of breath, to meet me but she just wouldn't." He moves around me like a shark circling his antagonizer.

"I think she had a breakdown, Hugh," I say. "She left Mark, and ran off with her shrink."

"I hate that word – shrink," he says, still pacing. "As she must have – well, at least at the start before she started up a relationship with him – no one wants to need to see a shrink." He sniffs his runny nose back up.

I bend down and gently pick the album up from the floor and carefully set down on the couch. I return to stand by him.

I can't be sure how I feel about what he is doing. Oh, it is so wrong, I know that much. It is completely weird and completely creepy and completely wrong on every level, yet I can't find a strong enough gut reason to take my leave and go straight to the Guards. Is he dangerous? Is this a criminal offence? Am I aiding and abetting? I have at this moment no idea. It seems more pathetic than frightening. It's very clear to me that it is a cry for help. It's more sorrowful than scary. He needs me. I won't let him down. We stand in the middle of this huge glorious sun-soaked room and I find a way to hug him. It feels so awkward and alien at first but when he hugs me back it feels so right. He holds me so tightly my breasts are sorely squashed into him. I hold him tightly back. I think we stand for literally minutes like this. As one.

184

I take a tiny step away from him after a while and ask, "You have been following these girls every day for the last month and taking their picture and then just adding Deirdre in, correct?" I am no technical genius. I need to clarify the ins and outs.

He nods repeatedly and closes his eyes tight in disgust at himself.

"What purpose, though, does that serve?" I ask him carefully.

"I don't know, Kate. I really do not know. I can't even begin to tell you how totally creepy all this makes me feel. It does, but at least I'm punishing myself in some way and that feels good. I know it won't make any sense to you but I want . . . I wanted . . . to see how her life would have been. I have to look at her face every time I add her into a new photo. I have to see what I did to Deirdre Collins. Who I took from the world. It first dawned on me when I was in bed one night after it all happened. It was a night that Wendy was calling and calling and was really hysterical so eventually I had to shout back at her. I always tried to talk to her, to convince her to meet me like I said, but this night I roared back at her that my life was ruined too. I have no idea why – a pretty pathetic selfish thing to say. Then I said sorry over and over and after every 'sorry' she quietly, calmly and eerily followed it with 'murderer'. She was just saying it over and over. Anyway, when she eventually rang off I lay staring at the ceiling, hating myself to my very core." He takes a slow deep breath, steadying himself. "I thought about Wendy. About how much she must miss Deirdre. I wondered what kind of things they did together? Did they meet for lunch regularly? Did they go shopping at weekends? Did they share their lives completely with one another? And it was then the thought hit me: I needed to see what Deirdre's life would have been like."

"Did you never go to the police about the calls?"

"I would never report her to the police, no, and this completely infuriated my folks too. They were victims also after all – their good names were associated with me – but I wouldn't let them go to the police either. Anyway, I was just thinking of her, of Deirdre – we'd had a laugh together at the hospital the night she was brought in even though she was in a lot of pain – she was really brave and never complained about the pain or the waiting. I secured a splint and gave her painkillers and we chatted as the X-rays came back and confirmed that her left leg was indeed broken. She had a comminuted fracture, which is that the bone in her leg had shattered into several pieces. She told me that was a bummer as she was going to Ireland in a few days to go back to college and that she and her friends had just signed up for dance classes during their free periods. She was just lovely. As I lay there, the phone began ringing again over and over and I put my pillow over my head. I saw her face. Deirdre's. As I did, as I still do every night. I wondered what she would be doing in Dublin now if she were alive, where she would be going, and I thought I just needed to be around her . . . her spirit, I suppose. I told my parents I wanted to get away from everything in my life. They were frightfully worried about me, sitting in my flat day after day, night after night. I know, I could see it in their eyes, the fear that I was going to take my own life. Some friends of my father's had this place and he asked them if we could rent it for a while – they agreed, so he got it for me. I have a pretty hefty mortgage on my flat in London but . . . em . . . I'm still being paid – I'm just on leave. They even drove me to the airport and told me to take some time out, that they would hold the fort until I returned. Stiff upper lip and all that, son. Dad patted me hard on the back as he handed me my boarding pass at the gate. I felt like such a failure."

He squeezes his temples and I say nothing, I want him to get all this out.

"Then when I arrived I just had the thought. I knew what college she was in, UCD, so I decided to track down whoever she hung around with, ask around, and the fact her college was fifteen minutes from where I lived told me it was some kind of a sign. I got into the apartment and took a cab straight to UCD. I asked a few subtle questions around campus – everyone knew the awful tale obviously and it wasn't long before her two best friends, who had been in London with her, were pointed out to me across the campus canteen. So I just started watching them, following them around . . . creepy fucking shit . . . I can hear this coming out of my mouth, Kate, and it's mortifying. The first day I saw the girls eating lunch I had the obscene idea of photo-shopping Deirdre into pictures of them. I got a picture of Deirdre. The one they used in the papers and the UCD magazine to write about her accident. Not normal, no, I fully comprehend that. Totally insane." He is biting on his nails now.

I don't know. I don't know if he was or is really unwell or if he's just really lost. But still I stay. I honestly do not know if I should get the hell out of here, far, far away from him, or if I should simply stop running from things that are hard and difficult and upsetting and just stay. See them through. So I stay. There and then I decide to stay and see 'this' through whatever 'this' might be or turn out to mean. I wasn't running any more.

We stand, facing each other. He is trying to read my mind. He can't tell if I am about to run for the hills or not.

"It's not normal, Hugh . . . no . . . no part of that is normal. . . but I know all about not having normal thoughts . . . do you know the movie *Flashdance*?" I cannot believe I am about to tell him this.

He nods and we both sway slightly.

"Well, whenever anything good happens in my life I have a flashback or an image in my head, I suppose you would say, of Jennifer Beals, the lead actress in the movie *Flashdance*, dancing across the floor – you know, at her audition for the prestigious dance school," I roll on, afraid to look up at him, "and when anything bad happens the image is of her falling on the ground, the needle scratching the record with those four judges looking down at her with contempt – and whenever anything good happens to me she dances exceptionally across my brain with those pointing fingers, sex on legs in her skintight black leotard and black leg warmers. I also don't exactly have any friends to speak of . . . my sister, Ciara, is really ill and desperately needs a bone-marrow transplant – that's why we were in Galway to find my long-lost mother who deserted us when I was eight leaving us in the care of my raging alcoholic excuse for a father. Both my father and I were a match for Ciara and donated – but the transplants weren't successful. So we are relying totally on my mother now to keep Ciara alive and just this evening she informed us that after her marrow is retrieved she'll simply go off again back to Galway – she can't wait around to see if Ciara survives as she must return to her home and look after her own mental health." I swallow and smile. "So there you have it. Slightly fucked-up Kate."

I look up now. I don't think that anyone else knows what I have just told Hugh. Even Ciara doesn't know about Jennifer Beals. We lock eyes again and he has the makings of a slight grin.

"That's so funny," he says. "I always thought Jennifer Beals was complete and utter sex on legs – I loved that movie." He pulls me tight and stares down into my eyes. He's a good few inches taller than me. "And I think you are complete and utter sex on legs."

He drops a soft lingering kiss on my lips and I slip my tongue into his mouth and press my body into his. I somehow feel we are at the point of no return. I pull away as he groans lightly into my mouth.

"You were correct earlier – we are a right pair of misfits," I say. "But, Hugh, you aren't a monster – you're just a very hurt man from a terrible accident that happened. It's so tragic that Deirdre lost her life, it really, really is, but both you and Wendy have to try and come to terms with it. Is there a court case by the way?"

"Next year some time – to be honest my solicitor has been calling me the last few days but I just can't face him yet."

"I understand," I tell him and I really do think I do.

"You think you can help me?" He starts to cry again now. Slow tears this time that fall in huge droplets down his face and bust open upon reaching his sharp dark stubble.

"No," I answer honestly and before he can speak I put my finger over his lips, "but what I can do is be here for you as you try to move on and rebuild your life. I have spent years rebuilding mine yet I am still half-consumed with dread of the people I tried to block out, my parents. I'm not sure exactly who I am or what I need either but I know this: I feel comfortable around you and I feel sexy and acutely alive so I'm thinking hey, that's a good sign, eh?" I laugh before I kiss him again now, his lips still slightly wet.

"I need a plan to go forward, don't I?" He holds my face in his hands. "I need some kind of professional help for sure. I sort of feel like I am waking up after a year in a bad coma."

"I'm probably not the best person to ask about that – I'm not a big believer in therapy – but in your circumstances, well, maybe it couldn't but help. I know one thing for sure: that album is full, Hugh. It is over. I couldn't support that. You must understand that but the fact you told me about it makes me think you know that it's over too?"

"Gosh, yes, of course . . . the relief I felt when I told you was like a lead balloon being released from around my neck. It was literally choking me." He looks at me, his brown eyes pleading for help. "But what do I do with the album?"

"What do you want to do with it?"

"I don't know." He takes a long breath up through his nose.

"Well, I tell you what . . . why don't we get it blessed?" The thought has just popped into my head for some reason.

"Blessed?" He narrows his eyes.

"Oh shit, yeah, are you a Catholic or a Protestant or what?" I never asked before.

"I'm a Catholic," he says and blesses himself.

"Yeah, okay, me too . . . so I think it would nice for you to go to a priest and get confession and get the photo album blessed and then ask the priest what to do with it? It would be respectful to Deirdre." I am really pleased with my own advice.

"Confess what I've been doing?" He's a bit shocked

"To a priest – you are a doctor, you know how all this works – these codes of practice – ethics and all that. He can't tell anyone but he can forgive you and that is the main thing – you need forgiveness, but you need to forgive yourself most of all. As I said I have never been in therapy but I can tell you that much for nothing."

"I think that's the best idea I've heard in a long, long time! I love it!" He grabs me and kisses me hard again. He runs his index finger down my side and I'm not remotely embarrassed by the rolls of fat over my hipbones.

"When will we do this?" he asks as he moves to sit on the couch.

"Right now," I say.

"Oh now?" He jumps back up.

"Grab your coat, Hugh Clover – it's time to forgive yourself."

As we push open the main door of our apartment block the sun hits us. Its warmth is almost a sign. It is where we both should be – out in the open air with the sun on our bones – yet I am well aware of my sister lying sick in her bed, and maybe that's where I should be right now, beside her, but I am also well aware that Da is staying in all night and I cannot bear being in that small contained space with him and his smell. Hugh takes my hand in his as he presses the lights at the pedestrian crossing. I have the red photo album tucked tightly under my arm. We walk in silence past Lily Bon Bons and up the road – we cross over Ringsend Bridge and the smell of the water soothes me. Familiar. Safe. The smell of Ringsend. People pass me by.

"Howrya, Kate love?"

"Nice day, Kate, thank God."

"Lit a candle for Ciara so we did last night, love."

My people.

Chapter Nineteen

The church feels cold upon entering and candles flicker brightly at the top and to the sides. Hopeful light. Scattered people sit around and pray, some kneel. A low hum of whispered prayer fills the church. At the candles people kneel on the soft brown spongy foam as they light them in hope or maybe just in thanks. I see the confessional box in the corner and I pull Hugh towards it. I still hold the red album tight in my left hand tucked up under my arm.

I pull the door hard as I have been told before and I stick my head in. The bench will easily fit us both, even with my bigger bones, I notice.

I nod my head to a nervous Hugh and I slide into the far corner. It's not roomy but it's okay. The bench is hard under me. Hugh squeezes in further beside me and we sit still.

The wooden slide over the little mesh window in front of us pulls back and I can see the shadowy profile of the priest through the mesh.

"There are two of us, Father, is that okay?" The sound of my own voice rings in my ears in this quiet small space.

"That's no problem – but pull the door tight like a good lad there, will you?" the priest says.

Hugh mutters an apology and pulls the door tight. It bangs with a touch of finality that I like. Upon its reopening I like our chances of Hugh feeling forgiven.

It's now quite dark in the box.

We are alone, the three of us. And God, I hope.

"Welcome," the priest says.

"Thank you," we echo together.

"Let's begin by making the Sign of the Cross. In the Name of the Father, and of the Son and of the Holy Spirit."

We bless ourselves.

There is silence and I suddenly remember my line. I whisper it closely into Hugh's ear.

He repeats: *"Bless me, Father, for I have sinned."*

"How long since your last confession?" The voice comes at us slow and steady.

It's hard to know how this is going to go but I'm here now and Hugh needs me.

"Well, Father, it's been a while and this is a bit of an unusual one . . ." Hugh lets a bit of a guffaw out through fear.

I nudge him and speak up. "I'm Kate Walsh, Father, as I suppose you know . . . well, I know you can't see me but it's me, Father."

"Ahh, is it you? How is Ciara, pet?" he asks.

It's Father Brennan – I now recognise the voice. "Em . . . well . . . I don't know yet, Father . . . she's going in for another operation."

194

"Oh I know, I know . . . I'll pop up to see your father again tonight after late Mass."

"Pop up where to see him?" I ask, slightly thrown off course.

"Up to the house. I've been going to see him of late – I see him most nights, Kate."

"Why? He never goes to Mass, Father – he believes in nothing except himself."

"Ahh, you're terrible hard on yer da, Kate Walsh – he's not a bad man at all, at all." Father Brennan tut-tuts.

"He is so too a bad man, Father, he's a very bad man – tut-tut yourself, Father Brennan," I say back to him, my heart rate rising.

Hugh stiffens on the bench beside me.

"Did Eoin Walsh do something to you, Kate?" Father Brennan is leaning right up against the window now.

"He did, Father, as a matter of fact – he completely ruined my childhood." I can feel the anger build in me as the darkened box becomes lighter to my now-accustomed eyes and I can now really make out the profile of Father Brennan.

"He is very sorry, Kate, truly sorry. He's going to the meetings now every night, you know, down on Pearse Street."

"Oh, good for old Papa! After he leaves the pub, is it?" I scoff.

"No . . . no . . . he's been trying to get sober for nearly seven weeks now – yes, he has fallen off the wagon once or twice but, boy oh boy, is he trying! He's been an addict for years."

I take a deep breath. "Father Brennan, I'm not in here to talk about me da, I am here to ask for your help about something else."

Hugh slides his hand onto my knee and squeezes.

"I'm sorry, Kate, please go ahead – I'm listening . . ." says Father Brennan, his voice trailing at the end.

"Okay . . . well, basically Hugh here is an English doctor – a surgeon. He had the terrible misfortune – that's not the right word but anyway it's all I can think of right now – of losing a patient under his care, a beautiful young Irish girl called Deirdre Collins. He was so overworked and exhausted he didn't administer the necessary post-op medication and she passed away. He's moved here for a while and has been very depressed and consumed with the thought of her. He is consumed with guilt and overwhelming sorrow at her loss. He blames himself. He has an album where he puts photos to keep her memory alive."

"Like a shrine of sorts?" Father Brennan asks.

"Well, yeah. He has been following two of her friends around and secretly taking pictures of them, but with the technology we have today he's able to take a picture of her friends and put this girl in the picture with them as though she were still alive. We have the album here with us. He is exceptionally remorseful and like I said guilt-ridden and, Father Brennan, he is a really good man."

Hugh squeezes my leg so tight it hurts and I have to pull my knee away. I refrain from rubbing it.

"Okay . . . okay, I see. Hugh, are you wanting to speak with me too?" Father Brennan asks softly.

Hugh coughs into his hand now and leans forward.

"Yes, Father." His voice is so small he could be a little boy.

"I'm listening, son." Father Brennan's silhouette leans back and so it begins.

196

Hugh talks and he talks and he talks and he talks and then he talks more. Words pour from him like water from a full water bottle full of holes. Gushing. Even I am now becoming conscious that six o'clock Mass is going on – we must be in here over an hour. Yet Father Brennan doesn't move a muscle. When eventually Hugh leans back, I am drained.

Hugh exhales the longest release of breath I have ever heard in my life.

"Thank you," he whispers and I'm not sure if it is aimed at me or Father Brennan.

"Father Brennan?" I say as we have now been sitting in silence for minutes and I find myself mouthing along to the words of the Mass outside.

"I'm just considering things, Kate," he replies and we continue to sit in the silence for so long the bells for Communion ring out.

"Hugh Clover," he says now and we both jump at the seriousness of his voice as though he is about to hand down a very grave sentence. "A doctor is a good man, no matter whether you think it wasn't the right thing for you or not. A doctor has a big heart – you helped and saved many, many lives. People need doctors. You are not a god. You are a human being with a great big heart. Human beings make mistakes because they are human. We are allowed to make them and allowed to ask forgiveness for them and move forward. As a priest I rain forgiveness on you, my son, and I grant you a fresh beginning. Whether you practise again or do not is up to you but I see it as a great shame if you don't. Try to take my blessing and forgive yourself. I absolve you of your sins in the Name of the Father, and of the Son, and of the Holy Spirit. As an act of contrition say ten decades of the rosary and help someone. Do a good deed. Make a difference in someone's life – a fundamental difference. That is your penance. But please remember that you must forgive yourself – that is the most important thing."

I nudge Hugh here to mark the fact that I'd had the ability to foresee this advice but he shrugs me away, listening intently to Father Brennan.

"What about the album, Father?" he asks.

"As for that photo album, well, I think you should take every picture out and destroy them but I think you need to keep that album. And fill it again. Fill it with your new life, son. Go in peace."

I am so stiff I can barely unfold myself and get out of the confession box. We genuflect and bless ourselves and our eyes sting as we leave the church.

The evening sun still shines brightly but I wrap my cardigan around my chest as a cooler breeze now blows that day away.

"Pub." Hugh points across the road to The Yacht.

I freeze and stop. "No, I can't. Da drinks in there sometimes."

"Didn't you hear Father Brennan say that your dad has been sober for weeks?" He pulls me by the hand and I allow him.

The pub is pretty empty as I scour every seat and we sit into the corner.

"What would you like?" He rummages in his tracksuit pocket and pulls out a twenty.

"Glass of Guinness, please." I remove my cardigan, fold it, put it on the ledge behind me and put the photo album carefully on top of it.

If he walks in I am straight out of here. Sober, me bleedin' big, cellulite-covered arse.

Hugh comes back with the drinks and pulls out a small round stool and sits opposite me.

"That was the most magnificent thing, Kate . . . I honestly do not know how to thank you . . . you know, I am going to go ahead with professional therapy but that was such a great start."

"I don't believe in therapy," I say.

"But that *was* therapy, Kate." He raises his glass in the air.

I look at him. "What's wrong with your glass?"

"Nothing," he says.

"Why are you looking at it like that then?"

"A toast?" he says.

"Oh right, sorry."

We clink and we drink.

"I can't believe how I feel . . . I actually feel excused . . . forgiven . . . I owe you so much, Kate . . . it's such a relief." He does look different. His shoulders don't sit up so high under his ears – it's as though they've been pushed down several inches.

"No problem – any time," I say with a smile.

"Now it's your turn." He spins the beer mat a few times before putting his drink on it.

"Exqueeze me?" Please tell me he's not going to go there.

"Look how great I feel after talking it all out . . . I'm know you don't believe in therapy and that's all fine but I do think you . . . we, if you will . . . need to talk to your father." He turns the glass on the beer mat now and avoids my eyes.

I smell the vomit immediately. I see the yellow-stained

fingers. I hear the slurred nonsensical words. The drunken rages. My heart starts to flutter.

"Alcoholism is a disease . . ."

He begins the familiar story and I stand up. It almost sounds the same as 'Once upon a time . . . a long, long time ago . . .'

"Please sit!" He pulls me back down.

I'm annoyed. He has stretched my grey cardigan. It's one of my favourites.

"I don't give a shit if you never want him in our lives but I do give a shit that you need to talk it out . . . you need to tell him how he affected your childhood, Kate. That is your therapy. Or, if not, you do need to talk to a professional."

I hear his words *"in our lives"* the loudest. He sees a future. I try to keep focus and stay in the moment. I try to compose myself.

"Da knows, Hugh," I say now but I raise my voice. "He fucking knows! What difference does it make now anyway? I can't get it back! I can't go to Glendalough in fifth class with everyone else because he has no money for me . . . I can't do the free gymnastics after school because he's in the pub and who will mind Ciara if he falls in aggressively? I can't make friends in school because how can I bring them to my house and let them see the state of him? I'd be pitied. I can't get a childhood back. He took it. It's over, I get it. I'm a grown-up now so it's over. I have closure. I don't need this therapy bullshit, I swear!" I am raging at Hugh now.

"Ya alright, Kate, love?" Morgan the barman asks across the bar, wiping it with a white stained tea towel. Morgan is sound.

"Grand, Morgan, yeah, sorry for the shouting."

Morgan gives Hugh a warning look and moves away.

"So why not talk to Father Brennan then?" Hugh asks.

"I don't want to," I reply.

He tilts his head at me, lowering his voice right down so that I can barely hear him. "Yet you thought it wise for me to go and talk to him?"

"That's different – he's not charging you an arm and a leg to talk about yourself. I don't want to talk to him because he knows me too well."

"Would you like to go out for some dinner and some wine tonight, Kate?" He changes the subject just like that.

I look across at him, confused. Then I smile. I know I have many issues but I don't need a lecture right now. Not with Ciara's condition. I detest the idea of telling some stranger my problems. They are too intimate. I would be too bare.

"Tell you what," I say, "why don't you go home and grab a shower and I –"

"Oh Lord, I must smell awful, do I?" he interrupts and recoils from me. "I was as sweaty as a flipping pig in labour when you called at the door and how long were we sitting in the confessional?" He lifts his track-suited arms and smells under his armpits. He pretends to fall off the stool.

I laugh. It's not that funny but I just find everything about him incredibly sexy.

"Yeah, a bit stinky now to be honest, pet, so go get a wash. I'll freshen up in the bathroom here and, if you don't mind, instead of going out to dinner I'll just pop over the road and get us a Chinese takeaway and a bottle of wine?" I stretch my arms high above my head. I'm stiff from sitting on that wooden bench in the confessional for so long.

"Even better," he says and drains his glass.

"What would you like to eat?" I leave half of my drink.

"You may as well find this out now rather than later. I'm a creature of habit with my takeaways. Indian is always Chicken Korma with pilau rice and naan bread. Chinese always sweet and sour chicken and egg-fried rice. That's me. That is the greatest Chinese meal takeaway on earth."

He grins again and my heart melts. We will be okay. I have an overwhelming feeling about him. I cock my head to the side.

"Really?" I say and I laugh as I grab my bag and head to the ladies'.

I am well aware I have left him alone with her. With the red photo album out there for him to take home. On his own. I am well aware that tonight together, after our food and wine and before we make love, we will lose those pictures and replace that album on the high shelf.

I don't know why but I feel as though I know Deirdre a little now. I feel protective of her memory. I know how much she was loved. Her face swims before my eyes. I see how much she was loved through the pain in her sister's eyes and I suppose because my sister is close to leaving me too it feels all the more real. Deirdre's life.

I push the silver-painted wooden door into the ladies' and the smell of bleach whacks me in the nose. I need to buy mints and deodorant wipes from the vending machine. I lean against the cool enamel of the sinks and all the way over to look closely in the mirror. I look okay.

Today I do look like Kate Winslet on her day off, papped as she does the school run or the groceries. Not a good enough look for her by any means but good enough for me. It's the grey cardigan, I'd say. Bit mumsy.

I stand on my tippy-toes to slot my two euro in the machine and I pull the little wooden drawer out hard to get my deodorant wipes. I go into a cubicle and shut the door. I wipe under my arms and everywhere else that I can reach. I feel I've done something really important today. I know if I ever tell anyone what Hugh was doing, like Phillip or Ciara even, they'll tell me to run a mile, that he is sick and that what he has been doing is totally weird and freaky but, somehow, I understand it. Somehow I understand where he is coming from. I remember now that day in Beggars Bush and the two girls, Deirdre's friends, walking by and how he looked at them. I thought he'd been eyeing them up and even then I was jealous.

I leave the toilet cubicle, splash water on my make-up-free face and leave the ladies'.

He has left and I say goodbye to Morgan.

"How's your da? Is he sick? I haven't seen him in here in ages. Me till is down," he jokes – not.

I almost laugh at the question 'Is he sick?'. I have to put my hand over my mouth. I smell the cheap tee-tree soap from my newly washed hands.

"I dunno, Morgan, I don't talk to me da much, as I'm sure you probably know."

I exit the bar into the late evening. That was a first. I always try to hide the fact me and Da don't speak. It felt good to admit to Morgan that we don't get on. So here is something I have learned. Something I honestly never believed in before. Life can change in an instant. Just like that. A snap of the fingers. All the thoughts about future and planning and thinking you know what is ahead is never a sure thing. I had resigned myself to the idea that life simply hadn't been kind to me. I wasn't blessed. I wanted to be one of the lucky ones whose life was filled with happiness and pink balloons. I know I used *The Secret* to prop up my couch, but still. All I wanted was to feel happy. I never craved loads of money, or fame, or anything bar happiness. And now I'd met some lovely bloke. But he's not just some lovely bloke, Kate, though, is he? He's very special.

I push open the door to Mr Top Top's and the smell is orgasmic.

"Two sweet and sour chicken with two egg-fried rice." Rice or rices, I'm never sure. Ciara would know. Her of the *elomucution*. "Can you throw in a bag of prawn crackers too, please?"

Always the same for me too. I never order anything else. Another sign. I think I should write down all the signs in my notebook. I sit on the grey hardback chair with the little cut-out at the back. I am never sure just why that cut-out is there. I hold my little square piece of white paper with Number 4 on it and I push it into my cardigan pocket as I pull out my iPhone to call Phillip.

"Greetings, dahling, where are you? What is happening?" he squeals at me and makes various kissing noises.

"I'm good. Looooads to tell you but how is Maura?"

"Oh darling, she is super-struttingly fantastic – just a virus, wiped the poor dear out so it did, in fact we are just out for the first time, we're in the queue for drinks to go see *La Cage aux Folles* in the IFI – can you call us after?"

"Oh sure, enjoy – I was –" But Phillip has already hung up.

This feeling comes over me. I rest my head back against the glass pane of the window. It is most strange. I try to put my finger on it. It's stirring some kind of memory and this always makes me nervous. But my heart's not thumping and my palms are quite dry. I retrieve it from my memory. I'm at the kitchen table in our house. Mam is peeling an orange and wearing that deep-pink tank top and blue jeans from one of the photos we have somewhere. Da is trying to tickle her. They have seventies hairstyles. I watch them both now in my memory, laughing, and I feel the relief flood over me. There was happiness. This feeling I have now is happiness. It did exist before. I was happy. I am happy now. Fuck me, I was happy before and I can be happy again. It is quite disarming.

"Number six!"

I jump and hand over my ticket. The girl in the long apron-coat takes it from me.

"No, number six," she says, pulling the brown-paper bag away from me and I apologise as a man behind hands over the winning ticket.

I take my seat again and she calls "Number four!" I don't know what she is shouting for as I am now the only person in here. I hand her the number and collect our dinner.

I pop into Centra and buy a bottle of red wine. I walk briskly towards the apartment and I think, if I can just convince myself Ciara will be okay, I am happy. I press the light and wait for the green man. I know Hugh is looking out at me but I don't look up. I do however squeeze my bum cheeks up as far as I can and hold myself tall. What is it they say? Tits and teeth. Me? A butt-cheek squeezer just because some lovely bloke is looking at me? Did I ever think I'd see the day?

When I enter through his open apartment door he is dressed in jeans, a black aertex-type shirt and black Adidas runners with red stripes. His hair is still damp from his shower and he smells of showel gel and a sweet aftershave.

"You came back!" he jokes as he takes the heavy brown-paper bag from me and kicks the door gently closed with his right foot.

I keep hold of the bottle of red wine. My phone rings out.

"You want to get that?" He nods to my pocket.

I glance at my phone then put put it down on the glass table in the living room. "It's only Phillip, no doubt, popping out to suck on his E-ciggy the second the film starts. He can't smoke it in the cinema. He is so annoying to go to the cinema with because he keeps getting up and down and therefore all the other people in the row have to do the same." I hold up the bottle. "Where can I find an opener for this?"

"Top drawer in the kitchen presses next to the fridge – it's a plastic-bottle-of-Budweiser-type opener thing." He looks into the bag as I follow him into the kitchen.

His parents' friends must be loaded to have this place and not rent it all the time. It's a huge kitchen compared to mine. White gleaming glossy presses and an American-sized double fridge. There are dark wooden floors throughout and a small picture of New York's Times Square. The one place in the entire world I ache to visit. I step nearer to it and lose myself in the brightness of its velocity.

"You keen on New York, Kate?" He rattles the plates as he takes two from the pile on the draining board.

"Keen?" I half-guffaw.

"No?" He moves beside me.

The feeling of him so close stirs me again. Jennifer dances across the floor; she is on fire.

"It's a dream I have . . . since I was a kid . . . to go to New York . . . I'd give anything to see that city. *Kramer V Kramer* . . . that was it . . . the first time I saw New York City and I just wanted to touch the screen. The colours autumn brings to New York are something else." I run my finger down the painting. Probably cost a small fortune. I step back.

"I've been a few times – it's just a mind-blowing city. I'd live there if I could. How come you haven't ever been then if you want to go so much?"

"I have never been to the UK never mind the US!" I tell him as I move away and pull open the drawer. Locate the plastic bottle of Budweiser and turn it around a few times looking for the wine-opener part. I'm confused. Is it some arty opener? If it is, it's crap. "This is a bottle-opener," I say, stating the bleeding obvious.

"Oh sorry, of course, wine-opener . . . eh . . . wine-opener . . ."

He rummages around the drawers as I watch him. He is perfect. The physical attraction I feel towards him is burning. He finds one and takes the bottle from me. Our hands touch and it is electric. He uncorks the wine with a pop.

"So where did you holiday as kids then?" he asks as I stare at his dimple.

"We didn't," I say and he is visibly shocked.

"What? Never? Even to Butlin's or the country or something?" He removes two wineglasses from the frosted glass-fronted press.

"No, Hugh, I told you. Da was a drunk, he was always drunk and we had no money. Mam did try her best before she left but it was never . . . well . . . never conventional. But strangely enough I remembered a day in our kitchen just when I was sitting in the Chinese. I remembered them laughing so I dunno – I guess at one stage things must have been reasonably okay?"

The wine floods loudly into the glasses and he hands me one.

I watch him now as he turns the wine expertly in the glass before sticking his nose right in and breathing deeply.

"*Mmmmm*, cherries, no?" He sniffs again and looks at me.

"I'm not much of a wine-smeller, Hugh, to be honest. I'm not much of a wine drinker to be honest. I drink to be sociable but I can take it or leave it. Phillip is always at me to smell this and smell that. I can see how it makes the food taste better though, I do get that. Phillip has been teaching me for a while now. He wants us to drive across France in a camper van visiting vineyards."

"Sounds amazing – can I tag along?

I nod.

"But when you take a drink – an alcoholic drink – is it enjoyable – tasty?" He sips his and holds it in his mouth now for a while.

"Ah here, let me see." I put the glass on the counter and take off my cardigan. I'm roasting. I pick the glass back up and swirl it, and then I smell it. "It was over thirteen euros," I take my nose back out and inform him before I smell again.

"I'm sure it was . . . it's delightful." His eyes glint at me and I know he is taking me all in.

I sip. I hold it in my mouth and I swallow, then I sniff again.

"Well?" He is amused.

I smack my lips together a few times. "Cherries," I lie because I have no idea what else to say.

He is thrilled. "See, I told you! And that's great but, tell me, do you like the taste?" He is genuinely interested.

This time I taste again and I say very honestly, "Yeah, it's lovely, it tastes of relaxation," and it does.

He nods as though that is good enough for him, puts down his glass and approaches me.

"I don't want you to get too relaxed now." He pushes himself softly up against me and I back into the glossy dark-grey laminate of the fridge.

He is hard and I stir wildly below.

"But, Hugh, what about our Chinese?" I struggle with wasted food.

"That, my dear, is most probably why Percy Spencer invented the microwave oven." His voice is low and heavy.

"It's never the same though, is it, reheated food?" I know it's not the right time to say this but I feel I have to. I detest microwaved food. Especially microwaved egg-fried rice.

I am still backed up against the fridge as he takes my glass from me and puts it on the counter top. He takes my other hand and pulls me forward and I hope against hope I'm going into his bedroom.

As we enter his bedroom I smell him deeper. He has a double bed in the centre of the room. Not pushed up against any walls. It makes the space seem smaller but I like it. It's different. The bed is unmade with one of those huge fat duvets on the floor and thick pillows in the centre. I imagine this is because his sleep is so restless. He has a small set of white drawers with a large pile of clothes folded neatly on top. We stop at the edge of the bed and he pulls me close and he kisses me deep and hard. It is not going to be an hour of foreplay, I know that much for nothing. I pull his top over his head and the feel of his naked skin makes me moan. His skin is perfect, splattered with large dark freckles and the curve of his muscular shoulders tells me that he once worked out. He pulls my T-shirt off and I know I haven't got the greatest body in the world but I don't think he thinks that. I can feel how much I turn him on. He slips a warm hand inside my bra and slowly we sink onto the bed. It's expensive, I can tell that much. I look forward to sleeping here tonight. I wrap my legs tightly around his naked back and he's pressed so hard into me it is slightly yet wonderfully painful. The kissing is deeper and deeper and I'm falling in love and I'm terrified as he pulls off my jeans and knickers and then his own jeans and boxers.

"I still don't have any condoms," he breathes heavily into my ear.

"Are you serious? Well then, we can't!" I say loudly back.

"Do you have any in your place?" he pants.

"No." I shake my head wildly.

"I'll go . . . I'll go buy condoms now." He moves to get up.

"Wait! No! Don't go . . . it's alright . . ." I heave out a slow breath. "Let's just wait. I just want to hold you and kiss you." I pull him closer and we kiss hard again. We devour one another. To want someone this badly is electrifying. I want it to last. I want to want him this badly for as long as I possibly can. We run our hands all over each other's bodies.

"*Chhhrrrrist*, this is hard!" He drops his face in my chest. We hold each other tight for a moment.

"Electrifying though," I whisper.

"I think you could be the greatest thing that has ever happened to me," he says as he rolls back on top of me now and stares into my eyes. His face sweaty and I can feel his heart pumping out of his chest.

"Oh, don't say that, Hugh!" I'm choking a little.

"Why?" He pushes my hair from my eyes and strokes my face softly. He really does have doctor's hands.

"Because I'm not strong enough," I hear myself say. Me? Kate Walsh, strength of strength, power of power, taker of no shit, is admitting this news to the new Englishman in her life. Well, I'll be damned.

"You are," he whispers.

"Am I?" I ask him. I don't play games.

"Yeah . . . you are, too." He kisses my mouth hard again.

"I want to make love to you so badly, Kate, but, you know, you're right – I'm also relishing the thought of it still to come."

He kisses me in such a way that it makes me feel of value. His lips open and close over mine like he can't get enough of me. I don't want to be anywhere else.

Soon our lips are swollen and we tear ourselves apart.

We lie on our backs.

"Am I your girlfriend then?" I hear the words tumble out and I feel my face burn red. Morto. What am I, eleven years old?

His perfect straight white teeth appear in a wide smile over me and he says, "I think that's something men should still ask, don't you?"

He gets up off me now and takes his taut, naked, still-excited body over to the edge of the bed where he gets down on one knee.

"Kate Walsh, will you be my girlfriend?" He isn't smiling now, he is deadly serious.

I sit up. It's so silly, I know it is, but I don't care. I don't even bother to cover my nakedness with the sheet. Bits fall here and rolls fall there and I couldn't care less.

"Ya know what, Hugh Clover – go on so – I will." I smile at him and it's one of the nicest moments of my life.

We kiss softly and Hugh hops back under the covers into the gorgeous warmth and we cuddle up and chat for a while. I have never felt so respected. I lie in the nest of his chest and when he talks I feel the vibration of the words he speaks. Nothing specific. We talk about favourite things, foods, films, music, books, TV shows, what we want to do in the future, shoe sizes, old fashions we wore, funny stories, bad habits, just really random getting-to-know-each-other stuff. These are first-time-only conversations. That is what makes them so special.

"Food?" I say after a while because my stomach has very unromantically started to rumble like a barking dog on the back streets of Mexico.

"Ahhh, please! Food!" he agrees and rubs his hand gently on my belly. It wobbles. I don't give a shit.

We pull on our clothes and I tie my hair up on top of my head in a messy bun. We go barefoot into the kitchen and I am so hungry that I agree to microwaving the Chinese food. We serve up two plates to be heated. He likes his rice mixed in with the sweet and sour, I like my rice on the side to add in when I see fit.

When the microwave has done its thing, we sit up at the breakfast counter. I can see the dryness of the rice but it's shovelled into my hungry mouth regardless. The chicken isn't too bad and I proceed to devour every forkful of its sticky sweetness. Neither of us fancy the wine now so he recorks it and pours us two huge glasses of cold fat-free milk. He finishes first and then starts dipping his fork into mine. I bat him away playfully but do spoon-feed him one forkful. Cheesy Kate.

My phone rings.

"I hate phones! So intrusive! I better check though in case it's Ciara – I'll let her know I'll call her back after we eat." I put my fork down hastily and it falls off the edge of my plate, bouncing onto the floor and scattering rice everywhere. "Sorry!" I say as I get down and begin to gather it up in my hand.

"Don't worry, don't worry, leave it," he says. "I have a lady comes in –"

I interrupt him as I look up, "You have a lady comes in?" I repeat in his accent. "How very posh you are. Not a cleaner, but a lady, I like that."

My phone rings again.

"Well, she's not my lady, you see, she's the owner's lady . . . even when they aren't here . . . which they basically never are apart from a few weekend breaks a year . . . they only ever rent to friends who want to come to Dublin for the rugby . . . anyway . . . sorry . . . she still is employed to come in once a week and clean. I mean . . . that is her job . . . the lady."

"Right," I say but still I clean up the rice.

The phone stops.

I don't tell him that I know plenty of cleaners in Ringsend – that I more than likely know the 'lady' who cleans his place. I know lots of strong Ringsend women who love their cleaning jobs. Not a speck of dust is left or an unbleached floor or unscaled bathroom. These women are fierce proud of their work. It was a job I considered before I took to the escorting game and maybe still a job I will end up doing one day. A lady.

I need to check my phone. I walk over to the glass table in the front room and pick up my slim-bodied phone. Entering my password, I slide my finger across and look at the screen. It is one of those few times when seeing that name on my phone has given me a dreadful feeling of foreboding.

Ciara Walsh.

My heart sinks as it rings again in my hand and I jump out of my skin.

"What?" I gasp into the phone.

"Katie! She's collapsed . . . Ciara's on the floor here! What do I do?"

My father sounds hyper yet eerily cold and immediately I think she is dead.

"She's breathing but . . ." he adds now as if reading my sick mind.

"*Ring a fucking ambulance!*" I scream at him.

"What's wrong?" Hugh drops his fork now with a clatter.

I hang up. "It's Ciara, my sister – she's collapsed!" I

run to the bedroom door. "I have to go, Hugh . . . now!"

"Let me come with you," he says and I don't even answer as we each find our own shoes in his bedroom and stuff our feet in.

I grab my bag and grey cardigan and Hugh grabs his keys. We slam the door behind us and we take to the fire escape. Two at a time. I clatter the green fire-escape bar and the door opens. I run all the way. Straight across the busy road as cars honk their horns aggressively at us. Past the library. Past the shops. Down Oliver Plunkett Terrace and into the flats, a shortcut to the houses. He runs alongside me. I don't see a fucking ambulance.

I arrive at the open hall door. People stand on the balcony of the flats opposite, watching with interest. Da must have been shouting on the street and anything out of the ordinary is of great interest around here. People stand around our wide-open hall door. Some faces I recognise and some I don't. They say nothing to me.

I see his butt-crack as he kneels over my slumped sister as we enter. She must have been peeling potatoes because half of one lies a few feet from her and still in her hand lies a small peeler. I fall to my knees and put my ear to her chest. *Flashdance* and Jennifer Beals is on the floor. Deep breathing.

"Did you ring an ambulance?" I snarl at him.

"I ran out onto the street, Katie, and Nanny Farrell next door rang one for me." He stands up slowly.

Huge takes over. "Okay, clear the space, we don't need to all be on top of her. Kate, what medications is she on? Go and find them, please." He is taking her pulse, holding her wrist and checking his watch. "She's breathing okay, pulse okay . . ."

215

"She's off everything right now," I tell him. "Mam goes in tomorrow – she was evaluated today – they did both their bloods though – maybe she's weak from that? She was supposed to go straight to bed." I can't stop staring at her.

I stand up now and turn, blazing, on Da.

"Did you have her making your fucking dinner? You fucking miserable selfish arsehole!" Father of the Year.

He stumbles back from my words against the sink.

"*Are you drunk?*" I scream so loud the word 'drunk' cracks and my throat hurts.

"No . . . no . . . I'm not . . . I'm sober . . . she insisted. I asked her not to make the dinner but she wouldn't listen to me . . . I told her I'd go across to Scotchy's for a one and one for us." He holds on tight now to the back of the chair.

"You know she hates you eating chips! Why couldn't you peel the fucking potatoes and make her something?" I yell.

"Okay, this isn't helping anyone." Hugh stands in and puts a strong arm around me. He turns to Da. "We need to call the ambulance again, sir."

Sir. I am about to tell Hugh that Da is no *sir* when a siren rings out in the distance, faint at first but becoming louder and louder.

Hugh moves to the door.

Da and I occupy the space on our own.

My sweet sister lies there.

"I am not drunk, Katie . . . I am very much sober and I – I am trying my best to stay off the drink. "He lets go of the chair and settles it in neatly under the table.

"Oh poor . . . poor . . . poor me another drink!" I spit

216

at him as the two ambulance men run in.

They begin to do their thing. We stand back useless except for Hugh who talks to them in a medical language Da and I do not understand and next thing I know I'm sitting by her side in the back of the ambulance on the way to St James's Hospital and she does not look like she is still alive.

Chapter Twenty

The next day goes by in a haze while Mam recovers and Ciara comes round. Her blood sugars had dropped dramatically – they were below 2mg/dl which Hugh explained was why she lost consciousness, not because she was peeling potatoes. She was given intravenous glucose. She quickly began to look better and Doctor Doyle said he was happy so she was prepped for the operation. The marrow only lasts seventy-two hours outside the body so time was not our friend. There were a lot of medical procedures Ciara had to go through and she asked that we all be around but not on top of her in the room. So we were all together in this very strange hospital world. It became our world. We were, to all intents and purposes, a real family. Family. There was the mammy and the daddy and the two daughters. All very normal. The word stuck in my throat yet here we all were, weren't we? Wasn't this what family was all about? Pulling together in times of need? Being there for one another. All this was true and now, to add to the mix, I had Hugh. He had been fantastic. Explaining things to Da and visiting Mam on her ward and making Ciara laugh. She thought he was, in her own clipped words "A bloody ride-bag".

I never told anyone his secrets of course.

Aplastic Anaemia. Two revolting words we were all hearing on a daily basis now. We had been hearing them for years. Ciara was simply the bravest thing on earth. She never cried or asked why or roared about the injustice. She just got on with it. I had listened countless times over the last few years as Doctor Doyle told us all about the procedure Ciara underwent and what the implications were if she didn't have a successful transplant but Jennifer Beals had fallen and fallen as he spoke repeatedly so I never really took it in. I wasn't mentally strong enough. I just wanted Jennifer to ask the judges if she could start again. But she was stuck. Freeze-frame.

I sat in the hospital canteen now, biting along the edges of my white polystyrene cup as Hugh explained it all to me.

"Ay. Plass. Tick. Uh. Knee. Mee. Uh." He kindly broke it all down for me, sounding out each syllable as I sipped my drink.

"Eh, yeah, thanks for that, doctor, but I have been living with a patient of the disease for quite some time so I can actually pronounce it. I just can't listen to anything about it or read about it any more. I don't want to know too much. I can't let my head go there. I have only ever known the basics. Too much knowledge isn't good in these situations I find."

"So you know what I know then? That this is a rare and serious condition in which the bone marrow fails to make enough red blood cells. I remember learning it originated from a Greek word meaning 'not to form'." He takes my free hand across the table.

"Yes, I know all that – not the Greek thing but, hey, you learn something new every day." I half grin at him, rubbing my thumb over his warm hand.

"Do you want me to tell you what I know in my own words, cutting down on the medical jargon? Probably still be a bit technical but I can give it a go and I will try not to be in any way insulting or patronising."

"If you like," I reply.

"Okay. So – anaemia is a condition that occurs when the red blood cells are low. Most of my college professors believed that aplastic anaemia happens when, for no known reason, the immune system attacks the bone-marrow cells. Actually Ciara is a great age to have a successful outcome from this, you know." He really is talking to me like a doctor. "So I know you donated and all that, but did you know what the procedure was after that?" He holds my hand tight.

"Yes, I did, doctor. The procedure – it failed," I say sarcastically even though I know I shouldn't as he really is only trying to help.

"Yes, it did on that occasion, Kate, correct – Ciara got an infection – but the great thing is we can keep trying. Do you know what Doctor Doyle does in the operating room?"

I shake my head. I never wanted to know, as pathetic as that sounds. I just wanted it to work. I just wanted Doctor Doyle to give me back my sister. He had offered to tell me all about it when my da was in too but I just didn't want to know. I was too scared if I knew the ins and outs I'd know how serious it all was. Head in sand. Head in hands. Head in the clouds.

"Okay, well, let me tell you then. Knowledge is power, Kate. Tomorrow during her transplant, which is very similar to a blood transfusion –"

"She's had and still has loads of those too over the years." I put my cup down, chewed to shreds.

"Indeed she has, exactly, first option . . ." He puts both his hands over mine now and he presses on, "Are you listening?"

"Have I a choice?" I open my eyes wide.

"So tomorrow Doctor Doyle will take your mother's donated stem cells, or bone marrow, and insert them through a tube placed in a vein in Ciara's chest."

I wince.

"Ciara won't feel a thing, okay? And once the stem cells are in her body they will travel to her bone marrow and begin to make new cells. Doctor Doyle was telling me about some medicines he feels Ciara should take afterwards. She hasn't had them made available to her before. It's keeping her immune system as healthy as we can and avoiding infection at all cost that we need to focus on. The serious life-threatening risk to Ciara is in possible infections post-op, as you well know." He stops.

There ya go. He said it. What I hadn't wanted to hear. She could die. I don't even blink.

"Hospitals are for saving lives, Kate."

He shuts down in front of my eyes. He's struggling being in this hospital, I just realise for the first time. I have been so centred on Ciara I haven't thought about how hard this must be for him. The memories. He is doing this for me. I sit up straighter now and give him my full, undivided attention. She will not die.

"Doctor Doyle was saying when he worked in Florida

some years ago he had a patient who recovered wonderfully from aplastic anaemia. He said the post-op medicines were the key. He confided in me, Kate, that they aren't readily available in Ireland. I offered to help with contacts in the pharmaceutical field I have in Manchester for what that is worth. Doctor Doyle is going to talk about Ciara's needs tonight at the hospitals admin meeting to see if he can order them from Houston, Texas. I'm going to go to the library later to look up some cases just for my own knowledge." He is very animated.

I am a little taken aback. As far as I can see Hugh is becoming a bit of a doctor again so I ask more. "How do the medicines help after the op?" I just want him to talk more.

He pulls his chair in closer to the table, almost severing the top half of his body in his apparent excitement. "Well . . . I know a bit but Doctor Doyle explained to me that these particular medicines combined should allow Ciara's body to start making blood cells again. They also help avoid the need for future blood transfusions. The three medicines, always given together . . ." he holds his hands up and tells me this like it is of the utmost importance I remember it before he continues, "can help the body's immune system and prevent it from attacking the bone-marrow cells. This is the biggest risk. They are antithymocyte globulin, cyclosporine and methylprednislone." He says the words very slowly.

"You know . . . this is the first time I have had any real confidence that she might just be okay." I squeeze his hand.

"It's a dangerous time, I won't lie to you."

I pull my hand away as quick. "Do. Please. I'm your girlfriend now, remember . . . lie to me a little."

He leans over the table. "She's going to be just fine," he whispers and kisses me on the mouth.

I dare to ask about him.

"How is it being in here?" I open my arms out wide, indicating our surroundings.

"Hard. The smell . . . it's like I never left the job in a way . . ."

I nod. We don't say more as we sit a while, lost in our own thoughts.

I am reading to Ciara from a *VIP* magazine that someone left her.

"See here, Amy Huberman is making a movie out of her own book," I say. "That is bloody handy, isn't it?" *VIP*. Full of people who find it too difficult to live in the real world. The great pretenders. The gas thing is they think we all believe what we read! That we can't see through the layers of make-up, hair extensions and really great lighting. That we believe their 'homes' are real and not just rented houses. Spare me.

"Please, Kate . . . go to a dance class . . . you need it, you need to let off steam." Ciara pulls the magazine from my hands. "I like *VIP* and I know exactly what you're going to do now: you're going to go through every page and tear everyone apart. It's my magazine and, believe it or not, I am saving it to read with my wonderful treat of one large cup of water that the nurse is bringing me in a minute. So if you don't mind, could you please just piss off for a while?" She pulls the magazine close to her chest.

"No. I want to sit with you. Doctor Doyle is preparing for that administration meeting later, about getting you all those big-named drugs – Hugh is doing some research in the library – he never broke down the pronunciation of those medicines for me so perhaps he is researching that. So I'm all on my own."

"He's so lovely, Kate, such a gentleman. I'm really happy for you." Ciara puts the magazine on the bedside locker and closes her eyes and I know she is tired so I stand up. She actually wants me to go so she can sleep, but she doesn't want me to worry.

"Sure, we'll see," I manage and I fix the blue cotton sheet up around her. "Has Mam been up to see you yet?"

"No, she is pretty sore actually, the poor thing," Ciara says wearily. "That friend of hers, who owns Yellow Posies – Gail – she is collecting her before I go to theatre in the morning. She called my phone – one of the nurses brought one to her."

I want to ask how it all went with Da on the dinner date but I know I need to let her sleep so I do what she told me to do and I go dance.

Chapter Twenty-one

Only when I push open the studio door do I realise how much I have missed Phillip. He literally leaps in the air towards me. He has badly missed me too. We air-kiss twenty times and then it is straight into it: the new mysterious relationship we left off talking about the last time I was over at his place has become a bit of a romance. However, as was my worry, all is not rosy with his newest beau. It isn't going according to plan and he is down. We both flop crossed-legged onto the floor and catch up like two gossiping teenage girls.

"I mean, you think I'm a great catch, right?" he sighs.

"Yes, of course I do – you are the best. Tell me more about him – all I know is what you said when we finished the movie that night which was that he was interesting, stylish and hung like the drapes in *Downton Abbey*."

"Yes, all of the above. But what has happened? Three guesses – no, one should suffice . . . the usual, chuck . . . we have been having fantastic, mind-blowing sex but now he thinks he might be straight!" He waves his hands dramatically, and I focus on his perfectly waxed arms.

It truly wasn't the first time I had heard this song sung.

"Ouch!" I sympathise.

"He is so gay, no question. I met him in Marks & Spencer's of all places! Like can he be any gayer? I helped him in the changing area. He was trying on these really awful pants and I took the liberty of popping out and bringing him a better option. He was thrilled. Bought them, he suggested coffee, I suggested after-coffee aperitifs, he suggested a stroll around Temple Bar, I suggested a nightcap and la-di-da we just happened to end up outside his flat on Eustace Street. So mind-blowing sex. A fantastic second date followed the next night – we saw some comedy in the International Bar, had some wine and some tapas, he came home with me, more fantastic mind-blowing sex, and I call him for a third date but he tells me sorry he's straight!" Phillip shakes his head.

"Sorry," is all I can really say.

"I know you are – story of my life, you'd think I would be used to it at this stage. I'm not crumbling this time, Kate. Britney spoke to me through 'Stronger' and Christina through 'Beautiful' last night in my bedroom. I love myself so he can go stuff himself. Shall we?" He stands and extends his hand to pull me up.

He trots over and puts on his favourite, the soundtrack from *Chicago*, and as the CD kicks in we move to the floor. We begin to warm up. He hasn't asked about me and I'm glad because I really don't want to talk about me. He flings his leg up high and pulls it in close to him by his calf.

"Am I right?" he asks in the long ceiling-to-floor mirror.

"Absolutely, leave it, Phillip," I pant as I turn and turn across the floor. Spinning. Spinning. Spinning. No time to think. No time to dwell. All my concentration on my movements. Freedom. My inner Roxie Hart explodes. My breath comes naturally and I glide across the floor. Turning, breathing, living. Dancing.

"Did I put him off though, I have to wonder? Am I too needy? Maybe I pushed him too hard? Too soon?" He jumps in the air, both his legs out perfectly straight, and falls into an effortless splits.

I am in front of the mirror now, using the bar, watching him. "I thought he was to go stuff himself? Are we changing our mind already?"

"He is, you are right, but am I really needy?" He looks at me with those puppy-dog eyes. A sweet, sweet soul.

"You are a bit needy but only when you throw yourself into a relationship. This wasn't that, this was a couple of dates. How needy could you have come across so soon?"

I lean into the mirror now, holding onto the bar with my two arms outstretched and focus on the makeshift dance floor. Always breathing deeper and deeper into my very core.

"You will fall in love, Phillip, one day and with someone who loves you back – otherwise what's the point?"

"Quite right!" He is satisfied.

We move into our routine. One of the first dances Phillip taught me that we could do together. It's the scene in *Chicago* when Velma Kelly starts telling the story about her sister Veronica. We dance in time, fast, making every beat in time to the music. *Bam. Bam. Bam.* Even after the hundreds of times we have danced this together, the hairs still stand on the back of my neck. Our timing is impeccable. We part. I catch my breath.

I say, "I love you, you know that, but when you find a

227

new boyfriend you always have to make out that he is The One three dates in. Why can't you just go with the flow? That's what I'm doing with Hugh," I pant.

He just looks at me so I try to soften my words

"Look, he's the one with the problem . . ."

He screams a high-pitched roar and I jump, presuming he's pulled something.

"Hugh?" he roars at me "Hugh bitch! Hugh have a boyfriend! How could Hugh keep this to yourself? I can't dance now – I'm flattened creatively." He stomps over to his office, raises the flap on the counter and dumps it heavily back down.

I finish my time on the floor before I grab my towel and follow him into his office.

"I didn't tell you about Hugh because there's nothing to tell." I don't tell him the truth and I don't know why. I think I'm afraid to harm it.

"Have you and Hugh had sex?" He fiddles with the mouse on his Mac.

"Not really," I admit carefully.

"How many times, not really?" He clicks on this and that in rapid succession.

"Twice. Just, together, ya know . . . we had no . . . yes, okay, he stayed the night in mine and then I went over to his. We were intimate, kissing, hugging, all that stuff." I pull myself up onto a high stool and wipe my damp face with my towel.

"*Aaaaaannnnnnnndd!*" He dramatically waves the mouse around in the air, his eyes now chewing into mine. He begins to type rapidly, hitting the keys hard, like the way people at airport desks do, faster and faster, searching and searching for the best seats available.

"*Aaaaaannnnnnndd whhhhhhhhaaaaaat?*" I fold my towel neatly over and over on my lap. Smoothing it out gently with the palm of my hand.

"And who is he? Where is he from? What does he look like? What is his job? Does he like cats or dogs? Sun or skiing? Children or goldfish? Has he baggage? Jennifer or Angelina? Age? Rivita or bread? Car or bicycle? Cock size?" He grabs a breath.

"Phillip!" I flick the towel now and hit him on the arm.

"All important questions, my dear." He shuts the laptop now with a bang and leans in closer to me as though I might have something on my face. "You like him?" he whispers, sounding out all his vowels.

He really should have been on Broadway.

I have no choice now but to come clean.

"I do, I like him. I mean it's nothing serious, you know me, and with everything that's going on in my life right now . . . but I like when he's around, I like spending time with him . . . okay, who am I trying to kid? He asked me to be his girlfriend!" I actually beam. I am beaming. Shoot me now.

"Sweet divine multi-Oscar-winning-Meryl-Streep!" He jumps off the stool.

"What?" I say.

He shakes me quite hard backwards and forwards.

"When did this all happen? Did I prick my finger and fall asleep for a hundred years?" He lets go of me and waves his dancing fingers in front of his face, checking every single finger and squashing them right up to his nose.

"It was all very quick, I'll give you that – he's staying in my building, we chatted a few times, then we bumped into each other in Beggars Bush, then we walked home together, then I we met again in a pub and I kinda invited him to my apartment –"

"You? You did what?" Phillip holds my head roughly between his hands now and pretends to look into my ears to see if my brain is still there.

"Very un-Kate Walsh, I agree." I push him away not so gently – he's being a bit rough.

"What does he do?" he probes now as the doors open and a class begins to fill up.

"He is, well, he *was* a doctor, and he's just taking some time out to weigh up his options." I feel proud as I say this – I don't know why – I didn't think I would be.

"Doctor Dreamy, hey? Well, bully for you, girl, I am swallowing green here with horrendous jealousy but I will get over it. When can I meet him?"

He is jealous, I see now, and a little pissed off with me.

"Soon." I don't quite know what else to say.

So I get up too and watch the class fill and I'm very impressed.

"All these people?" I point out to the floor. "What's the story?"

"I know – Maura and I literally blitzed Trinity College and UCD last week with flyers. Remember the way we did it during the summer a few years ago? Stuck up all those posters and flyers and got how many new bookings from the students for beginners coming back after the holidays? Well, it worked again, see – a little effort and we can go a long way. Thank God for Maura's support, otherwise I'd simply die. I couldn't go on. I'd be totally lost and on my own. I don't know what I'd do without her. Now Dickwad Donal downstairs says if I can get them all to eat lunch we might be able to come to a lease agreement."

He is trying to make me feel bad, I realise.

I felt bad already. I haven't been there for him lately. He has always been there for me.

"That's amazing – look, I'm so sorry I'm not able to help more," I tell him.

"Are you sorry or are you simply moving on?" He curls his hands now in front of his face and examines the clear varnish on the nails on his left hand intently.

"You are my best friend, Phillip. I will never move on from you. My free time is taken up with Ciara right now, you know that. As far as Hugh is concerned, if he does turn out to be a partner in the boyfriend sense, I won't see you every Friday night, but I will maybe see you every second Friday and then a Wednesday night. You will always be a huge chuck of wonderfulness in my life. I'll never, ever forget how much you and dance saved me." If I was a hugger, now is the time to hug him. I am improving so I cautiously approach him. He seems reasonably pleased with my speech but I know he wants more so I reach out and hug him.

"Oh my, a public display of affection? Who are you, chuck, and what have you done with my best friend?"

I have reassured him with this move.

"As soon as Ciara's up and running on her feet I will be totally on board." I hold him tight as I can.

"I know, sorry, I'm being a selfish brute – of course Ciara comes first. I was wondering, would you become a board member of The Phillip Stark Dance Company?" He turns to me now with that look he usually reserves for the moment he meets Panti Bliss. It's a look he has been practising since her infamous speech on the Abbey stage. Arty. Serious. Accepted.

"A board member?" I'm not quick on the uptake.

"I'm going legal, chuck, all above board. Maura talked me into it. I'm forming a legitimate dance company. I have even been in to meet The Arts Council – me, pottering along the carpeted halls in Merrion Square – who ever would have thought it possible?" He laughs childishly behind his hand.

"How did that come about?" I am seriously impressed.

"Maura took me – that's a story for another day – our Maura, Kate, she's a dark horse. Wait till I tell you!" He moves out to the floor and claps his hands loudly.

"Warm up, people, warm up, no passengers in this class! We'll be starting with 'La Vida Loca' so I want nimble hips. God wouldn't have given you hips if he didn't want you to *shhhaake* them!" He rummages through his CD's, selects the one he wants and pops it in.

Then he comes back to me.

"Sooooo . . ." he says.

I have been here a zillion times. When Phillip has really good gossip or news he takes an absolute age to tell you. It's completely draining.

"I have to get back to the hospital," I tell him and pretend to get ready to leave.

"Okay, okay, okay, okay, sorry! So you know we were googling her that time and, yes, we felt shitty and all that jazz . . . well, hear this. When I was in Dalkey – you were right, house is unreal by the way – anyway I so wasn't snooping before you say I was, I was simply looking for the milk for our hot cocoa and I found all these really old paper clippings."

"In the fridge?" I laugh.

"Shut your pie-hole! Anywhoo . . . there was our

232

Maura on the front of one of the *London Gazette*s in 1963 dancing in *Swan Lake* at the Royal Opera House with . . ." He shuts his mouth tight and expends air in and out in short bursts through his nose just as an exhausted yet exhilarated winning racehorse might at the end of the Grand National.

"Seriously, please stop!" I am extremely agitated.

"Rudolf Nureyev!" he blurts.

"No way?" I gasp.

"Way! Our Maura was in The Royal Ballet, Kate!" he gushes.

"No way José?" I don't believe it – well, good for our Maura.

"Way Jay! Our Maura is a way famous ballerina. I had to say it to her, I just had to – you know me, if there is something on my mind I cannot hide it." He claps with his arms extended out to the class to indicate he is on his way and goes on.

"But we could never find anything on her," I say.

"If you would let me have the floor? See, you leave me, this is what happens. So we weren't googling her proper name. She was once married – she danced under her maiden name – Maura Downey."

"Maura was married? She never said!"

"I know, she said we never asked! *Five minutes, people, I wanna see some sweat!*" he screeches right into my ear.

I flinch. "What happened to him?" I rub my ear.

"To whom?" He looks behind me and then out to the floor as though I am talking about someone in the class.

"To her husband, you tit!" I hiss and grab him back around.

"Oh, oh, oh, oh . . . well, he turned out to be . . . wait for it . . . G.A.Y." Phillip is beside himself with this gossip.

"That's so sad."

"No, not really. Maura didn't seem to mind at all, honestly. She said they were always more like friends. In fact he lives in San Fran and she visits him and his partner, and their two goats – and get this, she is going to take me at the end of the year. Now, if you don't mind, I have a class to teach." He wags those hips as he takes to the floor. He has, now I notice, acquired a long thin stick that he bangs on the floor. Gandalf in tights.

I grab my stuff and slip out. I must call Maura tomorrow and arrange a lunch downstairs in Macken's. How fascinating. I think it very sad that Maura didn't tell us about her success as a dancer or that she once had a wedding day. I wonder why?

I'm not too sweaty so I walk to the bus stop to get back to the hospital. I wait for the bus and when it arrives I am only seated a second when I feel my head nod off on the journey. I hadn't realised just how tired I am. Luckily I awake the stop before mine.

St Margaret's Ward is quiet and there is no sign of my English boyfriend, Doctor Dreamy, Hugh Clover, in the canteen or the waiting area. I go quietly into the ward and down the corridor. I peek around the cold plastic blue curtain and Ciara is sleeping still. I check my phone and no calls. I am acutely aware that just one floor down below my mother lies recuperating in her bed, most probably alone. How sad, I suddenly feel. I walk to the lift, press the button for a floor down and then walk away. I take the stairs instead.

Chapter Twenty-two

She is sitting up in the bed with a hard-back book open on her covers but she is writing a letter. I cough loudly to make my presence known.

"Katie, hi." She caps the pen and folds the letter. "How is she?" Her brow furrows.

Her nightdress is so old-fashioned I actually wonder for a moment where she might have bought it. That shade of purple is no longer seen – or is it lilac? Tiny lilac flowers imprinted on its whiteness. Three silver buttons down the front – I don't know but I imagine it goes all the way down to her ankles. Suddenly I think of her and Da having sex and I shudder. She must have had to have sex with him when he smelt of booze and fags and vomit and slurred and spluttered all over her.

I sit at the side of her bed.

"Yeah, okay, I think – she's asleep," I say quietly. "I'm glad – she needs all the rest she can get." I'm not sure how I came to be sitting here but here I am.

"That's good. I spoke on the phone with her earlier."

She smooths the covers with the palms of her outstretched hands. For the very first time I notice that she still wears her wedding ring.

"Thanks for doing this," I say now.

"She is still my daughter, whatever you think of me. I love her, I love you both." Still smoothing the bed covers and not making eye contact with me.

"I'm sure you do," I manage and sit back into the hard seat.

I have so many issues with these two, my parents, my givers of life. I'm so angry with them both it is eating me up. I am intelligent enough to know all this but it's a fact of life and no amount of talking about it will make it go away.

"What are you writing?" I say to try and calm myself down.

"Just a letter," she says.

"To who? Or is it whom?" I try to joke.

"Emm . . . whom I think . . . I never really knew to be honest. This one is to you, Katie, actually." She looks at me and winces a bit.

"Right, well, I'll be sure to put it in the biscuit-box thingy then. I haven't had a chance to look at them yet but I will do." I feel a bit awkward now.

"I hope that you do. Ciara has started hers and she is delighted with them."

"That's nice," I say.

A trolley is rattling around outside and I stand.

"Your night-time cuppa tea is here, I'd say. I'd better split so."

"I don't take tea at night, I can't sleep if I do. I don't really sleep so well, you see."

I get the impression she doesn't want me to go.

"Are you okay?" I look down at her old-looking hands.

"Yes, a bit sore. Sorer that I expected, old bones I'm sure. Why don't you sit again? The dinner with your father – would you like to hear how it went?"

She's been waiting to tell me this since I walked in, I realise now.

"I would." I sit.

She pauses as if trying to find the right words and I break the silence.

"Wasn't that a turn-up for the books all the same, Mrs Walsh? Breaking bread with the devil?" I say this to try to lighten the mood but the funny side of my sentence is lost on her. It was honestly only supposed to be a joke.

"He is so sorry, your dad, Katie. I am not asking you to speak to him – I'd never do that. I remember only too well the nights we had to take the big duvet down and sleep in the car out of fear. I remember him breaking the chain lock on our hall door to get in and terrifying the living daylights out of us. I remember how he threw the plate of spaghetti bolognese over my head because I hadn't kept it warm enough, I remember how he'd take my washing off the balcony and trample it into the coal bunker down below because I was annoying him or wouldn't give him any of my Children's Allowance for drink. I remember the vomit all over the house, I remember hating him so much and I particularly remember how hard it was on you. Heaven knows I remember it all. It was when I started getting really sick. But I have forgiven him. I have to and talking with him last night, a sober Eoin, after all these years, was really nice. He was just like he was before the drink. We had a lovely bite to eat – both of us had the cod and chips. He's a decent man deep down, Katie." She looks me in the eye for the first time now.

"That's good, Mam." I nod my head up and down. "I am happy for you and Ciara that you can both forgive and forget, I truly am." I have no energy to be sarcastic so I offer no other words.

In return, she lets it go. "Ciara tells me you've met a nice man?" she says, smiling lightly at me.

Did she now? Having the little confabs with Mammy, is she? But I'm kind of happy to talk about Hugh Clover and I am kinda happy to talk to my mam right now.

"I have – he's lovely all right," I tell her.

"I know, I met him earlier," she tells me with a cheeky grin on her face.

"Where?" I ask.

"He came in here earlier. Sat with me for a while. Ciara had asked him to drop me down a magazine she was finished with. One of those celebrity ones – how the other half live, eh? Of course he didn't say he was your fella – just mentioned he was a friend of yours and Ciara's." She is enjoying this gossip.

"Oh right." I'm amused.

"Hugh was telling me Doctor Doyle has permission to order Ciara those special medications in from America." She looks at me and says, "You know, he seems like a really good man."

"That's good to hear – about the medications – I thought we'd be told no. Nothing would surprise me with our health system, don't get me started."

"If you really need me to stay I will," she says and I can

see the fear creeping into her eyes again. "I've been thinking about how you reacted when I said I wanted to return home and you are right. I am thinking about myself but I'm just so frightened of letting my head get back to that place again. But it is selfish, I can see that."

"No, Mam, I understand. Sorry about how I reacted. I think I was just a bit shocked. It's okay, I can manage. We have only just found you and we don't want to lose you again. Go home and recuperate." I say it gently and I mean it.

"Thank you for your understanding, Katie. If I can make you understand and believe that I'd love nothing more than to be the woman I once was, to have the strength I once did, I'd be a happy woman. I'm just different now and I have to accept that. As horrible as the end of my marriage was, I think I was sick a long time anyway and really my leaving you and Ciara wasn't completely to do with your father. Yes, he was a dreadful husband and woeful father then but I couldn't cope with my own life either. I couldn't cope with being a mother. I honestly felt you were both better off without me. I'm too unwell still, but I thought today maybe I could try. I haven't taken strong anti-depressants in over three years now but I asked Doctor Doyle if maybe they could prescribe me something if the . . . if it . . . starts again. He told me no. Ciara would hate that . . . so I must go home."

I see her hands, one on the other, start to shake.

"Don't be silly, there is no way that you're going back on strong anti-depressants – I do understand, I promise." I put my hand on top of hers and I feel a calmness come over me. "Was he ever a good husband and father really?" I have to ask, now we are in this moment.

239

"Oh, he was, Ciara, before the drink got him – he was a very kind man." Her eyes well up with tears.

I say, "I tell you what, when she gets better . . . em . . . well, how about we come and stay in your spare room for a few nights?"

She pulls her bottom hand from our hand-pile and places it slowly on top of mine. Her chin moves slightly and her eyes glisten as she looks straight into mine. We hold the stare.

"I'd better go," I say before she can answer and I push back my chair and leave.

I feel really good that I haven't left her feeling dreadfully sad.

I am awoken with a bang as a machine beeps loudly and a nurse jogs in. Not a panicked run but she's not walking either. I try to move my neck but it's too stiff from the chair.

"Is she okay?" I ask, holding the left side of my neck tightly.

"Yeah, we just need to be aware of her blood pressure as this morning she is to have her two catheters inserted," the nurse informs me.

"Are these neck and left arm again?" Ciara asks despondently as she sits up.

"Sure are, Ciara," the cheery nurse replies, fiddling with wires and charts before she takes her blood pressure.

"What are they for?" I ask.

"Basically they allow us to give Ciara treatment fluids and some nutrition." She pulls at a bag of fluid and takes a small pen from her top pocket as she writes something on the chart.

"You don't remember all this, Kate?" Ciara pulls herself up higher in the bed.

"I tried to forget it all. I obviously did a very good job. Hugh has been explaining it to me all over again." I am trying to turn my neck from side to side to loosen the muscles.

"Why didn't you go home and sleep in your own bed, ya big eejit," Ciara says. "I wouldn't sleep in here unless I one hundred per cent had to, which I do." She shakes her bony finger with immaculately orange-polished nails at me.

"Ciara!" I shut my eyes tight in despair. "How many times have you been in hospital? How many times do they have to keep telling you? No nail polish!"

"Ah, go way, I'll take it off later. I can't look at my bare nails – my bare face is bad enough."

"She will be moved to ICU later this morning," the nurse says as she clips the chart onto the end of the bed. "To be prepped for op. And she will remain there – she can't remain on the wards due to the risk of infection." Her shoes squeak their way out of the room.

I always love the way nurses say "this morning" at five in the morning as though it's normal. Morning was any time after seven – that was normal.

"Right so." I dig my phone from my cardigan.

A text from Hugh: **called back to see you but you were asleep - i will be back at breakfast - let me know if i can bring you or ciara or emily anything" hugh x**

Emily is being discharged later this morning. I should really go back and see her before she leaves for Oughterard.

"So today's the day, eh?" I say to my beautiful sister.

241

She is leaning over to her locker to get her nail-polish remover, I see.

"Aye, 'tis, to be sure to be sure." She shakes the bottle and I hand her the roll of cotton wool from the bottom shelf. A big industrial roll wrapped in blue paper.

"It's going to work this time, I can feel it." I sound positive.

"I hope so." She opens the lid and the smell is overpowering. She wets the cotton and rubs at her nails.

It's slightly symbolic as we both sit and watch the beautiful orange disappear. The colour drain. Like her life blood.

"You know what, though, Kate? If I do get better, I'm getting a tattoo."

She puts the dirty orange-stained cotton wool on the bedside locker and I pick it up and take it over to the bin. "Okay," I say. "Whereabouts?" I stand on the pedal, the lid lifts and I drop it in. I remove my foot and the bin clatters shut.

"Why would you ask me where and not of what?" she says.

"Okay, of what then?" I reply correctly, doing as I am told, and sit down again. The space is so small and stuffy.

"Of my name," she says. "It will say in a nice stylish-font-type scribble down the back of my neck: *Ciara Walsh lives here.*"

"Okay," I say, not really sure what all that means.

"I just want to live again, Kate." Her eyes seem more determined than sad.

"I know." I swallow a lump the size of a golfball.

"Kate, when I go to theatre I want you to stay with Dad. I can't face it if he's going to be sitting out there all alone. He's trying so hard – can't you just give him one chance?"

She gazes at me, her face pale, and I can see she is clearly very upset about this. I cannot be the one to make it any worse. I'm not that selfish.

"Okay," I say.

"You aren't lying to me, are you? Well . . . maybe this is my dying wish right here and I want to know it's going to come true." With bare fingernails, she rests her hands on the blue hospital bed cover.

"You won't die, Ciara," I say.

"But, if I do, you will grant me my last wish, yeah?" She swallows hard and I hear it.

"Yeah," I whisper and I take her in my arms.

We hold each other and we are terrified. I can't face life without her. She is the most beautiful person I have ever met. She never thinks about herself. I idolise her.

Hugh come in and pulls us both back to reality. Neither of us is crying. We are way past that.

"How is everyone this sunny morning?" He is very cheery and he kisses my cheek and leans down and kisses Ciara's.

"Not too bad considering," Ciara says and we all laugh.

Doctor Doyle comes around now and he checks tubes that are hanging from Ciara's veins. Hugh slips in and Ciara and I make ugly faces at each other. There doesn't seem to be anything else left to do. It's all we can think of. All we are comfortable with. We pull the ugliest faces we can at the backs of Doctor Doyle and Hugh. Messers.

"Doctors are just so dreamy and so clever, aren't they, Kate?" Ciara says in her best Marilyn Monroe impression and we both fall around like kids. The laughter masking the fear in the pits of our stomachs, releasing the lumps in our throats. Laugher. The best medicine.

"I tell you what," Doctor Doyle sits at the edge of Ciara's bed, "when we are all better and full of new cells, why don't we do a pub quiz? You ladies versus us doctors?"

He is small in stature, Doctor Doyle, and I actually don't know the first thing about him. He always seemed too above me but now I ask.

"What's your first name, Doctor Doyle?"

"Dermot," he says.

"Well, Dermo, yer on," I say.

He stands and checks his pocket watch, then he excuses himself, saying he's going to scrub up and he will come and keep us posted throughout the day.

"I have this." He holds Ciara's hand and looks at her with very serious eyes.

She smiles at him. "I have every confidence, Dermot," she says with a wink and he leaves.

Da comes around the blue curtain now and for a minute I actually think he is another doctor and I have to do a triple take.

"Oh, it's great on you!" Ciara says as he sits on the other side of her bed. "See, I told you Mr Nolan was a brilliant tailor in his day! I knew he'd be able to adjust it for you!"

I notice now how he doesn't kiss her or touch her in any way.

He looks like he's ten years younger. He's had a short, back and sides haircut, the greasy strands cut away. He is wearing new glasses, a white shirt and a slightly ill-fitting brown pinstriped suit – despite Ciara's praise, Mr Nolan, to the naked eye, was no great tailor.

Hugh breaks the awkwardness. "Very smart, Mr Walsh."

"Thanks, son." He shifts a bit on the seat.

"Who cut your hair, Da?" Ciara asks.

"I just went into the barber's in Fairview. I used to go to there as a kid – short back and sides while I still have a bit to cut, wha?" He tries to laugh and it's so forced.

Two nurses come in now with the porters and Ciara is ready to be wheeled away.

"Smell ya later," I say as I touch her cold hand on the steel bar of the bed.

"Not if I smell you first," she laughs back and she is gone.

The three of us sit for a moment until Hugh rises and says, "Well, I'm ready for a bit of breakfast – how about you guys? There was a nice smell of sizzling bacon from the canteen when I passed, now that you mention smells."

"I'll just sit here – you go." Da cannot wait to get me away from him.

I know the feeling but I have made a promise and I will not break my promise to her.

"You may as well come with us," I say as I look at the gaping space where Ciara's bed once was. The floor a darker colour. I see her orange nail polish has fallen off the side table so I bend down and pick it up. I put it in my bag. I don't know why. I never paint my nails.

"Right so," is all he says and I am so glad that Hugh doesn't take my hand or pat me on the back or heap any type of physical praise on me for asking him because right now in this moment I would hate that.

We walk down the corridor to the big canteen and I just go for the coffee as does Da but Hugh gets onto the queue for the Full Irish. I watch, when he returns to the table, as he devours it and it actually gives me great comfort that he, with the knowledge he possesses, is able to eat. He must be confident enough, I think, as he spears his white pudding and winks at me, holding it in the air on his fork. I know he has great faith in Doctor Doyle – he told me as much. He puts his pudding into his mouth and chews it. Then he cuts his two sausages into little pieces and his rashers into two halves; he spears them with his fork and dips them into the ketchup he has squeezed onto the side of his plate. His egg is last and he puts this on top of his toast and picks it up with his hands. Not the immaculate eating manners from a Swiss finishing school I was expecting.

"What will be going on now?" I ask him, handing him a napkin for my sake more than his.

"Okay – so she's being prepped now. They'll be taking all the vitals, making sure she's okay for anaesthetic and then she will be going under." He swallows and dabs his mouth.

I jump as someone tips my shoulder and Mam is standing there with her small carpet-covered suitcase and Gail is beside her. She puts the suitcase down.

"We're off now," she says. "Is she in the operating room?" Her hands hold on to each other, resting under her chest.

I nod. "Hello again," I say to Gail and extend my hand. She takes it and her hand is warm and comforting. "This is Hugh, and this is Eoin."

She shakes Hugh's hand first and then Eoin's yellowing

one. "Pleased to meet you both," she says politely. "I will be praying for her, pet." She has a strong Galway accent. She hands me a piece of paper with a number on it. "That there is the new number of Yellow Posies, my café you were in – I have ordered the sure box to be delivered to Emily in the next week. Trying to get an exact delivery day and time in the country is near on impossible. Anyhow, I'm going to pick her up a mobile and a tablet on our way home, I got money out of our post office account. I live above the café so you can get me any time day or night – with news, I mean." She steps back close to Mam.

I thank her.

"Okay so," Mam says and takes a small step backwards.

I know I should get up and hug her but I am physically stuck to my seat and I just can't.

But then Hugh does. He gets up and embraces her, takes the carpet-suitcase from her hand and says, "Did you park in the hospital car park, Gail?"

"I did, Hugh," she says, showing him a parking ticket she has in her shirt pocket.

He takes the ticket and slides it into the back pocket of his jeans. "Okay, allow me to walk you ladies to your car."

Leaving me. Alone. Alone with him. I feel the panic rise.

Da stands like a true gentleman should as the ladies take their leave.

Then he sits and, without a beat of silence to follow, immediately says, "I was five years old when I had me tonsils out. I remember me da collected me from this very hospital. I don't think he ever visited me durin' the stay and in them days it was about two weeks long. But that day he brought me to Clery's on O'Connell Street and downstairs to the café where he bought me a jam tart and a glass of cold milk. He left me there and went out – I found out later that he went over to Mulligan's bar across the way – and I sat there, me feet swingin', not yet reachin' the floor, until they were moppin' under them to go home. They told me the place was closin' and I had to leave. Me throat was so sore and he had a prescription for me medication – painkillers, I suppose they were. I walked out onto O'Connell Street and the cold air . . . it was so cold that evenin'. . . I had no idea where I was or how to get home . . . or where he was . . . all he'd said was he would be back. I stayed always in me granny's and I knew it was on Townsend Street but I didn't know the exact address and I was too scared to ask someone, so I sat in a doorway down the side of Clery's all night until the sun came up in the mornin'."

I am listening because I know I have to. Because I have made my sister a promise that I will stay with him. I will stay with my da until my sister tells me it's alright to leave his side again.

"I was found by a policewoman, on the verge of hypothermia, and taken back to St. James's Hospital. It took the authorities a week to find out who I was and I developed an ear infection that resulted in the loss of hearing from me left ear, as ya know. Da never apologised. He did tell me I was the bane of his life and was it any wonder Maria, me mammy, died so young with me hangin' offa her hip all the bleedin' time. Me granny brought me up till I was eleven and I left school then because I couldn't hear right and I wouldn't tell them I was deaf in one ear, so they just thought I was bein' lazy or cheeky, ignorin' them, but sure I couldn't hear what they were sayin' at all. Ananyways when me granny died the council took back her room and I was out on me own again. I let on I was back livin' back with the da – he had a room above a launderette on Macken Street and some nights I did get in through the winda and crawl under his bed. He'd fall in at whatever hour and pass out and . . . and I used to steal any money that was in his trousers, cos I knew he'd have no idea of any money he might have left, bein' so pissed, and sure I'd be long gone be the time he woke up and headed back to the pub. That's how I survived. A lot of nights he'd fall in with no money in his pocket and I'd literally starve but he wasn't a bad gambler, believe it or not, and some nights I'd raid a lot of money and I used to be very careful with this and make it last."

"Are ya done with these?" a waitress asks and we both nod. She gathers up Hugh's dishes and dumps them on a huge trolley she is pushing around and takes her leave. The trolley squeaks away.

"So I had it tough. So did you, I know that – I'm not sayin' ya didn't but I wanna tell ya this ananyways like I told Emily the other night. I hid all this from her too, the poor woman. I battled through on me own and picked up jobs here and there. I never got into robbin' like some of the other lads out on the streets. I never took anythin' apart from what I took from him but I felt it was mine too – he had a duty to look after me."

I can't help it. I butt in. "Just like you had a duty to look after me."

"Yeah, just like that," he says back, deadpan.

We look across the table at one another. I can't feel

anything but anger still and the reality of his life slowly plays out like a scene from *Angela's Ashes* through the bitterness in my head.

"Go on." I lean in closer to him. He doesn't smell of booze, he actually smells of Ciara's Dove shower gel and it's like he's changing before my very eyes.

"Well, when that garage opened on the East Wall I would turn up every morning with me bucket and cloth and ask Mr Canavan, the owner, if I could clean his cars. At first he'd tell me to get lost but slowly he started to like me and threw me a few bob. Soon I was learning how to drive up the cars off the boats from the docks and parking them, and before I knew it I was employed. Mr Canavan gave me a job. I saved every brass farthing and laughed at the fuckin' mugs who drank their wages away in Barney's of a Friday night. I would walk to town and go up to Clery's department store, down to the café and buy two jam tarts and two glasses of cold milk – sometimes I'd buy four jam tarts – and I'd sit there in the evening till closin' and I'd walk back to the tiny room I had where I'd put me head down for the night. I was doing okay and then I met yer ma. She had fallen off a baby swing, believe it or not, in Ringsend Park and I went over to see if she was all right. I'd been sitting on the park bench eating a banana – mad the shit ya remember, isn't it, considering I can't remember the last ten years of me life? I'm glad I have these memories. She was okay, her knees were scraped, and we just got talking. Painfully shy she was and skinny she was. But real pretty – two long blonde plaints pinned up on top of her head she had. She was just starting a job the next day in the dry cleaner's on the top of Grafton Street and she was very nervous. Ananyways we started dating and I opened a bank account and we got married. Got the flat first, then the Corpo house in Ringsend and then you were born. Then he came back ta see me. He'd heard I got married and he had a granddaughter. It was the night after St Stephen's night and he was well jarred and I wouldn't let him in. I never told Emily about my shite childhood until I wrote her that letter – ya see, I wanted her to think I was strong and well brought up. I told her I'd lived in great comfort with me granny who I said only died before I met her. People said stuff to me over the years, about me da, but I never listened to it and it's where the first rows started to develop. She'd say somethin' to me that she'd heard and I'd have ta shout her down for fear she'd find out I was a good-for-nothin' scumbag. So that night I told him to go way and never come back. He took it to heart obviously as he was found almost in the same doorway where I was found after me tonsil operation as a boy – after bein' thrown out of Mulligan's he musta fell and hit his head and he died. Ah, he was a fuckin' bollix, Katie, no two ways about it. I had to hide it all from yer ma and you. It was so stressful, hopin' she wouldn't find out where I had come from. Then at the funeral, which I paid for, I took a drink. I drank a pint to the end of me da in Mulligan's and I never left."

"Excuse me, are you using that seat?" a girl in a dark-green school uniform asks us, pointing at Hugh's seat. The place is really busy now, I notice. She holds one white earpiece in her hand, the other still resting in her ear, and dance music blares out from it.

"Yes, sorry, my . . . we are . . . he's . . . he'll be right back," I tell her and she skips off, headphones back in ears, to find another seat.

"The dreaded drink, wha', Da?" I return to his gaze.

"Oh Katie – sorry – Kate . . ." He is mad with himself now for not remembering my name again and clenches his fists. "I just want you ta know this, I need ta tell ya all of this, and then I will go and wait in the corridor, okay?"

I could say no, too little too late, that I don't owe him anything, but instead I tell him to go on.

"The drink made me feel . . . wonderful. It made me so happy, so at ease in meself, that even a wife, a daughter and a new baby on the way couldn't match how it made me feel. Yer ma wasn't well either, I see that now – she's explained all that to me – I didn't understand depression at the time but I do now and she was always in the bed. It was another reason I stayed in the pub – to make her get up and take care of ya." He looks at me now to see if that last comment has upset me. It did.

"Come on now, keep to your story," I manage to whisper at him. I am not listening to him saying Mam's illness was a reason for his boozing. No fucking way.

"It's true but ananyways, okay, so I drank and I drank and I blotted out the horrible childhood I had and then I did the same to you. I see that now. The pattern. Hard, as hard as it is to believe, I did the same thing, I ruined yer childhoods . . ." His bottom lip covers his top.

"Yeah, yeah, you did," I tell him out straight.

"Jesus, I know, Katie – Kate, Jesus, sorry!" He slaps his knee hard now, furious with himself.

"The reason I hate you calling me Katie is because when you were drunk . . . like always . . . you would slur it so much you basically called me 'Kadee', it was so long drawled out. I wanted a new name, a sober name, something

252

with one beat if you will, so I started to call myself Kate."

"I don't remember much about youse growing up," he tells me.

"That's handy," I say and I rest my chin in my hands. Suddenly I feel absolutely exhausted, as though I have just pulled an all-nighter and I know it's time to give up the fight. I hope I can. If there is a towel to throw in, I'm almost bending down to pick it up. "You are sober now, I hear." I sit up straight, exhale slowly, shoulders down.

"I am over a month and a half now, no fall-outs. I can't tell ya how good it feels, Kate, I can't tell ya."

"How did you do it after all this time?"

"I woke up," he says.

"Just like that, after all these – what, thirty-odd years?" I shake my head slowly.

He nods. "I've seen them all die of the drink, all the ones who supported me, who understood me well so I thought – there's nothing like having fellow-alcoholics as friends. I met Father Brennan one night as I fell into the church to pay me respects to me pal Stephen Guest – he caught me be the arm and helped me into a pew. I kind of remember him handing me a plastic cup of hot coffee and I drank it and I listened to Stephen's daughter Caoimhe talking about her da. I was fond of Stephen actually, he wasn't a bad fella. She said things like 'this disease took him' – ananyways lots about 'this disease' – and I tried to stand in respect for my friend as he passed me in his box and me feet went from under me and I fell out onto the aisle. I remember being so, so embarrassed for Caoimhe – she'd done her best to give Stephen a proper send-off and as usual I fucked it up. And it hit me. It was all or nothing now – I had no desire to go on – just as so many friends before had lost their desire too. It wasn't living. I hadn't lived in years. I sat long after they left and then I saw the confessional and me, not havin' been near Mass in, oh, well over a decade, pulled meself over and sat in. I told Father Brennan it all and he asked me if I wanted help and I said I did and that was that. He actually walked me to Pearse Street and put me inta the AA meetin' and when I came out they gave me the number for a dry house in Rathmines and I went there for two weeks."

"Where did Ciara think you were?" I ask.

"Ah, she knew. I phoned her and she came and brought me clean clothes, just the once – she wasn't able and I told her not to come again – I wanted to do it for her too – ya see, her illness never really bothered me before because if she had died I was following her to the grave that night too or that day. There was no life for me without her. She has been my angel."

This maddens me and I don't know why but my shoulders jump right back up.

"Your angel? So what does that make me?" I hiss across at him. I wish Hugh would just come back now and get me away from this – my head is about to explode all over again. The towel remains on the floor.

"Kate, you did the right thing as did I with my da – cut me out – I always understood that. But Ciara somehow found this inner strength to stay with me. She didn't have to and I can tell you now, no matter what she says to ya, I was a bollix to her so many times. She kept me alive."

"I tried to get her to leave you, to come live with me but she wouldn't budge!" I am spitting the words at him, hoping they wet his face with venom.

"I know ya did – so I suppose I owed it to her to give it up. Kate, I know you and me are done – I finished any chance we ever had to have a relationship, I know that, and I'm okay with that now, I have to be. I don't deserve to ever get ya back. But I didn't ask for this disease, I was born with it. I'm in therapy and it's helping me. I can't say I will never fall off the wagon but I'm doin' the best I can ta stay sober day by day. That's as much as I can do. If the good Lord cures her, Kate, I promise I'll look after her for the rest of me livin' life."

He looks like a lost soul. Done up in a strange ill-fitting suit. Trying to please.

"You're right, Da, I can't forgive you, I just can't . . . it was too hard . . . you were too horrible . . . it was all just so awful. I know I'm a grown-up now and I see – I do see why and what happened – and I really wish you had told us the truth about your childhood. But, look, I had the same thing and I'm not a raging alcoholic nor is Ciara – I don't really buy the whole heredity thing . . ."

"I'm not making a case for that, Kate, although I do strongly believe I was born with it . . . I see myself now, sober, and obviously I could have tried to be sober years ago . . . I can't explain why I didn't try . . . I just don't have those answers yet, I maybe never will. I'm startin' to be alright with that."

"So what is it you're after? Do you want forgiveness? Are you afraid like your da of meeting your Maker with this daughter who hates you and won't forgive you?"

"No, I'm not asking you to forgive me – all I wanted to do was to apologise to ya."

"Well, go on then, get up and say the word and really mean it," I say.

He opens his mouth and then closes it again. "It's easy to say the word, Kate, I've said it before – but I'd rather show ya. But you won't let me, sure ya won't?" He stares hard at me.

I see his yellow fingers now, the curve of the onset of arthritis in them, and I see his sadness. But I am sad too. I am sad he did this to me, to us.

"I can't let you back into my life, Da, just like that, I just can't." I push back my chair and I swallow a huge lump in my throat.

"Okay, I understand." He scoops the small spilled grains of sugar from the table into his hand and dumps them into the empty coffee cups.

We both stand and face each other across the table.

"I can try to forget though," I eventually say and he sighs an audible sigh. "Let's go and sit together at ICU."

I wait for him and he falls into step with me. I cannot forget my promise to Ciara. We walk in silence and I notice how slow and frail he is. I look down to the floor and I see he has spent time polishing his cheap black shoes. They shine. I wonder what he was thinking alone in the house last night, sober and polishing his old shoes.

I am surprised to see Hugh sitting on the bench and reading the *Irish Times* when we arrive.

"What are you doing here?" I ask.

"Waiting," he says with a shrug and shuffles up to the top of the bench. "Hello, Eoin."

Da just nods in response.

"I reckon Dermot will be out with some news in . . ." Hugh pulls back his sleeve and checks his watch, "about fifty-three minutes or so."

Precise.

"Do you want a section?" He offers me some of his *Irish Times*.

I shake my head.

He catches my eye and opens his eyes up wide to indicate the silent question: am I am okay with this, with Da sitting here? I nod. I sit into the warmth of his recently vacated space and Da sits beside me. Not too close.

I can't stop staring at his polished shoes. They are moving me more than any words he has said. The simple action he took to look clean is overpowering to me. It speaks a thousand words. I'd heard stories from people in Ringsend all right that his da had been an alcoholic but that he had died in a street fight. Because Da would get so infuriated and angry anytime we mentioned his parents it became a big no-no. Rumours around Ringsend tended to grow legs so I just assumed it was a crazy story. We just believed his granny brought him up and he got a job in Canavan's garage after he left school. It was awfully sad, of course it was, and as I see him put his two feet together and place his hands on his knees I am softening again, just a little, but then my head swings me right back to his name-calling and drunken rages and his pure selfishness and I am consumed with hate again. The emotions are disturbing and exhausting.

I look away from the polished shoes and take out my phone. I text Phillip back. He sent me a text earlier to say he was thinking of us all today and to let him know as soon as we hear anything.

I know today will change my life forever. I know this is her last chance. Yes, they can go into the system again and look for donors but she won't do it again. I know that. Deep down Ciara is very religious so I know she's not as scared as I am. Her body is battered and I know she is sick to death of being sick and I don't blame her. I put myself in her shoes and I agree it is all too hard. But this will work, I grind my teeth and tell myself, as I think of her as a kid. I laugh and I know I have laughed out loud but I don't care. I can see her so clearly. Only three years younger but always weaker. She was always the sunny one. Picnic mad she was. Every Saturday all she wanted was for us to go on a picnic. Mam would have been in the bed then, I do remember that now. I think I was mixing up her being in the bed with her actually being gone. I'd make us thick ham sandwiches, and we'd put water into an old Worzel Gummidge flask and off we'd go, up to the strand. To Sandymount beach. Only a short walk but another world. It was a million miles away from the small house and dark dangerous atmosphere. We'd spread out our old pink bed-sheet and sit down on the sand and we would laugh. We would take off our shoes and socks and run in and out of the freezing sea. We were free. Ciara hadn't been well, granted, but neither was she too ill or yet diagnosed. She was never one hundred per cent but she had good days and bad. We just thought she had a constant cold because of the damp in the house and the lack of money to heat it. Here and now in my mind's eye I can see her flushed red rosy cheeks on the beach. I can hear the seagulls screeching up above. I can smell the salt and the seaweed. We would wait and wait until we'd get really hungry and then we'd tear the toilet paper off the sambos and devour them – never did bread and ham taste so good.

The black rubber doors swing open and Doctor Doyle walks out like he's just been in outer space. We all jump up and he pulls down his blue mask.

"All done, guys," he says, smiling at us.

"And?" I say.

He takes me by my elbow, sits me back down on the bench and sits beside me.

"Well, it all went really well as far as I am concerned. It is just a matter of time now, Kate. The drugs are on the way that will help her recover, so let's keep a positive attitude and we pray this time we are home and dry. As you now know only too well unfortunately, most infections happen in the first thirty days."

"When can I see her?" Da asks in a quiet voice.

"Oh, not for a good while yet, Mr Walsh."

"Thank you, Dermot. I know she could not have been in better hands," I say. I can see how fond of her he is. His eyes speak a thousand words.

Hugh starts to ask him all sorts of questions and it's like they're talking in some weird tongue. The two of them stand up as Dermot wants to stretch his legs.

"I know that feeling," Hugh says and falls into step with him.

My phone beeps. It's a number I don't know.

"Any news yet?" Emily & Gail.

Emily and Gail. Are they a couple, it dawns on me now? The joint post office account? Maybe? Who knows? Or maybe it's just easier that way for Gail to help Emily when she's not able to leave the house. I will never ask but I kinda hope they are. Emily deserves to be happy. Emily in the lilac nightie. I text back and tell them I will text again later and then I open my emails and scroll down through them. I have a few enquiries I haven't even looked at for jobs and then I draw a sharp breath as I see Mark's name come up in one of them. I open it. The internet is so slow it takes ages to download from the server.

Hi Kate, I just wanted to drop you a note to tell you that Wendy and I are back together and living in our house. Thank you.

I hope you are well?

Fondest regards,

Mark McMahon

I shut it off quickly. I am glad for him and I am especially glad for Wendy.

Hugh is back from his corridor walk with Dermot and I stuff the phone back into my pocket. They have parting words and Dermot goes back in behind the black plastic doors.

"Does Wendy know what you look like?" I ask him as he sits down next to me.

"Huh?" he says, his voice slightly high-pitched.

"Sorry, I know I'm a bit off track here with all this but I just got an email from Mark – they're back together. I'm assuming that Wendy knows what you look like?"

"Yeah, I should think so. There is a big bad internet out there. Why does it matter?"

He crumples his *Irish Times* and this time I do take the newspaper from him and smooth it down.

"Dublin is a small place – what if we bump into them?" I ask, folding the paper onto my lap.

"I don't know, Kate. I will meet her someday because I want to. I want to apologise to her face to face. She may attack me but that's alright with me too."

He doesn't want to talk about it now though, I sense that.

"Well, you will have to face her in court sometime – you will come face to face with her then, I suppose," I say.

"Yes, but that isn't definite yet – she still hasn't signed the papers to press charges so it's still just a threat." He leans towards me. "I don't really want your father to hear all this, not today, not here." His brown eyes are dark and worried and he pushes his index finger into his dimple.

"Oh, don't worry, he's stone deaf in the left ear," I say softly. "Besides, look at him – he's not even remotely listening to us – he's miles away – he hasn't heard anything we said."

"Anyway, can we just hold this conversation for a bit until we see how Ciara is?"

He takes my hand. Mine is cold and his is so warm. Mine fits into his perfectly. He also has black newsprint all over his hands, I notice, and I have a moment of how the hell am I sitting here with this man. It is the fact it feels so right that feels so strange. Almost like we have been sitting here, this comfortable around one another, for years.

"Yeah, of course we can hold it. I have some jobs here that I need to look at." I pause, choose my words carefully. "But I'm not sure how my work is going to progress now that I have a boyfriend. It's not really boyfriend-friendly work, is it? How'd you feel about me doing it now?" It's been on my mind for a while.

"Well, I don't want you to take this the wrong way or feel it is in any way controlling," Hugh says quietly with a glance at my da, "or any of my business for that matter, but I'm not sure I'm going to like you going out with other guys. And hear me out now – it isn't because of the job, it's because I'm terrified you might fall for one of them. Temptation is the greatest killer of relationships."

"That's so cute," I say. "I understand completely. If the shoe was on the other foot I would feel exactly the same way. I have a new business idea I'm already working on anyway." I squeeze his warm hand.

Da coughs.

Hugh reaches over for the paper on my knee.

I stare at the floor for a while. I feel so useless. I tap my feet. I just want to be in there with her. It's so frustrating. I can't stand waiting and doing nothing, never could. I feel useless.

I say, "I need to do something, Hugh. I can't sit here, I can't just do nothing while she is in there."

"May I suggest a corridor walk?" He looks at me over his paper.

He stands and so do I.

"I used to suggest this to the families of patients while they were waiting on the transfer to ICU. You count the steps. Like this . . ." We start to walk and he counts one, two, three, four and so on, until we reach the end of the corridor. "Sixteen, seventeen, eighteen, nineteen and twenty." He stops. "Okay, good, twenty – this is a good short corridor. Now you have to go back and sit and think of twenty things you like to eat and write them down. Doesn't have to be things you like to eat – it can be your top twenty movies or slow songs – one time a mother of one of my patients wrote down her twenty favourite sexual positions, I kid you not, and this was long before *Fifty Shades of Grey*. Shit, we have no paper, have we? Okay, let's go to the nurses' station and get paper and a pen . . ."

I stop him there by squeezing his shoulder. "Not really for me, Hugh," I say and I know what I need to do: I need to dance. But I cannot leave the hospital. The urge in me to dance is insane. My feet twitch and my head moves from side to side. I need to clear my head. It's my meditation. I owe so much to dance, to Phillip. Without it I'd have been a very lonely girl. It helped me get rid of fears and aggression in a positive way. I glance at Hugh. Maybe I can let it go a little now I have this man in my life. Maybe I can spend more time with Ciara at home and get along a bit better with my da. Maybe I can take weekend breaks in Oughterard with Hugh and visit Ma. And with these thoughts in my head I cry out inwardly, 'Please, God, let this work for Ciara!'

Hugh and Da are chatting now. A young girl stops in front of us with a hot beverage trolley. I order three coffees and pay for them. She pours in silence and as she hands them over she smiles at me and I smile back at her.

"It's not great but it is lukewarm and strong." Hugh makes a sour face when he says 'strong' – he's not really selling it to me.

I sip mine as I sit. I am still trying to clear my mind.

I close my eyes and listen as they go back to their conversation. I pretend I'm not listening but I am. I pretend I am trying to get a few winks of sleep. Forty winks or is it fifty? They are talking about religion of all things. Hugh is telling Da he was never that religious, that his parents always attended Sunday Mass but he didn't after the age of about fifteen, but that he is very spiritual nevertheless. Da is telling Hugh that Father Brennan saved his life. Now Hugh is telling Da that Father Brennan may have saved his life too and Da asks how and Hugh is about to tell him when I power my eyes open and go to stop them . . . just as Dermot and his masked team push out through the black plastic doors with herself on the bed.

"Ciara!" I jump up.

Now she is officially in recovery.

I run and stand by her still body.

"Not too close, Kate, please!" Dermot calls through his green mask. "She is going straight to ICU." He is being Strict Doctor Dermot.

I stand back as I watch them fuss around her, holding up tubes and wires and bags of clear liquid. I feel so helpless.

"You can talk to her, she can hear you, Kate," Dermot says then.

"Oh. Yeah. Right. Well . . . I was just sitting here with . . . with the Da, ya know, Ciara . . . the pair of us chatting away . . . he was telling me all about Clery's and his da and all that stuff. I know you must know all about his childhood but you knew it wasn't your place to tell me . . . I don't know how you are so wise and so kind . . . I suppose what I'm trying to say, Ciara, is that I understand now why you stayed with him." I know Da can hear all this but I don't care. It actually feels good.

One of the nurses presses the button on the lift and I can't see Ciara's face because I can't get that close to her. I wonder where she is inside her mind? Is she terrified? So I rabbit on because I know she will want to hear my voice.

Da and Hugh stand by me now and the tension is palpable amongst the three of us. I keep going like a wound-up toy.

"Anyway . . . or as Da says ananyways . . . what I'm saying here, Ciara, my darling sister, is that I kept my promise to you. Now if you decide to get better and get up off yer skinny arse, well, I don't see . . . I mean . . . I can't see why the three of us can't go down to Oughterard, to Galway together and visit Ma . . . now if that isn't a real *Little House on the Prairie* happily-ever-after ending for you I don't know what is."

I laugh and a bell rings out signalling the imminent arrival of the lift, then the doors open and they quickly push her in and as the doors close I fall to my knees and howl like a baby with the realisation that this is probably her last chance.

Recovery time ebbs by slowly as I avoid *VIP* and read old copies of *Take A Break* and *National Geographic*. Hugh is quiet. He is tapping away on his phone a lot.

We can't get in to see her but Dermot is constantly keeping us updated. Initial signs are good, her body is responding nicely. So we all get on with things, me, Da and Hugh. I clean Da's house top to toe every morning before I meet Hugh to go up to the hospital. I bleach it within an inch of its life in case she gets the all clear to come home. I have stocked up on hand-sanitizers and every other germ-killing product available on the market that I can get my hands on. Ten days in and Dermot tells us that they have detected a blood infection but they are on top of it. However, Ciara will remain in ICU for longer than he originally hoped. I would do anything to see her. I ache to see her face. I take in Dermot's news as I stop reading about a woman who drank eleven bottles of wine a night and how a reality star lost two stone in two days in a hot Jacuzzi.

I thank Dermot and turn to Da. He isn't coping well. His face is drawn and he pulls at his bottom lip, pinching the blood clear away. Calmly I tell Da this is all to be expected. Once they have it under control we have no need to worry. He paces the corridor, doing Hugh's twenty-something test.

Days pass and she seems to be recovering well. I keep Ma

and Gail posted.

Then Dermot informs us she has now come down with a bladder infection, which in her case has caused blood clots in her urine. Still I read on about the woman who married her son and I try to focus on the most magnificent pictures the most incredible photographers in the world have taken of our planet. I even read all about the reality TV stars and their drunken feuds.

"Entirely to be expected, Mr Walsh," Hugh tells a counting Da. It's like a scene from the movie *Awakenings*.

We just sit still and wait, day after day, as everyone else does with a loved one recovering in ICU. There is nothing else to do. The frivolous magazines have a purpose here, hey, have a real job in waiting rooms – they are so full of nonsense that you can, for a page at least, get lost in them. Suddenly I understand Ciara's love of *VIP* magazine and the vacant people who grace their pages.

Dermot updates us constantly. He tells me he read to her for an hour last night – he didn't say what it was but I can see now that he is actually in love with her. He keeps us upbeat and tells us all the signs are really positive, these little setbacks are normal. Thirty to one hundred days recovery. The biggest fear, that of graft-versus-host disease setting in, has not occurred. The immune cells in Mam's transplanted bone marrow have not recognised Ciara's body as foreign and attacked it. Maybe it was her mammy she needed all along.

Wait. Wait. Wait.

Tick. Tock. Tick. Tock.

Bong. Bong. Bong.

Then things turn around, twenty long days later. Her blood cell counts look good. She nails it. She can come home.

Chapter Twenty-three

The first time I saw her as she emerged from the ICU I cried. Not huge emotional sobs but a quiet, sophisticated opening of my tear ducts. She looked ill, of course she did, but she had a massive smile on her face.

"Home, James," was all she had said.

Da has the house spotless on the day she is discharged and I am impressed. We gently get Ciara from the ambulance, up the pathway and into the hallway. I have a disinfected chair left at the end of the stairs for her to rest. She sits. But not for too long before we help her up the stairs. I have plastic covers on the banisters to prevent dust. She is still incredibly weak and thin as I help her into bed. I have fresh hypoallergenic sheets and pillowcases on her bed and new organic cotton pyjamas for her to get into. Fuck you, Germs, is what.

All Ciara wants to do, is sleep.

"Do you want a cuppa tea?" I ask Da when I come back downstairs.

He sits heavily into the kitchen chair.

"Eh . . . that'd be lovely, Kate." He looks happily relieved that I'm not running straight out.

"Don't worry, Da, I will stay to take care of her with you," I tell him.

"Will you?" His eyes light up, the yellow fading slightly.

He is still so frightened, I realise.

"Absolutely. I'm meeting Hugh for a quick dinner at five but I will come back here straight after and get her sorted for the night."

He is drumming his fingers on the table.

"What about her tea? Will she wanna eat? I wouldn't know what to do there." he says. He knows I'm not going to react well to this.

I fill the kettle, click it on to boil, pull out the chair and I sit. I take a long deep breath.

"Da, after we have a cuppa tea, I have a while to fill so I'm going to teach you how to make a basic stew." I say this to him as you might speak to a naughty child. "Ciara's going to need something easily digested, like a stew – even if she just has the soup off it she'll be getting all the goodness from the meat and veg."

His look back to me is priceless.

"Ah here now, that's not somethin' I could do! Ask yer ma – I've never cooked a thing. I can peel potatoes and wash a cabbage but that's about it." He is shaking his head.

"Welcome to 2015, Eoin Walsh. Aren't you a changed man and all that? Time to live in the real world. I'm telling you, all Ciara will manage for weeks will be small bowls of healthy foods and you will need to learn how to cook them."

I know I can cook them for her but a part of me thinks he should learn to look after himself now too.

The kettle boils. I make us a pot and we have our tea in silence. I throw a few digestives on a plate. Neither one of us touch them. I study the gold buildings on my coaster. Then I stand and walk around the kitchen with my tea in my hand, checking the contents of the presses. I grab a pen from the drawer and some paper to make a shopping list for us. My phone beeps. I go to check it. It's Hugh confirming dinner plans for later in Pasta Fresca. I'm a little disappointed we aren't just staying in, I acknowledge, as I throw various gone-off items into the bin. I am craving sex with Hugh. I think about sex with him a lot. An awful lot. Sex just didn't seem right while Ciara was in the ICU – euphoria wasn't right, and it would be euphoric. Hugh was fine with that. We both want it to be special. He has been quiet the last few days but I have been so preoccupied I'm sure he's just giving me space. I can't get his naked body out of my mind's eye. I'd love to go to a dance class tomorrow. I open the fridge and throw out all the rest of the gone-off vegetables and meats.

"Honestly, Da, how can you not get the smell when you open the fridge?" I hold my nose.

"I dunno," he shrugs. "Whiskey nose probably."

I grunt at him as I finish the list and pull on my cardigan before gently placing the bottle of disinfectant and a cloth in front of him.

"Okay, Da, when you have scrubbed the fridge you need to buy what's on this list. Some stewing beef, carrots, parsnips, an onion, and Oxtail soup – there's a big bag of potatoes in the press."

His jaw drops and his yellow fingers dance around his chin. "I dunno about this, Kate – I could poison her." He is honestly fearful.

"You won't poison her – it's a simple dish. Fail to prepare, prepare to fail. Wash your hands well. I bought extra strong disinfectant soap. It's exceptionally easy. Sure didn't I learn how to cook it at ten years old? Are you listening to me?"

He seems miles away.

I pull my chair over beside him, just as close as I have to be. We both feel the tension of our bodies being so close. Again he smells of Ciara's favourite Dove shower gel so I relax a little. I twirl the blue ballpoint pen between my thumb and forefinger and smooth out the back of the page I have written his shopping list on.

"So, wash your vegetables well – your carrots, parsnips etcetera first and chop them –"

He interrupts, "With what?" Panic all over his old face.

"Sorry?"

"What do I chop the vegetables with?" he demands, slightly annoyed.

"Are you serious?" I drop the pen.

"Well, I'm bleedin' sorry but, Kate, I've never chopped carrots, or bleedin' par'isnips or anytin' like that before, have I?" He sighs heavily.

Weary at this stage, there is only one thing for it. I pull my iPhone from my cardigan pocket and type Google into my Safari, and I hope to God no one ever sees my browser history. **"How to chop vegetables."** I click videos.

I press play and he watches, genuinely enthralled.

"Would ya look at tha'!" He stares hard, squinting into the screen of the phone.

"Okay," I say when the mind-blowing vegetable-chopping tutorial ends.

"Isn't that yolk fantastic all de same," he says.

I nod and carry on. "Then just as with the carrots and parsnips, using the same knife even, chop your onion." The onion wasn't part of the last tutorial for some reason.

"An onion!" He cowers behind his hands.

"Yes. An onion." I am most definitely losing the little amount of patience I possess.

"They're awful things to cut up, Luke Griffin tells me . . . but go on, I can manage – I'll borrow them goggles Kieran O'Reilly the mechanic two doors down uses for welding."

"Okay!" I hold up my hand. "Please just let me get to the end now and we can google instructional videos after it all."

He nods slowly with a look a child might have when you tell them you are ambidextrous.

"This is the easiest stew to make. Now, I will also write all this down for you. I'm not expecting miracles – most likely Ciara won't eat anything much tonight anyway, or for the next few days. She has supplement drinks the hospital gave me. She said she might like some plain rice, but I want you to try and make the stew. You can use Ciara's phone for the video instructions."

He nods.

I say, "Heat some oil, a tablespoon, in the large saucepan and brown the 454g packet of beef. That means cook it until it's not pink any more but brown. Add the onion, carrots and parsnips and brown until they are lightly coloured. Bang in a bit of salt and pepper . . ." How I don't laugh at the shock on his face . . . His mouth is literally hanging open, like he's witnessing a home birth.

"Make up the packet of Oxtail soup, with 600ml of water – the instructions are on the packet and the glass measuring jug is in the press – add it to the vegetables. Place the lid on the saucepan and bring it to the boil. Bringing it to the boil means the pot of water should be boiling with bubbles. Lower the gas, turn the flames down, and let it simmer – that is, let it sit there for about an hour and a half but keep a watch on it so the water doesn't boil off. While this is cooking boil up yer spuds. Any questions?" I bite my lip so as not to laugh.

He has a very strong look of Father Dougal Maguire from *Father Ted*. I am aware of his confusion but I am kind of enjoying it. You want your place back at this table, pal, you bloody well earn it back.

"Jaysus," is all he manages.

"Okay, so that's it. I will type it into Ciara's Google videos for you – just press play." I point the play button out to him and he nods. "Have a bowl of stew ready for her to try for five o'clock and take it up to her on the tray with a pint of water. You never know, the home cooking may awaken her taste buds. I will leave her medication on the blue saucer in her room. Be sure she takes it. I won't disturb her now but you will have to wake her at five even if she is still sound asleep. I'm going to buy a bell of some description so she can ring it when she needs us. I'm having dinner in town with Hugh but I will be back here immediately after. I won't be long."

I get up.

"What if it's shite and she can't eat it?" he asks.

"I'm going to make her some rice now just in case – you can just heat that up – she said she fancied some plain boiled rice anyway."

He looks relieved. "Will I make a fresh bed up for you in your room?" he says as I make my way to the press to get the rice.

"No, I'll just kip on the couch," I tell him.

He says nothing, picks up his list and heads for the shops.

Then I spot the bottle of disinfectant on the table and realise I should have made him clean the fridge before he went. Afraid he might forget to do it, I heave a sigh and start to scour the fridge.

But he has another think coming if he thinks I'm looking after his belly. I'm convinced I will see the empty brown-paper bags of a Chinese delivery in the Green wheelie bin when I return later. I prepare some rice and put it in a bowl with tin-foil on top and pop it in the now pristine fridge. I leave him a note with instructions on how to heat it and I leave.

Town is alive on one of those gorgeous evenings that are rare, warm, bright and filled with music. A real Dublin picture-perfect evening. I stroll through St Stephen's Green and watch the lovers and the fighters. When the sun is out in Dublin there really is nowhere in the world I would rather be. I cross at the lights onto a bustling Grafton Street and weave my way between the street entertainers, the preachers and the clipboard muggers. I turn down onto Chatham Street and Hugh is seated at the window seat of Pasta Fresca. He waves at me and I wave back. The smells coming from inside make my mouth water and again I realise I am starvin' marvin'.

As I approach the table Hugh stands.

"Hi, Kate," he says with a smile as I slide into my seat opposite him.

God, he looks gorgeous, I hear myself say in my own head and am starting to become unfamiliar with myself. Swoony Kate Walsh. Heart-shape-hand-maker in training. He is wearing a denim shirt, top three buttons undone, black jeans and runners. Freshly washed hair still damp. He is sexy and yet cute at the same time. I want to hold his hands across the table. I want to kiss his dimple. He is fussing with his chair, pulling it in and pushing it out. He isn't quite himself, I see now, and he seems irritated.

"Are you okay?" I finally ask after he is happy with the position of his chair.

"Yeah, I'm . . . it's on a slope or something . . . I can't seem to get it right." He pulls back from the table again.

He stands now and starts pulling the table closer to him and the salt and pepper fall over as I grab the empty glasses just in the nick of time. I just stare at him as he next takes a napkin and folds it over and over before pushing it under the leg of his chair. He sits. Wobbles himself and then sees my face.

"Sorry," he says calmly.

"Quite all right," I say.

"How is Ciara doing?"

"She's doing really well, I think. She's resting and all the signs still look good. It's one day at a time as you told me. Dermot's been just . . . hard to put it into words . . . he's on the phone all the time . . . he's coming by tonight after his shift just to check on her." I take up the water jug, pour us both a glass.

"I'm so pleased to hear that . . . I think it's the one . . . with these medicines her recovery will take. I'm pretty confident about that. I think Dermot may be abusing the code of conduct though." He winks at me.

"Yeah, he's mad about her, isn't he?" I smile.

"Nuts," Hugh confirms my suspicions. He pours the wine he'd ordered before I arrived.

"That's great, I'm sure she really likes him too, so who knows?"

We clink glasses.

We discuss Ciara's triumphant return home then I ask him if we can go and see a movie tomorrow night. I've never actually been to the movies with a bloke before, imagine that!

"Like a proper date night," I gush at his handsome face.

"Yeah . . . no, sorry, I can't, Kate . . . I was just about to tell you . . . I have to head back to London for a few days," he says, just like that.

My heart sinks into the bottom of the deep blue sea. Lost. The Heart of The Ocean.

"Oh. Is everything all right?" I'm worried.

"It's . . . loose ends . . . things I need to tie up."

He pours more wine into his own glass but I've hardly touched mine yet.

I feel slightly on edge. It's his face. I can't describe it but it's hiding something.

"Did someone call you? Ask you to come back to London? I couldn't help but notice you were on your phone a lot at the hospital over the last few weeks." I'm a bit nervous now so I pick up my wineglass. The huge glass almost masks his face across the small table.

"That was my dad," he informs me and takes a long drink of the velvety red.

"Oh right – did he ring you or did you ring him?" My question is so dumb.

275

"Which time?" He looks at me, slightly confused.

"How many times did he call you?"

"A lot, he's been phoning me a lot. It's . . . private."

"Oh." I am starting to go red. I don't know what to say.

The waitress breaks the silence and hands us menus but I don't really see the dishes and I don't hear her specials and suddenly I'm not hungry. A couple come in and sit across from us. She is stunning. Dressed in a beautiful white dress with a thick brown leather belt and brown gladiator sandals. Copper-blonde hair all big and bouncy and bright red lips. I look at myself and for the first time in my life I kinda wish I'd made a slight bit of an effort. Hugh is studying the menu intently.

"Look . . . sorry . . . I don't mean private per se . . . it's just family stuff, Kate . . . I don't really want to talk about it." He rubs his right hand over the menu card on the table.

"Cool. No probs." I try a breezy voice but my heart is pounding.

"We've had enough to deal with the past few weeks, I just want to have a nice meal with a nice glass of wine and relax."

"Me too." I look up and give him a breezy smile to match my breezy voice as he picks up his menu again.

"Mmmm, all looks delicious, doesn't it?" he says from behind the square brown cardboard menu.

"Doesn't it?" I say, not having seen a thing.

We read in silence.

Hugh asks about my choice as he pulls the menu down from in front of his face

"Carbonara," I say. Cardboard would taste the same.

"With red?" He makes a face.

"Yeah, with red," I say. I'm starting to feel defensive.

"Okay, bit out there but hey . . . sounds good me too." He leans across and takes my hands.

I can see he is off. He can see I am off.

"It's no big deal, okay? I've always known that I have to sort my life out back home, Kate. I'm only renting here short-term . . . I can't run away from it . . . that's why Dad was calling . . . he is right . . . I never want to go back but I have . . . I have . . ."

Who do I think I am? What am I doing?

"Go!" I smile brightly at him and hold the smile for as long as I can. "God, Hugh, go home and sort your life out. It will be good for you. Closure or whatever they call it. I'm not going anywhere plus I'm so busy with Ciara and work and my own family stuff – which you have been so cool about by the way and so amazingly helpful. I'll be here when you get back. You must miss your folks and friends and won't they just be delighted to see how well you're doing? We are good, you and me. It's just nice the way it is, so let's just play it by ear, okay? We are good." I squeeze his perfect hands.

Baby steps, Kate. This is all too fast. I'm not a jump-in kinda girl. I have boundaries. Barriers. I'm falling too hard and too fast. I'm gonna get crucified.

We make chit-chat for a while but I can see he's not convinced with what I have just said – it's like he's struggling with it – but then the waitress arrives and we order our Carbonaras and I order a side plate of garlic bread with cheese for us to share and I quickly change the subject. I have no choice.

"Would you like me to dress like her?" I whisper

277

across to him as I nod in the direction of the gladiator-sandal-clad, Jennifer Aniston lookalike. I was always slightly put out by the beach-babe look, that long sun-streaked, tossed, messy mane of thick hair and those cool effortless-looking clothes.

"Goodness no! I have dated too many girls who spend way too much time on themselves . . . no time for it . . . you are a natural beauty, Kate. I love how I wake up with you and you actually look like the same person I went to sleep with. It's most reassuring."

He laughs now and I'm delighted to see he is more relaxed.

"Have you bought condoms yet?" I whisper.

"Well, yes . . . but I didn't think it right to tell you this ridiculous rubbery news while we were in a hospital and getting three hours sleep most nights, and we weren't physically together anyway . . ." He grins. "But I'm sure we can fix that this evening."

"I'm afraid it will have to wait now as I have to get back to Da as soon as we are done here. I have him cooking a stew – he'll most likely have burnt the gaff down." I laugh.

"The what down?" he asks.

"The house. You are more than welcome to come back for a coffee if you want?" I offer easily.

"You know, I'm pretty bushed myself. I'm happy with a good feed, some fine grape, the best company in the world and an early night."

That's good enough for me.

Our food arrives and we eat and chat. I feel more relaxed now. I can't foresee the future no matter how hard I may try.

Chapter Twenty-four

This job isn't one of the most interesting ones I have had to date, I freely admit. I am masquerading as a spectator at a gymkhana. The owners are trying to up the numbers. They just need bodies for the photos they are taking to put on their website and for their flyers and booklets. I have to be seen to be standing up and cheering. It's more a modelling job, I think now. I have been thinking a lot about my job and thinking of better ways to move it forward. I have decided to get new business cards made up this week. A new venture. The ponies are so cute and I clap and cheer and they clear the tiniest fences. I don't much like the smell of horses. Horse riding has always been a thing Ciara would love to do, so soon I'm hoping I can bring her here and put her up on a quiet schooled house.

I finish up before lunch and get my money. The owners are so sweet and tell me any time I want to ride just to pop in and it's on the house.

Going home by taxi, I check my iPhone. No messages

from him. I wonder how Hugh is getting on back in London with his folks; he left in a bit of a hurry yesterday. From what he has told me about them they seem lovely but I know they will try to convince him to stay and take up his position at the hospital again. I can't really let myself think about that. What if he gets back and he realises it is where he belongs? Well, I could move to London, couldn't I? Ha! And leave your family, my inner voice asks, and I actually burst out laughing in the taxi. Suddenly I see them all: Mam, Dad and Ciara. The Family. Who would ever have guessed this turnaround? It feels strange but good-strange, like a very old jigsaw with some missing pieces suddenly being found under the rug and the jigsaw completed.

Hugh will come back to Ireland, I know, because he has told me how much he loves the place. He doesn't love London any more, he never did. Whether he comes back to me is another question. The taxi takes me back to Da's in little or no traffic and I pay the driver and let myself in. I open the door and I'm hit by the smell of sizzling garlic.

"Ciara Walsh, are you out of that bloody bed?" I yell as Da comes out of the kitchen, his finger over his mouth.

"*Shhhhuusssh*! She's asleep!" He's waving a kitchen knife. An image that once upon a time would have paralysed me

Now I simply ask as I follow him in, "What are you cooking?" I stare at the various ingredients all over the counter tops.

The stew has been a resounding success. He has taken to cooking like a duck to water, even saying to me when I got home after eating in Pasta Fresca, "Ah, Italian food. I've been watching loads on how to cook Italian – ya know ya can actually maker yer own pasta? I can't understan' why anyone would buy those jars of sauces when it's much easier and adds much more flavour to make your own. I've been watchin' how to make them, easy peesy. I'm gona try a lasagne next week." He had proudly shown me the bowl of stew he had left for me to taste when I returned home after Pasta Fresca. Ciara had indeed eaten some and declared it delicious. Upon taste I was pleasantly proud.

"I'm doin' a . . ." He bends down and squints at the open cookbook. "A. Chilli. Con. Carne." He says the words like they are Japanese.

He has Ciara's iPhone set up on the chopping board and he presses play again.

An American voice booms out at me. He has the volume too loud.

"*Sooooo, once you have your gaaaarlic pressed, take your . . .*"

Da presses pause. "Ahh here . . . hang on, mister, will ya? Where's the fire? Jaysus . . . he goes way too fast, this bloke! Give us a second to press the bleedin' garlic! This is all new to me." He swipes his head repeatedly into the crook of his arm, wiping his brow. I watch him for a few seconds.

"Fair play to ya, Da," I say as I go and fill the kettle.

He takes his head slowly out of the crook of his arm and looks at me.

"Thank you, Kate," he says and I see he's delighted with the first ever compliment I have given him that isn't sarcastic. Eoin Walsh looks proud of himself.

He chops away in his new little world, pressing play and pause every few seconds.

I make a cuppa and I watch him cook as I sip and dip a chocolate digestive in and out. He's so into it I do my best not to laugh. He answers the professional chef all the time with a lot of "I am's" and "I'm not's". Then I hear the bell ring. She is awake.

"I'll go," I tell him as he swings to attention and drops his knife.

I take the stairs two at a time. I squeeze the antiseptic fluids on the windowsill of the landing onto my hands. I push open her bedroom door. The first thing I see is colour. Her face has colour and she looks like a different person. It's as though the black-and-white version of her in a colouring book has been carefully coloured in by a very talented child. All inside the lines.

"Seriously, if they are ever looking for people to play Rip Van Winkle in your dance place, I can't stay awake!" she says through a severe dry mouth, her lips stuck, and I hand her the glass of water from her side table.

"How are you feeling?" I ask as I help her sit up a bit and fix her pillows.

"Seriously, Kate, I can't stay awake long enough to find out," she says with a grin.

"You look good," I tell her.

"Do I?"

She knows it must be true. I don't lie. I nod up and down several times, taking her all in.

"What is that gorgeous smell?" she asks.

"That would be Chef de Walsh cooking up a storm in the kitchen."

"Huh?"

"Da – he's at it again. I think it's safe to say he has officially taken up cooking."

282

"This is mad – I thought he was winding me up when he said he made that stew – I'm not sure if it's the return of my taste buds but it was gorgeous!" Her eyes narrow. "I honestly presumed it was one of those expensive Marks & Spencer's ones. He must have a talent."

"Yeah, believe it or not, Eoin Walsh cooked that for you from scratch. We'd better hope he doesn't want to start making flambéed pancakes or we could be in trouble again!"

And then we start to laugh and laugh and laugh and we can't stop. Tears spill from my eyes. Tears spill from her eyes. It seems in this moment, to us, the funniest thing ever.

"Ahh stop, Kate, that's terrible." She wipes her eyes with the palms of her hands. "Here, pass me a tissue. He's doing so well, isn't he?"

"He is," I happily acknowledge as I pass her a Scotties hypoallergenic tissue.

"Dermot thinks I'm going to be fine," she dabs her eyes and says now, her voice suddenly serious.

"You will be, he will make sure of it," I tell her.

"He's amazing, isn't he?" She flushes a little.

"Truly a brilliant doctor and an all-round nice fella." I don't want to pry. I'm sure she will tell me soon enough that they like each other in *that* way. "Rest there now and I will bring you up a bowl of his chilli in a while – see how brave you really are, Ciara Walsh." I kiss her softly and she grabs my hands.

"I don't know where I'd be without you, Kate," she says.

"Ditto," I say.

"I love you, Kate."

"I love you, Ciara."

I walk out and go downstairs. I avoid the kitchen as the fumes are pretty heavy on the back of my throat. Smells spicy! I cough as I go into the sitting room and sit on the couch to call Phillip. I am on duty now. The fundraiser is all systems go. All our ex-pros have agreed to dance for us and Maura has managed to get a really famous English ballerina she knows, Nina Nunes (Maura has been a lifelong friend of her mother's – they used to dance together at the Royal in the sixties), to come to Dublin for one night only and dance *Swan Lake*. Well . . . our version of *Swan Lake*. Phillip has picked pieces from the entire thing and made a smaller-scale show. He has mood boards and storyboards up all around the studio. We are getting posters made up and flyers because I figure we need the advertising as we pretty much need to sell out the theatre. Rehearsals start with the others tomorrow and Nina the Ballerina comes into Dublin the Friday before the show on Saturday.

"One rehearsal?" I'm not convinced.

"Seriously? Is you mental? Is you? She is a world-famous *Swan Lake* ballerina – she is retired now but she can come out and do the Macarena for all I care!" He is spitting.

"We have to pretty much sell out Belvedere College to make this work," I tell him.

"And we will!" he snaps into the phone.

"Now, now."

"I'm edgy, alright? So anyway let's focus . . . the two local ballet groups are involved now – they're practising the routine I gave them and they are really eager which is fab. I sourced the most amazing gay orchestra, the Bander

284

Boys – they are the ones who play in The Den every Sunday afternoon and they are working away on their parts . . . everyone is rehearsing so well together, the studio feels magical . . . it's a no-brainer . . . you just need to sell it, leave the rest to me. I might even . . ."

My phone beeps in my ear and I take it away to look at the receiver. I hurriedly put it back to my ear and speak to Phillip.

"Can I get this? It's Hugh, he's in London – I'll call you straight back?"

"Whatevs!" He cuts me off.

I switch calls. "Hello!"

"Hi, Kate," he says.

"Hiya! How's it going there?" I am thrilled to hear his posh voice.

Silence greets my enthusiasm.

"Hugh? Hello?"

Silence.

"Hugh? Can you hear me?" I talk louder into the receiver and move quickly to the window to get better coverage.

"Sorry . . . I'm . . . I'm in The Portland," he tells me. The line mustn't be great his end.

"The Portland? Isn't that a maternity hospital?" I say, confused.

He goes quiet again before he says quite clearly now: "It is. I don't quite know how to say this, Kate . . . but . . . my ex-girlfriend is having our baby."

I drop the phone. Not dramatically. It just falls out of my hand onto the old threadbare carpet. I grab it up with shaking hands and push it back into my ear. His words fly around my brain. *Ex-girlfriend. Baby. Ex-girlfriend. Baby.*

"Huh?" I manage to speak the word and nod my head.

"Please, Kate . . . don't hang up . . . I know this is bizarre but I can explain . . . well, I want to try." His voice echoes on the other end of the phone.

"You are going to have a baby," I pant.

"Let me explain, please, give me five minutes – I was as shocked as you are when I found out . . ."

I find the words somehow. "Go ahead." My body is bolt upright, muscles tense. From the other room I can hear Da giving out to his professional chef.

"It's been . . . well, as you know . . . well, you don't know but it's been very complicated. Charlotte and I broke up long before I came to Dublin, and although she tried to contact me and talk to me after I just never called her back . . . we haven't been . . ."

"So are you back together?" I don't want to know the answer before I even ask the question.

"No! No . . . I don't want that . . . but I can't quite take in the fact we're going to have a baby . . . I'm all confused, Kate, you see . . . after what happened with Deirdre at the hospital, Charlotte was so kind to me . . . I told her I needed space so I shut her out . . . I didn't want to talk to her at all . . ."

I stop him there. "No, Hugh, the way I see it is you never acknowledged your pregnant girlfriend and started fucking me." I'm not shouting. I'm totally devastated.

"That's just simply not true, Kate," he says quietly. "I didn't know. We'd broken up."

We both just breathe into our phones.

I am so shocked that I could be capable of misreading someone so dreadfully badly. I haven't even hit any other emotion. I'm not this type of woman. You can't fool me like this. I'm not one of those eejits I read about in the crappy magazines who swear they really had no idea their boyfriend was secretly in a relationship with a pregnant girlfriend. ICU reading. Numbskulls, I called them, brain-dead. *Duh!!!!* Open your eyes and ears, stupid woman. Now I was she. The numbskull brain-dead blind woman.

"Kate? Are you there?" His voice is calm, not shaky as I would have imagined.

"Yes," I answer.

"Hear me out, please. I left London because I couldn't cope with my life . . . I was getting worse not better . . . Charlotte and I, we stayed together after a fashion after Deirdre's death but I wasn't present . . . I was on the verge of a nervous breakdown, as you well know. She tried to keep the relationship going by just calling over to me and staying in my flat, staring at the TV alongside me, but she got nothing back . . . one day she just stopped calling and I hadn't seen her in over six months before I left to come here. I solemnly promise you I didn't know she was expecting until I got a call from her. She had, rightfully, contacted my folks looking for my number . . . my folks had been very fond of Charlotte. Anyway she doesn't want us to get back together or anything like that – it's completely over. She just wants to be honest with me and wants me to have the opportunity to be involved in my child's life if I so wish. I'm just starting to feel like I can cope again, Kate. I won't run away from this, God no, but I'm . . . I'm scared of losing you now . . ." His voice is higher pitched.

"You better get off the phone to me, Hugh. That girl . . . Charlotte . . . is lying in labour with your child – grow some balls and go in there and support her and be a father to your child." I hang up. He won't like this Kate Walsh.

I pace the living room, clutching the phone so tight my skin burns. I've lost him, I know I have. I believe him that they had broken up and that he didn't know she was expecting and I don't know why but I still feel stupid. Like he was making an idiot out of me. I feel like a complete fool, like what we had was somehow fraudulent. Like he was never mine to begin with. I always knew this love thing was a farce, a joke – how did I fall so hard and so fast? But he had loved me back. He had, he wasn't that good an actor. I can't shake the feeling however that I have been taken for a big long jolly ride. I leave the room, grab my cardigan from the banisters and go into the kitchen.

"I have to go out for a while, Da," I say. "Can you take her up some food when it's ready?"

He nods in distraction and shoo-shoos me with his hand – he can't hear the chef. I grab my bag and leave, heading for the only person I know who can listen and not judge.

"The prodigal friend returns. I hope you are here to work – there are so many tickets to be sold still." Phillip is slightly miffed with me as he opens the door in a towel.

I barely make it through the door before I erupt into a spectacular waterfall of tears.

"His ex-girlfriend is having his baby!" I sob.

"Good grief, girl, it's like a Jilly Cooper novel exploded all over my doorstep! Come, come, come, come and sit!" He leads me into the living room. His towel falls and his big pink naked bottom stares at me. He doesn't even bother to retrieve the towel, he's so concerned to get me seated and to ply me with wine. Even now that I am desperately unhappy I know he cannot contain his excitement that there is drama. Phillip thrives on any kind of drama. He can't help it.

He is probably the only person who has ever seen me cry. I cry and cry as I fall onto the couch and as predicted he returns from the kitchen, now robed, with a bottle of red wine tucked under his arm and his claw-like grip holding two glasses.

"Spill." He curls his bare feet under him. His toenails are painted bright purple.

I compose my pathetic self.

"Can you believe this? Can you? He went back to London to sort a few bits but I felt he was being a bit off. Then, just now, he just calls me from the Portland Hospital. I casually mention that I thought it was a maternity hospital, thinking in my weird head he was there for some sort of job interview! Then he says: 'It is. My ex-girlfriend is having our baby.'"

"Sweet Dame Oscar-Winning-Aging-Perfectly Helen Mirren, that is unbelievable hashtag in totes and utter disbelief here, chuck!" He pours the warm red to the very top, his face flushed with the excitement of the drama.

This time I accept gratefully.

"What an asshole!" he says and, even though I feel Hugh is not an asshole, I don't disagree with Phillip. "Was he spitting the 'she doesn't understand me like you do' line at you?"

"No," I say.

"Do you believe that she is his ex?"

"I dunno."

"Do you feel stupid?"

"Yes," I answer.

"Well, you are not. You are not one bit stupid, Kate. He tricked you. Been there done that with Bobby – remember – he had a husband in Hawaii?"

"I think I'm in love with him though. I think about him all the time, I feel happy when he's with me, I need him, he's my happy drug. Look at all the good shit that has happened since he came into my life. Ciara is, please God, getting better, Mam is around in our lives again, Da off the drink . . . it's like he was sent to fix me, Phillip." I am in real pain. My stomach actually aches.

"Don't be a nana – all that stuff would have happened anyway and you know I'm still mad you use your copy of *The Secret* to prop up your couch. You allowed your mother to know you forgive her for leaving, you moved on with your newly sober dad. The Universe was supposed to make Ciara better and Hugh is just a big smelly prick with big smelly balls." He swirls his wine, world put to rights as far as he is concerned.

"He doesn't have smelly balls," I say and I have no idea why.

"Well, you know what I mean – now drink up, we're going out!"

"Do not make me go out! Look at the state of me!" I wail.

"He's not worth it. You deserve it all – the kindest, nicest man there is – and don't forget our forty-five-year-old pact. If neither of us is married by then we marry one another, right?" He extends his pinkie and I curl mine around it. "Come, little one, help Phillip dress."

I follow him into his bedroom. You would be forgiven for thinking someone had magically transported you to a red light district. It was that red. I sit on the bed.

"You can't make someone want you the way you want them, Kate." He drops the robe and pulls on skintight, second-skin red jeans over his Persil-white Y-fronts. "You taught me that." He pulls on a black tee and a green blazer. Grabs his massive leather bikers' boots with silver studs and stuffs his sockless feet into them, holding onto his door for support.

He is right.

"Out!" He is already Haloing a cab on his phone as he pushes me towards the front door.

Chapter Twenty-five

The pub is warm and welcoming, I have to admit, as we take a seat by the door.

"What will it be?" Phillip asks me as I remove my cardigan.

"Go on, I'll have another red, knock me out." I hear myself using alcohol to medicate my pain and for once I don't give a shit. I feel so rotten and so heartbroken and so dumb. But I'm not a thicko. Phillip is quite right. I can't make Hugh Clover want me as much as I want him. And, as desperately as I want to text him now, I know I never will. He has a whole new life to sort out and I, Kate Walsh, have too much self-respect.

I jump as Mark McMahon approaches the table.

"Hiya, Kate, what's the craic?" he says.

"Hi, Mark, not much, you?" I wish he would just go away.

"Just out for a quiet few with Wendy . . . she'll want to say hello to you . . . she's always raving about you . . ." He moves towards me and leans into my ear, "I told her about you – I hope that's okay?" He stands up and waves across the bar.

"Eh sorry, I'm not staying . . ." I'm not in the mood for this, not by a long shot.

"Wendy! Wendy!" Mark is waving his hand in the air.

I see Wendy and she breaks into a huge smile as she sees me. She starts to walk over to us.

"Kate! Hi!" She hugs me tightly and I don't flinch too badly.

Wendy is dressed in a crisp white shirt and a skintight leather miniskirt. Legs that go on and on and on. Kitten-heeled suede ankle-boots on her feet. Her elfin hair slicked back.

"Can I talk to you outside for a sec?" I say as I stand and pull on my grey cardigan.

"Sure," she says, looking a bit bewilderedly at Mark who just shrugs his shoulders as she falls into step with me and follows me out.

There is a picnic table and we sit.

"I'm not really sure how to say this or even why I am telling you but I feel an urge to do it. It's about Hugh Clover . . ."

Her eyes darken. "What about him?" she says.

"I was dating him when we spoke in the toilet at the Central Hotel . . . I didn't know then . . . about the connection between him and what happened with Deirdre." I look her in the eye.

"Dating him? How? He's with a girl called Charlotte, isn't he?" she says.

Her name stabs me in the chest again. Charlotte. Soon to be Mrs Charlotte Clover no doubt.

"I didn't know that," I say. "To be honest, I think they

broke up a good while ago, at least he says it's over . . . but, anyway, I want you to know this and I don't do bullshit, Wendy. He is torn to pieces by what happened to your beautiful sister."

The traffic roars by.

"Good!" she jumps in over the noise of a boy racer.

"I just wanted you to know the truth, Wendy," I say quietly. "I think you are a great person, I can't imagine your pain."

We look at each other for a few minutes and she pulls a packet of cigarettes from her ankle-boot. She opens the box and removes a cigarette and a tiny gold lighter from inside.

"You smoke?" She offers me the packet.

"No," I say.

"D'ya mind?"

"Not at all."

Wendy sparks up her cigarette and exhales slowly, the grey smoke curling around us on darkening night air.

"I was pretty awful to him, Kate," she says quietly as she drags hard again, the red tip of the cigarette shuddering.

"He understands that," I say.

"I wasn't in my right mind."

"He knows that."

"How did you meet him?" she asks.

"In my local butcher's." I half smirk.

"What did he tell you about me, about Deirdre?"

Honest as I am, that's just not my story to tell.

"That's for him to tell you, Wendy. All I can say is that he had a nervous breakdown, of sorts. He couldn't cope with life, he left his job, he never went outside his flat and then he came over here, to Dublin. He's been living in my local area the last month."

"Why Dublin?" She exhales on the words.

"I think he just couldn't let your sister go. He wanted to see what her life was like." I paused. "I know he'd love the opportunity to tell you how sorry he is some time." I don't have to do this for Hugh but I think he deserves it.

"I'm just so sad about it all now. Mark's been great, so great . . . we're getting back on track and we're trying for a baby. He told me all about you. I want a baby so much, Kate . . . this is my last weekend smoking, gotta kick this habit." She takes one last drag and then stands the butt into the grass. "I . . . we've dropped the lawsuit."

"That's great. Wendy . . . I have a younger sister who is . . . was . . . touch wood, really ill. She's had a transplant so she seems to be recovering well. I – I just wanted to tell you that."

"Oh Kate, I hope she gets well really soon. I will be crossing everything for her. I'm sure you are a marvellous sister."

"Well, good luck with everything," I say and I stand.

She gets up too.

"Oh, one more thing," I say and I rummage in my bag. "Would you and Mark be so kind as to buy some tickets for our fundraiser? It's a production on an amateur scale of *Swan Lake* in a few weeks at the Belvedere College? It's to pay for a long-term lease on our dance studio above Macken's pub on Townsend Street?" I hold out the pink tickets in my hand.

"I'm pretty sure Deirdre went there for some classes?" Her eyes are wide.

"Really?" I say. I hadn't recognised her from her

picture so our paths must never have crossed.

"That's too strange. I'll take four. My purse is inside."

We head back in as my phone rings in my cardigan pocket. I pull it out and stare at the four black letters on the screen. **Hugh.** I press silent and go back in to Phillip.

It's an easy night as I polish off two small bottles of red and we make plans for the fundraiser. I go around the pub and sell a load of tickets. Phillip is beside himself, thrilled skinny with me. I am back on his team.

My phone vibrates and vibrates in my pocket – Hugh every time – until eventually Phillip confiscates it.

"You can have it back when you're sober – no one with heartache drinks and dials – at least not on my watch, chuck. " He slips my phone into the back pocket of his red skin-tight, second-skin jeans.

I take my role as co-ordinator of the fundraiser seriously now and I sign some papers he has brought with him as a board member of his dance company.

"So basically we have the gay Bander Boys Orchestra for free – like I said, they are brilliant, and all soooo hot – and we have our ex-pros and the two ballet schools supplying us our extra ballerinas who have all danced *Swan Lake* before. Maura's girl Nina, our lead, will be amazing. I already have me and her on *Ireland AM* for an interview – everyone is fascinated about her, you know that? She used to survive on one calorie a day!"

"C'mon, Phillip, that's simply an urban myth." I can't help myself but out comes a sort of laugh. "Please do not say that on national television."

"She did! It's gospel! Would I make something like that up? Anyway we will raise this money, girl!" He's delighted with himself, probably mostly because he is appearing on

TV. He lifts his wine to his mouth but looks hard at me and puts the glass down again without drinking it. "It will be okay, Kate – the pain goes, I promise you it does." He smiles at me. "It's hard for you, I know – you have never been in real love before. It hurts. Throw yourself into this project for the next few weeks, save our dance studio for us, because you once told me it saved you. It will be something to distract you and never forget, chuck, we have each other. "

I nod. I am so incredibly thankful I have him. We smile at each other. I love him so much. He drains his wine.

"One for the road?" he asks with red lips and red teeth.

"No, not for me, thanks," I say as I signal to him to rub his lips and teeth. He does.

I watch him totter off to the bar and Jennifer Beals' needle scratches her record so bad. She falls and falls and she remains on the floor. I have the end of my glass and I'm still surprisingly sober considering. I wave over to Mark and Wendy and they wave back – they're talking to Phillip. When he returns they have paid him for the four tickets.

"Who else are they bringing?" he wonders.

"Dunno," I say.

"Fuck all talent in this shithole!" He leans back on his stool, arching his back and looks around. "Anyone watching me? Anyone?"

I look around. "I'm afraid not." I half smile.

"What is wrong with these people, Kate? I am a god." He shakes his head.

"Mostly married and worried about getting home for the baby-sitter, wondering how many times they will be up with the baby throughout the night, wishing they were in bed right now," I tell him.

"*Urgh*, that has totes depressed me, let's go." He flings the wine back in one go and bangs the glass on the table. "See you tomorrow, okay? We have a big day ahead – we need to flyer everywhere and sell, sell, sell."

We leave and he gets into the first taxi that stops. Chivalrous is not his middle name.

I hop into the next cab and go home to Da's.

When I get in he is washing up.

"Where were ya? The dinner's cold."

It's so ironic I can't even pass comment.

"I was in the pub," I tell him. A cruel twist of fate. "You microwave it for me?" I have no interest in food but I don't want to hurt his culinary feelings.

"Aye," he says and he takes the bowl from the oven and puts it into the microwave.

"She ate half a bowl." He raises his eyes to the ceiling. "She loved it. Dermot is delighted with her – look what he brought her!" He points to an enormous bunch of flowers. Red roses and white stalks, so beautiful.

I feel a revolting selfish lump in my throat.

"She can't have them in her room obviously but he showed them to her at the door – between you and me I think he has his eye on our Ciara." Da sticks his tongue onto his top lip as though he's just let a big secret slip out.

I nod in agreement and reach for my phone . . . bloody Phillip still has it!

But I wouldn't have texted Hugh, or called him.

I don't want to talk any more so I ask Da if it's okay for me to take my chilli into the sitting room and settle down for the night.

He tells me no problem – he has a late-night phone chat with his sponsor now anyway – as he gently twists my plate of chilli in front of me, wiping the edges of the plate with his tea towel. It smells great but I have no appetite.

"Are ya trying it or wha' before ya go inside?" He sits opposite me. His eyes look less yellow now with his liver regenerating and with the amount of antioxidants he is eating. He's even drinking two litres of water a day.

I take a bite. It's so spicy I cough. Poor Ciara!

"Bit of a kick to it, wha'? That's them Scotch Bonnet chillis." He laughs and coughs. He's still eating the fags.

When I catch my breath I say, "Wow, that's a fair distance from your taste buds, no? You of the corned beef and cabbage mentality?"

"Oh stop!" He gags. "Never again. I eat different now – bad memories all that boiled food." He gets up again, pushes his chair in and folds the tea towel over the draining board as Ma used to do. "I got one I'm doin' tomorrow offa that bird – sorry, lady – Nigella Lawson, ya ever hear of her? Brilliant cook so she is. Jaysus, she loves her grub though! I'm surprised she's antin' left to serve the amount she eats as she goes. I'm enjoyin' all the cookin' so I am. Right so, I'll leave ya to it. I'm off upstairs to chat to Peter. He's brilliant so he is, been through it all himself. Ciara is asleep again and Emily rang."

Here's the story . . . The Brady Bunch are back.

Apart from it being too spicy it is actually nice, and I manage a few spoonfuls before I dump the rest in the bin. I go in to my couch bed and pull the duvet over my head and beg for sleep. Hugh's face swims before me. I see it all, the past few wonderful weeks in a rush of images like I am playing old home movies in my head. I'm still in shock, I think. Hugh with a baby. I feel so stupid and that's the worst thing in the world for me to feel.

The tears stream down my face and I feel lonelier than I have ever done in my life. I am the loneliest girl in the world.

I throw myself fully into selling tickets for the fundraiser. I am like a woman possessed. I will not take no for an answer. Phillip has everything pinned on this and with me now a board member I have to be on my toes (Pardoned? Thank you). We blitz the local area with flyers and posters. We stop randomers on the street and sell tickets.

"Eh, can I have my phone back, please?" I ask Phillip as I see him on it.

He holds up a finger. "One minute – it's *Ireland AM,*" he mouths.

"Why are you using my phone to call people!" Seriously, he can really be annoying at times.

I leave him to it and I go into a huge office building across from Belvedere and ask the receptionist if I can leave a book of ten tickets and some information and call back later to see if there is any interest. She agrees.

When I come out Phillip is off the phone. He hands it to me.

"That . . . was Sinéad Desmond! She would like ten tickets purrlllesssssseee!" He jumps up and down.

"Fair play to her," I say, checking my phone. Twenty-seven missed calls from Hugh. Eleven voice messages. No texts. I push my phone back into my cardigan pocket.

"I'm on with her tomorrow morning with Nina – she's

a big ballet fan. I might ask her to join us for dinner after the performance." He is becoming shiny and very animated. I know what is coming. In the middle of the street he jumps high into the air and does a twirl.

"I'm pretty sure she will have plans for afterwards on a Saturday night, love," I say. "She can't exactly go out during the week, being up at God knows what hour for breakfast telly. Let's go. UCD time." I march on. A woman with a mission.

As we walk my phone continues to ring. *Hugh. Hugh. Hugh.* I don't answer.

"I'll give him one thing, he is persistent," Phillip says. "I had to get up in the middle of the night and flick it on to silent. Are you never going to answer him?"

"How can I?" is all I say. But here's what I am really thinking. Deep down where I can't go because it's weak, I truly believes that his relationship was over, I really do – I just think I'm too good a judge of character. But I'd never split up a family, ever, and now there was a baby involved that to me was a family unit.

We walk through the gates of UCD and I am straight into top ticket-seller Kate mode. Phillip, on the other hand, is soon lounging against a bicycle rail chatting up two boys in rugby attire. I continue without him.

"Would you like to buy two tickets for the Phillip Stark Dance Company's production of *Swan Lake*?" I say. "It's an amateur event so the tickets are only . . ." I have been too busy fussing with the stuck roll of pink tickets in my bum-bag to look up and see who I have stopped.

It's Alison and Victoria, the girls in Hugh's photos. I recognise them immediately. Deirdre's friends.

"Oh my God, we go there on Mondays – that sounds

great, we'd hate to see that place close down," Alison says.

Mondays. I never go to dance on Mondays – usually recovering from late-night TV-watching Sunday night. That's why I've never seen them there before.

"In that case they're on the house," I tell them and hand them the two tickets. I will pay for them myself.

"Oh no, it's for a great cause, let us pay!" they insist so I take their money.

When they walk away I am a nervous wreck, I realise, with a beating heart and dry mouth. I'm not sure why. I feel like I was spying on them too. I feel for these girls and their pain. I push through.

My phone keeps ringing and I switch it off. Until Saturday three weeks I am focused on one thing only: selling these tickets.

Chapter Twenty-six

How on earth do people dance in public? I look around the theatre as I put the programmes down and the doors are banged closed. It is a fantastic turnout – all the dancers sold their target of tickets to family and friends and we got a huge walk-up to the door, apart from the tickets we pre-sold. There are very few empty seats. Phillip was a resounding success on TV3 and we sold loads at the box office after himself and Nina were on. Booking from dance schools all over the country came in. We all put in three weeks of hard graft to move this show. I look around the theatre. The audience are such a mixture: young people, elderly people, locals, students and the families of all the dancers which is great. Everyone is aware it's an amateur production so there's no pressure. The atmosphere is light. It's a night out for a great cause.

I walk up and slip into my reserved seat in the front row. I look down along the row and they all smile at me. Mam and Gail are at the end with a bag of Dolly mixtures between them, Da in his brown oversized pinstripe suit sits next to them, an Eason's paper bag at his feet, no doubt another new cookbook in there. He's gathering quite the impressive collection. Last night we had his first attempt at an apple pie. He really has a talent – it was delicious. Dermot has his phone in the air, FaceTiming Ciara as he will be doing throughout the performance. He catches my eye and turns the camera towards me and she waves crazily at me from her bed, giving me two thumbs up. The weight gain is clearly showing and she looks so much better. We are by no means out of the woods but all we can do is take her recovery day by day. The same way everyone living has to take life day by day.

Phillip steps out from the side of the stage in front of the huge red velvet drapes. He is wearing a red tuxedo and black dickey bow, sockless feet in black pumps and he looks so handsome.

I can't sit still. I'm excited and nervous at the same time.

"Ladies and gentlemen, boys and boys, and you too girls, thank you all for coming out tonight. It's wonderful to see so many faces in the audience."

He talks a bit too closely into the mike and I wildly signal for him to pull away. He does.

"It is my great pleasure to introduce you to the Phillip Stack Dance Company's first amateur production of *Swan Lake*. We are beyond excited to have our soloist here tonight, the celebrated Nina Nunes. I am thrilled to share with you our own independent interpretation of Princess Odette, our heroine, this beautiful princess who has been transformed into a swan by an evil sorcerer's curse, and Odile, the black swan. Now please, sit back, relax and simply enjoy the performance."

He takes his leave and heads backstage. This is his stage tonight. I couldn't be happier for him.

I get shivers down my spine as the lights go down and the Bander Boys orchestra take flight on a long subdued heavy note. The oboe makes the hairs on the back of my neck stand up. The theatre is silent. Now the strings pick at me as their melody fills the auditorium and still I stare at the black box of a stage. I spot Maura in the front row opposite me. Not a young woman by any means but still a strong, proud, fit, wonderful dancer. The thick red drapes part and my eyes dart back to the stage. It is dark, then one beam of light appears downstage and we see the Prince take his flight across the stage. He is only seventeen and a local lad but he will go far. His movement is stunning and effortless. Then the set at the back rises to reveal our homemade scenery which really doesn't look too shabby at all. Someone has brought a child to the ballet and it's becoming noisy and is making me agitated. I love babies, don't get me wrong, but not at the ballet. Come on, people! I turn in my seat but can't see down into the darkness.

Four ballerinas dance now, graceful, almost un-human. Their bodies seem to fly. I think here and now that I am going to go and get myself ballet lessons. The thought amuses me as I see my large arse in a tiny tutu, but I don't have to wear that, I can just dance the dance. Maybe we should get Maura to start her own ballet classes in the studio – the thought excites me. I sit back and wait for Nina Nunes to take to the stage. The drums beat low. *Ba Dum, Ba Dum, Ba Dum. Thud, splat, crash, ping, doom. Boom. Boom. Bang. Bang.* Nina flutters out and her Princess Odette glides across the Belvedere stage.

Magnificent. Stunning. I sit in awe. My minds goes into complete focus as I watch enthralled.

The overall piece Phillip has choreographed, while admittedly amateur apart from Nina and some of our ex-professional dancers, has so much passion it actually moves me to tears. I'm amazed at the high standard of costumes Phillip has managed to beg and borrow. The piece runs through with no interval as it's a condensed version of all four acts. His set design of the magnificent lakeside clearing in a forest by the ruins of a chapel on a moonlit night is wonderful. How he has managed it all I have no idea. His palace set is simple yet effective, and Nina dances both Odette and Odile to perfection. Her Odette is vulnerable, gentle, caring, modest and warmhearted to her contrasted angry, dark, bitter, frightening Odile.

I take a second to glance around again and everyone is glued to the stage, watching intently. It all goes by too quickly and next thing I know I'm being dragged out of my seat onto the stage by one of the cast and I slip in amongst the row, beside an elated Phillip, and we all take a bow. Embarrassed at the fuss I turn and leave the stage and slip back into my seat amongst the standing ovation and banging of feet. It's then I notice that there isn't a dry eye on our row, apart from Da's. In fact, I think he might have been asleep. People stretch and remove themselves from the aisles. The mutterings are all contented, I feel. I make my excuses to the family who are all deep in conversation and I slip back into the Green Room to help organise the after party. Already the wine is being laid out in plastic cups on a long trestle table and the nibbles Phillip persuaded no-so-happy-Macken's-chef Tom to supply us are being laid out on paper plates by Maura and the Belvedere theatre ushers.

Suddenly everyone is piling into the invited-only after party and patting me on the back. Congratulations are thrown in every direction at me. I don't know where to turn but I'm loving the buzz. I really had no idea what to expect – I hadn't been to any of Phillip's rehearsals as I was too busy shifting tickets. What it showed was the passion the people on that stage had for dance. Some better dancers than others, of course, but all up there because they wanted to dance and more importantly to help Phillip. That spoke volumes about my friend. I decide to pop back out to the auditorium to gather my family together, as everything seems to be in hand in the Green Room.

"How's things, Kate?" Aidan Guiney asks as I walk straight into him. He is winking at me discreetly, holding hands with his mousy girlfriend Sue.

I had emailed everyone in my contacts to sell my share of the tickets. Every person I had ever met!

"Great, yeah, thanks for coming, you two," I say to them.

"I'll give you two a moment," Sue says, before she places her hand on my arm. "You are so brave how you handled your heartbreak and moved on." She walks off.

Aidan grabs a long sausage roll from a passing tray and Maura provides him with a gold napkin to eat it from. He delicately smells it and then takes a long bite, chewing slowly and nodding before swallowing.

"That is really good. Kate, I do feel rather guilty that Sue doesn't know the truth about us. However, I'm also a firm believer in what you don't know can't hurt you. I think it's for the best she never finds out. You gave me credibility and belief in myself and I'm hanging onto that, Kate. I've never been happier and nothing is going to spoil that. But, hey, I'm afraid to let my secret out but I know there is this guy in Oncology who could use your help . . . I can't tell him about you for fear he'll let it out . . . but there is a nurse he really likes . . ."

"I'll stop you there, Aidan," I say. "I'm not in that business any more."

And I'm not. I only just realise this myself. It's been swimming around in my head these last few weeks. So I fill him in quickly. I have had this idea to take my business in a new direction. My idea: 'Kate Kan'. I'm going to get shiny gold business cards made up, and open Facebook and Twitter pages. This pleases me greatly. I want to create my own website. Yes, I will still be escorting people to weddings, bar mitzvahs etc if they need me to but they are a different type of people. Let's say it's more Bingo and Bowls. A few weeks ago I advertised my services again, with my mobile number this time, on the board at Andrew's Resource Centre for the elderly in Ringsend. You would not believe how many old people are housebound without assistance. I got a lot of enquiries. It will of course be hard taking money from them but it is a business and I will never charge them too much, just enough for me to get by. I popped in to meet the manager, Morgan Jones, yesterday after I received so many calls, and he was such a gentleman. He even promised me a loan of their volunteer drivers and minibus in the evenings so I can take a few of them to bingo together and keep the costs down. It is going to be such a rewarding job. It's finally what I know I want to do. I can even collect old Mr

Dent which will be great. I will be taking them to family christenings, birthdays, Communions, Confirmations and the likes so they don't feel like a nuisance getting people to come and pick them up and leave them home. It's good. My life is good. This is the job I have been looking for.

I try not to think of what I saw this morning as I left my apartment.

Aidan thanks me all over again.

"Will you stop! Now go and enjoy your night with Sue," I say.

He kisses me on the cheek and I watch him go, dressed in skintight jeans, and a tight black polo neck. Mr Fashionista himself, though he could lose the man bag, I think.

I put a huge big smile on my face. Everyone is standing around and a huge cheer erupts as Phillip comes out from the Green Room. He is literally in Phillip Heaven.

"Thank you, thank you, too kind . . . really there is no need . . . oh . . . oh, you are all wonderful people . . . please . . . no more!" He is flushed and holding his long stick from the dance studio in one hand and a large glass of red wine in the other.

I try to make my way over to him but Wendy and Mark intervene. They both give me huge hugs and they are there with Wendy's parents. Deirdre's parents. Mrs Collins looks just like both her daughters. I want to hug her.

"Fantastic!" they all gush. Well, except Mark who has a crease-line down his face and I think he too might have caught the forty or fifty winks.

Jimmy from the Pork Shop hits me on the shoulder with his rolled-up programme.

"Mary, the Mrs, absolutely loved that and I have ta say, Kate, I didn't think I would . . . but, be God, I loved it too. Marvellous dancers the fellas, aren't they?" He's a bit gobsmacked.

I help old Mr Dent out of the aisle as all the people I know from dance classes file up to me. Jake the plumber and the rest of them sing out praises.

"Can we please get ballet lessons in the studio?" Jake asks.

"Yeah, I was just going to talk to Maura about that," I tell him and I look over to see Maura and Ma embrace each other like old friends, recognition and warmth written all over their faces.

I'm totally confused as they wildly beckon me over.

"Kate, you're not going to believe this!" Maura is flushed and flapping her hands around. "Your mother, we know each other – she worked for me in my house in Dalkey for years, way back – wonderful housework she did for me and we became such good friends. I always wondered what happened to her – I thought about her regularly. This is thrilling!"

"I don't believe you!" I look to Ma.

"Maura was the lady who helped me out with money," Ma says. "I'm sure I told you that . . . she was literally a godsend to me."

She takes Maura's hands in hers and I am smiling and shaking my head as they continue to grin wildly at each other.

And then I turn and I see them. Hugh holding a tiny baby, three weeks old to the day if I am to be perfectly exact, and a woman with them. I try to swing my body back into the crowd but still they come towards me.

Wendy and Mark and Alison and Victoria are inches away, talking with each other and some dancers. Alison is bending from the hip and trying a move with one of the very obviously straight dancers.

I can't swallow. Hugh's had his hair cut tight, and he looks like a teenager. The baby cries and I hear soft shushing noises from Hugh.

It's all becoming too much. Things start to spin.

"Kate?" He stands before me once more.

Instead of pudding he now holds his baby girl. What a difference a few weeks makes.

Her light pink Babygro and tiny pink earmuffs are all I can focus on. She has beautiful brown eyes and looks just like him.

"Kate?" he says again and now I look up.

"Hiya, Hugh." I ignore the two humungous elephants in the room.

"This is Bella," he shakes the baby up and down in his arms, "and this is Charlotte."

"Hi!" Charlotte steps forward, a huge multicoloured baby-bag crossing her breasts, dwarfing her small frame. She is blonde and blue-eyed with heavy make-up and dressed like she has just left the office.

"Nice to meet you, Charlotte." I can't look at Bella, I just can't, I will . . . in a minute. . . I just need time.

All around me people still shout and laugh and clap but I am in a world of isolation.

"Is that who I think it is?" Hugh nods towards Wendy who's with Alison.

"Yeah," I say as he looks at them and catches Wendy's eye. Wendy shifts her position, stands up tall and pushes her shoulders back. She raises a shaking glass to her mouth and sips her wine. They have a silent moment across the crowded room. Then Wendy returns her focus to Alison. Ladylike, in control, heartbroken but facing the future.

Hugh turns his gaze back to me. "She's not coming over?" He looks so frightened. "She . . . and Deirdre . . . they look so alike . . ."

"I know," I manage. "She won't approach you tonight. She will one day, but not here and not now."

He nods and makes an obvious effort to change the subject. "That was wonderful," he says.

"It really was, thanks, yeah," I manage to reply coherently.

"Can we talk?" he asks me.

I nod and say, "Sure, follow me." I'm pretty impressed at my light-hearted tone of voice as I lead them backstage into the empty dressing room next to the green room. It is empty now as all the dancers are showered and out and enjoying the attention and drinks before we take them all to dinner later.

I shut the door and Hugh hands beautiful Bella to Charlotte.

"Shall we all sit?" He points to the empty chairs, ever the gentleman.

Bella makes cooing goo-goo-gaga noises and I have no choice but to acknowledge her at this stage.

"Congratulations." I take them both into my eye line, "She's so beautiful." I swallow hard.

Charlotte just nods at me. This is horrific.

"Look . . . Charlotte, this is awkward," I say. "I'm not sure what you know about myself and Hugh or if –"

She stops me with her hand in the air. "I know

everything, Kate . . . why don't we just let Hugh get his speech out. . . God knows he's been practising it enough the last couple of weeks." She smiles and the lines on the sides of her eyes tell me she's more fun than she looks.

Never judge a book, Kate.

"Thank you, Charlotte." Hugh coughs and clears his throat.

I can see how nervous he is.

"Okay, well, as you can see, Bella has arrived, my . . . our beautiful daughter. I'm thrilled with her, Kate, I'm besotted. I didn't think I would be but I am." He stands now and walks to the water cooler and puts a plastic cup under the nozzle.

I sit, heart racing and underarms sweating.

He drinks.

"The thing is . . . I tried to tell you this at the start and I've been trying to tell you ever since but you won't answer me . . . Charlotte and I were over . . . I would never cheat, that's just not me . . . we've been over for a long time, way before I ever met you." He squashes the empty plastic cup in his hand.

My head shoots to her and she is nodding and looking at him intently, almost as though she has helped him with this speech. Go on, her eyes say.

"I didn't tell you about the pregnancy because she didn't tell me about it. I swear that to you. I swear I had no idea. Charlotte and I haven't been a couple for so long. After the accident last July I just shut down. I didn't feel I deserved happiness. In fact, we'd only been dating a short time before Deirdre died. I was really happy with you, Charlotte." He turns to her now. "You were so kind to me after . . ." He drops the plastic cup into the small metal in.

"I know." She smiles at him.

He turns back to me. "I realised I could no longer stay in a relationship with her but I hadn't the guts to tell her so I just shut her out. I was in no man's land. I stayed holed up in my place all that time like I told you until I came here. I wasn't able to let her back in even as a friend, was I, Charlotte?"

She shakes her head. She speaks. "When I found out I was pregnant I knew he simply would not be able to cope. I was the one who walked away in the end, not because he was so depressed, but because there simply wasn't enough there in the first place to fight for. I knew he needed help and I knew how much he was suffering. I didn't think this news could help. I wasn't in love with him any more but I did want to keep our baby. So, I made a decision to get on with my life and tell him whenever he was better. I always planned to tell him, it just never seemed like the right time. Then I met his mother – I wasn't showing or anything and she told me he hadn't left his flat in months, so I just faced the facts: I was having this baby on my own. It wasn't the right thing to do not to tell him, I see that now. It was only when David, that's my partner now, kept telling me as the due date got closer that Hugh had a right to know that I decided I was going to tell him."

Hugh takes over. "So what I am saying, Kate, is, yes, you are right. There was no excuse for keeping my relationship with Charlotte from you – I should have told you I had split from a relationship. But I'm not a cheat . . . I'm not unfair . . . I was just so happy to be with you." He scratches his short hair with both hands. "How do you tell someone you have fallen madly in love with that you

314

weren't even capable of being brave enough to properly finish your last relationship? Not very manly, is it? I tried to tell you that night in Pasta Fresca but I just couldn't find the words."

"He's not a cheat," Charlotte assures me.

"So when my dad told me on the phone that Charlotte had been in touch asking for my new phone number I told him to give it. I wanted to apologise to her. When we did talk she told me she was pregnant and I told her I would come to see her right away. I didn't know what to do yet. I needed to think and, what with Ciara's situation, I just thought it best to go and talk to Charlotte first. You had enough on your plate. When I got to London she went into labour a few days later. I wanted to tell you this to your face but it all happened so fast."

I don't say anything.

We all watch Charlotte take a bottle out, add formula from a small tub and get Bella settled for a feed. She gets the bottle in and Bella sucks quietly and contentedly.

"So why are you here . . . at this . . . at *Swan Lake*?" I ask.

"Phillip told me about it . . . he told me to give you some space for a while but that it might be a nice time to come back . . . to surprise you at the event."

"When were you talking to Phillip?" I ask, astonished.

"He had your phone, I rang, he answered it and we had a long chat. I ended up buying a few tickets from him for tonight."

"So you came back today?" I ask them. I'm all over the place.

"Well, I'm home. I came home yesterday but I flew over again this morning to bring these over here tonight.

I wanted them to meet you. A lot of flying."

I butt in. "But I saw a man at your letterbox this morning, at Number 6, opening his mail and then going up to your apartment in the lift."

"Oh, I'm not there any more – they won't rent it long-term. I rented a little cottage beside Ringsend Park."

A beam of hope is shooting throughout my entire body.

"I think Kate is confused, Hugh – you aren't really explaining yourself properly," Charlotte says loudly.

I like Charlotte.

"Okay . . . uh . . . sorry . . . look, I asked Charlotte to come with me so we can all talk this out, the three of us. Obviously we aren't ever getting back together, but we now have a daughter together who I want to bring up too. But I . . . I love you, Kate Walsh, and I want to set up a new life with you if you will still . . . if you still have any interest in me?" He looks like he's going to burst into tears.

"Yeah, I do," is all I say, my lip quivering.

"Ahhh, how lovely!" Charlotte says. "He's a great guy really, and he loves you so much. He deserves to be happy. It was a terrible accident. I wanted to meet you – just to tell you that and to see the woman who I'm presuming will be a constant presence in Bella's life?" She winks at me as she pulls the empty bottle from Bella's mouth. She puts her over her shoulder, rubbing her back gently. Bella lets out a loud burp. "Good girl, my beautiful Bella!"

I am trying really hard to hold the tears back.

"You want to hold her?" Charlotte asks now.

I'm not sure that I do as I am so emotional and babies never really seem to like me but I say "Sure," and she hands her over and I take her tiny squashed-up bundled body into my arms. She makes glorious baby noises in my ear as she settles herself on my shoulder. I inhale her.

"She loves you! See?" Charlotte claps her hands.

I stare up at Hugh. I know he is overcome with relief at getting me back. I can see that.

"I don't know about that," I say and she suddenly starts to wail. "It might take me some time – we have to get to know each other, don't we, Bella?" I say as Charlotte takes her from me.

"Why don't I leave you guys alone a while and I can wait outside?" Charlotte gathers all her bits again and Hugh helps her with the bag over her shoulder.

Then she leaves us alone.

He walks over to me and puts his hand on my hot cheek as I stand up.

"I can't tell you how much I have missed you," he says, breathing deeply.

"Me neither," I answer with pure honestly.

My game is finally over. It's time to just be honest about my feelings. To admit the hurt of the past and the pain I have felt. I can't hide Kate Walsh any more. I can't protect her from her future any more than I can protect her from her past. I feel the anger of the belly that has put up such a fight leave me. It feels wonderful.

"I should have told you about Charlotte," he whispers. "I wasn't thinking properly. You were so open with me and I thought I was with you too but I was all so self-absorbed, I see that now. Of course Charlotte was important to me – she helped me so much straight after the accident – I don't know how I'd have coped without her support."

I remain silent.

He says quickly, "But I couldn't have moved on like I did without you, Kate – firstly confessing to you and then you making me talk to Father Brennan – the weight lifted and although I'm still utterly devastated inside by that awful mistake I made, I know . . . with you by my side and professional help I can move on. I want to stop thinking about myself now, stop wallowing in self-pity and focus on you – on us – I want to move forward."

"I get it." And I did. I really did.

"So many parts of our lives are already taken, Kate," he whispers to me. "I can't take back my mistakes any more than you can take your childhood back but I want to make new memories with you, happy ones, the ones we deserve."

I know he is right and I lean into him and breathe in the smell of his neck.

"So what will you do here?" I ask as I come up and his two arms slide around my waist.

"I have an interview on Tuesday at St James's Hospital," he grins.

"You're going back to medicine – are you sure?" I can't believe this.

"Yes. And before you say it, I'm not going back because it's all I know and I now have a daughter to support. I have thought very long and very hard about this, Kate. No, it's totally my choice this time round. I think I always needed to know I was doing this job for the right reasons."

"That's great, Hugh," I say and he pulls me in tight.

"What do you make of Bella then?"

I squeeze my nose up tight. "Too gorgeous," I say.

"I'm so relieved that you're okay with me having her. I want her over in Ireland with us for holidays and stuff. I want to be a brilliant dad to her."

"Oh, I'm more than okay with that, Hugh. I think every little girl deserves a kind and loving daddy."

He kisses me gently on the lips. "This was meant to be," he says and we hold each other tight.

I think of the occasion, the people outside, the paths that have crossed and the paths that have been repaired by the crossings. There is still a lot of healing to be done both physically and emotionally but I know we will all get there.

"Oh, without a doubt I think that too," I say.

"I was thinking, Kate," he takes a step back and holds my hands out wide, "wouldn't it be lovely – someday – to ask Father Brennan to marry us?"

"It would, Hugh," I say and Jennifer Beals dances like she's never danced before.

The End

If you enjoyed
Already Taken by Caroline Grace-Cassidy,
why not try an exclusive chapter of a previous title
The Other Side of Wonderful
also published by Poolbeg.

The Other Side of Wonderful

CAROLINE GRACE-CASSIDY

Chapter One

Cara Byrne eased her foot lightly off the accelerator and the car pulled up slowly outside the hotel as morning was slowly stretching itself awake. It was an ungodly hour to begin her day but she'd better get used to it. This dark morning was the start of her brand-new life and her new career, as the hospitality manager at the Moritz Hotel, in the quaint old village of Knocknoly. She stared out the frosted car window before rubbing the condensation clear with the palm of her cold thin bluish hand. Her eyes devoured the building. The architecture of the hotel was uniquely beautiful, reminding her of a fairytale castle she had loved in her favourite torn storybook as a little girl. It was a perfect building, one of a kind, stonewashed white all over, with bay windows on the lower level and magnificent oriel windows on the upper levels. It looked to her like a perfect parcel, with the enormous wooden mahogany door a brown sticker to seal it together. A little spot of Irish paradise. The hotel sat in the middle of acres and acres of unspoiled green fields and was a truly breathtaking sight as the early morning stirred. The sky was bleeding shades of greys and blues, waiting for the sun to combine the two colours together.

She flicked off the engine and the lights on her trusty silver Ford Fiesta. She really had to get the heater fixed. She really had to do a lot of things. All in good time, she answered herself in her head. That was another thing she had to stop doing – talking to herself – because most of the time she did it out 'crazy lady' loud. The November morning was bitterly cold but crisp. The type of hour and air that made you really feel alive. It hit you full-on, like opening one of those huge freezers in the supermarket except you couldn't slam it shut again.

She looked at the hotel again. There were people silhouetted in some of the windows already. Upstairs and downstairs. Setting up for breakfast and for the hotel's day ahead.

As she watched them Cara took a deep breath. This was *the* job she had always wanted. She had gone back to college and studied hotel management at the Dublin Institute of Technology while continuing to waitress at The Law Top at nights and weekends. This job had really always been her ambition but life had side-tracked her before she'd had time to blink. Sometimes it took life to kick your arse bloody hard to make you realise what you really wanted from it.

Cara slid on the light-switch above the rear-view mirror and checked her face. She smiled widely at her reflection and then unsmiled as the crow's-feet jumped out at her. She rubbed at them gently then flicked the light off. Bloody face cream advertising all lied. There should be a law against it.

Starting over at thirty-five would certainly be a challenge.

She had tied her long, wild loose red curls up in a bun and added jet-black mascara to her green eyes and a dab of BB tinted moisturiser. BB tinted moisturisers were all in and, while she hadn't a clue what they did, she bought into the hype anyway. Cara bought into the hype of everything unfortunately – she was that kind of girl. If someone said something worked then she believed them. "It really works – honestly, I can't live without it," the counter assistants with their perfect skin would tell her every time and every time she fell for it. Nothing was ever what it seemed though. She laughed inwardly at that thought. How bloody true! She had always been too innocent. A sucker. That was the problem: she hadn't been able to see through the bullshit and the fancy packaging.

Cara's skin was dotted with light-brown freckles and she loved them. There was no point in piling on the make-up today or she would have to do the same for the next however many years she worked here. 'Start as you mean to go on,' was her new motto. Cara just wanted to be herself again.

She smoothed down her crisp white shirt as she sat in the driver's seat and was confident that the charcoal-black Stella McCartney suit she had spent a small fortune on would take her through the next few years – all she'd need were some different-coloured shirts and vest tops in summer. "Dry clean on your day off," Zoe Doyle, her course tutor, had said as she'd strongly advised her on the costly purchase. She took Zoe's advice. She had learned that skill only too harshly. She had finally learned to listen to people who knew what they were talking about.

324

Her mother Esther had bought her a sleek brown-leather Wilsons dual-pocket briefcase that would carry her laptop when she actually bought one of her own. She'd always wanted a sleek briefcase. Esther must have saved hard to afford this, or had a secret windfall at the bingo. In her old job as a waitress at The Law Top Cara used to watch the career women – the solicitors, the barristers and the judges – come and go with their all-important briefcases. She had felt so stylish but professional last night as she had posed in front of the mirror with hers. She was ready. She knew she was more like Melanie Griffiths than Sigourney Weaver in *Working Girl*, but she was working her way up. She was proud of herself. The briefcase somehow made it official. Cara Byrne was a businesswoman. She wouldn't look back. She couldn't look back.

She had better get in there and meet the manager. She hadn't met Mr Jonathan Redmond yet as she hadn't been interviewed here but at the sister hotel, the Zatlend in Cork, where the heads of the conglomerate and managers Amy and Graham Haswell had met with her.

Five more minutes, she decided, and slid the light on again. She picked up her notes. It was Steve, her dear friend and barman at The Law Top, who had seen the job advertised and passed the ad on to her. "Saw this and thought of you," he'd said as he slid the paper cutting across the bar to her, wiping as he went. He had circled the advert in bright red pen. She never in her wildest dreams thought she'd get the job. In fact, the night before the interview she had decided she wouldn't go. It was her mother who had talked her round over a large Toblerone and a pot of hot Barry's tea.

She licked her thin index finger and thumb and flicked through her notes for the thousandth time. The Moritz Hotel had been built in the eighteenth century and was a residence and stately home to the Harte clan. It had been passed down through the generations until the youngest of the sons, Emerson Harte, had sold his birthright to a moneylender in order to pay off gambling debts. How tragic, Cara thought once again as she flipped over the page. It had been falling into ruins until a famous Polish film director spotted it in the early seventies and used it as a location for his film *Thin Ice*. The filmmaker fell in love with the place and bought it. When he passed away it was sold to the American conglomerate that restored the old place to its original splendour.

The Moritz was now considered one of the more exclusive hotels in Ireland without being too posh or too stuffy. It was comfortable, it embraced you. It was immaculate, with great friendly staff, and an award-winning chef from Marseille, Delphine Coudray. It oozed a beautiful relaxed atmosphere. It was everything a hotel should be. Cara had visited for lunch before going to Cork for her interview and felt relaxed and pampered as soon as she entered the building. It wasn't huge by any means. It now had twenty-two bedrooms, four of them luxury suites, with a stunning bridal suite, and in the last few years they'd had the Haven Spa built onto the side, along with a small fitness centre and swimming pool. Down a long winding cobbled pathway opposite a wonderful courtyard there was the Breena Stable Yard, where guests could avail of complimentary horse-riding around the magnificent five-acre grounds and even down into the local village of Knocknoly. Cara had ridden only once as a child, on a donkey in Blackpool on the North Pier. The donkey had been called Buckles, she remembered now. She was looking forward to taking horse-riding up properly when she was a bit more settled into the job. She loved the idea of the freedom she associated with it. Ahh, freedom!

Cara rolled down the car window and let the freezing morning air fill her lungs. Someday she'd have a car that boasted electric windows and heated seats. She laughed as she pictured Esther's face as her bum got hotter and hotter.

The scent of freshly ground coffee mixed with the cold fresh air was wonderful. She would eat something soon – she knew she still had to put on over a stone. "Build yourself up, love, won't you?" her mother had told her as she left for Knocknoly. Esther had stood in the glass porch of Cara's Auntie Ann's house, and waved her goodbye and good luck.

Cara's life had been very tough over the last year and a half but that was all behind her now. She was a free woman, retrained, with an exciting new start. "Close that closet!" She whispered the mantra to herself, clicked the fingers on her left hand and smiled.

She had rented a beautiful small stone cottage in the village, just over the bridge from the Moritz. Mr Peters, the elderly owner, had more or less told her she could redecorate any way she pleased and she fully intended to do so. To be honest it must have been a few years since the cottage had seen any TLC. 'Musty' was the word that sprang to mind. But it was her very first place of her own and she planned to make it all hers. In fact, if this job turned out the way she was hoping it would, she might just try and buy the place one day.

She turned off the overhead light, rolled up the window, got out of the car and locked it. She zipped down and removed her grey hoody and opened the boot to remove her suit jacket and briefcase. She inhaled deeply before exhaling very slowly and watched her warm breath escape on the cold air.

"Welcome to your bright new future, Miss Cara Byrne," she whispered to herself as she began to walk and the stony gravel crunched noisily under her feet.